Anthea Ingham has published one previous novel, *A Latin Unseen*. At present she is studying for a PhD on the influence of Sappho on Victorian Aestheticism. She has five children and lives in Leamington Spa.

Sebastian's Tangibles

ANTHEA INGHAM

First published 2003 by GMP (Gay Men's Press),
an imprint of Millivres Prowler Limited,
part of the Millivres Prowler Group,
Unit M, Spectrum House, 32–34 Gordon House Road,
London NW5 1LP UK

www.gaymenspress.co.uk
www.gaytimes.co.uk

A CIP catalogue record for this book is available from the British Library

ISBN 1-902852-45-1

Printed and bound in Finland by WS Bookwell

Distributed in the UK and Europe by Airlift Book Company,
8 The Arena, Mollison Avenue,
Enfield, Middlesex EN3 7NJ
Telephone: 020 8804 0400
Distributed in North America by Consortium,
1045 Westgate Drive, St Paul, MN 55114-1065
Telephone: 1 800 283 3572
Distributed in Australia by Bulldog Books,
PO Box 300, Beaconsfield, NSW 2014

*"True and false are attributes of speech not of things.
And where speech is not, there is neither Truth nor Falsehood."*

Leviathan, *Thomas Hobbes*

CONFIDENTIAL

Combination Room
Wednesday
Dear Williams,   5/8/96

The enclosed ms has just arrived from Italy. What on earth am I meant to do with it? It is hardly suited to the shelves of the college library. I must say, my instinct is to destroy it. After all, we have been fortunate to have escaped from the most ghastly scandal, and I, for one, have no wish to be in possession of any Pandora's boxes.

I want your advice; you will, of course, have to read the whole bloody thing through, and will doubtless find it as distasteful as I do. I never liked Collins and he reveals himself in his true colours with his endless descriptions of in flagrante scenes with Salonière. Mind you, I should think they are mostly figments of his imagination. I cannot imagine him satisfying Sebastian, can you? Anyway, I find the whole 'gay' thing quite repugnant – and I must state here, Williams, there is absolutely no truth in Collins' snide and libellous reference to myself in this context. I never had the least interest in Salonière. Perhaps I escape lightly – at least I am not portrayed as a figure of fun. Collins was rather amusing about a personal mannerism of yours.

The whole matter is tricky; some of Collins' academic work is quite well thought of (The Swinburne biography, for example). I am not sure that we should dismiss the matter out of hand, although, of course, this is populist stuff and not in the least scholarly. Imagine what the tabloids would make of it: sex in the stacks, purloining of manuscripts – and as for getting government funding for tutorials, after Collins and Salonière, well!

To be honest, the manuscript upset me: I find its whole purport revolting and incomprehensible; and I am afraid I understand his references to 'tangibles' and 'epibiography' as little as I understand what the two of them did with the tea strainer and the Nutella. Thank God I am happily married.

I am extremely exercised over the whole thing. Come back to me if you can ASAP.

Yours,

George Atkins

<u>*Note*</u>

I have headed most sections (I do not call them chapters) with the name of an important object ("Pink-Suede Shorts", "Nutella" etc.). I append a complete list of sections below. I have been guided in this by two considerations:

1. *Such objects are more than the sum of their parts and often provide an manifestation of an inner truth ('Tangibles', Sebastian called them).*

2. *Objects such as leek sausages and Tupperware pots are – and I have only recently arrived at this understanding myself – the only unambiguous forms of reality we have and, as such, must not be underrated. (Sebastian, of course, always appreciated this.)*

There are a few sections to which I have not assigned a tangible titular object. The reader (if such there be) will appreciate that some sections are best left umbrageous.

Julian Collins

Contents

One
Chocolate Digestives

"Oh please, Dr Collins, do not ask me about Shakespeare, or Austin or Chaucer. I have been answering questions about them for two days now, and I think I have said all the right things –" he paused and regarded my greying auburn hair thoughtfully "– but I should so much like to talk to you, Dr Collins, about what really interests me."

He wore a lavender suit and had beads in his golden hair. He was the most beautiful creature I had ever seen, nor have I since seen another to equal him. Moreover, he was very young, not yet 17.

I had been interviewing youngsters for college places for some three days now. I had seen about 20 young people between the ages of 17 and 20. All were bright. No, that is a meiotic statement; all were extremely bright, some outstandingly so, as is the wont of those who apply to read English at Oxford. Every one I had seen thoroughly deserved a place. Glancing at Sebastian Salonière's forms as they lay on the desk in front of me, I thought it probable that he was the only one who did not.

Oh yes, the qualifications were all there – a dazzling array of 'A' grades at GCSE, 'A' levels taken early, very early, for he was still not 17. I glanced at his UCAS form; it spoke coldly of a great talent for literature ('although somewhat eclectic'). He was also, it appeared, an extremely able musician. On the intellectual front, he was undoubtedly formidable, but on the subject of character and moral worth, the school was resolutely silent.

It is difficult now, after five years, to convey an impression of Sebastian as he was at the age of sixteen, partly, I suppose, because this initial impression has been overlaid by others like the layers of paint on the Signorelli *Madonna and Child with Two Saints*. In some ways, his looks were conventional English good looks – wavy blonde hair, enormous blue eyes, lovely skin, full lips set quite close beneath a Roman nose. In build, he was gorgeous – tall and slim, yet broad-chested and long-limbed. I suppose he had a Rupert Brooke appearance; in fact, he could have served as a blueprint for Adonis. But this bald description does not at all convey the whole picture of Sebastian, for he exuded a vibrant magnetism – I suppose, if I am honest, what he really exuded was sexuality (but whether or not he was conscious of this, I have never been entirely sure. Certainly, he was pleased to please and to be pleased, but for all his myriad faults, I do not think he was in the least vain). And now he sat regarding me, without any of the usual adolescent nervousness, with a look that said, "I am awfully happy to be here, Dr Collins. I am waiting to see what you intend doing about me." I cleared my throat and put on my glasses.

"And what, Mr Salonière, is the subject on which you would like to talk to me?"

He allowed his eyes (perhaps 'larkspur' described them better than 'delphinium') to open enormously wide, and a dazzling smile illuminated his face.

"The subject which interests us both, Dr Collins, more than anything else."

"And what is that?"

He laughed happily. "Can't you guess, Dr Collins? Max Melcourt."

Max Melcourt! I had been struggling through some papers, forms and so on; it was a technique I applied while interviewing, partly to camouflage my natural shyness, but particularly, I suspect, in Sebastian's case to indicate the formality of the situation. He was, I felt, a little too confident for his years. Now I put down the papers. Actually, they fell from my fingers. Max Melcourt! No adolescent I had ever come across had the vaguest notion of, let alone *read,* the poet Melcourt. (He was unfashionable to the point of being virtually forgotten.) And in the whole academic world – or so I believed at the time (so *mistakenly* believed, as I now know to my cost) – only I knew and understood Melcourt, man and poet. I sat amazed.

I came out of my reverie and became commonsensical. Of course, the boy was no fool, he had expected to be interviewed by me and had had the sense to mug up on my specialist subject. Probably he had done the same for the other interviewers. It would not be difficult to expose his ignorance.

"Lord Melcourt, Mr Salonière? What is your interest in this very minor Victorian poet?"

"Oh, Dr Collins! I am sure you can't be serious! Nobody, I mean *nobody,* could call the writer of 'Charmides and Lysias' a 'minor' poet." He had an extraordinary smile, which started as a flickering in his enormous eyes and continued its journey across the perfect features, creating ripples and dimples until it reached his full, red lips, where it expressed an all-pervasive and absolute happiness; and when one looked (and one was compelled to look), one wondered by what right the boy's features should be suffused with a radiance that is denied to the rest of us. Actually, I found it extremely irritating! I looked forward to catching him out.

"And which couplet in that sonnet seems to you to suggest the essence of Melcourt?"

Still smiling, as if he found my question somehow amusing, he recited:

"You stole my joy and did not stay to share my sorrow
But laughed farewell and fled to find another's morrow."

Suddenly, he became quite serious. "Of the two readings, I prefer 'another's' with an apostrophe 's' to the more common 'another'. I mean, it definitely suggests possession…"

For a sixteen-year-old, he spoke with amazing authority, but there was no suggestion of smugness or self-satisfaction. In fact, he looked at me for reassurance and added, as if suddenly uncertain, "... doesn't it, Dr Collins?" However, I think now that he did so merely to flatter me. Sebastian was always very definite in his views.

I would put the young man through his paces. I suspected I would find his knowledge superficial. Indeed, I believe I wanted to find his knowledge of Melcourt deficient. Perhaps I even resented the boy's intrusion into my territory. The poetry of Lord Melcourt was not to be read and understood by a schoolboy after a few hours' reading, no matter how bright he might be – or how attractive.

"Would you like to start with the biographical angle, and then move on to discuss how this affects his poetry?"

"Yes, of course, Dr Collins. I'll tell you what Reginald Somebody-or-Other says in his very dull biography, *Melcourt: A Life*, and then I'll tell you what I think."

He certainly knew his stuff. He went through the early years at Melcourt Hall, at Eton, at Oxford. He quoted from poems written at these times: "Not awfully good, is it, all that rhyming of love and dove and above... ?" He went on to speak of the years after Melcourt had left Oxford, his essays and verse plays and so on. And then he stopped and looked at me meditatively as if he knew, or rather as if we both knew, he had not yet touched on the essential Melcourt. I avoided his glance.

"Please continue, Mr Salonière."

"Well, none of this early stuff was much good, really, was it, Dr Collins? I mean, the *Lime Trees* and so on are quite pretty, but Melcourt hasn't really lived before 1893. I mean there's no real source of inspiration."

"And what," I asked, "happened in 1893?"

He looked across at me thoughtfully (he had just the faintest hint of golden stubble on his chin).

"He started writing his really great poetry, the cycle of Chrysippus Sonnets and 'Pausanius and Argilus', all full of his love and anguish. Shall I quote, Dr Collins?"

"Please do, Mr Salonière."

I met my lover laughing with lilies in her hair
Their petals fell like snowflowers and perfume filled the air.
"Oh, why do you bring lilies when musk roses are in bloom?"
"Roses throb with life, my love, but lilies line a tomb."

He looked at me gravely. "You see, Dr Collins, Lord Melcourt had fallen in love."

"And who was the lady concerned?" I asked. "Do you consider, with Dakyns, it was his cousin Lucy Lambourne?"

He laughed delightedly. "No, Dr Collins. Of course I don't. It was a young man."

"Indeed?" I was somewhat shaken to have my ruse so easily discovered.

"If Melcourt is writing of a man," I said, "how do you account for the pronoun 'her'?"

"Oh, Dr Collins!" Sebastian looked at me, full of innocent reproach, "Victorian gays always switched the pronouns. Addington Symonds does it all the time, and so does Swinburne."

He gave me a look such as a young teenager being interviewed for an Oxford place does not usually give a don. It was not exactly a 'come hither' look. Nevertheless, there was in his expression something that held the suggestion of an invitation. I thought I understood why the school had little to say concerning Sebastian Salonière's mores. I regarded him coldly and changed the direction of the conversation. I would not ask him about Toto.

"What can you tell me about Lord Melcourt's death, Mr Salonière?"

"Well, I suppose it could have been murder… Anthony Roberts might have murdered him, but the verdict was suicide, wasn't it?

"How do you know so much about it?"

"I followed up your references, Dr Collins. And then I read the Symonds' letters in the Bodleian."

"Did you really?"

"No. They wouldn't let me in. I just guessed."

Suddenly he looked very young and terribly sweet, sitting there in his lavender suit. He was, after all, only sixteen. I felt I owed it to him to ask him something straightforward, but before I could frame a question, he continued. "But there's a verse of Melcourt's which does suggest..."

"Which verse?"

"You wove a silken thread, my love, a web for love, you said
You had a noose, so loose, my love
And set it round my head.
With fingers light you pulled it tight
And hanged me from my bed
With sky-blue eye you watched me die
And not one tear you shed."

"Mr Salonière, I am not familiar with that stanza."

"Nor was Lord Melcourt," said Sebastian, unabashed. "I thought of it first."

I should have dismissed him there and then, crossed him off my list. He had no right to be taking a university place from the worthy and meritorious. Instead, I asked him, "How do you account for your interest in Melcourt?"

He thought for a moment and said, "Well, in the first place, an English master at school used to read me Melcourt's poetry..." I thought I could imagine the scene and wondered if it stopped with the reading.

"And in the second place?"

"I do not think people change very much, Dr Collins. It interests me to look at people in the past and draw parallels."

"Could you explain?"

He regarded me for a moment, obviously deciding whether his words would be well received. Then he said, "Well, Dr Collins, you, for example, do look a bit like the portrait of Lord Melcourt, the one in the Faber anthology, and..."

I interrupted. "There I think you will find the parallel ends, Mr Salonière. I, alas, am not a poet, nor am I a peer of the realm."

"No," he responded demurely, "but there's..." I resented hearing him intrude on what was to me, then, a very private subject. I picked a particularly difficult sonnet out of my first edition Melcourt, and told him to look through it and analyse it. Of course, he made a few adolescent mistakes, but his analysis was sharp and intuitive. I was somewhat annoyed.

"Did I do all right?" he asked. I smiled non-commitally and asked him if he had any further questions he would like to ask me. He smiled shyly, and for the first time seemed a little abashed. "Well, Mr Salonière?" I asked, somewhat apprehensively. Whatever I had expected, it was not his next remark.

"Chocolate digestives. A whole packet." The voice was wistful.

"Biscuits?"

"Yes. You've got a whole unopened packet of chocolate digestives behind your telephone. I was hoping... ?" The lashes lifted and the eyes looked at me pleadingly. "You see, I thought, perhaps... I mean, I have been wondering... although, of course, I am awfully interested in Melcourt... whether you were going to open them."

Of course, I should have had them open. I had bought them to serve with coffee. The thought of pouring coffee and offering biscuits came to me every year when I did the interviews. Every year, I bought the biscuits, and every year I chickened out of the whole coffee business; it seemed riddled with pitfalls somehow. I am not a man who finds social intercourse easy.

"I am afraid..."

"Only, you see, I do *love* chocolate digestives. In fact, I love eating; it's my favourite thing. I wanted to put it down on my UCAS form under 'Interests', but the school wouldn't let me."

I held out the unopened packet. "Take it," I said, "courtesy of the college."

"Really?" He reached out for it, and his whole face became suffused with joy. "What a lovely end to the afternoon. I have had such a nice time, Dr Collins. Melcourt and chocolate biscuits, my two best things." He smiled sweetly and engagingly, and, for some reason, I did not doubt his sincerity. Nevertheless, I was not prepared to let him off the hook.

"I hope you can contain your hunger pangs for a few more minutes," I said. "I shan't detain you much longer." I asked him to recite a verse of his choice.

I had learned from experience that this simple test often exposed weakness in the most confident of candidates. Sebastian, however, seemed to relish the opportunity.

"Melcourt?" he asked.

"If you wish."

"May I stand?"

"Certainly."

He stood up and stationed himself (biscuits in hand) facing me, extremely close to my desk, thereby affording me (whether intentionally or not, I could not be sure) an opportunity to inspect him frontally as he recited.

"Please begin, Mr Salonière."

"Like wild, white wind you swirl about my soul
That flutters fearful; you make hot my cheek.
You are the missing part that makes me whole,
Your youth gives strength, where age is weak,
Yet Flora frowns to hold your flowers furled
In hard green tightness, not in petals' plume:
Ah, do not hide your brightness from the world
But bring your bounty to the bursting bloom,
And tarry not, lest winter's freezing frost
Blight beauteous blossoms yet unborn
With all their scented sweetness, withered lost

When all might grow in dewiness of dawn.
For sun and snow and wind and storm are ours,
If yield you will to passion's pulsing powers."

He recited beautifully, with the beads in his hair moving as he spoke. He gave the impression of enjoying the whole exercise, and being a little amused by it. I, on the other hand, felt distinctly embarrassed, both by his choice of subject matter, and, indeed, by the whole situation. I rapped out the first obvious question which came to mind.

"How is this poem titled?"

"*The Unripe Rose,*" he replied. "It is dedicated to A.R., but he really meant Toto, didn't he?"

Sebastian Salonière had certainly done his homework. I had had enough. I stood up and thanked him, and told him he would be hearing from the college in due course. Then I shook his hand – which rested a little longer than courtesy required in mine (the other one held firmly on to the biscuits).

"Would you phone me," he asked, "and tell me if I get in?"

"Certainly not. The college has extremely strict rules."

"Of course," he said sweetly. "Thank you, Dr Collins. I'll ask God, instead."

"I beg your pardon?" Surprise made me frame the words in a tone of irritation. I was disappointed that an interesting interview should end on a note of schoolboy silliness, but before the words were out of my mouth, I felt I was wrong; he wasn't being in the least facetious, he actually meant what he said. He regarded me gravely.

"I always ask Him things."

I was at a loss for words. Sebastian Salonière smiled his dazzling and uninhibited smile. He was completely unembarrassed.

"I'll ask Him to remember you specially, Dr Collins."

"I... er..."

"For the biscuits. It was awfully kind of you."

Wordlessly, I watched him depart. His firm, taut hips were much emphasised by the close cut of his trousers – but, of course, the tightness about his hips might well have been the result of a spurt of schoolboy growth. He was, after all, only sixteen.

I thought a great deal about Sebastian Salonière before the interviewers' meeting: he was bright, persuasive and original, of that there could be no doubt; that he would be interesting to teach was undeniable. Yet I should not argue for him. He was, after all, I reasoned, just another one of those sharp, rather silly kids one sees too much of at Oxford. He had boned up on Melcourt, flattered me and imagined that was sufficient to get him a place. Well, he was mistaken. He was also much too young; let him wait a year and try again – if he was still interested; but he was just the sort of boy to have got another fad into his head by then.

Actually, I was not altogether honest in my reasoning; probably the chief factor affecting my decision was self-interest: I had never come out, and I did not wish to make a parade of my own homosexuality. There were no two ways about Sebastian; he was extraordinarily pretty. I felt that a wrong interpretation might well have been put on my motives if I were to speak in his favour. I think I was also frightened: I suspected that he was dangerous. My life was very well as it was, thank you. I looked through the details of the other candidates again. I elected an earnest young girl who had expressed an interest in twentieth-century women poets.

It is strange, is it not, that one can decide on one thing and do another? I didn't argue for the young woman at all. I argued for Sebastian, and I wasn't alone in this; two of my colleagues wanted him, as well: Williams, who always liked to make a deal of business over things, said he had already discussed the matter with a 'great number of people' and there could be 'absolutely no doubt...', and he blew his nose vigorously, as if that clinched the matter. Atkins pronounced Sebastian Salonière 'a lad with a brain'. I was amused by his inadvertent use of the word 'lad' (Atkins is a Housman authority, and everybody knows what A.E.H. means by 'lad'!). Actually, in the end, even the women wanted him. Sebastian Salonière met with universal approbation. He was to be offered a place.

Anyway, in the event he was offered no place. He had taken advantage of his last unsupervised night in Oxford, got drunk, stolen a moped, was arrested and subsequently packed off back to school. We all agreed that it was a pity that such a talented youngster had thrown away his chances, but there it was. For a long time, I thought no more about him. Well, actually, that last remark of mine is not strictly true: I thought of him every time I read that wretched Melcourt poem.

Two
Lord Melcourt: A Biographical Sketch

At the age of ten, I had (like every schoolboy in 1956) been made to read and learn by heart *Lime Trees after Rain*. From that moment began my life-long devotion to its author, Maximillian, Lord Melcourt. The poem brought the smell of lime-flowers to my nostrils, the scent permeated my senses and my soul. I sheltered beneath the lime's hooded green leaves, and heard nightingales sing from its branches. And when other boys jeered at my red hair and podgy body, I saw rainbows reflected on the leaves' dew drops, and I was comforted.

I was a lonely boy, bright, diligent and bookish; what would be termed nowadays, I believe, 'a geek'. But it is a mistake to think a geek cannot be a sensualist – all too often, I suspect, he is exactly that. But he lacks the advantage of his peers, since he does not know how to approach the crude outlets of adolescent sexuality at which they so readily snatch. He, too, hears the laughter in the other room, but he cannot burst through the door and discover the delights within. He turns instead to the shadow on the wall, images of all kinds: pictures, sculptures, and, in my own case, poetry. A single line acts as a symbol, a substitute for that which is unattainable. And for me, Melcourt's *Limes* was an early signpost pointing the way to delicious secrets. As a child, and later as an adolescent, I read with passionate curiosity. I also discovered that Melcourt shared my unfortunate physique; he was built (or so it would seem from a photo I used to keep under my pillow) as clumsily as I. Later still, I discovered that Melcourt had auburn hair. Then I read more Melcourt and I discovered the Toto Sonnets.

> *'Like wild, white wind you swirl about my soul*
> *That flutters fearful; you make hot my cheek...'*

I said the words over and over to myself, not knowing what they meant, only that in some indefinable way they held the key to a dimly perceived, but nevertheless glorious, mystery. And as I repeated the words in the silence of my lonely bedroom, my cock grew hard. Other boys went to parties and had girlfriends, I read Melcourt and savoured the mystery of life. In a way, Melcourt became my life.

I suppose an unkind person might say I have had little else to put into it; life. Obviously, I have not married, and my parents (who always seemed immensely old even when I was a small boy) have long been dead. I have a couple of second cousins, and am, in fact, godfather to the daughter of one of them; I am very dutiful, and send decent presents at Christmas and birthdays, but they have not asked me to visit since the Christening. I have no other family to speak of. I have always had acquaintances rather than friends. It is not, I think, that people dislike me, but because I am rather hard work, difficult to talk to, reserved to the point of taciturnity. Actually, I quite sympathise with their reluctance to bother. And then I am fussy and old-maidish. I liked my flat (which contained some objects of great beauty) to be just so; I did not encourage visitors. Nevertheless, at the time about which I write, I wasn't an unhappy man: I was respected by colleagues, I enjoyed my work and I took pleasure in my flat. As for sex, well, I suppose I must be honest; I paid for it when I needed it – outside Oxford. Money is a great facilitator in such matters, and I was very fortunate in that my father's death had left me extremely well off.

Anyway, for whatever reasons, Melcourt was the chief interest in my rather unexciting life.

At the time of Sebastian's interview – I suppose it was about

November 1992 – I was trying to complete my magnum opus, my definitive Melcourt book. I had several books behind me, mainly on the Victorians or late Victorians (most notably, three biographies of minor Victorian poets – Cory, Swinburne and Roden Noel – all, as it happens, homosexual) and, of course, I had published countless papers and articles, many of them on Melcourt, or in which Melcourt played a large part. I suppose I am reasonably well regarded in the literary field, and my books have met with the sort of success that middle-of-the road academic books usually do. Unlike many of my colleagues, I have always tended to write very simple and straightforward prose, perhaps because, in many ways, I am a very simple and straightforward man. Anyway, the Melcourt book was important to me; moreover it was to be the culmination of some 20 years' work.

It was a literature-based biography. I examined his life through the medium of his poetry – and his poetry through that of his life; and the greater, or rather the easier, part of my work was complete. It was concerned with the first 28 years of Melcourt's three decades. In case you are not familiar with the poet, let me sketch an outline of Max's life.

Melcourt's early years are what you would expect: born 1868, the second son of the Earl of Melcourt. His childhood appears to have been happy: some diaries of his mother and letters from a cousin tell of picnics, birthday parties and hours of riding, or roaming the extensive grounds of Melcourt with his brother and cousins of both sexes. He and his brother were educated by tutors at home until the age of 12, when they were sent to Eton. The elder brother, Thomas, was a wastrel, but Max was a prize-winner: modern languages, Latin, Greek and English, he excelled at them. Yet, he was no angel, and was regularly beaten for the usual schoolboy misdemeanours: 'caught drinking porter in the town', 'lateness for mathematics' and 'the making of unseemly remarks' are comments to be found in various 'books of misdemeanours'.

The years of his boyhood appear happy and carefree. He formed no romantic attachments – to either sex. The poetry he wrote as an adolescent was not concerned with love. There is a great deal of indifferent pastoral stuff, influenced by his Melcourt childhood. There are also some neat, witty and extremely obscene translations from Martial and Catullus.

When he was 17, he left Eton with a scholarship to Oxford, ready to leave, and Eton as ready to say farewell to him. Anyway, he embarked upon university life with easy confidence – as well he might.

He was tall and rather shambling (at the age of 12, he was six foot). There is a portrait by Frederick Leighton (I possess it myself), done when he was in his late twenties, which, I suppose, gives a good idea of the man. The dominant feature (apart from the abundant auburn hair) is undoubtedly the large, sensuous lips. The nose is rather carved, and the eyes hazel-green and a little on the small side for the size of the face. The complexion is pallid: it is perhaps an ugly face – but not an unpleasant one; there is an integrity there, and even – yes – a touch of naivety. I am only describing Leighton's impressions of Melcourt, which may be totally misleading. I must admit now to something else – the picture I have given of Melcourt is, to some extent, a description of myself when I was younger. There was something uncanny about our physical similarity – Sebastian, had noticed it straight away. In other ways, we were totally dissimilar: Melcourt possessed those qualities that are absent from my own character; self-assurance, wit, and (in his pre-Toto years) levity and a carefree attitude to life, an easiness with those about him. Enviable qualities indeed!

While he was at Oxford, two events occurred which were to alter the course of Melcourt's life. First, he fell in love. She was one of the many cousins with whom he had spent the happy years of his boyhood. Perhaps, through this attachment, he sought to prolong the period of childish innocence. Perhaps, if he had married her, he would have succeeded, and his whole life would have remained a childish idyll. Anyway, she refused him – the reasons are unclear; perhaps it was judged unwise for cousins to marry, or perhaps she simply did not reciprocate his affection. She announced her engagement to a military man, and she passed out of his life. To be honest, I do not think he was particularly heartbroken. Admittedly, he wrote *'April's laughter is my August tears...'* at this time. I am well aware it is in every school anthology, but I do not consider it great verse; it is little more than a poem written by a child for a lost kitten. Melcourt, at 20, knew nothing of passion. It was the sound of the words, not their meaning, which prompted him to write, 'I will wed Darkness, if not thee'. Nevertheless, utter them he did, and spoke more prophetically than he knew.

The second event that was to alter the course of his life was the sudden death of his elder brother in a riding accident. There is no doubt in my mind that this time the grief was genuine. *'Shall I lay my childhood on thy grave?'* is a cry from Melcourt's heart, and he had never wanted the responsibilities of the estate, the title and all the duties of an eldest son – and, as it happened, the Earldom itself, for his father died a year later, 'of a broken heart', says a contemporary source, but actually from acute alcoholism.

His carefree childhood was over. What was he to do with his life? He took his degree (a First in Greats) and went back to Melcourt to look after the estate. But Max was not a jovial, land-owning, huntin', shootin' type. He might write (rather poor) eclogues, extolling the virtues of rusticity, but in fact, I should say, he was pretty bored by country life. He began to entertain a great deal; there was a lot of talk of the 'wild parties at Melcourt'. Such rumours were put about, I think, by those who were not invited. Certainly, Melcourt's friends were artists and writers, and undoubtedly a great deal of discussion went on about Baudelaire and Swinburne and de Sade; but I believe it was all very innocent. And besides, Melcourt was welcome at all the great houses. Many a mama paid court to the eligible Lord Melcourt, but they met with no success, Max had learned his lesson. His name was linked with one or two actresses and even a lady poet, but I wonder now if such liaisons (if liaisons they were) were a cover for other activities. About this time, Max Melcourt's acquaintances began to include a number of handsome and amusing young men – of all sorts: there were aristocrats and actors, grandees and grooms, lords and liverymen. All the same, I don't think there was much in any of it; Melcourt was merely testing the waters. And, of course, he had begun to write in earnest.

He made his name overnight with a verse drama, *The Tears of Niobe*. It is fashionable nowadays to sneer at epics like these; it is easy to pick out weak lines such as *'Her stone eyes wept stone tears'* or *'Fast were the dreams in the naiad's fair young breath'*. Very easy. But only read them as a whole (but who cares to read more than twenty lines nowadays?) and you will see, admittedly, not great poetry, but a few exquisite lines that contain within them the seminal worth of the poet Melcourt was to become.

His success had been phenomenal; there seemed no reason why it should not continue indefinitely, for Melcourt himself was fast becoming as much an object of idolatry as his verse.

I have given here the mere bare bones of his first 28 years. The main focus of my book, the one I had been working on for some 20 years, was not concerned with his early life, but the two years prior to his death. And that was exactly what I could not discover. I had, of course, read *everything* from the three weighty tomes of Kains-Jackson written in 1923, the pedantic and inaccurate biography by Sylvia Newton, the miserable and scrappy book of Reginald Roberts, the acrimonious correspondence of Blythe and Placket, etc, etc. I knew every extant source, every letter, original manuscript, photo, reference and cross-reference. There was nothing I did not know about the early years. But the last two years were a different matter. Let me explain.

In the spring of 1893 (it could have been the May) Max Melcourt met Anthony Roberts, whom he was later to call Toto. The poetry of those last two years proclaims the passionate nature of their relationship, and, in every way, points inexorably towards his horrible and mysterious death.

Who, then, was Anthony Roberts? It was doubly difficult to establish fact, firstly, since Roberts is an extremely common name, and, secondly, Toto was obviously good at hiding his tracks. Since there were (or so I believed before my visit to Reg and Joyce) no extant letters between Melcourt and Toto, I had to rely on other contemporary sources. Reg Turner to Oscar Wilde is perhaps our best source: 'Saw Max yesterday with his divine young Wickchamist friend A.R., now I believe at Balliol.' But this is confusing; Winchester has no record of any Anthony Roberts in the 1870s or 1880s; and, besides, Melcourt knew a host of people, an artist Arthur Rigley for one (not that there was any Arthur Rigley at Winchester, either). But surely the word 'divine' can only describe Toto?

And then, after June 1894, there is no more mention of A.R., Anthony Roberts, or any Roberts. He (and I had not been sure hitherto if it was he) has become Toto. Dawson comments: 'Max left after the second act; I saw him later at Willis with Toto.' Benson writes to his brother: 'Max is in Paris with his beautiful friend. I think we should all have a Toto, don't you?'

What was frustrating, too, was lack of pictorial evidence for Toto, particularly as there *was* a portrait. 'I have drawn Toto for Max', writes Rothstein. 'I have never had a worse sitter – even though he is so very beautiful. He would not sit still, and was by turns restless and arrogant; I think I have caught the likeness, but I do not know whether Max will like it.' The picture, of course, disappeared. It was probably sold with the rest of Max's things. There is a photograph of Max with an unidentified young man, but the boy is wearing a boater and his face is turned away from the camera – and yet, there is something: a grace, a careless arrogance, perhaps even a reluctance to have his likeness caught and preserved?

There was then no tangible evidence of Toto's appearance, but after the interview, which I mentioned in the last section, a strange thing happened: when I turned my thoughts to Toto I found I was modelling him on Salonière, which, as I am now aware, was very foolish, since there was no reason on earth why Sebastian should look in the least like Toto.

Then, on 3 June 1898, Melcourt was found in his gun-room

bleeding to death. His success and suffering had ended. In true Victorian fashion, the unsavoury death of a peer of the realm was hushed up. The Coroner's verdict recorded accidental death; the proprieties were observed. And Toto? Where was he? History does not divulge; he becomes even more shadowy than before. It would seem that he left England, and there is some connection with Venice; Horatio Brown in 1901 writes, 'I saw Toto on the Zattere with Lady Ellen Blythe; I hope the poor lady has not fixed upon him as a husband.' J.A. Symonds writes, 'I hear Melcourt's dear young friend has been seen on Italian soil. I wonder how he lives?' However he lived, it was not for long, for in 1915, Lord Alfred Douglas was looking for his grave on the cemetery island of San Michele, but he did not find it, not has anyone else. Toto was as elusive in death as he was in life.

Had Toto shot Melcourt (as I had suggested in my paper referred to by Sebastian at his interview), or had Max shot himself? Contemporary sources had little or no light to throw on the subject. Some years ago I had had an acrimonious discussion with Williams on the subject: he maintained that Melcourt's death was a simple accident, and I asserted that there was a mystery that needed solving. He picked his nose and abruptly lost interest in the subject. But, for years afterwards, he took a perverse pleasure in needling me: 'How's Miss Marple getting on?', he would say, or, 'Has Morse cracked the code yet?' It was mildly irritating, and was possibly a contributory factor in my book's non-completion. I wanted some proof. Over and over again, I read the last poems and examined the relationship – that it was passionate and stormy was apparent, and also that it was Melcourt who suffered at the hands of his young lover, if lover he was. But more than that, I could not discover.

One way and another, then, I did not bring my book to a conclusion: I was waiting for a new impetus and more material. I was to receive both: I fell in love with Sebastian, and I discovered the Melcourt papers.

Three
Bacon Sandwiches

It was Atkins who told me. We were walking back after a formal dinner in Hall. "That young scamp," he said, "he's got himself here after all."

"Who?" I asked, but I knew instinctively, and I experienced both fear and a sense of elation.

"Sebastian Salonière, the blonde youngster who stole the bike."

"Oh," I replied laconically; there are some advantages to being shy and taciturn: at least one is prevented from blurting out words one later regrets.

"Yes, he did rather an intelligent thing."

"Oh?"

"He sat the Cambridge step paper, did rather well, and someone wrote and more or less promised him a place. You know how they are there."

"So, why is he here?"

"He photocopied the letter and sent it here to coincide with the A-level results. I believe he spoke to Williams. Anyway, it seemed pointless to let a youthful escapade stand in his way. Rather better for us to have him than them."

"I see." I wondered which of them had engineered it. Williams probably, since Atkins does little but lurk nervously about in the closet, while Williams enjoys exercising power about as much as he likes picking his nose, and often produces successful results from both.

"You sound rather censorious, Collins. You don't think the boy's a bad lot, do you?" He peered at me. I took so long over my reply that he rapped out sharply: "Well, do you?"

"I don't know," I said slowly. I remember pulling my gown around me; I suddenly felt rather cold.

"Well, you must think something," he said irritably.

"I don't know whether he's a bad lot or not," I said finally, "but I do remember him expressing some sort of belief in God. I think he possibly operates on a different moral scale to the rest of us."

"Oh, well, he'll have to adjust his moral scale to ours if he's going to stay here," he replied comfortably. And then, just in case I should imagine he had any unseemly interest in the boy, he said, "I expect he'll create havoc amongst the fair sex."

"I daresay," I replied as I watched him make a speedy departure across the quad; but I felt that we were both aware that it wasn't the fair sex who were in danger.

I did not teach him in his first year at Oxford, but I was aware of him, not only because of the interest he had excited in me at his interview (and because he was quite extraordinarily beautiful), but because everyone knew of Sebastian Salonière. He was active in the Union, obtained a blue for cricket, acted in the OUDs, and was noticed academically. He was a young man to watch – and he was *very* young, only 17 when he came up. Perhaps success went to his head, I do not know, for I had no experience of him in his first year. Perhaps he did too much at the expense of his academic work, or perhaps he had simply lost interest. He failed Mods spectacularly. Meetings were held and heads were shaken. He was bidden to re-sit, succeed or leave. He took 10 papers. In six, he gained Alphas.

Maybe his earlier failure had made him disillusioned with his work or maybe he had proved his point with his Alphas. Whatever the reason, and he never offered me an explanation, he virtually disappeared from university life. He played no sport and did no more acting. This was, of course, partly due to the fact that a student's second year is spent out of college, and Sebastian lived a long way away, on the Iffley Road. Then, in the Lent Term, he began to skip tutorials and supervisions – it was rumoured that his friends were at the rough end of the gay line – nor did he attend any of the meetings of 'Erebus', the exclusive college dining club to which he had been elected.

I don't believe I thought about him very much at that time, after all, I didn't teach him and our paths seldom crossed. Sebastian Salonière was an interesting and desirable young man certainly, but he was no concern of mine. Then, I had a strange encounter with him.

I was walking back through the Parks – I had been in a long and tedious meeting at Magdalene and took a detour home. It was early March, one of those deceptively warm and sunny days – a false spring. Suddenly, the weather changed dramatically; it began to pour, and thunder rumbled overhead, and I did what one is always told not to, I sheltered under a large oak tree. I was extremely annoyed to be without my umbrella, and stood with the water running off my ridiculous hair. Suddenly, out of nowhere, came Sebastian on his own leaping and running and whooping as he went. I expect he was high on something. He was wearing a T-shirt and thin trousers and his clothes clung to his body – everywhere. When he noticed me, he paused and called out *"Blow winds and crack your cheeks! Rage! Blow! You cataracts and hurricanoes, spout."* He looked terribly pale and his whole body was trembling with the cold (or possibly something else, since his pupils were enormous). I felt overcome by a rush of emotion – a mixture of compassion, curiosity, fear and – lust.

"Sebastian!" I said, although I suppose I should have called him 'Mr Salonière'. He gazed at me for a moment, and then remarked, "Your hair is quite straightened by the rain; how strange it looks hanging like red threads!" He reached out, almost as if he would touch it, then changed his mind and went leaping off into the rain. The incident unsettled me for weeks.

I overheard gossip about him in the Senior Common Room; it was rumoured that he was taking cocaine and incurring huge debts.

Subsequently, more meetings were held, more heads were shaken and his university career was touch and go. I actually believed he would be sent down. Perhaps I, or Melcourt, saved him.

In the Summer Term, I always gave my lectures on the late minor Victorians, in particular Stephen Phillips, Roden Noel, Addington Symonds and, of course, Max Melcourt. From all that I had heard of Sebastian, I did not expect him to turn up and was surprised (and somewhat flattered) to see him sitting diligently taking notes in the front row. At the end of term, most of his other exam papers were 'iffy'; his papers on the Late Victorians were quite outstanding. Sebastian's university career was safe.

The following October, a new Sebastian appeared. Gone was the lank hair and emaciated appearance; here was an immaculately turned-out young man who had fulfilled the promise of his early beauty. He had also grown his hair, which flowed all golden about his shoulders. He was, to put it mildly, quite stunning. I wasn't the only don to be found in the college quad when Sebastian was on his way to a supervision. I was amused to note that Atkins was often to be seen rigorously dead-heading the climbing rose that grew over the North Wall at such times.

In the Hilary Term, I became his tutor; he had quite naturally chosen Melcourt for his special subject. I knew I must, in these days of political correctness, be extremely careful, all the more so when he began, as he had at his interview, to flirt with me. I had always been circumspect; Sebastian was not the first young man at Oxford to catch my eye, but I had always resisted the temptation. Quite frankly, the risk was too great. I suppose I might as well admit here that sex was quite important to me. No, I wasn't obsessed by it, but *physically* I needed quite a lot of it. I used an agency in London. I won't pretend it was entirely satisfactory, but it served. Love did not concern me; I had never experienced it, and did not expect to. Sex, pure and simple, was what I wanted, and sex was what I paid for and had. So, Sebastian posed a problem: I wanted him, he knew I wanted him, and I did not know in the least what to do about it.

The tutorials were farcical; they consisted of Sebastian, me and a bright, earnest young woman. Without Sebastian she would have shone. Sebastian knew almost as much about Melcourt as I, and he was brilliantly intuitive as well. The girl would read out her essay, often of some merit, and Sebastian would listen gravely. Afterwards, he would politely demolish her arguments and, all the while, he would wriggle his hips in his chair and gaze meditatively at my crotch.

I remember the girl on one occasion saying, "Melcourt's imagery is strikingly vivid and original. Take the line, *'Thine eyes are founts of bounteous health...'* I think here..."

"Oh, Rosemary," said Sebastian, who was, I think, wearing one of those ridiculous baseball caps, "how can eyes be fountains? Tears go down, not up and down. I know it's different for you, but for me there's only one part of the body that produces a fountain. I'm sure Dr Collins would agree. And how can eyes produce health? Nobody has invented elixir of eye, and *'bounteous health'* sounds a bit like a muesli bar, you know, something new at the deli. Buy your bounteous health bars here! What was it you admired in the line, Rosemary?" Halfway through the term, the girl decided to transfer to the Tennyson option, which was taught by a female researcher. Sebastian and I were alone. I asked him to dinner.

I must state now that I did not do this with any ulterior motive. In fact, I do not think I thought through my intentions, I simply wanted to be in his proximity. Perhaps, too, I wanted to impress him with my flat, particularly my piano, not the Steinway I was later to buy, but a nice enough instrument. I took enormous trouble over the preparation for the meal: I scoured the Covered Market for unusual items, I went and sought advice from the college steward. Finally, I went down to London to Fortnums for their homemade passata. I made a superb meal (I am a very good cook), based on a dish that I had once eaten in Tuscany. At 8 o'clock, I put it on the table; at 9 o'clock, I returned it to the oven; at 10 o'clock I threw it away. He never came. I drank the champagne on my own and wept. (I cry very easily; it is a failing of mine; one, however, which I believe Melcourt shared.)

I was very cold to him at the next tutorial, and made sneering and quite unjustified criticisms of his essay. He accepted them quite humbly and asked if he might come and play my piano one night. I replied nastily that only my friends were permitted to do so. He nodded amicably and did not pursue the subject. He continued to produce quite outstanding essays, and I asked his permission to use some of his ideas in my forthcoming book about Melcourt. He said he would be delighted if he could do *anything* for me.

Shortly afterwards, I gave him a treasured first edition of the Melcourt Sonnets. He arrived one night without warning at my flat, carrying blue delphiniums. He asked to play my piano and I replied that he might. He played Prokofiev quite brilliantly for 20 minutes, and then asked for bacon sandwiches (food, I was to learn, often meant more to him than sex). I fried a dozen rashers (cutting off the rind), and I buttered eight pieces of bread (cutting off the crusts), and cut four rounds of sandwiches, which I topped with a chervil leaf.

"Are they all for me, Dr Collins?" he asked.

"Yes," I replied faintly.

"Oh, goody," he said. I sat and watched him eat all 16 of them. (I had been thinking of having a couple myself.) I made polite (and, no doubt, extremely awkward) smalltalk to show that we merely enjoyed a little social chit-chat. I even spoke of work I must do that evening. He nodded, acquiescing gravely, and disappeared in the direction of the loo. He was gone for some time and I became rather nervous, I rattled plates and cleared my throat, but I met with no response. When I finally plucked up courage to seek him out and ask if he was all right, I could not find him. I searched all six rooms; five of them were empty; my own bedroom, however, was not.

He lay, naked, on top of my bed, reading Melcourt and idly playing with himself. Lazily, he smiled at me.

"In Autumn, Love plucks apples one by one
And bites and sucks until sweet juices run...
And Bacchus with his thrysus high upheld..."

I did not wait to undress; I pulled my trousers down about my legs, flung open the bedside drawer, grabbed a condom, dropped it in my haste, reached for the lubrication and squeezed out too much, eventually got condom, lube and all in the right place, and flung myself on him. I had had many boys, but had never had one to equal him. I came, sweating and groaning and shouting his name. He stretched out his body luxuriously and laughed.

"We have made the most frightful mess of your trousers," he said. "Why don't you get undressed and we can do it again properly?"

He stayed the night, or at least part of it, for I know I had him twice again. In the morning, however, I awoke to find him gone. My first reaction was to feel relief. Perhaps, in my folly, I was even a little smug, self-congratulatory even; I had done what I had wanted to do for some months, even some years. I had had him several times, enjoyed him, and, well... I remember getting out of the shower and putting some of that stuff on my hair that stops premature baldness. Well, there was an end to it. I savoured the triumph of the successful male animal. I towelled myself, looked in the mirror and thought my skin a little less pasty than usual. The eyes looked wise and knowing. I even hummed a few bars of the previous night's Prokofiev.

This sense of exhilaration lasted, I suppose, for some 10 or 15 minutes; and then I came down to earth; my smugness vanished and the more I thought about the previous night, the more worried I became. What had I done? Simply played straight into the hands of a scheming, penniless student. Ghastly pictures began to appear before my eyes. There were headlines in all the newspapers, 'Oxford Don Rapes Innocent Boy'. I was led off to the police station, summarily dismissed from my job, shunned by all my acquaintances, forced to live in... for some reason, I cannot imagine why, I fixed on Dieppe as my place of exile. I passed my days there, eventually dying of alcohol poisoning.

I made my matutinal Earl Grey tea. My hands shook but as I poured it through the strainer (I never use bags) I became rather more sensible. I hadn't raped Sebastian, he had enticed me of his own free will. Moreover, I brightened at this thought, he was over 18, and, anyway, there was no reason for any trouble. He had, after all, thoroughly enjoyed himself, I had seen to that. And if he did choose to exact money from me, it wasn't the end of the world. I sipped my tea and felt better. I had nothing to worry about as long as I was sensible. I had had sex with him. We had taken mutual pleasure from it, but there was an end to it. Actually (I took a wafer biscuit; I like them with early morning tea), it was a good thing; the fuck had got him out of my system. I didn't desire him any more. Absolutely not. The tea went down reassuringly inside me; a pleasant feeling of warmth spread about my body. I made a decision; I would never fuck him again. I felt strong and purposeful.

I cancelled the week's tutorials on the pretext of illness, and when we resumed the following week, we neither made reference to the incident – until the end of the hour when he told me he was 'terribly short of money, Dr Collins'.

"Do you intend to blackmail me?" I asked, with a calm that I did not feel.

"Of course not," he replied sweetly. "I simply imagined the act of giving would bring you pleasure." I wrote out a cheque for five hundred pounds and told him I would give him no more.

"I should think not," he replied indignantly as he pocketed the cheque. "You have been much too generous." He came to the next tutorial with a bowl of hyacinths (blue, of course). I can catch the scent of them now.

"For you, Julian," he said, and I understood, with a mixture of trepidation and delight, that we were to be on first-name terms. However, I pursued my policy of resistance, I behaved in a sternly pedagogical manner and the term came to an end. I congratulated myself on my successful obduracy.

On the second day of the vacation, he arrived in a flurry of snow. He stood shivering outside my door; he looked almost as wet as he had that time I had encountered him in the Parks.

"I haven't anywhere to go," he said piteously, and my heart was wrung, as no doubt he had intended it should be. I told him to come in and insisted he take a warm bath. I ran the water myself and handed him a bathrobe, so that propriety might be observed while I dried his clothes. While he bathed, I sat in my study, pretending to mark essays. I read not a word.

Eventually, he emerged, smelling of Armani (I had a penchant for it at that time). He was quite engulfed by the bathrobe. I could hardly bear to look at him. I do not mean that I was overcome by lust – of course I wanted him – but it was something more, an unbearable feeling of tenderness for a vulnerable creature. I imagine a man might feel something of the sort for an infant son. Anyway, I did my best to resist. I spoke sternly.

"I have made up the bed in the guest room. I suggest you get some rest."

"I should be awfully lonely there," he replied, the bathrobe slipping from him. He advanced across the room and put his arms around my neck. "Jules," he murmured. I had him, there, on the floor.

I had resisted his charm; his vulnerability I could not resist. And now I had no strength at all with which to fight him. I had him over and over again that night and, when I was not having him, I poured out incessant words of love; I had lost all control over myself. I told him the truth; I told him I worshipped him. Rationally, of course, I didn't imagine he would return my love – how could he, in his beauty and his youth, feel anything for a dull ungainly pedagogue more than twice his age? But, unfortunately, one isn't rational in such matters: I begged him for words of love and, when I received none, I wept. He was very sweet about it. "Don't agonise, Jules," he said, "just enjoy it." He added as an inducement which I'm afraid I did not appreciate, "God likes us to enjoy ourselves, you know." The next day, he went home.

The following term, he avoided me. I did not even have the pleasure of the tutorials, for the course had ended with the Michaelmas Term. He made no effort to come to the flat and, although I discovered his address from the accommodation people, I lacked the courage to knock on his door. Once I went and parked the car down the road, but some youth came and jeered at me and I drove away. I watched him about the college, and I did not like the look of his friends. He waved merrily and called out a "Hi, Jules!", and I smiled grimly and passed on my way. I suffered horribly, but I could do nothing. I was, however, sensible enough not to write to him.

The Summer Term he spent working. I used to see him in the Bodleian, with his hair all loose about his shoulders. I made a point of going into the Duke Humfrey's Library, which he seemed to have chosen for his studies. I would walk past and smile, but I met with no response. I didn't mind too much; at least I knew where he was. Nor did I take his lack of response personally; I knew the intensity with which he gave himself to his needs. (Not a murmur escaped from him when he made love; 'I have to concentrate, Jules'. It was the same with food; he liked to give it his full attention.)

He got his First. I knew before he did. He got Alphas in eight of the 10 subjects and Alpha plus in the remaining two, one of which was his special subject, Melcourt. A week later he arrived at my flat (the first time for six months) with a bottle of champagne. He told me he was going to do research into gay poets of the 1890s, and Melcourt in particular. We had an idyllic week and I begged him to live with me. He said he would think about it. The following day, I returned from a meeting early and found him in my bed with someone else. I threw them both out and thought about killing myself. I went on holiday instead. On my return, I bumped into him outside the Radcliffe Camera; we went back to my flat and stayed in bed for two days. Then he went off to Turkey for the rest of the summer. God knows what he did there.

He returned in October and started on his PhD. Our relationship continued in the same old way: passion and love and money on my part, charm and beauty and promiscuity on his. I was, of course, supervising his work on Melcourt. I talked to him about buying a place in Tuscany; he took me off to a car salesroom and persuaded me to buy a Porsche instead. I had not seen him drive before and I was amazed. He was quite spectacularly terrible; I forbade him to ever get behind the wheel of my car; it was the only thing I categorically refused to let him do.

I was anxious to keep him amused, and took him to London once or twice; we dined at my club, The Athenaeum, and I was gratified to see how heads turned in his direction (and, to some extent, in mine; in amazement, I suppose). I also took him to a pretentious country house hotel, simply because it looked like Melcourt from the brochure. It was, of course, nothing at all like it, but it had a nice rose-garden, and I remember picking a pink rose, tucking it in his buttonhole and kissing him. Anyway, it was a time of great pleasure for me.

In the Easter Term, he was very promiscuous. I was concerned about Aids.

"It's all right, Jules," he assured me, smiling sweetly. "We use condoms and stuff, and God won't let me die of Aids."

"What about me?"

"No, nor you, either."

"How can you know that?"

"Because He told me." I may not have mentioned that Sebastian was a Catholic.

The Easter Term came to an end, and Sebastian remained in Oxford for the holiday. He lived in a flat in St Aldate's; he advised me not to visit him there, and I complied with his request. Halfway through the holiday, he arrived at my flat one afternoon to discuss his thesis. He stayed two weeks (on and off), and I forgot all my past worries in the joy of his company.

I was still at work on the Melcourt book, and we spent a good deal of time discussing him (Sebastian's thesis was entitled *Gay Codes in Late Victorian Poetry*). I can picture him now as he sat at my yew table, his golden hair about his shoulders, writing some thoughts that had just occurred to him in his beautiful, gothic script, with great concentration. It was, as I say, a very happy time for me.

Four
Steiner's Book

The idyll was interrupted by various predictable peccadilloes on Sebastian's part, which I shall not go into now, and a quite unexpected blow from a source unconnected with Sebastian. It was dealt by an American man called Steiner (he does not merit a Christian name). He brought out a coffee-table book. It was entitled *Max Melcourt: The Gay Lord*. It was banal, bland and bad, and I was appalled.

Full of coloured pictures that had little to do with Melcourt or his poetry, it rode on the bandwagon of the present vogue for prurient interest in homosexuality. But it had a kind of bogus authority. There were a great number of shiny, coloured pictures of the outside of Melcourt Hall and the Dorset countryside, generally inappropriately captioned by a quotation from Melcourt. There were pictures of other gay writers of the 1890s: Oscar Wilde, Addington Symonds, Housman, André Gide (none of whom Melcourt knew), entitled 'Others Who Shared The Secret'. There were Melcourt's more explicit poems, written in large print (as if they could not stand on their own). There was a page of Victorian guns, (some actually not Victorian at all, but of the eighteenth century) entitled 'Phallic Symbols of Death'. In short, the whole thing was quite loathsome.

It was not that I regarded the book as being in any way a rival to my own gestating work – how could it be? Mine was scholarly, a *'ktema es ae'*, a possession for all time; his was naive and ephemeral. However, I felt soiled and cheated, as a gifted pianist might who had been invited to the Albert Hall for an entirely new performance of a Mahler symphony, to find the venue taken by the Spice Girls performing their own populist rendition. I was utterly dismayed. There was only one thing that slightly comforted me; Steiner had even less idea about the reasons for Melcourt's death than I had. He contented himself with an artist's impression of the dying Melcourt, and a sweeping conclusion: 'Thus it was that the magnificent Max Melcourt met his bloody end. Who knows if by his own hand, or by the fell design of Destiny?' The end was typical of the whole, crass and banal. I was furious.

Even Sebastian, who was seldom put out for long, was distinctly annoyed.

"I know what we'll do, Jules," he said. "Have you got scissors?"

Little did either of us know that the provision of scissors was to lead to an extraordinary chain of events that was to have a cataclysmic effect on both our lives.

We sat in bed and cut up the whole book into rectangles which we placed in a neat pile in the lavatory. The glossy surface made its usage uncomfortable, but, nevertheless, it seemed the best and most consolatory thing to do. I was actually about to put it to such a use one afternoon in May, when a tiny line of writing caught my eye. It must have been from an appendix of credits at the end, for the writing was smaller than the usual vulgar large print. Because it was only a fragment, I could read only the one line, '... thanks due to Reginald Roberts, son of Toto, Melcourt Hall, Do...'

I replaced it on the pile, selected another piece for my purposes, and, when I had concluded the operation, I went off to tell Sebastian.

On chilly afternoons, I would sometime make a log fire in my study. It was, of course, strictly illegal, but I am not much bothered by prohibitions of that nature. I kept a store of resinous pinewood in the subterranean underbelly of the flat – where I garaged my Porsche. As I say, I would sometimes light a log fire – on the off-chance that *he* would unaccountably appear to spend an afternoon or evening or even a night with me. I liked to think of the rosy light of the smouldering pine playing upon the pallor of his flesh.

"Look!" I said, clutching my rectangle of paper. "Look, darling."

He was asleep on the rug in front of the fire (he always lay with his hands folded behind the blonde hair of his head). Sleep was one of Sebastian's 'needs'. He had a number of them, they tended to rule his life and form his code of ethics.

To be truthful, the sight of Sebastian on the rug, all golden and flushed and a little bit hard, rather put the thought of Reginald Roberts out of my mind.

I advanced towards him over the rug. The thought of Reginald Roberts hovered momentarily and departed. It was quite some time before I was in a position to broach the subject again.

"I have a surprise for you, darling!"

"Goodness, Jules!" He regarded me meaningfully from the rug.

"No," I said, "not that sort. Look at this." I handed him the piece of Steiner.

"It can't be!" exclaimed Sebastian regarding the rectangle of paper. "Not R.R. Roberts, not the author of *Max Melcourt: A Life.*" His astonishment was understandable. I shared it.

Reginald Roberts' book (to which Sebastian had referred at his interview as "that very dull biography by Reginald Somebody-or-Other") was exactly that – miserable and meagre, sparse and spare. It dealt with Melcourt's life, certainly – if you can call an endless stream of dates and geographical place names a life. Human touch there was none, evaluation or even a modicum of humour or human interest, there was none. It was (and you can see from this assertion how very bad a book it was) even worse than Steiner's! The greatest mystery had always been, for me, why anyone with so little interest in Melcourt should have chosen to write about him. And now here was Steiner, claiming this very man was Toto's son!

I suppose once, many years ago, it might have crossed my mind that R.R. Roberts might be some relation of Anthony Roberts (if that *was* who Toto was); but that such a miserable book could have been written without a single mention of the fact that the author was Toto's son dispelled any such thoughts. After all, Roberts is a common enough name and, besides, one hardly thought of Toto as a marrying man.

"Here it is!" said Sebastian, who was rummaging through my neatly arranged shelves of Melcortia, and he came over with the thin grey book. Together we examined the dust-cover; there were no autobiographical details of the author.

"Well," said Sebastian, "we learn as little about Reg from the cover of the book as we do about Melcourt from its contents." He shivered and made for the door.

"Where are you going?" I asked. I was always nervous when he made sudden departures from a room, never knowing if he would return.

"I'm going to put some clothes on. I'm freezing – unless you want to lend me your dressing gown?"

"No," I said, "I am less happy than you to exhibit my somewhat limited attractions."

My body has always been a source of embarrassment to me; not only was I overweight but I am also excessively hirsute (ironically, it is less offensive now, the red is fading and I am no longer overweight).

"Why is Reg at Melcourt?" yelled Sebastian from the bedroom.

That was easy to explain; some years previously, in search of material, I had motored down to Melcourt Hall and found it turned into an old people's home, surrounded by retirement bungalows. It had become a hideous travesty of itself; the whole interior had been gutted and turned into neat and tidy bedrooms; (I had been shown round by a harassed and uninterested warden) almost nothing remained of the original interior. Reginald Roberts (if he was Toto's son) had obviously returned to the old stamping ground of his father.

Sebastian returned in T-shirt and jeans, carrying the fruit bowl from the kitchen.

"Lovely bananas, Jules," he said, "and all sorts of goodies." He sat down on the rug, crossed-legged, and bit into a peach. "Heaven!"

"Don't drip peach juice over the rug," I said. I suppose I enjoyed telling him off.

"Now, Jules," he replied happily, juice dripping down his chin, "I did not notice you so worried about damage to the rug some minutes ago. In fact..."

"Yes, yes," I replied somewhat tetchily. Sebastian smiled and regarded the remains of the peach. "Now, why doesn't Reginald Roberts write a proper book about his father?"

"I have no idea, Sebastian. Have you?"

"No." He spat the stone into the fire, and it made a soft sizzling sound as it hit the scented pine logs. "But I'd like to find out, wouldn't you?" He was peeling a banana with the extraordinary concentration he gave to matters appertaining to food.

"Yes, I shall write to Melcourt Hall."

"You could ring."

"No, I shall write in the first instance. Anyway, why me, not you?"

"You're so much more organised than me, Jules."

"Don't throw the banana skin into the fire, it'll smell horrible."

"Do you mind if I eat all the grapes?"

"You know I don't mind," I said indulgently, taking the banana skin from him.

"How did Steiner find out who Roberts is, Jules? It surely can't be that he's smarter than we are."

"Oh, Americans. They go bulldozing into everything."

"Still," he said. He spat grape pips into the fire.

"Oh, it's just the sort of street-wise thing that a populist writer like him would think of."

Sebastian held out an empty stalk. "Sour grapes," he commented.

"What is interesting, Sebastian, is why Steiner hasn't followed it up."

"Mm. Oranges are difficult, aren't they?" He was peeling one with great concentration. "A double mystery, really. Reginald Roberts writes about Melcourt without mentioning Toto, and Steiner writes about Melcourt without mentioning Reg Roberts." He tucked into the orange.

"You'll give yourself diarrhoea if you eat any more fruit."

"But think what opportunities that would afford me for examining the Steiner in the loo. I might discover all sorts of other vital information if I was there for long enough."

"Diarrhoea isn't noted for taking a great deal of time."

"No, but the aftermath is." He thought for a moment. "Why hasn't Steiner followed it up? Why hasn't he taped a hundred interviews with Reg and put in all in his horrible book?"

"Perhaps Reg is dead," I said. "He must be very old."

"Or gaga," he suggested, licking orange juice from his fingers.

We did some sums. The trouble was, we didn't know when he would have been born, or even who Toto had married, or indeed if he *had* married at all. The only meagre clue was the Horatio Brown letter, claiming to 'have seen Toto (in Venice) with Lady Ellen Blythe'. And when had he died? He must have died before 1915 because of the letter of Alfred Douglas, 'looked for Toto's grave but couldn't find it', written in that year. So Toto's son (Reg?) must have been born between 1897 and 1915, so Reg must be anything between 90 and 100! He *could* still be alive. I allowed myself to be optimistic: "We might find out anything – even the truth about Melcourt's death!"

"Come now, Jules," he dimpled at me, "is it really likely that this Reg Roberts is going to say, 'Actually, Dr Collins, my old dad shot Lord Melcourt'? Particularly if he's about 105."

"Well, perhaps not exactly in those words, but…" I was struck by a pleasing thought. "Wouldn't it be one in the eye for Williams? He never misses an opportunity for telling me the Melcourt book is a waste of time."

Sebastian stretched out on the rug and laughed. "Don't you mean one in the nose? (Williams' nasal activities really were legendary.) But, Jules, you won't have any excuse for not finishing your book."

"Well, it's not a question of excuse, but…"

"However –" he reached out luxuriously for an apple "– will you pass the time?"

"I expect I can think of something to do," I said, and made a grab for him. We fought amiably on the rug in front of the fire. The air was full of the smell of banana, orange and pine. And, of course, I had to say: "I adore you, Sebastian."

"Don't spoil it, Jules." He got up.

"Does it spoil it?"

"Yes." He zipped up his jeans. "I must be going."

"No. No. Don't, Sebbie, please."

"Must."

"But there's a lot to talk about and…"

"Write the letter, Jules." He put an apple in his pocket. "See you."

"But, darling…"

"Bye, Jules. Stay happy."

I did what I always did when he left; I sat and wept. Then I went to my Sheridan writing desk and wrote to Reginald Roberts.

I heard nothing from either Sebastian or Reg for six days. No, that's not entirely true. I heard Sebastian's voice frequently every time I phoned him. He had a penchant for ridiculous answering-machine pronouncements. Even now I can remember it verbatim.

"Hi, Seb here! Well, no, of course I'm not here, otherwise you would be speaking to me, wouldn't you, instead of listening to my voice? Let's start again, shall we? This is Seb's voice, but it's not Seb – although, of course, it was Seb when he made this recording. So what this disembodied thing that you are listening to now is, I have no idea, but obviously you're enjoying listening to it because you haven't put the receiver down. Or rather – let's get our tenses right – you will have not *put the receiver down. Future perfect. But what really intrigues me (*will have *intrigued me) is how much of this drivel you have been prepared to listen to in order simply to speak into my machine…"* and so on. Ten bars of baroque music ensued. I felt frustration and anger.

"Oh," I shouted down the phone, "I see we have been reading the 'Ladybird Book of Philosophy' and have got as far as 'D for Descartes'. How fortunate you chose to do your degree in English and not in P.P.E." I was upset by his neglect, but afterwards I felt sorry for my remarks. Sebastian, for all his looks and glamour, was only 21 – little more than an exuberant schoolboy. It was cheap for an old pedant like myself, twice his age, to score off him. Besides, there was nothing mean or petty about Sebastian; *he* never made nasty remarks about others, or bore any resentment from those made against him. "Oh, Jules," he would say, "it's such a waste of time being nasty when you could be eating or fucking instead."

Of course, I had no need to listen to the whole of his rubbish time after time; but I did, persuading myself that this time he would switch it off and speak to me himself. For the first three days, I resisted making further responses to it; on the fourth, I made an involuntary reply.

"Sebastian, I miss you terribly; I want you desperately. Darling, sweetheart. Please ring me."

There was, of course, no reply and I bitterly regretted having made such a fool of myself. I vowed not to ring again.

On the sixth day I broke my vow, but I had a valid reason for doing so.

"Sebastian, listen, it's Julian... Sebastian, please phone me back. I'm not being a nuisance; I've heard from the warden of Melcourt Hall. She says we can go and see Reg Roberts on Thursday. He's alive! Well, obviously. Apparently, he told her to ring me. You will come, won't you, Sebbie? Please. Ring me ASAP." I paused, and added what I knew was best left unsaid: "I love you, Sebastian."

He did not return my call, and I had to endure the answering-machine message a further three times. At the fourth, the message had changed (so he must have been back). "Hi, Sebs here. I'm awfully sorry. Can't talk to you now because I'm busy doing all sorts of lovely unmentionable things. Do talk to me after the Palestrina, won't you?"

I went down to Melcourt on my own.

Five
Reg and Joyce

I sat in a back pew in the church of St Michael, Melcourt, and thought of many things, but obscuring my thinking was anger. I had been to the church once or twice some years before, when I was researching into Melcourt from a biographical angle. I had been disappointed then and I was disappointed now. This time it was not the church that upset me, it was Sebastian. I was furious with him for not coming with me. I rationalised my fury; his thesis was on Melcourt, he ought to have come. He was interested in Melcourt, wasn't he? He knew what a marvellous opportunity this was. Why, why had he ignored my call? Why was he so irresponsible? He ought to have supported me – he knew I wasn't good at social chit-chat; his presence would have made everything smooth. He ought to have come.

There was a great, fat, self-important, blue-rinsed, middle-aged, middle-class woman arranging the flowers by the pulpit. I could tell she resented me being in her church, she glowered at me over the gladioli. I glared back. I wasn't glaring at her, though, but because of Sebastian's rejection. I wanted him with me at Melcourt. It was not simply the question of the difficult interview that lay ahead, although our unique and mutual interest in the poet should have made his presence imperative. It was far simpler than that; I wanted him at all times and in all places: I wanted to be on him, in him, under him, over him, or, failing that, simply with him. I loved him intensely as Melcourt had

41

Anthea Ingham

loved Toto. Unfortunately, for both Melcourt and myself, our love was not reciprocated.

"I am afraid I shall have to ask you to move." She looked at me, full-bosomed and full of righteous importance.

"Oh. Why?"

"I have to dust the hymn books."

"I should be obliged if you would leave my pew to the end."

"I'm afraid I can't do that."

"Why not?"

"Because I always start here." She was wearing a blue overall, and it swelled with indignation. Each pew-end had a carving of a contorted face, presumably of a soul in torment. I could tell she would have liked me to join them. I am pretty meek and reserved by nature, but my misery over Sebastian needed an outlet.

"I am afraid I do not feel inclined to move."

"Then I shall have to get Mr Spriggs, the church warden."

"Does he help with the dusting?"

"No, of course not. I shall get him to... to –" the bosom surged out alarmingly "– to... ejaculate you."

"My dear lady, eviction I can accept, ejection I can accept at your hands, ejaculation would be impossible." Actually, I did not say the words at all, but merely rehearsed them in my mind, not only since I dislike discourtesy but, as so often, I lacked the courage to put my thoughts into words. I was rather pleased with my unspoken bon mots, but they didn't make me feel any better about Sebastian or the prospective interview.

I went and sat on a hard, uncomfortable wooden bench outside the church. It was covered in bird shit but I didn't mind; it accorded with my mood. Besides, I was sitting opposite Melcourt's tomb, and I liked that.

The grave was not particularly prepossessing. Indeed, the church was not very attractive, either, being late Victorian (Max's father had paid for its construction), but while the church owed its ugliness to the

42

meanness of the Earl, the exiguity of Max's grave was due to quite another cause. The mysterious nature of his death had meant an absence of a grandiose tomb, the mighty mausoleum that the name of Melcourt might have commanded. Max was put to rest hastily, the stone placed above his head before anyone might question how he had arrived there. I traced my finger over the spare wording: MAXIMILLIANUS HENRICUS MELCOURTUS, POETA ET HOMO LITTERARUM HIC SITUS EST AETAT XXXI. RESQUIESCAT IN PACE. Poor, dear Max. At least I'd managed to live another 20 years more than he.

I looked at my watch. It was time to go. Had Sebastian been with me, he would have laughed. 'Oh, Jules, there's oodles of time'. But he wasn't, and I hated to be late. I left the churchyard and made my way to the village duck pond, by the side of which my Porsche was parked. I sat and combed my hair – it was, at the time of which I write, still rather bright. I wore it rather long, after the style of Max in his portrait (I think my hair intrigued Sebastian: not only had he made that comment in The Parks, but sometimes, if the sex had been especially good, he would take hold of the lock above my ear and twirl it round a finger and smile) – and then I drove to Melcourt Hall.

Melcourt Hall is approached by a drive of some one-and-a-half miles; it is lined with fine lime trees (perhaps the inspiration for the famous poem) on either side. Perhaps they were there in Max's day, I don't know. Probably not at the end of his life; I daresay they were chopped down for timber and others have since replaced them. Anyway, I gained a frisson of excitement to be where Max had once dwelt. By such a building had Max been nurtured. It accounted for the staid, traditional side of his nature, the side with which I empathised so well, for I, too, have been born from such a mould. I do not mean that I am an aristocrat; far from it. My father was a self-made man, an industrialist; he had succeeded in making a great deal of money before I was born. I think his thoughts were more upon the making of money than the engendering of babies. I was the only child of elderly parents, but, like Max, I was brought up in the country, not in such splendour as Melcourt, of course, but in a pleasant enough, small manor house. Perhaps it was its isolation that made me so bookish and shy.

The Hall came into view. In Max's day it had been a fine, rather austere Palladian building (I had some early nineteen-century prints of it). Max would not, however, have recognised anything else beyond the drive and the façade of his house, for the whole forecourt had been built over with horrid little bungalows, and the house itself bore the legend 'Melcourt Acres: Residential and Retirement Home'.

I parked the car outside No. 5 and wished, for the hundredth time, that Sebastian was with me. However, he was not, and I must do the best I could. I hate to be late, and I made my way down the narrow path that led to two plastic buckets of geraniums either side of the front door. I glanced towards the impassive frontage of the Hall. Perhaps my own feet lay on the very spot where Max had once walked. Perhaps he, too, had stood where I was now standing, (with my finger pressed on the doorbell), wishing for Toto to be at his side.

I had to wait some time before I heard slow movements at the door; bolts were drawn back by an unfirm hand. A key turned in the lock. I held my breath – I waited to see Reg Roberts, the son of Toto. It was not, however, Reg Roberts; it was, or rather she was, an old lady in a pink courtelle dress and a hand-knitted cardigan. She supported herself with a stick in either hand. She reminded me of Tenniel's drawing of the old sheep who kept a wool-shop in *Alice Through the Looking Glass*.

"Yes?" She looked at me without interest.

"I... er..."

"Are you a Witness?"

"A witness? I'm afraid..."

"A Jehovah's Witness?"

"No... My name's Collins. I..."

I hate such situations; I am ill at ease myself with new people; it is terrifying to me to have to put others at their ease. I have developed strategies for everyday academic life: I can lecture (rather well) after I have got over the business of introducing myself; I can chair meetings and outline agendas, I can listen and make the right noises while others speak to me of their problems, but I am an intensely private man. I suppose I have never spoken of my inmost thoughts to anyone, except Sebastian. Nor then has it been a case of my *choosing* to speak, rather some inner compulsion that caused me to blurt out inarticulate words of love.

"I was expecting – I... er... believe... My name is Collins."

"No," said the old lady "my name isn't Collins." She regarded me mildly and without curiosity through blue-rimmed spectacles.

"Actually... er... I know your name isn't..."

"Thank you very much," she said, "but we don't want to buy anything."

"I, um, don't..."

"No, not Collins," she repeated firmly, "Roberts."

"Mrs Roberts?" I had not thought of Reg having a wife; but there again, who would have imagined Toto marrying? "I wrote Mr Roberts a... ah... a... letters. He was kind enough..."

"Are *you* Mr Collins?"

"Yes..."

"Mr Collins, the schoolmaster?"

Should I try to explain? What would she make of 'Research Fellow', and how to explain it? In the event, I didn't need to.

"You'd better come in," she said.

The bungalow smelled of old flesh; the smell pervaded the narrow hallway with its patterned wallpaper and its bunch of tired silk flowers; it filled the sitting room. It was the sitting room of an old couple who did not have much money. It seemed strange that the son of Toto, he who was possessed of so much beauty, should be so lacking in taste. I stood awkwardly conscious, as I always am in a new situation, of my size. I felt too large for my surroundings.

The room seemed to fall into his part and hers; hers was by the window, denoted by knitting and some women's magazines. His had

45

the benefit of the electric fire and the bookcase. There were some cheap china figures of cats on the mantelpiece and a tapestry-work picture (obviously done by her) of a kitten. There was nothing of any interest whatsoever.

"Sit yourself down, Mr... um... I can't seem to remember names now." She indicated an orthopaedic chair and my heart sank, not so much because of the chair – its straight-backed sides looked unwelcoming enough – but because the subject of poor memory was not one with which I wanted to associate any member of the Roberts family.

"Collins, Dr Collins. Please, call me Julian."

"Oh, I didn't know you were a doctor, I thought you were more of a schoolmaster." She smiled at me dimly but not unpleasantly; she had a large brown wart on the side of her nose; it gave her a rakish air. I decided not to try to explain the ambiguity of the word 'doctor'. I embarked, instead, on my campaign.

"This is a very exciting day for me, Mrs Roberts..."

"What did you say, dear?"

"This is a very exciting day... I have so many questions to ask Mr Roberts about..."

"It's his trousers."

"I beg your pardon?"

"His trousers, he's gone to change them."

"Oh... ah... quite..." I started again. "I wonder, Mrs Roberts..."

"You can call me Joyce, if you like, Mr... um... The warden here does and the lady who brings the puddings. Of course, Reg doesn't like it, but I don't mind." She smiled at me brightly, and I smiled back and nodded; I thought I would find 'Mrs Roberts' easier to manage. I regarded the chair; I wondered if I would fit into it.

"Do sit down, Mr... um... Reg and I, we like these orthopaedery chairs." I sat; I found it extraordinarily uncomfortable, and I thought how ridiculous I must look, perched upright, wedged in by my bulk. Nevertheless, I persevered.

"I hoped to ask Mr Roberts about his father and... Lord Melcourt..."

"What did you say, dear?"

"I wanted to ask Mr Roberts about his memories of his father..."

"Oh, he doesn't say much now, not since the stroke..."

"I didn't know, I'm sorry... I..."

"He doesn't speak hardly at all in the afternoons; he's better in the mornings." She regarded me happily, and her eyes strayed to her knitting.

"Perhaps he might manage a few words about his parents?" I asked wistfully.

"No, dear, I shouldn't think so." She spoke quite decisively. I imagined I knew what it was; after a lifetime of being married to Toto's son, she had become weary of anecdotes. Perhaps Reg's stroke had come as a relief to Joyce. She picked up the knitting. "Of course, Reg wasn't brought up here, he was brought up abroad."

I wanted to shout, 'Yes, yes, I know! Toto went to Venice after Max's death!'

"His mother was a real lady." Another corroboration, surely? Toto *had* married Lady Ellen Blythe. "But he can't remember now. He couldn't tell the American gentleman anything, either."

"Mr Steiner?"

"Was that his name? He came to ask Reg about Lord Melcourt, but, of course, he couldn't tell him much after the stroke. He sent a book about Lord Melcourt, but we didn't read it. Reg doesn't read now, but there were some nice pictures of the Hall, and that."

I could almost feel sorry for Steiner. So near and yet so far. But, still, there was no need for me to gloat; if Steiner could find out nothing, I was unlikely to, either. And, moreover, Steiner had made the all-important discovery that Reg was the son of Toto.

"Lovely view of the Hall, isn't it?" she continued, pointing with one of the two knitting-needles at the window. "I like to look out."

"Yes, I..."

"Of course, *I* was brought up here."

"Really?" This was a surprising new factor. Reg had been the one associated in my mind with Melcourt, not Joyce.

"Oh, yes, my mother was housekeeper at the Hall, as was my grandmother." I was all attention. What had they told her? Goodness, either might have been there when Max died!

"Can you remember any stories, Mrs Roberts?" I leant forward from the excruciating orthopaedic chair.

"No, dear. It's a long time ago."

I saw, or I thought I saw, another difficulty. Of course, Joyce didn't want to talk about it; after all, her husband's father might well have shot Lord Melcourt! I would not press her at present. I would ask her, instead, about her meeting with Toto's son. Perhaps with Toto dead in Venice (I remembered the Alfred Douglas reference), his mother (Lady Ellen?) had brought Reg back to England, to Melcourt Hall, even, and Toto's son had wandered among the Melcourt acres, seeing the ghosts of his father and his father's lover... and there he had met the housekeeper's daughter?

"Then how did you... how did you meet Mr Roberts?"

"What did you say, dear?" She had obviously given up on my name. "I'm rather deaf, you know." She regarded the knitting critically. "I don't know that I really like the blue."

"How did you meet Mr Roberts?" I seemed to have become wedged in the chair.

"Oh, Reg? Oh, he came down to Melcourt doing some... I don't know what you call it... getting information for his book. I was in the P.O."

"The Post Office?"

"Yes, dear. I was a clerk."

"And you settled here?"

"Oh, no, Reg didn't want to stay here, not once we were married. We went to Swindon; he was a schoolmaster you know." She looked suddenly very proud. "A boys' school, only young boys, like a young boys' school..."

"A prep school?"

Joyce looked puzzled. "It might be."

"And then you came back here, to Melcourt, to retire?"

"Yes. We saw the bungalows advertised, very reasonable, and... Of course, you don't earn very much as a schoolmaster..."

Her words were interrupted by a shuffling noise. Anthony Roberts' son was making his appearance. What had I expected? If I had expected to see the reincarnation of Toto (with allowance for another 70 years) I was to be disappointed.

I saw before me an anonymous, bent old man in carpet slippers. Nor could I so much as glimpse his face, since it was pressed down against his chest and the whole front of his head drooped forward. He guided himself with a stick into his chair.

"Mr Roberts," I said, standing up awkwardly, "this is very kind of you." He did not reply.

He was certainly very old, probably 10 years or so older than his wife, whom I judged to be about 80. So he had come down to Melcourt to research his book? Well, the book bore little evidence of personal research. I remembered its hundred-or-so uninspired pages. Had he wanted to write a book to vindicate his father's part in Melcourt's death, and then found evidence to prove Toto guilty? No, it was not very likely. After all, Toto's name had never been mentioned at the inquest, nor was there any evidence to suggest he had left England immediately afterwards. He must have gone to live in Venice some time after Melcourt's death. Perhaps Reg had merely developed an interest in Melcourt from hearing his father talk of him. And if so, why had the book been so meagre and miserable?

"I'm very pleased to meet you, Mr Roberts." There was no reply. Joyce nodded her head as if pleased to be proved right in her assertions as to Reg's taciturnity. She clicked away, and I wondered what to do. She turned her bland face in my direction.

"I expect you'd like a cup of tea, Mr... um... Dr... um..., I should say."

"I shouldn't want to put you to any trouble."

"Oh, it's no trouble; Reg and I always have a cup of tea about this time, and a piece of cake. He likes a piece of cake."

Very slowly, his head came up off his chest.

"Not the sponge," he said. "I don't like that sponge."

As the face rose up and made its pronouncement, I formed two impressions almost simultaneously: firstly, that the face was not a nice face, and, secondly, that the eyes had once been those of his father. When I say it was not a nice face, I do not mean that age was responsible for robbing the visage of its worth, that if the face had been younger it would have been that of a fine, upstanding man. No, the face was simply rather unpleasant. As to the eyes, even sunk and narrowed as they were, the colour was still vivid – it was a colour I knew well – time and time again, Melcourt spoke of the colour: 'The devil hides in your delphinium eyes', 'Sapphires dull beside you…' and so on. Not only had I read Melcourt, I was also familiar with Sebastian's large blue orbs.

I was filled with fresh hope. He *could* speak, *had* spoken, not of Melcourt, but words, nevertheless. I wondered where to start. I could hardly believe that after all my years of working on Melcourt, wondering, postulating, surmising, here sat the man who might well hold the key to it all. I cursed myself for a fool. Why had I not made a list of questions to ask? I had come all this way without properly preparing myself. I must start straight away.

"Mr Roberts, I should be so interested to hear of any memories you have of your father." There was no reply. Joyce was getting her sticks into position.

"You'd like a cup of tea then, Mr… um…?"

"Thank you. I wonder, Mr Roberts, if…"

I needn't have worried about my failure to bring a list, since he showed no indication of having heard me. He continued to regard the floor.

Joyce smiled cheerfully. She said, "There's nothing like a cup of tea, is there?"

I stood up again. "Can I be of assistance?"

"Oh, no, dear." Joyce picked up her sticks and made her way towards the door.

A kind of low rumbling came from Reg. I trembled with anticipation.

"I beg your pardon?" I could not catch it.

"Oh, it's only the irises," said Joyce. "He always says how Lord Melcourt had blue irises in a blue vase in the Library." I turned to Reg, all attention.

"Did your father...?"

"Oh, no," said Joyce, "my mother said it once. Of course, it's just a story. I've forgotten the rest."

I could see it was an effort for him to keep his chin up, but nevertheless he watched his wife out of the room. Then he did a surprising thing, the blue eyes slithered warningly towards the kitchen and he put a finger to his lips. Then, with the other hand, a tremulous hand, he drew two blue envelopes out of his pocket and jerked them towards me. He pointed to my pocket. I don't know which of us had the more tremulous hands, he with old age and subterfuge, or I with delight and amazement. Both envelopes were in handwriting which had become familiar to me over a period of 30 years. The writing was that of Maximillian Melcourt.

"I... I..."

He tapped his lips once again with his finger and then allowed his head to sink back once more on to his chest.

I pocketed the letters as he had indicated, and if ever the expression 'burning a hole in the pocket' had held any meaning for me, it did now. For a while, I sat in silence looking at the sunken head of the old man. I racked my brains for some conversational gambit that wouldn't involve mentioning the letters, but would elicit information about Melcourt and Toto.

I said it must be pleasant to be back in Melcourt, particularly for Mrs Roberts, who I understood had spent her youth here. I said (mendaciously) how much I had enjoyed his book. I added that I myself was writing a book on Melcourt with help from a colleague. To all of this, Reg made no reply, though I fancied a slight sneering cough when I mentioned the book. But he spoke never a word. If I had not been able to feel the presence of the letters in my pocket, I would have believed him incapable of action.

Joyce's head appeared at the hatch. "Could you help me with the tea tray, Mr... ah...?" I made some feeble attempts with teapot and cups and, between us, Joyce and I assembled cups and plates. Mindful of Reg's words, I declined the cake and sat balancing my cup and wondering how I could elicit more information.

Tea was disturbed by a ring at the bell. I offered to go, but Joyce was up again with her sticks. It was a treat for her, I think, to see a fresh face. Probably, she did not have many treats in life; it could not be much fun living with Reg.

"It's the pudding lady, Reg," Joyce announced from the hall, "she's brought a lovely baked custard."

The pudding lady looked as if she made good use of the leftovers of her trade. She was enormous, and clad in a particularly unlovely turquoise tracksuit. She thrust herself into the sitting room, making me, for once, feel quite sylph-like.

"Here," she said, thrusting a bowl of something loathsome at me. I took it meekly, and gazed down at it with dislike and embarrassment.

"I've given it to your son, Mrs Roberts," I heard her say as she returned to the hall.

"Oh, no," came the reply, "he's not my son, he's a doctor."

I feared I should be called upon to give advice upon obesity, but the door closed and she was gone. Joyce returned, indefatigable, with her sticks.

"Do you like a baked custard, Mr... ah...?" Actually, I loathe baked custard, and this one looked particularly unappetising. I felt the whey sloshing around in the base of the Pyrex dish, and the congealed yellow top was covered with a thick tarpaulin of skin.

"I... um..."

"I'll put you up a portion in a Tupperware pot."

I was about to refuse this suggestion, when it occurred to me that the Tupperware pot would make an excellent excuse for a return visit.

"Well, if you can spare..."

"I like a bit of baked custard, but Reg now, he doesn't care for it, do you, Reg?" A grunt.

"How many are you, Mr...?"

"I'm sorry?"

"In your family?"

"Oh, there's just me, Mrs Roberts."

"Oh, you're not married, then?"

"No."

"Not met the right young lady?"

"No."

"Ah, well, there's plenty of time, I was forty-three when I married."

Yes, that would fit. Reg did his research at Melcourt, met Joyce, married her and brought out his book.

"'Maid of Melcourt' they called me when I was young," she said, making her way to the kitchen to 'put up' my baked custard. She paused a moment and smiled, and for an instant I saw Joyce, wartless, a smiling young girl in a sailor suit. I suppose she had missed her chance of a husband after the First World War, and had settled for Reg. And he? Why had he married her? Perhaps I should find out, perhaps I shouldn't. Anyway, Joyce was the least of my concerns. There was a host of unanswered questions. Why, I had barely started.

I was not, however, to have any of my curiosity satisfied over tea. Reg crumbled his cake (she had given him the sponge) and nodded off. Joyce started yawning. They were tired; it was time for me to go.

I thanked them both for the visit – and the baked custard, which I clutched somewhat nervously – and I asked if I might come again. Joyce looked unforthcoming, but a grunt emerged from the orthopaedic chair. I felt encouraged enough to ask again. Somewhat ungraciously,

Joyce offered me the following Thursday, "when the foot lady's gone". I thanked her again and she looked at me with her aged, expressionless eyes. I felt I had not made a particularly favourable impression on her – but then, I suppose I don't on most people.

Joyce was slowly closing the door on me, when she suddenly opened it again and stuck her head out.

"Mr... um...!"

I turned. "Yes, Mrs Roberts?"

She paused and her eyes blurred behind her glasses. "He – Reg – he didn't give you anything, did he?" I am not mendacious by nature but I felt no compunction about lying now.

"No, Mrs Roberts. I've only got the baked custard." As much as Joyce was capable of registering emotion, she registered it then. A look of relief passed across her face.

"Goodbye, Mr... um..."

I felt slightly guilty; I supposed she knew about the letters, and believed them valuable. Well, if they were, I should pay her for them – handsomely. One thing I have, fortunately, never been short of, is money.

Six
Aubergine Curry

As I drove away from Melcourt, I felt exhilarated; my mission had succeeded beyond my wildest expectations. I may not have learned a lot from the aged Reg, or his wife, but I had the letters – perhaps all the extant Melcourt letters – or, possibly (oh, glorious thought!), they were the first of many others I should receive from the trembling hand of Reg. And, shortly, I should handle and read the letters. The sense of anticipation was glorious. However, my happiness was not unalloyed; there were other thoughts of a more practical and immediate nature: where to jettison the custard before it did some irrevocable damage to the Porsche (I could hear it swishing about on the passenger seat) and an urgent need to find somewhere to empty my bladder (a thing which my natural reserve had prevented me doing at the Roberts'). Then I must phone Sebastian; for spread over the surface of my thoughts, like the odious skin over the baked custard, lay a film of misery; where *was* Sebastian? Why had he not come?

I passed a rustic gate at the side of the road, and, stopping, put an end to two of my problems, at least. I drove on in search of a suitable pub; I did not expect to find anything pleasing or even tolerable (there are, in fact, only a handful of places I find entirely satisfactory in the whole country).

The first pub I stopped at was hideous – I had thought to sit out in the garden and read the letters among the flowers and leaves, but the patch outside was full of flies, plebs and the children of plebs. The interior contained a jukebox, three fruit machines and a clientele suited to the ambience. I could not – would not – read Max's letters in such a place. All the same, I found a phone and tried Sebastian's number. The reply was predictable: *"Hi, Sebs here; I'm awfully sorry I can't talk to you now, I'm busy doing..."*

I did not wait for the Palestrina, and put the receiver down. Of course, I picked it up, redialed, endured the whole fatuous message again (*and* the Palestrina).

"Sebastian," I said, "I've been to Melcourt." And although I had meant to ring off and leave him tantalised, I did not. I told him all about the day's findings. "And now," I concluded, "I'm going to read the letters." Although, of course, I had to add my usual idiotic remark: "Sebastian, I love you." I replaced the receiver, and went back to the car and drove off in search of another pub.

The next pub was not ideal but it was a vast improvement on the previous one. I did not this time attempt the garden; I found a quiet corner in the rather hideous lounge bar, and ordered a Campari and soda. I sat down and drew out the letters, but did not allow myself to examine them straight away. There was a question I had been putting off asking; now I must pose it: were the letters, in fact, genuine? In all probability, yes. After all, why shouldn't Toto's son possess the genuine article? Why should an old man of ninety present me with forgeries? Nevertheless, every researcher knows that wanting a thing to be genuine does not make it so.

I made myself look first at the envelope. I had been reading Melcourt's manuscripts for 30 years – on and off: I had actually handled all the original stuff in England (most of it in the Bodleian and the British Library, and a few bits and pieces in the States), but I had facsimiles of more or less *everything*. I knew Melcourt's writing as well as my own. Now, I steadied my nerves with a sip of Campari and forced myself to be critical: were the bottoms of the 'f's too rounded? Was the cross-stroke of the 't' too pronounced? Well, no, I didn't really think they were. I took out the letters and forced myself to scan them as 'patterns'. Well, of course, I should look at the facsimiles and get the letters properly authenticated as soon as possible, but nevertheless, there was absolutely no doubt whatsoever in my mind: I held in my hand the original letters of Maximilian, Lord Melcourt. I was filled with a sense of fearful wonder. It was akin to my feelings on waking in the morning and finding (all too rarely) Sebastian at my side, possessed of a magic, a beauty, that seemed to me so marvellous that I was unworthy to possess, or touch it. Such was the feeling I had now at the thought that my fingers might lift a page to turn it where Melcourt's hand had held it, that my eye might behold the very first thought of his brain – here might be a crossing-out done with impatience, and there a word deleted uncertainly; the words might run easily, yet, on the next line, they might stand crabbed and awkward. All these things were very wonderful to me; I paused as one might pause before a sanctuary. Then, with '70s Muzak in my ears and Campari on my lips, I began. I was not to be disappointed; the letters exceeded every expectation.

I append the letters below sequentially, since Max never dated his letters. Initially, in my eagerness, I read them in the wrong order:

Melcourt Hall

Dear Mr Roberts,

Thank you for your delightful letter with its excessively kind comments on "The Somnolent Endymion". Your own sonnet was delightful (even if it was not quite original; Swinburne used 'impossible pangs' in Dolores*), but the sentiments were admirable. It did not naturally (and happily) bear the stamp of maturity – that may come – but there was a sort of innate romanticism about it which I liked. I think you have the makings of a poet; the muse Euterpe looks over your shoulder.*

I have, I think, spent long enough in earnest pedantry; I have never been an admirer of that worthy gentleman Signor Gravitas. I consider him a poor mentor, since he is discouraging to the novice, and to the expert he merely condescends. I can do without his company. I prefer his younger sister Frivolita; not only is she seductive in her charm, but wise enough to slip a nugget of Truth (whatever that may be) beneath the brittle appearance of her offerings, rather in the manner that the Neopolitan confectioner constructs his sugared almonds.

So, my dear Mr Roberts, I shall cease to offer you earnest advice. Gravity has effected an introduction between us, now I shall bow to him formally and swiftly make my adieux, as one makes an escape from a tedious partner at a ball, making post haste for the friend whose company is dearest.

You must, then, expect to be addressed without formality, even with levity. Do not, however, be misled; Frivolity is one of those duennas who, whilst seeming merry and irresponsible has, in effect, two eagle eyes which she keeps firmly fixed upon her maiden charge, Decorum.

Your handwriting intrigued me; it had a strange languid grace which I dare to hope reflects the nature of its writer. To find beautiful thoughts presented beautifully is as unusual as to come upon an exotic bloom with an exotic scent. You must be a flower – a lily or a rose – which, I wonder? Perhaps you will allow me to find out. May I give you lunch at The Athenaeum on Thursday at half-past one? We shall have no difficulty in recognising each other; my face will be well known to you (I am as ugly in the flesh as in my pictures), and you I shall recognise by your petals.

I am sure you will not mind tearing yourself away from lectures for our engagement. When I was up at Oxford (isn't it strange that we both belong to the same college?) I thought it my duty to attend as few as possible.

Yours,
Melcourt.

Melcourt Hall

Dear Roberts,

Since Propriety does not need to be accompanied by Formality, I omit your title – as I should wish you to omit mine – at least when we are à deux; I think Roberts and Melcourt will enjoy each other's company rather more than Anthony Roberts Esq and Lord Melcourt. We will behave after the manner of two schoolboys who, away from the master's eye, will abandon their jackets and caps, the better to enjoy their play. My butler, a splendid old fellow (I should like you to meet him) likes nothing better than to keep my silver wrapped in brown paper when the house is free of guests. Even I am often compelled to take my viands 'e fictilibus', which earthenware I greatly prefer, it seems to give the food more savour. Only amidst my guests am I allowed to glimpse the argentine glory of my tableware. Let us be advised by the butler; together we shall feast off Melcourts and Roberts, in company we shall use the full complement of titles.

I was right, of course: you are a flower, but I cannot – although I have frantically thumbed a thousand books of botany – decide which sort. At first, when I saw you enter the dining-room so willowy and wan, I thought you a wild flower, an anemone perhaps, swaying wind-blown in a woodland, or frolicking amidst the ruins of a deserted Sicilian temple. But when we sat and ate and talked, I saw you were too cultivated to belong to the woods and the ruins – even Sicilian ruins. Your place was in a garden, not a neat town garden, of course, but one resembling my wilderness at Melcourt – order in disorder. Yes, I think you would not be out of place at Melcourt. Shall I transplant you? And what kind of flower? In Spring, in this wild garden of mine, in late March or early April, I walk out and see before me a Bacchic throng of white and gold narcissi who dance, gloriously throwing their heads back in their delight at the wind and the sun to which they owe their souls.

Are you a Narcissus? I think I see a little of him in you; you are certainly white and gold, and certainly you wear your profuse golden locks with as much abandon – no, not as much, for you, I think, toss them in perfect consciousness of their beauty. You must take care that you do not fall too much in love with your own reflection – you must leave that for another to do.

I am coming up to Oxford on Wednesday to give a lecture at Balliol. I think they wanted Ruskin, but found out at the last minute he is no longer with us and were forced to try me in his stead – I think I shall serve the purpose, for although eccentric, I am not mad, and I also have the (possibly dubious) advantage of being still alive. I talk on 'Pathless Parnassus' – I tossed up as whether to call it that, or 'The Paths of Parnassus' and then I cheated, since I thought it easier to talk hot air on something that does not exist than be earnest upon something which does – hence 'pathless'. I will call for you at one o'clock. Do not attempt to see me before the lecture; I am inordinately nervous before such events, and furthermore have to work with a great industry at my spontaneity and extempore remarks.

Your friend,
Melcourt.

I append a poem.

'I wandered listless through the land
And found a lily blowing free
I reached for it with eager hand
And laughed aloud in pagan glee.
But ere I plucked it from the ground
It spoke aloud with iv'ry lip:
"Beware the fair thing you have found
The flower is white, but red the tip".

I stood surprised and wondered much
What lay within that ferrid flower?
Could there be poison in its touch?
Could it bear malignant power?

"I do not fear your flower," I said
"The scent is sweet within the bell
The petals are more white than red...
But pluck or not? I cannot tell."'

I have, of course, dedicated it to A.R. Perhaps he can suggest a title.

Your friend,
Max.

I read (what Sebastian and I were later to term) 'the Melcourt letters', and I trembled; I read them in order, out of order, forwards and backwards. I read them analytically, passionately, dispassionately and endlessly. The pub Muzak moved from the '70s to the '80s to the '90s, and then started all over again and repeated its whole cycle.

I had in my hand, next to the glass of Campari, what nobody in the world had – the first love letters of Lord Melcourt to Toto. My good fortune seemed so great, I hardly dared believe it. But there before me were Melcourt's very words. Once, some 100 years ago, he had sat down at the table in the library at Melcourt, with a bowl of blue irises before him, and written words to a young man at Oxford which were to change his life, and, ultimately, end it. I laid the letters down and dreamed.

"Excuse me, are these seats taken?" A peroxide blonde stared at me aggressively. Instinctively, I put my hand over the letters. Melcourt should not be subject to scrutiny by such as she.

"I am just leaving." Carefully, tenderly, I gathered up the letters and made my way back to the car. The Porsche smelt of baked custard, but not even that could spoil my happiness.

I turned to other questions: Why had Reg Roberts given me the letters, the first important letters? How many more did he have? Did he *have* any more? If so, how many? Where were they? How could I get my hands on them? A Metro overtook me, hooting and flashing. I put my headlights on main beam and followed neatly behind. Why had he given me these previous letters? Did he have some wily plan? After all, he was Toto's son. Or did he hardly know what he did? I turned the headlights off. I am not aggressive by nature.

My brain whirled with a myriad of questions. I went over and over the letters in my mind – I knew them off by heart. More than that, I knew the mind of Melcourt as he sat by the irises, penning his first letter to Toto. I felt his amused interest as he stretched out his beautifully manicured hand with its enormous signet ring, the one with its embossed and intricate bee (the origin of the name Melcourt is connected with the Latin word, *Mel*, for honey), to read again Toto's (undoubtedly) unashamedly fulsome letter. And even at this early stage, I thought, there was a hint of his lack of scruple. Had he not tried to pass off another's words as his own? I saw the swift smile flicker across Melcourt's face as he determined to play the young man at his own game and answer flattery with flattery. And yet, he *was* intrigued; something in the young man's letter had caught his imagination. And, undoubtedly, he was not disappointed. I drove the last stretch into Oxford (always a trying run, beset with cyclists and speed bumps). How would it have been, that first meeting between Melcourt and Toto? I pictured the scene.

I suppose I had better admit now to a weakness for fantasising (although I prefer the term 'imaginative reconstruction'). It was a habit I had begun as a teenager, after reading Melcourt; and, of course, I often accompanied such fantasies by masturbation. I am afraid both habits have followed me throughout life – although, after I met Sebastian, I never thought of anyone but him when I indulged. Anyway, the discovery of the letters set in train an imaginative reconstruction of that first meeting…

"My Lord!"

"Yes, Buxton, what is it?" Melcourt looks up from the desk where he is writing letters in the smoking room of The Athenaeum.

"There is a… er… Mr Roberts for you, My Lord. I do not believe he is a member."

"I don't believe he is either, Buxton."

"My Lord, I…"

"It's all right, Buxton. He comes at my invitation."

"I beg your pardon My Lord… I…"

"Oh, show him up, Buxton."

"Certainly, My Lord."

The door opens, and, one by one, the members raised their heads. The young man is slim and blonde; his eyes are the blue of irises. He is very young and wears a suit of lavender cloth. He is quite extraordinarily beautiful. There in an armchair sat the adventurer, Burton, the scar on his face glinting in the firelight. He grunted appreciatively at the young man's appearance. Frederick Leighton looked on appraisingly; perhaps he would put this young man into his next picture as Bacchus or Theseus. Horatio Brown sat more upright in his chair, the boy reminding him of a Venetian gondolier friend of his…

"Won't you sit down, Mr Roberts? Pray, do draw up a chair." Melcourt smiles courteously, his red hair hanging straight about his austere features. Did he feel in those first few moments some intimation of what was to be?

"What shall be the subject of our discussion, Mr Roberts?" The light from the chandelier overhead caught in Toto's hair so that it glistened as if full of coloured beads.

"Oh, Your Lordship, there can only be one subject."

"And what can that be?"

"The subject that interests me more than anything else – your

Lordship's poetry."

"And what exactly is your interest in this very minor modern poet, Mr Roberts?"

"Your Lordship!" The young man leaps to his feet with perhaps feigned indignation. "Nobody could call the author of 'Charmides and Lysias' a minor poet!"

Burton grunts ironically, and Leighton smiles to himself, but they return to their own thoughts (Horatio has already nodded off); tacitly, they admit that already the young man belongs to Melcourt.

"And what would you say was the poem's essence, Mr Roberts?" The young man looked thoughtful; a coal in the grate crackled ominously.

"The destuctive power of love, My Lord."

A cyclist glowered angrily at me; I abandoned my imaginings and concentrated on getting home.

I garaged the car; I have a service flat, and the parking arrangements are in a subterranean area underneath the building. The whole thing was rather a business, keying in numbers and so on; I have to admit, I did not always bother. I entered my flat (more security devices); I rang Sebastian.

"Hi, Sebs here..." I replaced the receiver.

I went into the kitchen; it is of a Mexican design, all oranges, reds and painted wood. There is a great deal of ethnic terracotta, that sort of thing. There is even a Venus flytrap, which Sebastian and I had, on occasion, taken turns to feed. I liked it well enough when bought, but think it rather pretentious. I set about cooking. If I was not eating out, I always cooked. I enjoyed the preparation of a meal. The process was akin (I used to think) to the writing of biography; out of disparate ingredients one created a delightful feast. The most elaborate meals I cooked were for Sebastian, although he could not always be relied upon to eat them with me. I set about making curry; aubergines were to be the main ingredient. Then I opened a bottle of Chardonnay, very good

Chardonnay. I drink only good wine.

And then there was the second letter. The poem. As he wrote it, did he remove the irises from the blue vase and sniff at them delicately? Did he, perhaps, in the fingering of them, upset the vase upon the letter – for it was a little browned in one corner? I peeled the root ginger very carefully; the smell is exquisite – I know nothing like it – but it must be grated very fine. It must blend with the other ingredients absolutely, not obtrude. Blended in pestle and mortar and added to garlic treated similarly, it makes a happy union. I had a special knife for onions; it was particularly sharp; besides, even after being washed in the dishwasher, the pungent odour still clings. Onions must be browned extremely slowly. Fifteen minutes is the very least they take.

The kitchen was a little daunting when one had had a few glasses; the ochres, earth-reds and clay-brown tended to move heavily about and produce all kinds of coloured fancies. Sitting on my habitual cooking stool, I prodded the onions and thought of Melcourt and Toto, and then of myself and Sebastian. I picked up the phone, endured the message and then, without introduction or explanation, read him the letters. When I had come to the end, I thought how stupid I was to have told him everything and not to have made him wait; then, instead of ringing off abruptly, I said – as if I was asking a favour instead of just having granted him the enormous privilege of hearing the letters – "Please come, Sebastian, please."

I took out the heavy copper pan I used for the making of curry. It is important to add the spices in the correct order, and to allow exact intervals of minutes and seconds in between. You may do untold damage by adding turmeric *before* rather than *after* coriander seeds. The sweating spices smelled delicious, hinting, suggesting truly exquisite pleasures in store. *Did they return together to Toto's rooms – for whom to seduce whom? Or did they do none of these things, but part company outside Balliol? I wanted to know – I must know. But should I?* You must be extremely careful with aubergines – salt them first to remove excess moisture.

It occurs to me now (although I had no such insight at the time) that my curry was an interesting example of the essential emerging from the tangible. For what could have more solidity t han my aubergines in their episcopal purple or my many-layered globular onions? But I had only to mix them together with their attendant herbs and spices for an exotic aroma to arise. And what, you may ask, was that aroma; a mere piece of intangibility? No, no, no! It was the distilled essence; the very 'curryness' of curry. I digress, but the digression is, I think, an important one.

I lifted my aubergines gently and continued with my deliberations: Reg Roberts had given me the first two letters. Why should a man, the son of Lord Melcourt's lover, with such material at his finger-tips, have written a book devoid of such material? I had no idea. Moreover, he had given them to me surreptitiously, without Joyce's knowledge. Why had he done that? And where were the other letters? Were these, for some extraordinary reason, the only ones he had? That would be horribly cruel. It would be like giving Tantalus (after 6,000,000 years in Hades) two single grapes and then removing the bunch again from his grasp. I saw myself as the baulked Tantalus, Reg, the King of Hades himself, and somewhere loathsome in the Fields of Asphodel strode Steiner, waving his loathsome book.

Another yet more horrible scenario sprang up; perhaps Reg Roberts was as appalling as his father. Perhaps he did have *all* Melcourt's letters to Toto and intended withholding them from me? Wild schemes appeared to me: I would kill Reg and burgle his home; I would hold Joyce ransom and demand the letters; I would take out an enormous loan from the bank and bribe them with the best retirement home in England. More reasonably, I should call again and ask nicely for them. The waters must swirl and gush before the wild brown rice goes in. My brain teemed with notions, not only for obtaining the letters, but with queries as to what *had* happened at Oxford after 'Pathless Parnassus'. With the rice, I put in a pinch of golden saffron and a single blade of lemon grass; as the waters settled to a heady brew, appeased by these golden offerings, so my mind settled to a feverish calm. Perhaps the yellow water prompted it...

"Your hair is so very golden, I cannot believe that it can be Nature's unaided work."

"As I am quite perfect in every other respect, why should my hair require the help of Artifice?" They were walking through the cloisters at Brasenose, and the dappled gloom had brought their voices to a hushed whisper.

"What I find so enticing about you, my dear Anthony, is the delicious contrast between an angelic person and a diabolic soul."

"And are you enticed?"

"Oh, certainly I am; but should I yield to the enticement?" Toto's eyes glinted in the cloister's gloom.

"I do not think that either of us deals in 'shoulds'. Ours is a currency of 'shalls' and 'wills'."

"A rather debased coinage; I think you speak of a currency of hedonism. I have such coins in my pocket also, but I have others of greater weight."

"And what are those?"

Melcourt turned away from Toto and spoke hoarsely. "Position, duty, integrity..."

Toto tossed his hair and laughed. "I think your pockets will soon have holes in them, weighed down by such ponderous items."

Melcourt was (I stirred the rice to prevent it sticking) a man of high moral standards; like most men of his time, he believed that homosexuality was a sin, something to be repressed, repudiated and fought against. His motives were superior to my own in my resistance to Sebastian: I had merely been fearful of the spectre of political correctness; he had resisted because he believed the thing wrong.

I opened another bottle of Chardonnay and thought about the four of us – it was easy to draw parallels: I looked like Melcourt, Sebastian resembled Toto (although, of course, I had no actual evidence for this beyond the fact that both were beautiful). Melcourt and I were both considerably older than our lovers, but the parallel was not exact: as I had told Sebastian in his interview, I was neither a peer nor a poet. I might have added that, although wealthy (undoubtedly more so than Melcourt), I was not witty, congenial and urbane, but taciturn, introverted and awkward. And as for Toto, I felt he was not like Sebastian, for Melcourt's poetry reflects the unhappiness Toto brought him, rather than joy, and while Sebastian's absences and rejections brought me misery, his presence brought me intense happiness (a fact I have never forgotten). Sebastian was extraordinarily sunny-natured, hardly ever out of sorts, while Toto, I felt, was difficult, petulant and given to complaining. Perhaps, I reflected, as I drank the first half of the bottle (I am rather a heavy drinker) we were mirror-images, each possessing all the vices and virtues lacking in the other.

The rice absorbed the water and became as yellow as ribbed sand. The sweet and delicate flavour blended with the scent of aubergine and coriander. My meal was ready. It was perhaps a little disappointing. So often the titillation of the senses arouses expectations that Actuality does not fulfill. Only with Sebastian was the anticipation matched by its consummation, but he was not here to share in either my fantasies or my food. Well, I must manage without him. During the meal, I made plans for the rest of the evening; I should check the letters against my facsimiles of existing poems, estimate their dates from expression, vocabulary and so on. I should go through them again with a fine-toothed comb and see if there was anything I had missed.

Actually, I did none of these things; I had drunk far too much wine to be analytical. I went to bed instead and dreamed about us: Melcourt, Toto, Sebastian and me. Most of all, I dreamed of Sebastian. My dream brought me some physical release, and I woke the following morning ready to work. I forbore ringing him and got down to the letters in earnest.

Of course, my interest was not entirely scholarly. What I really wanted to do was to understand Melcourt's earliest feelings for Toto and compare them with my own. I could not get away from a belief that, by understanding Melcourt, I should understand myself, and by understanding myself, I should understand Melcourt. How foolish. How little I understood about the nature of perception, and how terribly I have learned the extent of my wrong-thinking.

I worked through until late afternoon when I was disturbed by the doorbell. I dared not hope it would be he, and schooled myself against disappointment. But when I opened the door, he was standing there, beautiful and unabashed.

I think I ought to pause here and make what is an obvious point, *viz*, I can in no way vouch for the truth of what I have set down. I do not mean, of course, that I have deliberately set out to tell lies; not a bit of it. I have, in fact, tried to do the opposite, to report the truth, but as Sebastian would say, 'There are so many shadows'. This is a subject I shall return to later. Suffice to say, some of the scenes I have described I do not remember very clearly – I hardly remember my conversation with Reg, Joyce and the church warden. I have recreated them, for that is simply the best thing I can do. And some scenes remain more clearly (or *seem* to do so) than others. Amongst the most vivid (oddly) are my imagined scenes between Melcourt and Toto; I also remember distinctly *almost* everything that passed between Sebastian and me and, most clearly of all, I remember our lovemaking.

Seven
Pink-Iced Buns

"Hello, Jules," he said. "Are you going to ask me in or are you terribly cross with me?"

I regarded him with fearful severity to disguise my feelings.

"The answer to each of your questions is in the affirmative. They are not mutually exclusive."

"I hope you're not going to be pompous all afternoon."

"Very probably. You are wearing a beautiful shirt; one which was not given you by me."

"No, Jules. You don't have the monopoly on giving me prezzies."

"Obviously not."

"Don't be cross, Jules. You know you're awfully pleased to see me really."

"Oh, come on in," I said.

He looked unrepentant, but quite beautiful. The shirt was exactly the colour of his eyes, as no doubt its donor had also noted. His hair was in a pony-tail, and I followed his denimed hips into the sitting room.

I suppose the man in the street, whoever he might be (no doubt Sebastian would have known him), would describe my flat as 'posh'. I prefer to call it tasteful; at that time, it gave me pleasure.

The sitting room is pale pink, like the inside of a shell or the blushing of a tea-rose. It is hung with some rather good pictures; there is a Watts and a late Burne-Jones; but far more enticing is a pencil drawing by Simeon Solomon, entitled *Love and Sleep embracing in Flight*; the two winged figures (possibly angels) kiss tenderly mid-air, Sleep's wings gently touch Love's cheeks. It is quite extraordinarily beautiful – and Love looks almost exactly like Sebastian. There are seven other rather valuable pictures, including a Henry Tuke; it depicts a number of boys bathing. That, too, gave me great pleasure. The rest are pretty, but not worth describing. There is a sofa in deep-rose and a chaise-longue in a deep-crimson velvet, rather the colour and texture of a peony. The carpet, an Aubusson, in a pattern of peacocks and pomegranates, echoes these shades; there is also a touch of leaf-green in it. There are one or two easy chairs in cream and chintz. The curtains are lily-of-the-valley on pink silk. They, too, are rather pretty. There are a number of bookcases containing, for the most part, Victorian first editions (among which feature a large number of Melcourts). On this particular occasion, the round yew table was covered in books and papers, and, of course, the letters. I had been working on them earlier in my study, but the sitting room seemed somehow more attuned with Melcourt. Sebastian made a beeline for the letters.

"Oh, wow!" he said. "Can I touch them, Jules?"

"Yes."

He glanced up from the table and dimpled at me. "Jules?"

"Yes?"

"Have you got any buns – those sticky ones?"

"I have buns in the freezer, yes."

"For me?" His hand hovered over the letters, but the buns were uppermost in his mind.

"Yes. I put them there last time you failed to turn up."

"Perhaps it's as well I didn't."

"Why?"

"Because if I'd come then, I should have eaten the buns, and there wouldn't be any left now."

"I should have bought more buns."

"Should you?"

"You know I should."

"Oh, Jules, you are kind. And lapsang souchong in the big jade pot?"
I went stumping off to the kitchen and left him to Melcourt.

When I returned with the tea tray (buns and jade pot) he was leaning over the table. Sebastian absorbed information very quickly; he had finished with the letters and was on to my notes.

"I don't agree with your dating of June 1893," he said without looking up. "The poison-lily sonnet does not contain the word 'fervid'; he always used 'fervid' in the Lysias cycle."

I put the tray down and went and looked over his shoulder.

"He uses 'fertile'," I said. "He was simply feeling his way towards 'fervid'."

His shirt had parted company with his jeans, exposing a small area of soft brown flesh. I put my hand on it.

"Are you feeling your way towards 'fervid'?" he asked, still bent over the papers, as my hand crept down the back of his jeans. I didn't reply; my hand was enjoying the firm hillocks inside the denim; they were both hard and soft – hard because the buttocks were strained gloriously with the leaning towards the papers, and soft because his flesh was always soft – like the feathers in the Simeon Solomon drawing. Sebastian was, in his physique, entirely perfect. He straightened up and I removed my hand.

"Do you want to do Melcourt or me, Jules? And no, it's *not* the same thing. You may have copious amounts of red hair – on all parts of your body – but you aren't Melcourt and I'm not Toto." He stood laughing at me, but I knew he would be acquiescent when his other appetites had been satisfied.

"Eat up your buns," I said.

"Pink icing! To match the walls; oh, Jules!"

I cleared a space on the table. "Don't put your sticky fingers anywhere near the letters, or on the surface of the table."

"I promise."

"How do you want it?"

"Well...?" He bit into the bun and raised an eyebrow.

"The lapsang."

"Weak, please. Oh, there's no strainer."

"No, I threw it away – after our last tea party."

He looked at me with his eyes dancing. "Oh yes, I'd forgotten. Not one of my more successful ideas."

"So we have leaves. Do you want to tell our fortunes?"

"No, Jules."

"Why not?"

"Because... Oh, you know why not. Lots of me doing bad things and lots of your being miserable. Tell me about your visit to Melcourt. You know you're dying to tell me."

"I told you on the phone," I said sulkily.

"You might tell me some more."

"No!" I felt I did not want the aged faces of Reg and Joyce intruding into our conversation. "Let's talk about the letters instead. What do the letters tell us?"

He licked the icing from the bun. "Hundreds of things." He popped the denuded pastry into his mouth. It disappeared rapidly.

"A quick synopsis, please."

He took another bun and bit into it, regarding me attentively. "Well, I would say, Toto writes to Max around May 1893."

"Because the narcissi are over?"

"Mmm. He makes a dead set at Max, who is suspicious but intrigued. They meet, and Max is simply bowled over."

"But still suspicious; no, not suspicious, apprehensive. And I think we can assume the 'poison flower' sequence of sonnets starts around then."

"How much more has Reg got? Can we get hold of it? Can I have some more tea?"

I poured out the last few drops from the jade pot. "We shall have to go down and see, shan't we? Will you come this time?"

"When are you going?"

"On Thursday."

"Great."

"You'll come?"

"Mmm."

"Really? Will you?"

"Mmm."

I wouldn't pursue it – then. "I have the telephone number, too."

"Did he give it to you?"

"No, I took it off the dial."

"Very smart work." He regarded the last bun. "Jules, I suppose the letters are genuine. I mean, have you had them authenticated?"

"I'm not entirely naive, Sebastian. I have facsimiles of all the Melcourt letters – well, you've seen them, haven't you? I spent the entire morning comparing them. I would say they're identical; and there's another thing which may have escaped your notice."

"Ah, you mean the watermark on the 1892 paper?"

"The paper is exactly the same as he used in that letter written to his bankers."

"So, you're satisfied?"

"Yes, I'm satisfied."

"Oh, good. Can I have the last bun?"

I am (I may have mentioned this before) a large man, and I have often taken comfort from the fact that Melcourt (at least to judge from the few remaining photographs), like me, had a tendency to a paunch. Undressed, I made a displeasing contrast with Sebastian who, admittedly, was always very nice about it. 'Don't worry, Jules', he would say, 'I like size'. As he finished the buns, I stood regarding him with a mixture of envy for his svelteness and pride in his beauty.

"I don't know how you can eat all the time and stay so slim."

"Oh, it all gets recycled, lots of Steiner used."

I frowned. "Go and wash your sticky hands and we will have another look at Melcourt."

"If that's what you want."

"No, of course it isn't, you know perfectly well what I want."

"Oh, good. I'll go and have a shower, then." Sebastian was by nature practical rather than romantic.

I took the tray into the kitchen and put the cups in the dishwasher. I could hear him singing snatches of Schuman in the shower. Then I went and undressed, and got into bed.

My bedroom is rather nice. The walls are covered in Lambert and Osborne wallpaper, flamingoes and swans amidst water-reeds and lilies, and the curtains are made of a similar design. The bed is a four-poster, naturally; it is swathed in the green of the water-reeds, with touches of flamingo-pink. One wall contains an original portrait of Melcourt, which I was fortunate enough to pick up at auction. Of course, I paid a great deal of money for it, probably much more than it was worth; the agent told me afterwards that I would never make the money back on it, should I wish to re-sell it. "I shall never re-sell it," I had replied. I suppose in those days I imagined that I could learn some truth about Melcourt from his portrait. The bay window looks out on the Isis. In the days before Sebastian, I used to enjoy watching the eights go sculling past, but after I fell in love with him I hardly noticed the bodies of other young men.

The wall facing the bed contains a large mirror. This, of course, had been Sebastian's idea, one day quite early on in our relationship. He was lying across the bed, relaxing after a rather athletic and mutually satisfactory session.

"What a pity," he had said, "only us to see us."

"What on earth do you mean?" I had retorted angrily; I thought he was asking for an audience.

"It would be fun. I mean, if there was a mirror on the ceiling, we could see if the mirror-people liked it as much as we did."

"You could; I couldn't."

"Well you *could*, Jules. It would just mean…"

"All right," I said.

But the next day, he had done one of his disappearing tricks and, to be honest, I lacked the courage to find someone to ask to fix mirrors over the bed, so I bought a large Victorian mirror from an antique shop, and hung it on the wall myself. The surface was a little pitted (I should have had it restored, but I wanted to have it in place for Sebastian as soon as possible). It never gave a particularly good reflection, but, needless to say, it had its moments. I shall be returning to the subject of the mirror later on.

What else did the bedroom contain? It's odd, isn't it; only a year or so has passed, yet I can't see the room in my mind's eye with any clarity. And I had chosen my things with such care! Ah well, as Sebastian would say, if you can't recall *things*, how can you possibly know anything else? Oh, yes; there was a pile of black velvet cushions screen-printed with Burne-Jones' *Laus Veneris*, a rather sweet carriage-clock, and a curious, elevated chair (actually from Lord Houghton's celebrated collection of erotica at Fryston), cunningly angled, with raised leg rests and so on. There was little that escaped the Victorians! It was, I suppose, a very pretty room. Sebastian liked it, anyway, and that was all that mattered to me.

Eight
Sausage, Mash and Onion Gravy

"Come here," I said, "I am going to give you pleasure." I made him lie down on the bed facing the mirror (Sebastian was always acquiescent in my demands; he was, in some ways, very unselfish). I wanted him like this: stomach down, buttocks raised, not so much to observe myself fucking him (although I admit I was not averse to this), but in order to see the sweetness of his face, particularly the expression in his eyes as he came. I imagine most people would describe me as 'buttoned up'. When I gave tutorials, I allowed my students to talk, rather than myself. Even at High Table, I had little to say. My size and red hair make me a conspicuous-enough object. I do not wish to draw further attention to myself by uttering inanities. So I say little; I do not enjoy activities that involve hysteria, such as football matches or any sort of pageantry. My interests are those of a refined and cultured man: I like going to concerts, I enjoy the theatre, literature, art, food, good wine, pleasant surroundings; in short, all kinds of beauty. Such things as I have mentioned, I enjoy moderately and quietly. It was not so when I made love to Sebastian; I was incapable of making love quietly.

It was such a wonder to me to be inside him, to thrust into him, all the many emotions of my heart translated into this one ecstatic exploration; my love, my feelings, my desires, even the hurt of his betrayals all lost, all given away into his glorious grasping arse. And I am a man easily aroused; my cock swells quickly and my need for orgasm is very great. I groaned from the depth of my being in my desperation to come, and coming, I groaned in an ecstasy of pleasure. Yet I fought for control over myself so that it should be best for him, so that he might prolong his pleasure, trembling on the delicious brink before he came, bursting and spurting into my face.

"Was it nice?" he asked. "It sounded as if it was. Would Max have approved?"

"Max would have approved. Would Toto?"

"Oh, yes, I enjoyed it every bit as much as Toto – twice." I remembered the lovely spurt of him as he came. I pushed his head down on the pillow and stroked his warm, dry hair back from his face and gazed at his wonderful body. He had the most adorable line of soft honey-coloured down running from chest to waist, but below, he was smooth, hairless, glorious.

"I worship you," I said, "I am besotted with you. There is no part of you I do not consider perfect."

His head moved impatiently. "Oh, don't, Jules."

"Why don't you come and live with me?"

"Because I don't want to, because I am a tart, because I like fucking around."

"Come to Italy with me."

"Perhaps. Maybe."

"Just for a few days."

"Perhaps. Let's do Melcourt first."

"You'll come with me?"

"Yes. I've said. Thursday." He yawned.

"I love you. I want to spend the rest of my life with you. Every minute of every day, every second of every night."

"Jules."

"Yes, darling?"

"I want to go to sleep."

"All right, my angel."

"Jules?"

"Yes, my love?"

"Can we eat something when I wake up?"

"What would you like?" I nibbled his neck.

"Sausages and mash."

"Yes."

"Sausages –" his eyes began to close "– with lots of leeks in them, and onion gravy."

"If that will make you happy."

His eyes opened. "And lots of cheese in the mash. Will you, Jules?"

"Yes."

I kissed him, and fell to fondling him gently so as not to wake him; then I fell to fondling myself, but less gently and I knew I could not keep quiet. Sebastian must be allowed sleep; I left off, got out of bed and covered him over with the duvet. Then I went into the kitchen; I took leek sausages out of the freezer. Then I found potatoes and peeled them and set them to boil in the pan; I put the sausages in the Aga and chopped the onions. Tears sprang to my eyes; it didn't matter, I was used to crying over Sebastian.

I stood in the kitchen, waiting for the potatoes to cook, and fried the onions. I got out a dish for the gravy – Bisto, which I kept for him; I personally do not like it – and peered at the sausages. I grated the cheese and, once the potatoes were soft, added it in. I must have presented an extraordinary picture: naked, thick red hair about my genitals, my greying red hair flying about my face as I thrust madly at the potatoes. At last it was done, I put it into a Le Creuset cast-iron bowl and placed it in the oven. The gravy I would make at the last moment. I opened a bottle of Burgundy and went back to the bedroom. I stood and looked at him wonderingly, and felt acute happiness; the most beautiful boy in the world was lying asleep in my bed. Soon we would drink red wine and eat sausages and mash and discuss the life and poetry of Max Melcourt, after which I would make love to him in a number of different and possibly innovative ways (but not with the tea-strainer). Life at that moment seemed particularly sweet to me.

"Oh, goodness, Jules..." His blue eyes opened; he awoke as

effortlessly as he fell asleep. "I've got to go."

"Go!" I echoed incredulously. "What do you mean 'go'?"

"I'm going to Amsterdam."

"Amsterdam! You're fucking-well not!" As he rose, I took him by the shoulders and began shaking him. "You're not, you're not! I forbid it!"

"Oh, all right." He extricated himself neatly from my hands.

"What on earth are you talking about?" I asked, appeased by his capitulation. "You never said anything before about Amsterdam."

"A friend. A party," he said, stretching carelessly. "Never mind, I'll go tomorrow."

"What friend?"

"Don't ask, Jules. You wouldn't want to know."

I thought of the sort of people I had seen him with and knew he was probably right. I looked at him, as he stood idly brushing his hair with my silver-backed brush, in the mirror. I knew it was no good to express anger and bitterness, or, indeed, even feel it. Sebastian was Sebastian and if he needed to go to Amsterdam, he would go whether or not I minded. I was powerless to stop him. Besides – common sense asserted itself – Amsterdam might have him tomorrow, as undoubtedly the friend would, but I had him tonight.

"Jules," he said suddenly, "you smell of onions. In fact –" his entire face lit up "– the whole flat does. Have you really made sausages and mash?"

"It was what you wanted. We are both fortunate; we both have what we want – you a meal and I your presence."

"Don't be bitter, Jules," he said, coming over and linking his arms round my neck. I watched my cock in the mirror respond to his embrace. "You know what I'm like."

"I'm going to mix up the Bisto for your gravy," I said savagely.

"Can we eat it in bed?"

"No! I don't want sausages in the sheets."

"Nor Bisto in the bed?"

"Very funny. All right," I said, "just this once."

"I'll make the gravy, if you like."

"No. Just get into bed, look beautiful, and I'll put the food on a tray and bring it to you."

He smiled rather sadly. "Will that give you pleasure, Jules?"

"Great pleasure, but not as much as the pleasure I intend to have afterwards."

We sat side by side in bed, the curtains absorbing the pungent smell of onion; I supposed it would hang around for days. We shared the tray. I was not a great lover of bangers and mash, but I had a sausage to keep him company, and a little of the potato. It was quite acceptable. Sebastian loved it all. As he spooned up his gravy, his eyes wore the look of fixed intensity which they had during sex.

"Do you think that we'll find out the truth about Melcourt and Toto?"

"Do you mean Melcourt's death?" he asked, obediently wiping his fingers on the linen napkin I had provided.

"Yes, the answer to the old riddle; did he commit suicide, or did Toto kill him?"

"Well, as you know, I've always thought Toto killed him. I am sure he was totally despicable, even worse than me." He took another sausage.

"I wonder," I said, "if we *shall* find out. It would be marvellous, wouldn't it?" I was so carried away, I even helped myself to some onion gravy.

"I don't know –" he stuck his fingers in the potato and licked them "– how much we ever really know of people, alive or dead. To be honest, Jules, I have a problem with the whole biography thing."

"Well," I said rather irritably, "I do have some experience in this field; I have spent twenty years writing biographies." In fact, I've done a great deal of work on the nature of biography. "I..."

"Well?"

"To give an accurate picture, of..."

"Accurate or subjective?"

"Well, obviously there must be a certain amount of subjectivity."

"Not a certain amount, the total amount. Nobody can *know*."

"I think..."

"Well," he said, picking up a sausage in his fingers and poking it into the mashed potato, "how well do his colleagues know Julian Collins? I daresay you are considered able, quiet and rather reserved. Probably, there is some speculation about you. You are a man of taste, with enough money to indulge your tastes, but what do you do in your spare time? Probably, you are gay, but you have not come out as being so. In fact, you cut a shadowy Housman-like figure, whereas..."

"Whereas..."

"Whereas..."

"Use the serviette. Your fingers are covered in potato!"

"Whereas, I see a very different side of you. Who can say who is right?"

"You are all right, my colleagues and you."

"But the whole truth cannot be perceived by one person."

I took over the job of wiping his fingers. "That is not what you said at your interview."

"Good heavens, Jules, surely you don't remember what rubbish I said then?"

"I remember everything about you. You said you liked to draw parallels between people from the past and now."

"The trouble is, Jules, we both see Toto through Melcourt's eyes and we perceive Melcourt through our own. And besides, you imagine their relationship to be like ours. I bet you've had all sorts of fantasies about them."

"Of course I haven't!"

He laughed. I knew that he could often see through me; he seemed to posses an uncanny knowledge of my secret thoughts, and now I felt a kind of shame that he should be aware of my Melcourt day-dreams. If he knew those, he must also know of the hours I spent fantasising about him – although, of course, he wouldn't have given it a thought.

'Jules', he would have said gleefully, 'yet another excuse for wanking!'

"It's awfully dangerous," he continued, "mixing up two sets of people – particularly when one set is dead. When are we going to Melcourt?"

"Thursday. I told you. No, don't move. Stay there like that. Please, sweetheart."

"I smell of onions."

"You don't; you smell lovely. So lovely, I'm going to get rid of the tray."

"I'm awfully full. You'll have to be very gentle with me."

I took the tray out into the kitchen, but didn't bother putting the things into the dishwasher. I came back and undid the great swathes of curtain that surrounded the bed and let them conceal him from the mirrors. Then I got in beside him. I quoted:

"When my lover lies at rest
My thoughts are green and I am blest.
My world becomes a song-bird's nest
When his lips to mine are pressed
His hair in golden gleam is tressed
And shines as sunshine in the west;
I hear his heart beat in his breast
And from his body all undressed
The sweetness of his loins I'll wrest."

He pulled a face. "It's not awfully good, is it? In fact, I should say it's dreadfully bad."

"Well," I said, allowing my hands to explore the delicious places of his body, "even Melcourt nods, but as a directive on how to proceed, it speaks perfectly."

"Oh, Jules."

"Mmm."

"Do remember the sausages, won't you?"

Making love to him with exquisite care and tenderness was as much a delight as to attack him with unbridled passion – opportunities for which occurred on three other occasions in the small hours and the longer hours of the morning ("Wake me up from time to time, Jules. I shouldn't want to miss anything."). I did, and he didn't, which was as well, since, when I finally woke up, he was gone. He was horribly prone to do this and it was a perpetual bone of contention between us. I would try to explain that it wasn't simply a question of sex, but the joy of… well, I suppose, possession. Anyway, he had gone and my heart was filled with misery; the word 'Amsterdam' came into my mind. I had never checked that he would be back in time for coming down to Melcourt with me. I picked up the phone. My heart sank when I heard the answering-machine:

"Sebastian Salonière has gone to Amsterdam to see 'the little mouse with clogs on, going clip-clippetty-clop on the stair'. Of course, he hasn't gone solely in the interest of musology. Amsterdam has, he believes, other more tangible attractions. He will be so pleased to hear from you after the Palestrina, of course."

It didn't sound as if Sebastian intended hurrying back.

Nine
A Miserable Cup of Coffee

"Is that Mr... um...?"

"Julian Collins, yes."

The voice was old, reproachful and rather common. It was, of course, Joyce. "I keep forgetting your name, Mr..."

"It really doesn't matter. How nice to hear from you, Mrs Roberts."

"Yes. What did you say?"

"I said how nice to hear from you. I'm so looking forward –" I raised my voice "– to coming down to Melcourt on Thursday."

"I can't hear what you say."

"I said, I am looking forward to my next visit – on Thursday," I bellowed.

"That's why I'm ringing. You can't come then."

I ground my teeth. "Oh dear! When *would* be convenient?"

Her voice became querulous; it was all very difficult – the lady from the social was coming and then there was the young lady who did her hair and (a mysterious being entitled) the sheropody; and Mondays, she did the washing, and Tuesdays, the man came with the fish. When, then, could I come? It couldn't be until Thursday week, Mr... um... The receiver went down abruptly. A fortnight was an inordinately long time to wait, but I supposed it was not the end of the world, and at least it would give Sebastian time to come back from Amsterdam – something which he showed no sign of doing.

Actually, I was very much at a loose end: the Summer Term had come to a close – the round of garden and cocktail parties and summer festivities had passed – I had marked finals papers and sat on the last of many committee meetings. The Michaelmas Term was too far off to bother about. I felt I had come to rather an impasse with my Melcourt book, for there was really nothing I could do until I knew whether there were more letters or not, and the figures of Melcourt and Toto flashed about my brain like spots before the eyes. Scenes between the two of them appeared with extraordinary vividness and I consoled myself for Sebastian's absence with a portrait of an equally treacherous Toto. I believe it was during this period – i.e., while Sebastian was in Amsterdam and I between two visits to Melcourt – that I first entertained the idea of abandoning, or at least postponing, the completion of my existing book on Melcourt and writing a psychological biography of Melcourt. For no one understood as I did (certainly not Steiner or Reg Roberts) the feelings of a large, ungainly, red-haired, middle-aged man possessed of literary ability, for a beautiful, blond, unscrupulous man half his age. In the meantime, I bought some maps of Southern Italy and planned some routes – on the off-chance that Sebastian would come on holiday with me when he got tired of everything else.

Ten days passed extremely slowly. Sebastian's answering-machine message remained unchanged (a sure sign that he was not in Oxford). Obviously, he had forgotten all about coming to Melcourt with me; had, in all probability, never intended coming at all. I tried not to think of what he was doing in Holland. I was deeply unhappy and I knew I must go down to Melcourt a second time on my own.

I slept extremely badly on the eve of my visit to Dorset; I was pent up, frustrated by my period of enforced inactivity, and, of course, I wanted Sebastian. I do not mean only to satisfy my physical longing for him, but to bring me the extreme happiness that his presence always inspired, and the closeness he brought to me with Melcourt. I hated to think of him in Amsterdam.

I resorted to sleeping pills, but when I did sleep, my dreams were hectic: Joyce, Reg, Sebastian and Toto filtered in and out of my consciousness, mocking me in different ways. Joyce held the Tupperware pot of baked custard before me: 'Eat this, Mr... um...' she said. Reg raised his chin and said slyly, 'No blue irises for you!' Toto merged into Sebastian and he stood, naked and laughing, before me. 'Goodness, Jules', he said, 'you're not wanking again, are you?' Only Melcourt smiled at me, but the gentleness of his smile upset me more than anything else; he was so dreadfully vulnerable. Nevertheless, the night passed, as such nights do, and I was on the road by nine. Without Sebastian's presence and its concomitant delays, I made good time. I was too early.

I parked the Porsche and stood and looked at Melcourt Hall. There was a slight drizzle and the air was chilly. I put up my umbrella and stood regarding Max's home. I tried to shut out the hideous modern annex built along the side, and the horrible modern bungalows that seemed to me as acne on the face of the Melcourt Estate. Once, Max had walked here, perhaps stood on the very spot where I stood now and composed verses of great beauty and great sadness. Doubtless, too, he had thought of Toto as I thought of Sebastian, and wondered about the joys and dangers in possessing so beautiful and unaccountable a lover.

I walked past the miserable, shrivelled geraniums and rang the front doorbell. Joyce was a long time answering; I supposed this was due to the exigences of old age, but she did not look very pleased to see me.

"Oh, it's you, Mr... um... You're very early."

"I am sorry," I replied stiffly, "I hope I do not inconvenience you."

"Oh!" She had either not heard or not understood. "You'd better come in, but the sheropody is here." It was my turn to be non-plussed.

"The sheropody, Mrs Roberts?"

Joyce's eyes, behind the now familiar blue-trimmed spectacles, expressed surprise, and the wart nodded a little, as if in sympathy.

"I should have thought you would have known about a sheropody, being a doctor."

She made her way to the sitting room, and I followed along behind the sticks; all was revealed, for there sat Reg in his corner of the room with a footstool and feet protruding before him on a pouffe; beside the foot and the pouffe sat the chiropodist. I had hoped great things of Reg and had purposely planned an early visit, remembering Joyce's assurance that he was 'better in the mornings'. But her 'here's Mr Collins come early' elicited no response from him; he made not the smallest effort to lift his head from his chest; even the bare foot remained impassive. Not so the chiropodist; I think she was the smallest woman I have ever seen, but what she lacked in stature she made up for in vocal volume. She spoke loudly and incessantly, and Joyce looked on impassively.

"Oh, I've heard all about you from Mrs Roberts. A book-writer... just lift your foot a little, dear, that's it... I'm a great reader; always got a book in my hand. They laugh at me, my son and daughter: 'Another book,' they say. I read anything, though I like a story. I always go by the cover. You can always tell by the cover. I never look inside until I get home. What's your name now? Oh, Collins... Not *Jackie* Collins, I can see that..." I smiled, showing a wan appreciation of the wit. "And you're writing a book about some poet in old times. That's very nice. Just wiggle your big toe, Mr Roberts. A bit more, dear. Good."

Joyce and I regarded Reg's foot in silence. I wondered if Joyce would offer coffee, but the sheropody had a half-empty cup at her side, so I supposed the hour had passed; furthermore, as much as I wanted coffee, I saw the sheropody's cup, and believed myself better off without coffee. I wedged myself into the orthopaedic chair and gritted my teeth, wondering how much of this I should have to endure, but a new character appeared, quite unannounced. This was no knocker-upon-doors but a putter-of-a-head round. The head belonged to a very gaunt body; it was not unlike that of a very old horse. Its neck wear explained its purpose.

"It's the Reverend," said Joyce, "with the parish magazine." I swear I heard Reg give a groan; the sheropody didn't look very pleased, either.

I, meanwhile, weighed up the pros and cons: would the arrival of the Reverend hasten the departure of the sheropody? Or would each prolong the stay of the other? Was the Reverend an even greater threat, or could he be brought in as an ally? Already, he was straining his neck in my direction. The sheropody, who was clearly still aggrieved, took a vicious jab at Reg's foot, and Joyce announced that I was Mr... um... book-writer.

"Oh!" said the Reverend, "that is very interesting – extremely interesting." I saw my way in.

"Yes. I have come to chat to Mr Roberts about Lord Melcourt, the poet."

"Really? How very interesting."

"I understand that Mr Roberts knows a very great deal..."

"Ouch!" It was Reg's first word.

"You must sit still, dear."

"I wonder," said the Reverend, "if I might be permitted to put the kettle on and make us all a cup of coffee?"

"He's a devil for his coffee," said Joyce, uttering what seemed a particularly inappropriate personification for the Reverend. The sheropody was finished. She set about gathering up the tools of her trade. She gave a tug at Reg's foot as if she would have liked to put it in her bag along with the rest of her implements.

"I can't stop, dear. Three more calls to make before lunch. I never stop, me. That will be the usual £7.50, dear. Nice to meet you, Mr... You must tell me the name of your book. I like a good read."

She had not been hard to dislodge; for staying power, she was not in the same league as the Reverend. He went through two cups of coffee and half a packet of squashed fly biscuits, which he ate as if he had not eaten for a month. Not for him any fear over uncleanliness of crockery. We had the organ fund, the church fête, the ordination of women, the over-70s and the under-threes. Joyce quite enjoyed it; Reg went off to the lavatory. I wondered if he was going to find me some more letters, but it was a vain hope; he came shuffling back empty-handed. When we got to the flower festival, I had had enough. I had sat for an hour, making polite noises, and had heard nothing about Max. I could restrain myself no longer; I butted in rudely.

"Mr Roberts was telling me last time I was here of Lord Melcourt's fondness for flowers."

"Yes," said Joyce, "Mr Roberts gave Mr... um... an interview."

"And I wonder –" I went bull-dozing on "– what Mr Roberts will tell me today."

"Ah!" said the Reverend quite nastily; he was cross, I think, at being balked of the flower festival.

Reginald lifted his head slowly and looked at me with his old violet eyes. "My feet hurt," he said, and he shuffled off to the bedroom. He did not return, but the Reverend told Joyce all about the parish supper. I had drawn a blank. I stayed for another half an hour and prepared to make my departure.

"Did you bring back the Tupperware pot?" asked Joyce as I stood at the door. I apologised profusely and asked if I might call again to return it. I said how much I had enjoyed the baked custard. The Reverend, who seemed to have settled in for the day, looked up at this point and gave me a nasty look.

"I like a baked custard," he said reproachfully. It was time to call it a day.

I returned home, full of bitterness. My disappointment was to be compounded; I rang Sebastian and heard the familiar voice telling me about Amsterdam and mice. I replaced the receiver.

I sat down at the kitchen table and wept; I didn't cook anything but drank half a bottle of gin and most of a bottle of claret. I was horribly sick afterwards, and felt desperately weak. I filled a hot-water bottle and went to bed. In all my misery, it brought me small solace.

Ten
An Unusual Blend of Coffee

I felt dreadfully washed out the next day. I lay on the chaise-longue with a rug over me, and drank a good deal of luke-warm water. At lunchtime, I managed a coddled egg and some soldiers. The one good thing about my weakened state was that I felt incapable of continuing resentment; it seemed too much effort. I felt I no longer cared about any of it – the Melcourt letters, Roberts, Sebastian, Italy, Steiner – or rather, I knew that I would care again in a day or so, but that, now, I was somehow in remission from these worries. My mind was not free to consider them. I read a couple of Dorothy L. Sayers' Peter Wimsey novels, *Clouds of Witness*, I think, and *The Nine Tailors* – I don't know, I can't remember now – and in the evening I was strong enough to go to a concert of chamber music. Of course, it had to be Palestrina, but even that I got over. Oddly enough, I had a good night's sleep; such a good night's sleep that it was 9 o'clock before I had showered and collected my post.

My post!

How extraordinary it is that one's whole being can be changed in seconds by inanimate objects! Having been plunged in the deepest of despair, I was now to be filled with delight and exaltation.

There were a great number of letters. I corresponded with a large number of people, mainly on academic matters. Such correspondence brings in its weary train large numbers of reports, papers, journals and the like. Some are interesting, most are not.

That day, I received only two missives, and I did not know which to look at first, so great was my delight and astonishment at both. The first was a postcard: It came from Sebastian.

It was chosen for its extreme vulgarity – indeed I was amazed it had been allowed into the country – for it had been sent from Holland; it contained four stanzas of Melcourt's *Humble-Bees*:

'*How sweet the taste of honey*
That gushes from your comb,
No mountain stream that rushes
Can bring such silver foam.

Your honey smells of violet, of clover
And the rose
It swells so sweetly over,
My lips are loth to close

Your honey on my lips is ripe
Like scented thyme
No tunes upon the pipe
Can so move this heart of mine

And oft I read in books that treat
Of herbal lore
That honey pure is sweet
But mixed, entices more...'

He was in Amsterdam, and he had thought of me! He had sent me Melcourt, and some of Melcourt's most explicit verses.

I have often wondered since why he sent me that poem; indeed, why he bothered writing to me at all from Amsterdam. Was he moved by guilt – remorse, even? Or was it done at the prompting of his companion? Did they laugh together at my fond incredulity? Well, it is pointless to speculate. Anyway, I was very happy. I was so happy that it was some minutes before I looked at what would otherwise have leapt out at me. The envelope of the second piece of post was addressed in shaky writing, as if its author had found the task difficult. More importantly, the postmark was Dorset.

I took both the postcard and the letter to my desk and carefully opened the letter. It was written on paper, water-marked 1892. I shook it for modern enclosures. There were none. If it was from Reg, he wasn't 'letting on'. I have no difficulty reading Melcourt's writing for, despite his affected flamboyance, his writing was very regular and neat. It was not one letter, but two; it seemed that Reg liked to give letters in pairs. I placed them in the correct order:

Melcourt Hall

My dear Anthony,

I have spoken to you of pedants, pedagogues, schoolmasters and mentors, Gravitas and Formalitas; I told you I had eschewed them all and banished them from our company. Now I shall eat my words (rather easier than eating my hat – as I saw a chap do whilst I was at Magdalene). There are times when only these wearisome creatures will do, and now I have demanded their return. Gravitas approaches, resplendent in black; he walks with measured tread and frowns as he advances. Formalitas comes behind, preceded by a hunched lictor complete with fasces. He wears, of course, an inordinate number of medals. In their wake come a whole academy of pedants and pedagogues; some wield sticks, others brandish grammars, books of mathematics, horrid tomes of logic. Where are they bound, you ask, why have they been summoned? I will tell you. They are bound (they approach in horrid throng) for the chamber of one Anthony Roberts, they have come at my bidding and they are intent on chastisement! And I follow in their wake, a gentler mentor, for while they prepare their instruments of torture, I plead your cause.

'Only spare him,' I entreat. 'It was only his modesty that caused him

to withdraw his acceptance and say he would not after all come to Melcourt (although his word was given). Spare him, gentlemen, I entreat you. See! He capitulates already. He repents his hastily written refusal.' And with that, I drive them back with their very own weapons. Already they retreat, I have vanquished them all. I deserve, do I not, the rewards of the conqueror?

Of course you must come! You said you would come. You shall come. Let me hear no more of this nonsense: 'I have nothing to wear'. That in itself must be an advantage – at least for the rest of the world, if not for you. The rose needs no false petals. However, to save your blushes I enclose a cheque. You may use it as a fig leaf or for the purchasing of seemly garments, but whichever you do, you must arrive punctual to the instant on Tuesday. (I will send the fly to meet you at the station.)

As I told you, there will be a dozen or so rather less than tedious people staying from Friday to Monday (I think you will like the Blythes; Lady Ellen is particularly amusing). I have sung your praises to all of them, and if you do not come, they will all be rending their garments in grief, and then <u>nobody</u> will have any clothes. So you see how you must come. (Besides, they all depart on Monday so then we may be together.) I want you to know Melcourt; in its essence, I mean.

It is well you will come too late for the narcissi; but I have whispered of you in the rose garden and the place has become a hot-bed (sic) of dissension: the pink roses have turned red from furiously blushing at the thought of so much beauty, and as for the white roses, they have turned yellow with jealousy at the very thought of you treading amongst them. It is hard to believe, is it not, that sweet and soft blossoms conceal thorns of such sharpness?

Your affectionate friend,
Max.

P.S. Send a telegram. 'Veniam' will suffice.

This is the subsequent letter:

Melcourt Hall

My most beloved Toto,

When I first set my eyes upon you – that day in the Savoy – I was as an explorer who comes across a secret cave and sees the glint of gold within. Bemused, he stands upon the threshold, wondering if it be safe to enter. For a while he walks about, advancing, retreating, now turning to the right, now to the left but always returning. At last he can bear it no longer, he throws caution to the winds, he enters and there before him lies a great trove of treasure, a mighty hoard such as they say old Norse kings amassed or the great ruler of golden Mycenae. And yet he dare not touch. You are following, are you not, my most beloved Toto, the story of this traveller? He does not touch the gold; at first no doubt he is frightened lest the treasure conceal a nest of serpents or scorpions, or is held by an ancient curse. Evening draws nigh, the cave is bright with the glistening of the treasure. The traveller forgets his fears, so great is his desire for the beauty before him. He reaches out, and yet he dare not touch. Now he is assailed by a new terror; perhaps, so great is its beauty, the treasure will vanish away at his touch, for it is surely not possible that a mortal man should possess such riches. No, it must be a mirage such as thirsty men in a desert see, imagining they behold water whilst it is only an illusion. Better, this traveller thinks, to preserve his illusion than to touch and find bitter disappointment. So he gazes before him, sometimes reaching out a hand only to withdraw it again. Then, oh then, I do not know whether his spirit compels him or it is some injunction of the gods, he stretches out and touches, gathers, grasps and garners.

I am that traveller, I have dared to touch my treasure, I have dared to fill my arms with gold, nay I have lain upon it, I have become intimate with every part of it. I have possessed it utterly and it has not vanished from me. It is mine, all the beauty, all the treasure of the world. My most beloved, it is mine. How should the traveller speak? How can he tell of his joy?

Oh, my dearest one, we are one flesh, one mind, one soul, let us be together until the Day of Doom when God's trumpet sounds upon the world. Nay, that will mark but the first millennium of our love, our passion will pass beyond the bounds of time into eternal union.

I worship you,
Max.

I sat down on the sofa, tears pouring down my face. All my life, it seemed to me, I had been waiting for this moment, for Melcourt's declaration of love to Toto. Our lives were not distinct; they were transformed and seared together by love, for whatever I felt for Sebastian, he had felt for Toto. I experienced envy, too, for I held in my hands the letters of a man who had enjoyed his lover's body and had been able to put into words the feelings it had inspired. I had never been able to do this – often, I took hold of my lover roughly after love and told him of my passion, my devotion and my undying love. And yet I could not express myself as Melcourt had done; I could only utter inarticulate expressions, ill-sounding, unoriginal and inelegant. And he? 'Don't spoil it, Jules', 'I know, Jules', 'I want to sleep', were all the response I could elicit from him. And yet had Melcourt fared better? What had been Toto's response? My thoughts were disturbed by the coffee-machine, which made the sudden vulgar noise it used to make on announcing the completion of its labours.

I drank, at that time, a very unusual blend of coffee; the man at the delicatessen got it for me – he claimed his brother imported it from a small village in Southern Turkey. I suspect the brother (who was small and dark, and the shiftiest man you ever saw) imported a very different brand of goods, or perhaps there was poppy seed mixed up in the coffee, for when I drank it, I could conjure scenes of Max's life with Toto with extraordinary ease:

They had dined late, and the balminess of the June evening had induced them to walk into the gardens, the roses glimmered in the starlight and a full moon swept the garden with light. Toto took his arm.

"Was I a success?"

"Ah! Now you ask for compliments, and I am not sure that compliments are good for you, they make you toss back your petals and a smile of overwhelming delight plays upon your rosy lips."

"But was I?" The young man turned to him eagerly. "Did I please?"

"You cannot help but do so. Lady Blythe made enquiries of you. I believe she thinks you would suit her daughter, Ellen."

"You are teasing me."

"You like being teased."

Melcourt stopped to pluck a rose of the palest pink. "Let me put it in your button-hole; my pledge of... affection. And what will you give me in return?"

The young man laughed. "Look," he said, "it is coming on to rain."

Suddenly, the whole sky darkened. A few large drops of rain fell; almost singly at first, but the pace increased until the rain fell with hard incessence; and yet neither of the men felt inclined to move. It was as if each waited for the other. There was silence between them, and only the sound of the rain as it fell upon the dense foliage of the rose-garden. For minutes they stood silent, regarding each other – Toto's eyes were bright, his pupils huge.

At last he said, "Your hair is quite straightened by the rain, how strange it looks, hanging like red threads," and he reached out gently and wound a damp lock round his finger. The rain intensified the scent of the roses, intermingled with the wafted perfume of honeysuckle; and still the two stood in the rain, allowing their clothes to hang wetly about them. Melcourt gently moved his hand from the young man's hair and, placing his fingers beneath his chin, drew Toto to him and kissed him lightly on the lips.

Almost upon the meeting of the lips came a tremendous clap of thunder; a blinding flash of lightning forked across the sky and the rain fell in torrents.

"It is my pledge!" cried Toto, and, pulling himself away from Melcourt, he began running, laughing wildly, and Melcourt ran after him towards the house.

I drank a second cup of the strange coffee. It had the property of being both acrid and sweet. You felt you would like to drink for ever. I took my cup into the sitting room and lay on the sofa; the coffee induced a kind of feverish somnolence...

"Max!"

"My dear!" Max got out of bed in alarm. "Whatever is it?"

Toto stood in the doorway, bare-foot, in a nightshirt whose folds engulfed him. He trembled, and the candle he held flickered with his trembling. He put it down and advanced towards Melcourt.

"I am so cold." Melcourt felt the young man's arms about his neck and he, who had feared the danger inherent in the young man's beauty, was overwhelmed with sweet tenderness for his very vulnerability. He took off the boy's nightshirt and took off his own, so that the warmth from his body might penetrate into that of his friend. He led him to the bed. They lay together beneath the covers, and all Max's love was sweet tenderness. But when he felt the slender arms of his companion close about him, and the hard white body press close upon him, and the pouting rose-bud lips meet his, then the tenderness became longing and the longing an ache; and the tenderness fled and overwhelming desire came upon him. He was conscious of nothing but a terrible need to plunge himself again and again into the yielding core of the boy's compelling beauty.

I reached for the phone; I needed to speak to him.

"Sebastian Salonière," I was informed, "has gone to Amsterdam..."

I decided to write to him instead, or rather, to send him a letter. Everything I wanted to say to him had already been written, so I photocopied Melcourt's last letter: '*My own beloved Toto...*' I put a line through Toto, and wrote 'Sebastian' next to it. At the end ('*I worship you – Max*') I crossed out Melcourt's name and wrote 'J'. On the back, I wrote 'Am going down to Melcourt on Thursday, leaving at 9.00 a.m.; will wait until 9.30. Please come'. I added, as an inducement, 'I'll take you out to dinner at the Randolph afterwards'. Then I bundled it all into an envelope, and walked down to the post box with it straight away: if I waited, I should be too ashamed to send it.

Eleven
Pink-Suede Shorts

I may have given the impression that I was eremitic, reclusive, a social outcast, interested only in my own company, my researches and – Sebastian. This is not entirely true; while I was not a gregarious man, I had always attended the plethora of functions with which the college presented me. I went to dinners and lunches, sherry parties, teas, suppers and what-have-you, and was conscious of a duty to return the hospitality I had been offered. On the other hand, it is fair to say that in these days of the summer vacation, in between visits to Melcourt and wished-for visits from Sebastian, I had avoided socialising, and had certainly not invited people to my flat. However, there was a long-standing invitation to four or five members of my department (with wives, etc.) that I had arranged before the Melcourt business had arisen. That I had arranged, that I must stand by. I had said nothing of it at the time to Sebastian; I never said anything that might deter him from coming to the flat, and if he should arrive, well, I was not averse to people knowing such a glamorous figure was a friend of mine.

It was a fairly successful dinner: I am, as I have mentioned, a good cook and I had cooked well; the food had been enjoyed by a congenial company. I would call it a pleasant evening. At 11 o'clock, enough food, wine, conversation and polite controversy had been ingested and digested, and there was a general murmuring of departure; I was not sorry that the evening was coming to an end. I had done what was expected of me. Then, there was a ring at the bell.

It was Sebastian. My heart pounded. He was back; he had come in response to my letter. He had come to tell me he loved me/would spend the rest of his life with me/would collaborate with me on a Melcourt book/would... On the other hand (common sense asserted itself), he neither looked like a man with a serious purpose in view, nor appeared disconcerted to find my flat full of people.

He stood there in boots, T-shirt and (admittedly, it *was* a hot evening) tiny pink-suede shorts, his golden hair loose about his face. He gazed about him; he was all innocent curiosity.

"It's an orgy and you haven't asked me, Jules."

"Young Salonière," said Atkins who was waiting impatiently in the hallway for his stout spouse, "if it had been an orgy, you would most certainly have been there."

"Gosh," said Sebastian, "I don't know whether to take that as a compliment or an insult."

He smiled sweetly, and I suspected that he had fucked Atkins somewhere in the course of his four years at Oxford. "Wow!" he continued, as Dorothy Atkins emerged from the lavatory. "What an extraordinarily beautiful dress." And Dorothy Atkins, who had probably not been complimented in the last 30 years of her life, or even in the previous 10, blushed. He had made her happy. He oozed gently into the hall, and inquired after the Dobsons' twins (I had totally forgotten that the twins existed). He asked after Dr Wood's batik business, and suggested a shop in London called 'The Dying'; he knew the owner. He greeted the aged Rossetti in Italian. The latter lost no time in inviting Sebastian to stay with him in Milan.

I longed for them to go; I tapped my fingers up and down on the hall table; I replied to questions in monosyllables. I felt acute hatred for all of them. I wanted only to be alone with him. I glowered at all my guests and finally, since none of them seemed inclined to go, I glowered at Sebastian. He laughed happily.

"It's *so* nice," he said, "to see everyone looking so *jolly*."

Perhaps I create an impression of a machiavellian character; a heartless and insincere manipulator of the naive. This is not the case. To start with, my colleagues (and their spouses, most of them) were highly intelligent people, not material for ocular wool-pulling. And, to continue, Sebastian was *not* insincere; the concept of sincerity simply did not enter his mind: his intuition told him what people wanted to hear, and he was happy to accommodate it. He would compliment Mrs Atkins on her dress, or speak to Signor Rossetti in Italian because he knew it was what they wanted. A recipient of happiness (through the gratification of his needs), he was equally (or almost as) keen for others to enjoy the sweets of good fortune as himself. Before they left, there was not one of them who had failed to ask Sebastian to something or other.

"I thought you would keep them all talking here for ever," I said, as the door finally closed. "I thought they would never go." The pink-suede shorts preceded me into the kitchen. "Where have you been, Sebastian? What have you been doing in Amsterdam? Did you get my phone calls, did you...?"

"Can I finish everything up, Jules? Heavenly avocado soup."

"Sebastian..."

"Much too late for questions, Jules." I sighed angrily, and he laughed. "Don't be silly, Jules. What does it all matter?"

He was right. As I gazed at the bulge of his cock beneath the silver buttons, I knew I didn't care about the answers to my questions. I ran my finger over the shorts, but, as so often with him, the desire for food prevailed over desire for sex; at least, the need was more immediate.

I watched him move about the kitchen, exhibiting signs of joy as he spooned in soup or found a left-over piece of garlic bread. I suppose I had drunk a fair amount; I could think only of the pink-suede shorts, or what lay beneath them.

"Sebastian..."

"Boeuf Bourguignonne: why do you never make it for *me*? And broccoli, lovely broccoli; all those flowers going down inside."

I stood leaning against the fridge, watching him, desiring him. "Where did you get those shorts?"

He scooped up melted butter and helped it down with pieces of parsley.

"Amsterdam."

"Did you buy them?"

"No." He sucked in noisily a number of French beans.

"Someone gave them to you."

"Mmm."

"Who?"

"A Dutchman, obviously. I was in Amsterdam. Oh, look, there's half a bowl more here of avocado soup."

"How did you meet him?"

"He picked me up at the station." He concentrated on the new potatoes, and I steadied my nerves by refilling my glass.

"How long did you spend with him?"

"Oh, I forget. A couple of days, maybe. Lovely carrots, all caramelised."

"Did he give you great pleasure?"

"No, he gave me the shorts – and lots of money." He began extracting button mushrooms from the Bourguignonne. Suddenly, he looked up. "Oh Jules, don't keep on."

A strange expression flickered across his face; I could not identify it; I thought then it was indicative of boredom, or impatience at my insistent cross-examining. It disappeared as quickly as it had come.

"Why didn't you ask me if you wanted money?"

He made no reply, but peered into a Pyrex bowl. "What was this, Jules?"

"Chocolate roulade." He regarded the empty dish sadly. "All gone. How greedy your guests were!"

"Why do you want money? Are you taking drugs again?"

He lifted reproachful eyes towards me. "Of course not. What succulent grapes! Did you get them from Arcadia?" He held up the bunch, and began plucking grapes with his teeth. I was consumed with lust.

"Stop eating. Come here." He laid down the grapes obediently and stood before me with his eyes modestly downcast. I began undoing the tiny buttons which served as a fly. He had found the remains of the crème brulée and spooned in the crunchy top with his right hand, while, with his left, he lazily unzipped my suit trousers.

"Come," I said abruptly.

"Where? I imagine you mean in the sense of 'follow' rather than... "

"Come," I repeated, "where I can have your undivided attention. My attractions are not sufficient to compete with the remains of the crème brulée."

"Oh, Jules!" We went into the bedroom, and I dimmed the lights. Not because I liked making love in semi-darkness; I preferred to see Sebastian. But tonight, for some reason, I felt very conscious of the portrait of Melcourt.

"Undress," I said, "and stand by the mirror."

I undressed myself, watching him as he removed his boots, T-shirt and shorts. Obediently, he stood by the mirror. I sat on the bed observing him, and his reflected doppelgänger.

Sebastian was easily aroused, and his appetite demanded immediate attention. I knew so well the exact state of him, not simply from his swollen cock but from the look of total absorption that he fixed on me. I advanced on him, wishing to excite rather than satisfy. I began with his nipples and worked downwards, purposefully ignoring his cock, which nodded at me indignantly, and a little viscous droplet oozed from the end. He began to press himself against me. I felt with increasing lust the hardness of us both, and, staring into the pitted surface of the mirror, I watched my counterpart take hold of his lover's buttocks.

"Turn round. Press yourself against the mirror." He did as he was told, and we watched as Sebastian's cock thrust and fused into that of his beautiful double. Then his lover, the larger man behind him, driven by intolerable desire, entered his beloved and in his thrusting and plunging moved his lips desperately in an attempt to crack the mirror with his cries, but he could not. Of the four fixed figures, only I cried my pleasure aloud. My thoughts grew less and less coherent and disappeared into the sound of groans and rhythmic movements of my body. Yet, as thought receded, I became aware of being in the presence of, even in the possession of, reflections of Melcourt and Toto, who stood at the other side of the mirror to form a perfect equation with Sebastian and myself; we were meeting at a point outside time and space and only the thickness of the glass prevented a supernatural union.

Reflection, vision, thought and dream; suddenly all was gone. Sebastian's cock jarred violently and the mirror clouded with semen. His convulsing body brought me exquisite release. With the mirror's opacity, Melcourt, Toto and all things that did not belong to the world of my beloved and myself vanished. As I took him into bed, I said nothing of my impressions.

But he laughed. "No, Jules, it wasn't."

"Wasn't what?" I replied, easing myself down next to him and putting my arms about him.

"It wasn't Melcourt, and it wasn't Toto."

"I didn't say..."

"No, but I knew perfectly well what you were thinking."

"Did you, darling?"

"Yes, Jules. You're awfully easy to read."

"You are always saying nobody can read anyone. Anyway, I think it *was* Melcourt and Toto."

"No, Jules. The fact of the matter is that you have drunk an awful lot of wine, and I've noticed that your intellectual powers are not at their clearest when..."

"But, didn't you feel...?"

"Obviously. Look at the state of the mirror."

"Oh, Sebastian!"

He turned over abruptly. "Jules! Can't we even fuck without them? Look –" he regarded me with smiling tolerance "– I didn't think Melcourt was coming through the mirror to screw me, and I didn't think that I had hold of Toto's cock. Actually, I thought that you were fucking *me*, Jules." He regarded me gravely. "As for what you thought... "

"What do you think I thought?"

"Well now..." He came wriggling down beside me. "You might have thought that *you* were fucking Toto, or you might have thought that you were Melcourt fucking Toto, or that you were *you* watching *Melcourt* fuck Toto, or that you were *you* watching *Melcourt* watching *you* fuck *me*, or..."

"You're wrong."

"Am I?" He raised an eyebrow.

"Yes. In the first place, I've told you; I don't fuck, I make love, and in the second... I really don't want them, Melcourt, Toto... in all my life, darling, there has only ever been you. Melcourt and Toto were only understudies, substitutes. Oh, darling. There has only ever been you."

He seldom frowned; very often, he smiled and almost always he looked extraordinarily cheerful. When he needed to be serious, he opened his eyes wide and concentrated hard. But he seldom frowned. Now, however, an unfamiliar crease appeared between his beautiful eyes, and a look – puzzled, confused, distressed, I don't know – flickered there.

"Julian, I..."

"Darling?" But he remained silent; the look passed, and he yawned. "Shall we go to sleep now? I'm awfully tired, aren't you?"

"Well, yes, I suppose I am," I admitted reluctantly.

"You know what it is, Jules?"

"What?"

"Well, fucking one guy is tiring enough, but why've you got to fuck for someone else at the same time?"

"Go to sleep, darling," I said wearily; but, of course, he was asleep already.

I lay awake, as I liked to do, believing I was watching over him, protecting him, from the dangers of the night. Of course, I was deluded, for the result was that, when I finally did go to sleep, I slept far too heavily, so far from protecting him that in the morning I found my bed empty. He had, as so often, woken up and disappeared.

I lay wondering why he was so reluctant to spend a whole night with me. I could never get a proper reply from him when I asked. 'Jules', he would say, 'nobody could sleep through your snores; it's like being on the edge of a volcano'. But I do not think that was the reason. Sometimes I thought, miserably, that he liked the two-mile walk to his flat in the early hours of the morning, for the opportunity it gave him for casual sex; but I do not think now this was the reason, either. I think it was fear – fear of the love that waking beside someone induces. He was, I think, apprehensive of love, perhaps because he knew little of it. His personality attracted admiration rather than affection, and his childhood had been lacking in love: his mother had died when he was six (of cancer, I believe), and his father had been more interested in his career than in his son. Sebastian had been packed off to boarding schools and relatives. Perhaps that's why he looked on God as the only reliable source of love.

Anyway, he had gone; it was the morning of the Melcourt visit, and I had forgotten to remind him. There was no answer when I rang, and I had no means of knowing whether he would come. I imagined he would not. I got up, cleaned the mirror and prepared to go down to Dorset.

Twelve
Two Helpings of Black Pudding

I waited for him, of course, until 9.30; and then, in case he had been held up or unavoidably delayed (I invented a hundred reasons why he should be late), I waited another 10 minutes, and then another five. He did not come. I made a business of getting in the car and revving it up, but still he did not come.

I went to the local garage and filled up with petrol; as I was coming out of the shop, he came strolling round the corner, his arms full of flowers. He was dressed as I had seen him on Graduation Day, in an extremely expensive suit. He looked so beautiful, I could hardly bear it. I scowled at him horribly as I got into the car. He smiled amiably and climbed in, throwing the flowers into the back and ignoring the seat belt.

"Where the hell have you been? I have been hanging about for you for at least an hour."

"I went to get some flowers for Mrs Roberts, and to put on my best clothes."

"Well, I don't know why you couldn't have said, instead of creeping out first thing."

"I didn't creep; actually, I went banging about, but you know what you're like after a good fuck: you sleep like the dead."

"I don't fuck."

He smiled contentedly: "You could have fooled me."

"I make love."

"Well, you'd better put your foot down, or we'll be late. You know how you hate being late for things."

"I set great store by punctuality." I felt violently irritated by his remarks. He had washed his hair; it was wavy and glistening. And I couldn't find my keys.

"What a curiously archaic expression."

"What is?" They were in my pocket after all.

"'Set great store by.' Oh, do stop faffing, Jules." He leant back happily and stretched out his long legs, the expensive cloth of his suit falling in enticing ripples about his lap. I thought of the metaphor, 'to set great store by'. How well I understood its meaning, and all the labour implicit in the word 'store'. Like the ant, I had laboured painstakingly for his love. And he? Like the grasshopper, he had gambolled heedless.

"Why didn't you come back to my flat?"

"Because I knew you'd fill up with petrol here. I thought you might be a bit short of juice after last night."

I glanced furiously at him. "Are you going to tell me about Amsterdam?"

"No."

"Why not?"

"You wouldn't want to know." I didn't pursue it.

"Are you going to come to Italy with me?" I was trying to get out of the garage into the main street. Nobody would let me through. Every time I edged forward, another car appeared out of nowhere; then came a cement mixer, very large and slow, and finally what appeared to be the year's entry for the Tour de France. He laughed happily.

"If you keep barking questions at me like a sergeant major, I shan't even come with you as far as the end of the road."

I said nothing, and eased the car out into the traffic. He laid his head on my shoulder.

"Don't be grumpy with me, Jules. We're going to have a fun day.

Aren't you happy to have me here?"

"Of course. That is why I am so cross."

"Cross that I make you happy?"

"Cross that you know you do."

He lifted his head. "Don't waste time being nasty; I've just been reading *Marius the Epicurean* – you know, Pater's thing – which says you must get the maximum out of every moment, and burn with a hard, gem-like flame. Let's do lots of burning, Jules."

"St Paul says it's better to marry than burn," I retorted gruffly.

"I'm much too young to marry," he said lightly. I knew I mustn't pursue the subject. We got through the traffic lights, and were on our way.

He began rummaging in the glove compartment in front of him. "Do you still have your Thelonius Monk CD?"

"Probably. My life is littered with things you have made me buy, that I keep on the off-chance you will want to enjoy them with me." I don't think I spoke in bitterness; probably resignation, or perhaps (now I reflect on the matter) some intimation was stirring in my mind of the importance of objects.

We had left Oxford behind us, and were heading south in the direction of Basingstoke. I do not admire suburban countryside, and I made some disparaging comment about it.

"Don't be so critical, Jules," he said, "it's very nice. Most things are, really."

The sound of saxophone filled the car, and I pondered his happy disposition. Happiness, I thought, is like sunshine; it pervades and becomes part of its object. Certainly, it was integral to Sebastian's nature – and to his beauty. He loved food, sex, music, good literature and speed, all manner of things. Unlike the rest of us who spend our days dreaming of much and attaining little, Sebastian desired and had. He was selfish, but quite unspoilt, like the very wealthy. I do not mean a man like myself, who can spend £1,000 pounds on a suit and not worry about it; I mean the legendary rich, princesses and sheiks and dukes who own half of London. Such people go where they will and find welcome everywhere. They move with ease upon a friendly world. They do not suffer constraints as the rest of us do, particularly a man like myself. How much of my life I spent agonising, 'Do I dare to ask where the lavatory is?', 'Shall I speak in French, or will they think I'm showing off?', 'How shall I reply to the college porter when he wishes me a pleasant holiday?' No such problems for the rich or the richly endowed, like Sebastian. He wanted, he took (most courteously) and his enjoyment and happiness were boundless. It illuminated him and gave his beauty a new dimension. Sebastian himself had once given me a simpler explanation: "God's grace, Jules."

"Oh, Jules, look!" He pointed gleefully. "A whole field of lesbian cows." I frowned at this display of urban naivety; I had been brought up in the country.

"Don't be silly."

"Awfully difficult to imagine getting pleasure out of banging your udders together."

"There are certainly simpler ways of obtaining pleasure." And then in case Sebastian should start thinking of them, I said sternly, "Now I am going to tell you all about Melcourt," and I started to relate the saga of Reg and Joyce once again.

He listened attentively, but, after a while, interrupted: "Jules, I need a pee. There's a sort of trucker's caff in a mile or so."

"I will *not* take you to a trucker's caff. You will have to wait for the motorway place."

"I'm bursting."

I gave him a look, and continued talking about Melcourt. He sighed, and the far-away look came into his eyes. I stopped at the motorway services. He paused getting out.

"Will you get me a huge all-day breakfast thing? All of it, and loads of black pudding."

I watched him unhappily as he headed off for the lavatories. Perhaps he *did* only want to relieve himself.

I went and stood in a very long queue behind a school party. It took me exactly 17 minutes to procure the breakfast (I only wanted coffee). I conveyed the refreshments to the smoking area; I knew he would want to smoke, as one of the few things I denied Sebastian was cigarettes in the car. I sat down and looked at my watch; it was 10.20 a.m. At 10.30 a.m., I stood up and sat down again; I could not leave the congealing breakfast. Probably, he had thought of that. I tried not to think of what he was doing. At 10.38 a.m., he returned, very happy. I said nothing and neither did he, but he took my hand and stroked it gently before tucking into his revolting breakfast.

"Go on telling me about Melcourt; the Hall, I mean, and Joyce and Reg," he said.

"Yes," I said, "all right, sweetheart." I shouldn't remonstrate with him. What was the point? What was done (if it had been done) was done, and now he was sitting opposite me, happily dunking sausages into egg yolk. Anyway, I *wanted* to tell him all about it.

I was still telling him when we returned to the car and continued on our way. I drove very fast, as he liked me to do.

The countryside was improving; it was more rural and Hardy-esque. I felt excited at what lay before us. I was even inclined to boast a little about my previous successes.

"Now come on, Jules," he said, laughing, "you haven't done so amazingly well."

"What do you mean?" I was indignant. "I have obtained some wonderful letters."

"Yes, but by luck, by serendipity. You haven't adopted any proper campaign."

"I have brought you in." I slowed down; I had a feeling there was a police car in front.

"Yes, but so late."

I thought of all the times I had rung him and listened to his answering-machine. I spoke with icy reproach: "I couldn't get hold of you any earlier." I expected an apology, but he was seldom repentant.

"But, you see, you should have been decisive, and you should have taken flowers. You shouldn't have allowed yourself to have been defeated by the Rev., nor by Joyce. Don't you see, he *wants* to give you the letters, but you don't give him a chance."

"There may not be any more letters and, besides, she is obviously against him giving them."

"Of *course* there are more letters – I don't like this CD. I think we need something more of the period. Wagner would be ideal."

"You took my Wagner CDs."

"Then you should ask for them back. Ah, no, here's one. There are obviously more letters, because the ones he's given you are in strict sequence. If that were all, he would have said so. And you don't really know that she *is* against you having the letters. Flatter her and get her on your side. You haven't used your brains: take her out to lunch, go shopping, get her pension for her, anything."

"And what part will you play in this?"

"I'll talk to him; he'll like that."

"It's all very well saying this. You haven't been there. It isn't as easy as you imagine."

"But, Jules, you forget how persuasive I am."

I glanced at him briefly. "No, I never forget that. What will you talk to him about?"

"I have no idea. This Grünhilde bit is wonderful, isn't it?"

"I had intended stopping off for a bit."

"Oh, really! Where?"

"There is a sort of copse where I had a pee and emptied out the egg custard."

"It sounds a delightful spot; I wonder English Heritage don't put up a plaque."

"But I shan't now, because we're late. You wasted all that time in the service station." I hadn't meant to refer to it again, but the words came by themselves. I am not a good dissembler.

"It wasn't wasted, Jules."

"No, I don't suppose it was."

"I had a lovely time." An infuriating smile spread across his face. I took refuge in sarcasm.

"I'm so very glad you enjoyed yourself; delighted, charmed to think... Oh, for fuck's sake!"

"Interesting use of personification, Jules, but what has 'fuck' got to do with it?"

I calmed down, ready as always to be reassured: "Well, what was so good about the services place, then?"

"Where else could I have had two helpings of black pudding?" He hummed quietly to the music.

When we approached the village of Melcourt, we got stuck behind a tractor. We were rather late; normally, I would have been annoyed. Punctuality is important to me, but now I did not mind because the road was very lovely, and Sebastian's hand lay not altogether idle on my cock. "Recite to me, darling," I said.

"The Elderflower now forms a bower
And elms embrace about my head
And speak the words I have not said."

"That's not Melcourt."

"No, it's Sebastian Salonière. Do you like it?"

"I like everything you do."

"No, you don't."

"I like your hand there."

"Even with the tractor driver in front?"

"Unfortunately, both his pleasure and mine are short-lived. This is the turning to Melcourt Hall, and we are 15 minutes late."

"What a master of self-restraint you are."

He was not entirely right. I parked the car next to an ancient Escort so we were obscured from prying eyes. I drew him to me and kissed his lips gently. "Melcourt might have made love to Toto here," I said.

"Shall we see if it's a lively spot?" he asked.

Summoning up all my self-control, I removed his shameless hands and kept a strict control on my own. I brushed my lips against his designer stubble and murmured involuntarily, "I love you, Sebastian."

A little sigh escaped his lips. "I know," he murmured sadly. "Poor Jules."

He got the flowers out of the back and I took the Tupperware pot out of the glove compartment.

"What on earth is that?"

"It contained the baked custard."

"The thing you pissed into?"

"I didn't piss into it."

"Of course you did. It was the obvious way of getting rid of the custard."

"I didn't piss into it," I said angrily.

"Yes you did." He stood smelling the flowers smugly.

I had driven a hundred miles; I had had an exhausting night. I was anxious about the visit (*and* we were late). But I wasn't simply tired; I was tense with excitement. I was *there*, at Melcourt with Sebastian; together, we were having a great adventure: it was immensely important to me. And all he could do, however, was to make totally irrelevant comments about a stupid inanimate object. Furthermore, with his uncanny knowledge of my foibles, he had guessed right; I *had* pissed into it.

"I did not piss into it," I said, virtually shouting at him. I was conscious of the sound of a window opening behind me. "I did not piss into it," I repeated sotto voce.

"Oh, I think you did."

"I didn't." Tears welled up in my eyes; the wretched blue plastic pot now encapsulated all my misery. I wrenched off the top.

"Look, it's quite clean. Look." I thrust it at him. He laughed. I became quite incoherent with grief and anger. "Why does it matter?

118

What does it matter? Okay, then, I *did* piss into it. If I could piss *now*, I would *piss* over *you*, over your fucking suit and your fucking flowers."

I stood, ridiculous, overweight, ginger-haired and middle-aged, while he, for whom I cared more than anything in the world, mocked at me, laughing and beautiful, callous, cruel and promiscuous. Tears began to pour down my face. As we faced each other there in the sunlight, in the place where Melcourt had once walked, his attitude to the pot was in every respect identical to his attitude to me. Both were risible and of no importance, each was available to be picked up or put down at will, each was unbeautiful, uninteresting, utilitarian. The pot might hold food, or serve merely for the receipt of such detritus as the body might exude. So too, I. "Oh God," I said. I held on to the side of the car. I felt I would faint.

His expression changed immediately; despite everything, there was great sweetness in Sebastian.

"Jules. Don't be silly." And because he knew it wasn't about the pot at all, he said gently. "I do care about you. I came here with you because you asked me to come." I stood staring at him, yielding. "Come on, Jules, give me the keys and that silly pot, and I'll put it back in the car." I handed them over.

"Sebastian!"

"Yes?" He locked the car.

"Say you love me."

"I love you, Jules." But I knew he lied.

Thirteen
Roast Chicken and Dorset Apple Cake

I opened the little wicket gate and led him past the buckets of geraniums.

"It's here," I said. "I'll ring the bell."

"Super!" He was relieved to find I had reverted to my usual laconic self. Joyce could be discerned sticking her way to the door. I could hear her struggling with the bolts.

"Oh, Mr... um... We thought you weren't going to come. I see you have brought a young friend with you." She regarded Sebastian with far more interest than she had afforded me. "I thought you were a young lady for a moment, with your hair like that, and all the flowers." I effected an awkward introduction. Sebastian smiled, and held the flowers out to her.

"They are for you, Mrs Roberts. Look, the roses match your cardigan perfectly. If you have a safety-pin, I could make you a little corsage."

"Well, you'd better come in, and Mr... I can't remember your name."

"Can you manage, Mrs Roberts? Let me take your stick, and you give me your arm." Joyce beamed. Sebastian had achieved in two minutes what I had failed to do in as many hours. Nor were his conquests over; no sooner had he eased Joyce into her chair than he was over in the far corner of the room.

"Mr Roberts! How do you do, sir? You *are* kind to let us come."

If Reg had been slow at raising his chin to scrutinise me, he was not so tardy now. He fixed his violet eyes on Sebastian, and his face immediately creased up, though whether from surprise or delight, it was difficult to say.

"Good morning," he replied, in tones as clear as any I had heard him use. The presence of Sebastian had produced a kind of electricity into the room.

"Reg," Joyce was saying, "Reg, Mr... I-don't-know-your-name... (interrogative look in Sebastian's direction) reminds me of someone, but I can't think, I don't..." His chin was still up, angled towards Sebastian. "That picture you used to have, Reg (the chin descended), the one I gave you. It came from the Hall, didn't it?" She looked at Reg for some kind of corroboration.

My brain whirled; the picture – she must mean the missing Rothenstein portrait commissioned by Melcourt; it had been given to Reg by his father. And I had been right: Sebastian *was* exactly like Toto.

"Oh," I cried, excitement getting the better of my reserve. "Have you still got it? Can I see it?"

"I often see likenesses in people," said Joyce, gathering up her blue knitting. "Now you, Dr... put me in mind of that comedy man on television who tells all those naughty jokes." I avoided Sebastian's glance.

"But the picture, do you still have it?" I felt rather less sanguine now – I could think of nobody who resembled myself lest it be Melcourt and certainly no 'comedy man with naughty jokes'. If this was a measure of Joyce's judgement...

"No, dear," said Joyce complacently, "we don't have any old clutter now. Reg threw it all away when we moved from Swindon." Old clutter! Melcortia, clutter? Toto gone to be replaced by tapestry kittens! I clutched at straws:

"But you must have..."

She regarded her knitting critically. "Not now."

"No," said Reg, mournfully.

She took a look at Sebastian and was struck by a new thought: "All that golden hair of yours, Mr… ah, it puts me in mind of my cousin's little Emma."

It was my turn to give Sebastian a look, but it was small comfort for the disappointment of the picture. Unlike me, he did not waste time crying over spilt milk. "Much better," he was saying (I suspect as a tease for me), "to get rid of old junk." A few old photos, he intimated, were all one needed. Could Mr Roberts, perhaps, remember whether he had any?

Reg said nothing, and Sebastian continued. "Perhaps we could have a look for them and see. Might I help you, Mrs Roberts? We could find a safety-pin, too, and I could make your corsage; and if you could tell me where to find a vase, I'll put the flowers into water for you."

Clever as Sebastian was, he was unused to old people, and had tried to move things forward too quickly.

Suspicion had been aroused in Joyce. "I can manage, thank you," she said, but made no attempt to get up. I shot a 'I told you so' look at Sebastian. Perhaps it would not be so easy, after all. I had had experience of the Joyce-and-Reg ménage; I knew the many obstacles – the Reverend, the pudding lady, the sheropody, Reg's silence. Sebastian, I felt, although a skilful pilot, was ignorant of the hidden reefs and shoals beneath the apparently placid ocean of Melcourt. But he was used to getting his own way, as I knew to my cost; like my Porsche, unassailable in beauty and power. And yet, the analogy was a false one. It was actually *I* who had paid for the Porsche and took the risks; Sebastian merely reclined at my side. Well, I supposed that was how it must be. I was, after all, lucky to have the Porsche, and even luckier to have Sebastian. Perhaps, between the two of us, Sebastian at his ease and I doing the work, we might meet with some success where Reg was concerned.

Sebastian continued to express an interest in old family photos, when suddenly there was scuffling and a high-pitched squeaking outside the door, followed by the appearance of two aged heads.

"Oh, Mrs Roberts, we were so worried. We wondered… oh, dear, there they are."

Two very old ladies, one extremely tall and fat, the other very small and thin, gazed up at Sebastian and me with horrified fascination.

"I hope you don't mind us poking our heads in, only we heard..." said The Small, addressing Joyce.

"But perhaps they are friends of yours," suggested The Tall, indicating Sebastian and me with an incredulous stare.

"Well," said Joyce, who seemed as puzzled as I, "I don't know, I'm sure."

"I'm sorry if we have intruded," said Tall, in a tone which suggested she was anything but sorry, "but we heard your two gentlemen with raised voices shouting outside our window and Emily said, quite rightly in my opinion, when we saw them come in here, we should just check and see."

"And a funny car," said Small, "like a salesman's car."

Sebastian threw me an ecstatic glance. When he had initially persuaded me to buy the Porsche, I was not as rapturous as you might expect the new owner of a car to be; it wasn't the money or the challenge of driving a powerful car (I am a good driver) but the fear of what people would think. I have always had a horror of drawing attention to myself. I was afraid everyone would laugh at me. Actually, I was pleasantly surprised when, far from being mocked, I found I was acceded a new respect on my replying in the affirmative to the question, 'Is that your car, sir?' Complete strangers would come up to me and ask questions about the car, and to my surprise, I often found the ensuing conversation quite pleasant. Even colleagues whom I hardly knew would smile and acknowledge me as I was parking. Students, whom I suspect had previously regarded me as something born before Noah, actually spoke to me. I have always collected beautiful objects: pictures, antiques, books etc., but they had been seen only by me. Now my good taste had, as it were, received public acclaim. I rather liked it when I overheard the college porter say, 'No sir, I couldn't tell you Dr Collins' subject, but I can tell you he drives that green Porsche.' And, I must be honest: when I had

Sebastian beside me in the car, I enjoyed (what is the expression?) a 'double whammy'; to be the possessor of a Porsche and the most beautiful boy in Oxford, if not in England. No wonder Sebastian was laughing at me; he knew, of course, with his extraordinary intuition, all the complexities of my pride in the car.

"I'm so sorry to have disturbed you," I said stiffly, "it was quite unforgivable."

"This is the doctor and his friend," said Joyce, "they are our guests." Joyce, it seemed, was indignant at the intrusion. Perhaps, like me, she didn't want to share Sebastian.

"Well, I beg your pardon," said The Tall.

"Yes," said The Small, "we only came out of concern."

"Thank you," said Joyce, and Reg mumbled a contribution.

"Thank you so much." That was Sebastian.

"Yes, thank you," I concluded.

"They are always prying," said Joyce as the door closed behind them. She added, inconsequentially, "That's what comes of never being married."

I felt, on the whole, that Tall and Small had done us a service. Their intrusion had brought us closer together and, furthermore, Sebastian and I were injured parties. Some reparation should, I felt, be made to us.

Sebastian doggedly continued on the track of photos; he would simply love to see some family photos.

Inevitably, there were plenty of them. Joyce brought out her album; the theme, however, was *not* Melcourt, but Joyce's cousin. Also to be viewed were the cousin's husband, the cousin's three children, their four cats and a large number of neighbours.

"Fascinating," murmured Sebastian. I saw him glance at the clock on the mantlepiece and I could see he was wilting a little, "but I should like to see photos of your father, Mr Roberts, and, of course, you, Mrs Roberts," he said, treating Joyce to his devastating smile. But Joyce said she couldn't remember where they had put the album. "He doesn't know either," she added.

Then the window-cleaner appeared at the window; he was very slow and methodical but took a great interest in viewing us. He was full of bonhomie and waved his rag at me from time to time as if to invite me to share in his labours.

I embarked on the first of my prepared questions. Did Mr Roberts remember his father telling him anything about Lord Melcourt? Joyce looked as if she might speak; indeed, she put down her knitting and opened her mouth, but then seemed to decide against it. Reg maintained his silence, and I began to think that he was, in some perverse way, enjoying himself. I had a whole fusillade of questions, and I overcame my reserve and prepared to fire them off. Did Mr Roberts have memories of his father or, indeed, of Lord Melcourt? Reg said nothing; his chin descended once more on to his chest. Joyce said sharply that Reg 'wouldn't know now', an irritating comment, suggesting that had I come at some earlier point I might have been given a reply. Staunchly, I continued. Did Mr Roberts ever hear his father speak of Lord Melcourt? No reply. I had wanted to ask how old Reg had been when Toto died, but my usual reserve prevented me asking, and Sebastian was engaged with Joyce. Did Mr Roberts remember his mother, perhaps? No reply. I understood Mr Roberts had been brought up abroad; Venice, perhaps? Reg emitted a kind of groan, and I did not know whether or not to interpret it as an affirmative. Sebastian smiled irritatingly. I grimaced at him, and leant forward, trying to dislodge my arse, which had become wedged in the narrow straits of the orthopaedic chair.

Next to appear on the stage of what was becoming our very own farce was the warden, obviously alerted by Tall and Small to the danger presented by Sebastian and myself. She had a small, vicious and evil-smelling dog with her; it spent a long time sniffing at my trousers as if considering them suitable for urination. I thought (even at the risk of my trousers) to enlist her on our side.

"We were chatting about Mrs Roberts' photos," I said, but the warden, a hardened woman, had obviously seen pictures of the cousin before, and took a hurried departure.

The time-scale had gone all wrong, that was it. I had timed our arrival for 11 a.m., mindful of Reg 'being better in the mornings', but, of course, thanks to Sebastian's activities at the service station, we had arrived late. Now, having wasted time and having achieved nothing, Meals-on-Wheels arrived. It was clearly the cue for our departure.

However, despite his carefree, pleasure-seeking appearance, there was, as I say, a steely side to Sebastian, particularly when he did not get what he wanted. I was afraid that the sight of Meals-on-Wheels ('Mr Roberts doesn't eat lunch', Joyce assured us) would have the effect of making Sebastian consider his own stomach. Not a bit of it; it made him decisive and masterful. Apparently, he never ate lunch, either, and, really, he didn't think that fish and chips smelled very appetising. How would it be if his friend, Dr Collins, took Mrs Roberts out for lunch? He had seen a delightful public house in the village. Dr Collins would be only too pleased; it was the least he could do after she had been so kind.

At first, she didn't understand; she hadn't been out to lunch since 'the parish outing in March'. No, she didn't think she wanted to go; besides, Mr Roberts wouldn't want her to.

Joyce and Sebastian began to duel, the outcome of which was a foregone conclusion. It was not possible to vanquish Sebastian. "You'll love it, Mrs Roberts."

"Well, no, it's very kind, Mr… , but I should have to change, and I…"

"You certainly don't need to change, Mrs Roberts, you have that delightful cerise dress on. Now Julian, you bring the car round to the front."

"I don't think I should like that car; I saw Dr Collins stoop right down to get into it."

"Oh, it's very comfortable, Mrs Roberts, and I shall help you in."

"But you won't be there to help me out."

"Dr Collins will help you out, won't you, Julian?"

"Oh... Oh yes, certainly."

"Go and get the car, Julian," he ordered, pointedly.

"What do you think, Reg?" Joyce asked.

I thought Reg would maintain his normal silence, but the chin rose up: "I should go," he said.

"But will you be all right, Reg?" He didn't reply but I swear there was a twinkle in his violet eyes.

Joyce wavered. "It seems a pity to waste that nice fish and chips."

"I shall eat it, Mrs Roberts."

"Do you like fish and chips, then?"

"I like everything." Sebastian smiled happily. He had triumphed. And Joyce was happy that he had; her eyes glinted behind the glasses and the wart nodded gleefully. He bent us all to his will.

The 'outing' was not as bad as I had feared, as is often the case with dreaded social occasions (I detected a note of malicious glee in Sebastian's farewell glance). It took a little while to get her (sticks and all) into the car, and even longer to get her out of the car and into the pub but, once there, seated in a corner with a glass to hand ('I don't mind a glass of sherry, dear'), she began to enjoy herself. She had me read out the menu several times. She didn't like the sound of those foreign ones but could fancy some roast chicken. I hate anything hot at lunchtime, and had a ploughman's.

I started by asking Joyce about her grandmother, the housekeeper, and even about her own childhood, but she either couldn't or wouldn't remember. I attributed her reticence to the ancient scandal surrounding her dead father-in-law, but I was determined to have another go at finding out all I could about Reg, particularly his childhood, for there, perhaps, I might find Toto.

"I should be so interested to hear about Mr Roberts' childhood."

"Oh, yes, dear."

"He must have told you some stories about his father... and his mother, of course."

"No, dear, I don't think so. Very nice thick gravy; I do like a bit of gravy, it makes all the difference to the veg."

I persevered; I *would* find out about Lady Ellen. After all, Joyce had said on my first visit that Reg's mother was a 'lady'. *And* Melcourt had mentioned Lady Ellen Blythe in his letter.

"Mr Roberts' mother had a title, I think you said."

"A title?" Joyce looked puzzled.

"She was a Lady," I continued doggedly.

"A very nice lady. Reg was very fond of her. I never knew her. Both his parents were gone long before I met Reg." She looked at me almost, I thought, with satisfaction.

"And you don't remember her name? It wasn't Ellen?"

Joyce looked up from her vegetables. "Nell, she was called."

I felt a frisson of delight. Ah! So Reg's mother could be Lady Ellen – I had discovered something! "Do you know anything more about her, or her husband? Mr Roberts must have told you about his father. After all, he was quite famous, as the friend of Lord Melcourt."

"What did you say, dear?"

"Mr Roberts' father; they called him 'Toto'."

"I don't know, dear. Lovely carrots these are, nice and fresh. I don't like those frozen ones." I tried a new tack.

"I expect you remember your husband writing Lord Melcourt's biography."

"No, I don't think so, dear." She took a spoon to the gravy. "I expect it was a very nice book."

"Didn't you read it, Mrs Roberts?"

"No, dear."

The chicken disappeared and the question of pudding was raised. Joyce fancied a bit of Dorset apple cake. Her eyes glowed at the thought. "I *am* having a lovely time, Mr... it's very good of you to take me out. I expect you'd rather be entertaining some nice young lady." I replied quite truthfully that I would much rather be with her, and she beamed again. I pressed on. Had her grandmother told her any stories about Lord Melcourt and Anthony Roberts? She looked as if she might say something, but the Dorset apple cake appeared, and the moment passed. Once, I thought sadly, her grandmother must have told her of Lord Melcourt's life at the Hall, but 70-odd years had passed, and there was nothing other than the predictable, 'Very nice gentleman, I think', and 'He died in a shooting accident'.

"Did your grandmother talk about his death, Mrs Roberts?"

"Yes, dear, I said; it was a shooting accident. Don't you fancy a pudding?

"Er, no, thank you, Mrs Roberts."

"But you like a pudding. You liked that baked custard I gave you?"

"Oh, yes, indeed. I must let you have the Tupperware pot back."

"Yes. They're very useful. I put all my left-overs in them." She tucked into the apple cake, and I mentally checked over what I had asked and discovered: information about Reg's biography: nil; information about Toto: nil; information about Max, virtually nil. Anything else? Yes, Reg's mother might have had a title, and she had been called... Ellen? Perhaps. There seemed to be little else to ask. My thoughts turned to Sebastian; I wondered what he was doing. As if Joyce had telepathically interrupted my thoughts, she looked up from the debris of the apple cake and remarked, "He's very good-looking, your young friend."

"Oh, is he? I hadn't noticed."

"Yes," she said, and returned to her apple cake. As she laid down the fork, she suddenly remarked, "He hasn't given you anything, has he?"

I was momentarily confused: "Who? My friend?"

"No, dear, Reg. He hasn't given you any letters, has he, or sent anything? Sometimes he gives letters to the warden to post." There was one mystery solved! I had wondered how Reg had got the letters to the post box.

For a moment, I wondered if I should own up to being in possession of four of Lord Melcourt's letters, but decided against it. I would wait and see if Sebastian had come up with anything. Certainly, I didn't intend cheating the Roberts! When I was sure I had everything I wanted, I should be happy to be as generous as they wished.

"No, Mrs Roberts, he hasn't given me anything."

I paid the bill and embarked on the lengthy business of getting Joyce into the car and back to the bungalow.

Nothing could have been pleasanter than the sight that met our eyes on our return. Mr Roberts was fast asleep and Sebastian was sitting quietly at his side; they might have formed a picture: *Old Age Guarded by The Innocence of Youth*. He smiled sweetly at us and put his finger to his lips, but Joyce was not to be silenced.

"I've had ever such a nice time, Reg." The old man stirred a little in his sleep and then began to snore loudly.

"There," said Joyce, getting into her chair, "I think I'll do the same."
It was time to go.

Sebastian stood up and took Joyce's hand. "It's been lovely meeting you, Mrs Roberts," he said. "Next time, you must let *me* take you out." Joyce's ancient face creased into wrinkles of delight, and the wart moved vigorously up and down.

"I should like that, Mr... ah."

I, on the other hand, fidgeted about and, mindful of my earlier visit, tried to pluck up courage to go off to the lavatory. Sebastian, of course, knew exactly what I was thinking.

"Just as soon as Dr Collins has washed his hands, we must be on our way," he said. Life was always so much easier for him.

Once in the car, I assailed him with questions, but, disappointingly he had little to report. Reg had remained silent, the vicar had called and angled for the fish and chips, so Sebastian had eaten them himself, along with the spotted dick and custard. Reg had fallen asleep and Sebastian had done the crossword. Oh, and put the flowers in water.

"Didn't you have a look round?"

"Of course not."

"Of course you did."

"Well, I didn't find anything. Stop off at a shop, Jules. I want some nibbles."

"You're going out for a meal tonight."

"Well, it's not tonight now, and I'm jolly hungry. Unlike you, I have not been eating gourmet meals at the pub."

When I came back from the shop with Mars Bars and Monster Munch, he was asleep. His head rolled on to my shoulder, and I managed to keep it there all the way back to Oxford. I woke him as we came into the city on the Botley Road, but he refused to come back to my flat, and said he would meet me at The Randolph at 8 o'clock.

"Do you promise, Sebastian?"

"My word is my bond."

"Promise!"

"No. Will you drop me at Blackwells?"

"It will be shut."

"I'm not going to Blackwells." I dropped him off. He leant through the window and smiled at me.

"Don't worry. I'll come. Oh, and Jules, I'll show you some letters."

"Letters?"

"You didn't really think I'd come away empty-handed, did you?"

I watched him turn into Holywell Street. The suit fitted him like a glove.

Fourteen
Dinner at The Randolph

I sat in the bar of The Randolph and had a gin and tonic; I didn't order one for Sebastian lest I tempted fate. I had fallen into the habit of playing such childish games with myself on the many occasions I had spent waiting for him: 'If the next person I see is male, then Sebastian will come', 'If the next sentence I hear spoken contains a pronoun, I will wait another five minutes', 'If I can't think of more than five artists beginning with H, I know he won't come'; exactly like a love-struck teenage girl.

So now I sat, musing about Sebastian's cache of Melcourt letters, but wondering more about him, whether he was going to show up and whether, if he did, he would spend the whole night with me. I thought of times he had stood me up: when I was taking him to Glynbourne, and missed it myself because I went on waiting for him rather than go without him; the time I waited for him to collect the results of his finals (pasted up inside the porter's lodge) and he never came. 'Why not, Sebastian?', I had asked when he turned up at my flat a week later. 'Because I knew I'd got a First, anyway'. 'How could you possibly know?' 'God told me'. 'Oh, don't be ridiculous'. 'Actually, He did, Jules'. 'Well, anyway, you could still have come: I told you I would be there, I waited three hours, walking to and fro in the quad, looking like an idiot'. 'But Jules, I didn't *ask* you to wait three hours'. 'Well, I shall never do so again'. But, of course, we both knew that I would. I poured the rest of the tonic into my glass then went over and ordered another.

And what I hate – hated, I am different now – was the exposure to other people's looks and surmises; I could almost hear them saying to each other, 'That fat man over there with the ginger hair has been stood up. I don't wonder. I shouldn't think anyone would be anxious to meet him, look how ridiculous he is and at the same time how dull and prissy...' I took out a pocket version of Melcourt's sonnets and studied it intently, but I don't suppose I fooled anyone, least of all myself; I had known Melcourt's sonnets off by heart for at least 30 years. It was while I was drinking the second gin and tonic that I knew he had come. I always knew (as I did when I picked up the phone) when it was he. A kind of ripple went round the bar; Sebastian had come through the swing doors.

"Hi, Jules," he greeted me effusively, as if we had not met for years. "Wonderful to see you! Have you got me a g & t?"

His hair was loose and silken upon his shoulders, his eyes wide and blue and his shirt of the palest pink. We all looked at him, everyone in the bar and I; we all admired him, but none of them admired as fervently as I. I would not allow him to know this. I frowned severely.

"I have drunk your gin and tonic while I have been waiting for you."

"Much the best thing; I did the same with the fish and chips and the spotted dick. It's a wonderful day for food – all that black pudding and lovely greasies at that wonderful service place; and then the Meals-on-Wheels, perfectly congealed custard, wonderful colour, quite saffron, and now this meal." I caught the barman's eye.

"Two gins and tonics," I said.

"And, Jules, what have you done with that junk food I asked you to get? You've hidden it." He sat down opposite me, his eyes sparkling for whatever reason, the shirt exactly the same pink as his cheeks.

"It's in the car."

"You've left it as bait to lure me back."

"Very probably."

"What did you get?"

"Two Mars Bars, some Monster... Oh, never mind. Have you brought the letters?"

"Oh, Jules, I *am* sorry!" He looked at me, repentant.

"What do you mean?"

"I've left them in the flat!"

"You've left them in the flat, the Melcourt letters? You haven't bothered bringing them?"

"No, Jules, I forgot."

"Forgot!"

"Yes."

"Have you read them?"

"No; I've been busy."

Anger got the better of me: "It's too bad of you! You *know* how much I want to see them, and you can't even be bothered..."

"Oh, Jules," I felt a hand rest lightly on my thigh beneath the table; the fingers ran briefly along my cock. "However shall I make it up to you?" I moved my legs away to show he was not forgiven.

"Tell me how you got the letters. How many have you got? Did Reg actually speak? Did he say why he was giving them? Joyce was awfully worried about Reg giving things away."

He smiled radiantly. "Let's forget about Melcourt for a bit, Jules. I'm starving."

And, of course, he created exactly the same stir about him as we went into the dining room. Everyone stared at him – and at me; 'Beauty and the Beast', they were thinking, obviously. We were seated in a corner and, although I wanted to maintain a reproachful silence, I couldn't, for Sebastian's glee was infectious. Besides, I wanted to learn how he had got the letters.

"I'll tell you in a minute, Jules. Let's enjoy it all: I *love* The Randolph."

Waiters hovered about, proffering menus and putting napkins on Sebastian's lap, removing plates and replacing them with others yet more splendid.

"What do you want to drink?"

"Champagne, of course. A good one." He flashed his eyes at the waiter. "Will you bring the list of champagnes?"

"If monsieur looks, he will see them on this page."

"Is that all? Don't you have something a little special?" The sycophant scurried off.

"Do tell me, Sebastian!"

"Yes, I will, I will; but you know how I like looking at menus and can never decide. What are you having?"

"I shall start with oysters."

"Horrid and slippery. What will you have next?"

"I haven't decided; what do you want to start?"

"I don't *know*. I want the smoked salmon thing, but I want the pheasant terrine, too. Oh, what shall I have, Jules?" The blue eyes implored me. I do not mean to intimate that Sebastian play-acted or calculatingly turned on the charm; in some ways, he was very straightforward; when he wanted something – food, sex or music – he wanted it with his whole being and his body expressed his wants (I remember having to satisfy him surreptitiously during the first night of Wagner's Ring Cycle at The Apollo). But it wasn't as simple as that; because he was bright, he knew instinctively the best way to achieve his goals. If he wanted an alpha in the Chaucer paper, he would go to the Bodleian and read every available text. If he wanted someone to give him food or sex, he would open his blue eyes very wide; it was a sensible thing to do.

"Why don't you have both, the smoked salmon and the pheasant terrine?" My question was intended as a sarcastic one, as I sought to obscure my adoration of him by dry severity of tone.

"Oh may I, Jules? Really? Both? What a marvellous idea. How lovely!"

The top three buttons of the pink shirt were undone, little golden hairs winked at me.

"You can have what you want, darling. You know perfectly well I can refuse you nothing." I looked away, ashamed at self-betrayal; I began furiously breaking up bread sticks. He leant forward and touched my cheek gently with his finger.

"Stop worrying about it, Jules. Just enjoy spoiling me; it makes us both very happy, you know."

The waiter returned with the news that there was an excellent Bollinger '85. I nodded. He wanted to know how I would spend the next hundred pounds.

"Smoked salmon mousse and pheasant terrine..."

"A very wise choice." He smiled approval.

"And oysters. I will have the oysters."

"If monsieur could repeat...?"

"My friend will have the smoked salmon mousse *and* pheasant terrine."

"But monsieu..."

"He wants both."

"Yes," said Sebastian, smiling at him happily, "I like strange mixtures. I've already had black pudding and cold custard today."

The waiter blanched, but he was well trained.

"And I will have the oysters."

"Does monsieur wish for the terrine and the soufflé on one plate?"

Sebastian beamed. "Oh, yes, definitely. It will be such fun to mash them up together. I may have invented a new dish, like Peach Melba."

"What do you want to follow, Sebastian?"

"The fillet steak, definitely. I do think one needs butcher's meat, don't you?"

It was the most expensive item on the menu. "Make it two," I said.

"Two for monsieur?" he asked of Sebastian.

"Good heavens, no," said Sebastian in horror, "I have a very poor appetite."

The waiter bustled off to carry out Sebastian's orders. I endeavoured to restore some vestige of normality.

"Tell me about getting the letters." But someone else brought the champagne, and Sebastian watched gravely as the napkin was held swaddled about the neck of the bottle, and the cork eased out with a sigh. Champagne spurted decorously. It was given to him to taste.

"Quite delicious. And a couple of bottles of Chateau Haut Brion to follow."

We excited some attention in the dining room; couples bent towards each other and looked at Sebastian, waiters stood together and conversed with animation. I frowned at him severely and dropped my napkin on the floor. He picked it up and tucked it back in. "Now stop glowering at me, Jules, and I shall tell you how I got the letters." What could I say?

"Well, after you had gone, I tried chatting him up, but it wasn't any good and I was awfully fed up, because I didn't want you to be proved right, and me not get anywhere. After a while, he sort of nodded off, and I thought I'd go and have a look round. Actually, I was awfully scared – the champagne's nice, isn't it? Can I have some more? – because I wasn't sure if he was really asleep or not, and I don't know, Jules, I didn't really trust him. Anyway, I took the flowers as a sort of cover; I thought I could pretend I was looking for a vase or something. I do hope they won't be long, I'm so hungry, and you know how I can't wait for anything. No sooner had I got into the bedroom – ghastly flowered coverlet and matching curtains – do you think that's my sal'n'pheas coming? Oh, no, it's going to that American in the corner – no sooner had I got there, than there was a knocking at the door – I jumped a mile. It was the Rev. after the fish and chips, not to mention the spotty D. So, of course, I make short work of him... look, it's the starters!"

"Pheasant terrine and salmon mousse for monsieur."

"How scrummy!"

"And oysters for monsieur."

"Thank you."

"You must be careful, Jules; people meet horrible deaths from surfeits of oysters."

"Lampreys, Sebastian, not oysters."

"Monsieur, the chef advises you to eat these separately; he says..."

"Oh, but I never take advice. It looks quite delicious, such pretty colours, please tell him from me."

"Thank you; it looks absolutely fine."

"Can I take two rolls, the white one with the poppy seeds, and the curly-whirly one?"

I let him eat. The oysters were very good.

"Are they nice, Jules? Are you happy now?"

"I am happier. Go on telling me."

"Well, I got rid of the Rev. He's a dreadful man – he kept on and on about the church choir. I can just imagine, back in the vestry, can't you? All that unrobing."

"Don't be annoying. Tell me about the letters."

"Try a bit of the pheas 'n' salmon mix." He held out a forkful at me. "Go on, tell me what you think."

"It's very nice." It was; I really think he *had* invented a new dish. I often meant to try it, but I never have.

"So, I got rid of the Rev., had another go at Reg, all to no avail; I ate the fish and chips..."

"And the spotted dick."

"Now, don't interrupt me; I went back into the bedroom and had a poke around. I opened a few drawers, but there were only Joyce's knickers and things, and I thought I'd go back into the kitchen and make a pot of tea, so I could pretend that's what I'd been doing all the time if he woke up. Oh, here comes the claret; do gulp down the champers, Jules."

"Did you like your mashed fish and game?"

"Yes, I told you. It was lovely." He reached across and touched my hand. "You're very sweet to me."

"Are you happy?"

"Radiantly. Now, where had I got to? Oh, yes. I made the tea, filthy pot and everything and I went back to the bedroom – I felt sure the letters and anything else must be there – for a final recky. And, Jules, suddenly I looked up and there he was! He must have moved so silently. Staring at me with his gentian eyes. Well, of course, I began to babble, but even for me it was difficult; you don't make tea in a bedroom. Look, here comes the steak; they're going to do all sorts of sizzling and stuff here now."

I watched impatiently while burnished pewter pans received our pieces of beef. Sebastian asked the waiter what his name was and if he was married. He inquired after the names of his children, and said he had always had a hankering to have a little boy called Shane. I sat in silence until the ritual was completed and the waiters had withdrawn.

"And what did he say?"

"He didn't say anything; it was really very unnerving but, after what seemed like hours, he put his hand, all trembly, into his pocket and brought out the letters and sort of thrust them at me. And then he went shuffling off to the lavatory. Of course, I pocketed them straight away and busied myself about the tea. Mm, the steak's *gorgeous;* I wish I had had two now. Can I?"

"You can have two puddings if you're still hungry."

"But that would look so greedy."

"Go on. What happened next?"

"Well, he came shuffling back and I did feel rather embarrassed. I followed him into the sitting room and explained all about your book and things, and how much you wanted the letters, and so on; I ended up by pointing out that he had given you the last four, so obviously I'd imagined he would want to give you the rest."

"And did he answer?"

"Never a word; he just went off to sleep."

"What do you think he wants done with the letters? Do you think he wants me to write his father's biography?"

"Well, actually..." I refilled his glass and he stopped mid-sentence, regarding his wine thoughtfully. "I don't think he knows what he wants," he continued, but I got the impression that this was not what he had first intended saying; but, as so often, I resisted questioning him. Would events have taken another course if I had? Pointless to speculate now.

"He's very old, you know. I don't think he's got very long." He suddenly looked very sad.

"Well," I said brusquely, "at least we've got the letters."

"Or some of them. What shall we do with them?" He regarded my plate with interest. "Do you want all those potatoes? Can I have them?" He scooped them off my plate and I poured him more wine.

"Listen, darling," I said, leaning forward, "I must tell you: ever since I have received the letters, scenes between Melcourt and Toto have been so vivid in my mind; I almost know how it happened. I feel I could write such a book."

"See, Jules?" he said, eyeing a stray carrot left in the silver chafing dish, "I *told* you you fantasized about them, but you denied it."

"Never mind what I said. I know how Melcourt felt for Toto because I know how I feel for you."

"You're on dangerous ground, Jules. Nobody knows how somebody else feels." I ignored his comment and placed my knife and fork together.

"I want to write a new book, Sebastian."

"Good heavens, its taken you twenty years to write this one!"

"The one I'm doing can stand – all the lit. crit., the early years, and so on; a sort of primer on Melcourt. The *real* opus will be a re-creation of Toto and Melcourt, a sort of psychological study."

"Goodness!" He finished off what was left of my potatoes.

If I had not drunk gin, champagne and the best part of a bottle of Chateau Haut Brion, I daresay I should not have spoken of my ambitions.

"Darling, I want us to write the book together. As Melcourt conceived beautiful verses as a result of his union with Toto – well, we shall conceive a biography; if I know how Melcourt felt, you know about Toto."

"I'm not sure that's terribly flattering, Jules."

I continued: "To write a study of Melcourt and Toto would be something quite extraordinary, the supreme consummation of everything. To do it together would be like making love."

"No, it wouldn't."

"Oh. Why wouldn't it?"

"Two reasons; alpha, it would take about a million times longer, and beta, it wouldn't be nearly as much fun." He helped himself to the last of the red cabbage, but I was not to be deterred.

"It was only an analogy, darling. And I haven't finished yet." I wanted to hold his hand but, of course, I couldn't there in the middle of the dining room. I reached under the table and put my hand on his thigh. "When I speak of consummation I speak also of the result of the consummation. I see the book as a child, our child – the child, if you like, of the four of us: Melcourt, Toto, you and I."

"I hope it won't have two heads."

I ignored this. "It will grow from the babyhood of the Melcourt letters, through the childhood of ideas, the awkwardness of adolescence –" I removed my hand from his thigh and gesticulated wildly. I was getting confused myself "– the child, the book-child, grows into maturity, becomes elegant, beautiful, wise, and goes out into the world where it captures the hearts of civilised men." All drivel, I know that now, but at the time, I spoke what was in my heart.

He smiled. "I wonder what's for pudding; do you think it will match up to the spotted dick?"

Then the waiter arrived with the menus, and I knew I had exposed my heart enough. The waiter gave Sebastian them both, as one would to a mother with a small child. I glowered at the two of them.

"Would you like me to choose for you?" he asked wickedly, hanging on to my menu.

"No, I should like to choose for myself. Give me my menu, please." I felt irritated by this abrupt return to reality.

He humoured me and indicated to the waiter that I should have a menu. "Compote of almonds," he said, perusing the list of desserts. "Almonds are wonderful, they make me think of hectares of pink blossom in the Hindu Kush, a compote of almonds, cherries and apricots; how delicious! What will you have, Jules?" They both (the waiter and Sebastian) stared at me, Sebastian all wide-eyed wonder, the waiter as if nothing, however crass on my part, would surprise him. I felt very cross.

"Oh dear," I said sarcastically, "there is no vanilla ice-cream, Black Forest gateau, or sherry trifle."

"He will have the almond compote with me," said Sebastian to the waiter, "and, oh, yes, I think a light dessert wine; a muscat, perhaps, nothing very serious." The waiter relieved us of our menus; I think he was pleased to get mine back in one piece.

"Now, Dr Collins," said Sebastian, "let's have a proper grown-up conversation, shall we?"

"What shall be talk about?"

"Why Reg wrote that miserable book, when he had all this glorious stuff to work from!"

The compote arrived. "Very well, then," I replied smugly, "I shall tell you." I leaned back in my chair with an air of triumph. "I learned from Joyce today that Reg's mother was called Nell – and she may have had a title." I paused for his comments.

"What a sleuth you are, Jules. But where does this lead you? Lovely, lovely apricots."

"Firstly, that Toto did marry Lady Ellen."

"A bit tenuous."

"I don't think so. Perhaps it was she who stopped Reg writing an explicit biography."

"She would have been dead by the time the biography came out.

Look, here's an apricot stone. What a pity I can't crack it open. The kernels are delicious."

"In the 1940s, one had to be terribly circumspect."

"Much more likely that she'd nagged at him for years to write the biography, and he was so bored with the whole thing that he did the least possible. It's dreadful when people keep telling you to do things."

I looked at him crossly. I had wanted to impress him with my theories. "Well then, we have absolutely no idea why Reg didn't write a proper book. In fact, we don't know anything, not even why Reg has given us the letters."

"Nor why," he said, picking up almonds in his fingers, "Joyce doesn't want him to."

"I don't know what Reg's motives are," I said, "but I suppose Joyce knows the letters are valuable, and doesn't want them given away. I do feel rather guilty. Eventually, I'll have to decide what to do about them. I certainly don't intend stealing them." Having delivered myself of this moral fusillade, I stared at him. "And nor, I hope, do you, Sebastian." His upper lip was delightfully downy.

"Good Heavens, is there no baseness of which you regard me incapable?"

"No," I said, "none." Of course I was only teasing.

He had finished his dessert, and was idly dipping his spoon into my fruits of the Hindu Kush. "I don't like Reg much, do you, Jules?"

"No, I don't think I do. Don't eat *all* the cherries."

"Mean and selfish."

"I'm not; I've just stood you the most stupendous meal."

"Not you, silly, Reg. Did you notice in that horrid little room everything is designed for *his* comfort, not hers. He's got the best chair and the electric fire."

"Well, I suppose he takes after his father."

"But you don't really know what Toto was like, do you? Can I have some more of the fabulously expensive Muscady?" I poured it out for him. I watched him drink, leaning back and stretching his long legs out under the table, replete with all the delicacies I had bought for him. "I mean, I know you think he was like me, devouring all Max's substance just like I'm devouring all your cherries now, but you don't *know*, do you?" I pushed the plate over towards him. I had drunk a great deal of wine, I had driven a long way; all in all, I had had a tiring day, and yet I knew Sebastian had touched on something vitally important, the parallel between Melcourt and Toto, and I and Sebastian. My brain, befuddled as it was, cast about to make some sense of it.

I imagine my thought processes went like this: I have no doubt that Toto's chief aim in pursuing Melcourt was money – as much money as possible. Perhaps, in view of the sonnet he had sent to Melcourt, he wanted to pursue a literary career and was anxious for Melcourt to use his influence on his behalf. Sebastian, too, is interested in money, and during the course of our relationship he has relieved me of considerable sums (directly in cash, or indirectly through presents, such as meals, clothes and the car). Like Toto, he is interested in a literary life and he may see me as one capable of pulling strings for research fellowships and the like, but this I doubt. Certainly, he has never asked me. Money, then, is of the essence in both cases, but I do not think in either, money is the only factor. The other is, of course, sex. No, that is to oversimplify. Both Sebastian and Toto clearly have gargantuan appetites for it, but both (because of their beauty) could satisfy their appetites where and when they wish. 'When you have cast your seed by the wayside, I glean where others have reaped,' Melcourt wrote. I do not need to detail instances of Sebastian's casual promiscuity. So, both are capable of getting sex. So what, then, was it, this factor that brought Toto to Melcourt's side and kept him there for so long? What is it that causes Sebastian to return to mine after repeated defections? Both Melcourt and I were not exactly *ugly* men, but certainly unattractive in the conventional sense. Toto and Sebastian were quintessentially quite beautiful. How, then, why...? It is perhaps the awareness of the discrepancy in our physical appearance, the lacuna between extreme beauty and plainness, that drives us desperately to find ways of keeping them: we spend, we spoil, we indulge, but that is not all. Love taught us;

I do not know if Melcourt satisfied Toto sexually, but I *feel* he did, and, certainly, there is nothing I do not know about Sebastian's body and his sexual preferences. I have learned him as a musical instrument, and because he makes love silently, I have learned the sound and significance of every breath he takes, every tremor of his body. And I know by the way he stretches out his glorious body afterwards, and the glimmer in his eyes, I have pleased him. Of course I'm not enough for him any more than Melcourt was enough for Toto; but I think that there is something, more than sex, less than love – shall we call it 'eros'?

"Sebastian," I said, suddenly, and the loudness of my voice surprised me as much as it surprised the other diners. "Are you going to spend the night with me – all of it?"

One or two people, especially an earnest young man with a beard, obviously on his first date with a plain girl with glasses, showed signs of alarm, and Sebastian told me afterwards he had heard one middle-aged woman declare, 'They should all be castrated'. Sebastian was, as always, master of such situations.

"Of course, we'll have an orgy –" he raised his voice and cast his eyes about the room "– and ask all these nice people to come." Fifteen pairs of eyes swivelled frantically towards us, towards the ceiling, towards each other before fixing themselves on the plates before them with grim intensity.

I drank a great deal of black coffee. It wasn't my Turkish variety, of course, but it sobered me up wonderfully. I paid the bill almost without blinking, and we took a taxi home.

Fifteen
In Bed

Amazingly, he was still beside me in bed the next morning. I am a heavy sleeper, particularly after sex and Sebastian had no compunction about getting up and slipping away when he had had enough of me. So it was with delight that I murmured:

"You shook the gold laburnum of your hair
Against my raw soul's face.
And with the blossom gently blowing there
I knew the benison of grace
And love, both mine and thine, to share."

I broke off abruptly and reached for him. "Darling."

"Oh, good," he said rolling over obediently, "I'd much rather have you than Melcourt."

An onlooker, a voyeur, might have dismissed what ensued as a simple fuck, an ugly middle-aged man screwing a sexy kid. Indeed, he would have seen all he expected to see: I roughly shoving my cock into my lover, working him first rhythmically then violently, groaning and sweating, and Sebastian, his blue eyes wide open, breathing shallowly, silent even at the end when he shuddered and convulsed repeatedly and lay still. It would have been, in the onlooker's eyes, a crude act. But for me it was not like that because I made love; the ache of my cock was the ache of the love I had for him, and when I came I gave him the love that lay within me. It was a tangible thing for him, a gift better even than food, and one that blessed the donor and the recipient equally. (I have only given him one greater gift, but that was much later – quite recently, in fact. I shall not come to that for some time.)

Afterwards, I turned him gently towards me. He was flushed and damp with sweat and sperm, and he settled, sweet and still into my arms. There are some moments of one's life that one would think worth a thousand years in purgatory. This was one such moment. And then, of course, I had to break the spell with foolish words:

"There is nothing in the world I want beside you, there is nothing to put beside you. I adore every particle of your body; I live only when you are with me; my life, when you are away, is empty, dross."

As always, when I made such remarks, some foolish part of me hoped against hope that he would reply, 'And I love you, Jules, I want to spend the rest of my life with you'. He didn't.

"Hush," he said, rolling over on top of me, "I keep my love for God."

"Oh really!" His blind Catholicism never failed to infuriate me. "I do not imagine how you can possibly do this, and expect to go to heaven."

"Of course I shall." He smiled, rubbing his cock against mine. "I shall make sure I receive divine unction, and all my sins will be forgiven me."

"It may be some time until then; had you not better settle some old debts with God first? What about now, for instance?"

He rolled off me and laughed happily. "I'll say some Hail Marys," he said. His eyes closed piously and his lips began to move.

"And what am I meant to do while you're at your devotions?" I was getting hard again and could think of better things to do than be at his side while he prayed.

"Well, you can't lie here all morning." He sat up and became brisk and business-like. "I suggest you get dressed and go out and buy us some croissants and pains au chocolate, and then we can read the Melcourt letters."

"What?" I sat up, filled with indignation. "You said you hadn't got them. You said you had left them in your flat."

"So, what a pleasant surprise it must be to learn that I have brought them with me after all. Do get up and get some food, I'm awfully hungry."

"Have you read them?"

"No. I told you. I was busy."

"Let's read them now."

"No, it's breakfast time. You will buy Nutella, won't you?" In spite of my indignation, I couldn't help smiling.

I had forgotten his passion for the glutinous chocolate spread. He would have it straight from the jar with a spoon – as well as in other, more original ways.

"Oh, and honey for you, the runny kind."

"Of course," I replied, reluctantly getting out of bed. I could not resist quoting:

"Oh Sweetheart, suck the honey clear,
In firm swift sips
Your nectar be on mine, my dear,
And mine, on your sweet lips."

I put on my Y-fronts.

"What a pity Melcourt didn't know about Nutella," he said, settling himself into the pillows.

"Why?" I was irritably trying to fit my reluctant cock into the pants.

"It's so difficult to find rhymes for 'honey'. 'Money' and 'funny' don't have the right ring, somehow."

"There's 'bunny' and 'tunny'," I said crossly. I wanted to get back into bed with him.

"Don't be silly, Jules, Nutella's much better."

"How?" I surveyed myself in the mirror; my trousers bulged out ludicrously. "I can only think of 'cellar' and 'Sam Weller'. And anyway,

I'm going off to buy your breakfast and then I shall read those letters."

"Yes, of course."

But as I went stomping off past the front of the flats, I looked up to see my bedroom window open. A naked Sebastian gazed out. He waved merrily and, leaning out dangerously, proclaimed:

"Jules is a hell of a feller:
He likes honey instead of Nutella.
But whichever you pick,
Let's put it on thick,
It will..."

I refused to stop and listen to the last line. I set my face resolutely towards the bread shop.

Sixteen
Nutella

It took me some time. I bought the croissants and pains au chocolat first; but they didn't have any Nutella; nor did the corner shop, so I had to walk half a mile in the opposite direction to the supermarket. (I should have taken the car, but it was always such a bother getting it out.) Anyway, I was staggering back under the weight of the bread and the rest of it, when I bumped into Williams, dressed in the suit he always wears to meetings (he has worn it, to my knowledge, for the last eight years).

"Goodness, Collins. Are you going into the wholesale bakery business?"

"No." I stood like a guilty schoolboy, clutching my bags.

"Just opening a little patisserie, then?"

"I have been purchasing some breakfast."

"You're supplying the college?"

I didn't want to stand listening to Williams' wisecracks. (He was chuckling irritatingly.) I wanted to get back to bed with Sebastian and read the Melcourt letters. I was also conscious of being none too fresh, and needing a shower after the night's activities.

"You'll have to excuse me. Must be getting on."

"People staying?"

"Yes."

"Ah." He picked his left nostril briefly. "You're coming to the A-level assessment committee meeting? As you know, I've been heavily involved in the whole business."

"I'm afraid I can't make it." I had, of course, forgotten all about it. "Too much to do."

He looked critically at my trousers and sweatshirt. "You look a bit seedy, Collins. You need a holiday. Get out and enjoy yourself a bit. You spend too much time on that book of yours. You look as if you have been up all night."

"Yes," I said, (I couldn't resist it) "I was up a number of times." I gathered my bags together and set off back to the flat, with Williams doubtless staring suspiciously after me. I felt curiously distant from him and academic life in general: it seemed to me then that the only true reality lay with Melcourt and Toto, Sebastian and me.

Sebastian thrust his croissant into the Nutella jar and brought it out all covered in chocolate. I watched it disappear into his mouth, and turned my attention to the first of the letters. Now I had the letters, I almost couldn't bring myself to read them: that I should be reading Melcourt's letters to Toto, to Sebastian, seemed complex, and if the letters revealed indifference (or worse) on the part of Toto, as I suspected they would, how would I bear to read to Sebastian what, in effect, was a taboo subject between us, in respect of our own relationship?

I began: "*Melcourt Hall. My dearest Toto...*"

Sebastian interrupted. "It's the first time he's called him that; Toto, I mean." He peered regretfully into the jar. "I suppose I'd better leave the rest," he said as he reached over for a croissant.

"And don't drop crumbs all over the bed."

"Of course not; the crusty bits are agonising. Read on."

"*It was with delight that my eye fell upon your letter, my heart leapt up, and my hand seized upon the envelope, but how soon was joy to fade and the hand to drop beneath the burden of such cruel words...*"

"Oh dear," said Sebastian, "anyone can tell Toto's not written about Nutella." I frowned and continued:

"You do not often write to me, my dear, nor have I expected it: you have youth's carelessness; it is part of your boyish charm. I have taken pleasure in imagining the innocent antics you have preferred, to the dull wielding of a pen: perhaps you sported upon the cricket field, clad in white, or sculled upon the Isis, or urged on some horse as high-spirited as yourself. Only when you had finished your sportive play would you write – some whimsy, perhaps. Solid letter writing I did not expect..."

"Quite right; it's horrid writing letters." He put his finger into the Nutella jar and regarded it with interest. I continued:

"I was wrong on both counts; your antics were not innocent and you had determined to write an earnest letter, indeed a most serious and, in its way, an honest letter; you had supposed (wrongly, as it turns out) that I had discovered your antics with a back-street renter. You were anxious to ask forgiveness – I like to think from a sentiment of repentance, but I fear it was to clear the way for a new request; you have a 'small gambling debt'..."

"Ah!" said Sebastian.

"You throw yourself on my mercy; in effect, you undertake to avoid the enticing distractions of the Albany Street Barracks and The Hundred Guinea club if I clear your debts..."

I paused; I found it difficult to continue.

"Go on, Jules."

"Very well: 'Forgive me, Max', you beg. 'Dearest Max, please do not be hard upon one who is no more than a boy'..."

"Oh dear," said Sebastian, his mouth full of Nutella, "poor Melcourt."

"Shall I read on?" I was sarcastic, annoyed at so many interruptions and his cavalier attitude to it all.

"Mmm."

"Of course I forgive you. I suppose I shall always forgive you whatever you do." I sighed; the words might so easily have been mine. I took refuge in severity. "Please listen, Sebastian, and don't do that while I'm reading."

"Yes, Jules, and no, Jules."

"*But I cannot understand you, Toto. I believed we were all in all to each other. That you could do, what we did in love to each other, to another, a common telegraph boy, simply to satisfy some lascivious craving, that I cannot understand. Do you care nothing for me? Is it only I who loves? Is your love only prompted by appetite? Or is your motive a more sinister one? Is it my fame that attracts you? Do you envisage using my name to further your own feeble literary efforts?*"

"Nasty!"

"*Or even more horribly...*' Don't take the last pain au chocolat, I haven't had one yet."

"But I'm so hungry, Jules."

"Oh, very well. Now I've lost my place..."

"'Or even more horribly'..."

"'*Or even more horribly... you have not even the artist's excuse; it is simply my money that interests you? Well, my dear, let me disabuse you of any false illusions. I am not a rich man; almost every penny I have is eaten up by the estate. I simply do not have large amounts of...* I can't read this word."

"Cash," said Sebastian. He had finished the pain au chocolat and was wriggling down the bed with the open jar of Nutella.

"*Cash. Perhaps I should have told you this before I spent so much upon you, somewhere in the region of £2,000 in presents, subs and meals. Perhaps I should have told you before that I am not an inexhaustible source of cash; but I feared to lose you. In my heart, I have trembled lest your affections were venal. Did you plan, when you wrote your first charming letter to me, to compel me to fall in love with you and use my money, while you continued to pursue your own interests among the London renters –* Don't do that, Sebastian!"

While I read of all the sufferings of Melcourt at the hands of his treacherous lover, what was Sebastian doing? Was he listening gravely, sympathetically aware of how cruel the parallel was between us? No, he was not. He was preparing to coat my cock with Nutella.

He moved up the bed and put his arms around me. "Jules, don't get upset. This is Max Melcourt writing to Anthony Roberts more than a hundred years ago. It's not about us."

"Yes, it is," I said, pushing his arms away, "it is exactly that." My eyes filled with tears and I turned away in shame. He removed the last croissant from its wrapping and placed it carefully on the ashtray at his side of the bed. Then he gently wiped the tears from my eyes with the corner of the paper bag.

"Give me the letter, and I'll read."

"No. You don't know the writing well enough, and your fingers are covered in Nutella."

"The trouble is –" he took a bite out of the croissant "– that what neither you nor Melcourt has ever understood is that you like us, Toto and me, *because* of the way we are. Melcourt knew what Toto was like after the first letter, or else why did he write about poisoned flowers? And you knew when you interviewed me for my college place. It was all in the UCAS form, wasn't it? Anyway, you must have guessed about Johnson, the guy who taught me English, when I told you he used to read Melcourt to me."

"Did he?"

"Yes."

"Anyway," I said sternly, "there was nothing in the UCAS form that spoke of bad character. I would not have argued for you if there had been."

"It wasn't so much what there was, but what there wasn't. Did anyone write of my worthiness, good conduct, diligence? Was I Head of House, Prefect or Monitor? Had I done anything at all of merit?"

"I made my judgments."

"Exactly. You chose me for my looks and my charm."

"I chose you for your obvious ability. I was proved right. You obtained an excellent First, and you are now doing a PhD."

"You chose me because, for the first time in your life, you saw something dangerous and glittering and you desired it."

As usual I could think of no suitable reply. I resumed reading: "*Well, Toto, I shall not continue to berate you. What would be the point? Probably you would not even read it, if I did continue. You would smile your charming smile and toss the letter away. Then you would go to the mirror and smile again. Perhaps you are not even alone as you read this. Perhaps you read it laughingly to another as he gives you what you so frequently desire.*

"I have spent long enough in recrimination. If I have been tedious, forgive me as I forgive you. Come to Melcourt on Tuesday, and I will see about your debts. If you can manage to come earlier, come. I have some people to see about estate business, but I will put them off. Toto, I must see you, hold you in my arms, and give you the love that is in my heart. Your adoring friend, Max. Well, Sebastian, what do you say now?"

"I say it's time for a short intermission. One Melcourt letter is quite enough for one morning." He reached for the jar of Nutella. "Shall I tell you the last line of my limerick? It's awfully appropriate."

"If you must." I shall not set it down here, since it verged on the obscene. Besides, 'tell yer' and 'swell yer' do not really rhyme with Nutella.

Seventeen
Lord Melcourt's Last Letter

"Jules," he said, some hours later, "I simply have to play your piano."

Music was another of Sebastian's needs. My piano (a Steinway) had been one of the many things, such as dinners, clothes, holidays, even the Porsche, which had been bought either with, or for, Sebastian, or simply as an enticement to bring him to me. I myself am an indifferent pianist; I play with some accuracy, but little flair. Sebastian, of course, managed to beat me on both counts; he had a perfect ear and played with wicked panache. He also played at great length. I hid the Tchaikovsky scores (a composer I loathed) until I found he knew them anyway.

"What about the remaining Melcourt letters?" I put my dressing gown on, and followed him into the study.

"You read them, while I play." He began leafing through the music I kept for him. "I'll find something desperately sad."

"How do you know the letters are sad? You said you hadn't read them. You *have* read them, haven't you?" I was full of reproach. "I wanted to think that we had read them together for the first time!"

"Did you, Jules? Oh, this will do." It was Stravinsky, and it looked fiendish.

"I don't think you should play the piano with no clothes on." But my words were lost. He had begun to play.

I settled down to read: "*Melcourt Hall. Dear Toto, Once I believed that you and I... oh, how much sadness lies contained within that little word 'once'. It comes from the realms of childhood. How often have I sat at the knees of my nurse and heard those magic words 'Once upon a time lived a prince', 'Once there was an enchanted garden'. 'Once'. Thence I believed I, too, should go and dwell for ever in enchanted places... Once then, Toto, I believed that you and I should go thither and dwell in perfect happiness. Once, indeed, for a short space, I believed we had discovered the garden of joy and made it our dwelling place. But the child grows older, I will not say wiser, for surely the belief in the possibility of perfect happiness must be formed in a mind of wisdom, and to turn from that dream, a fall from wisdom. The child grows older and he discovers, amidst the flowers and trees of his garden, noxious plants, serpents and pestilent creatures beneath the grass. Ah, what a time was once.*

"Satis. I will come to the point before I weary you. You are bored, I daresay already scanning the letter eagerly, not for words of love, but a favourable reply to your demands. Nevertheless, Toto, read these words of mine, mark them a little, my dear.

"Some weeks ago, you received a letter, a letter of such sweetness... never mind, perhaps you read it, perhaps you did not; words of endearment are of little moment to you. You put it into your pocket and forgot about it. My letters are, after all, cheap enough things, if one is lost, another will come. So there it lay in your coat pocket. But that, in itself, was no crime, to forget a lover's letter is nothing. Nor must I blame you for setting my love at naught, and preferring the embrace of boys bought off the back alleys of Holywell Street, youths vicious, venal and various. Affectionate love was nothing to you. Appetite was all. Of course, it is not long before some fellow, vicious and vile, but not stupid, given, no doubt, the run of your rooms, sees his opportunity – a letter from Lord Melcourt to his lover! Gold indeed!

"And now you write and ask me for money to buy it back! 'It is you, Max, I think of', you write, as if your motive was one of altruism. 'I could not bear some disgrace to come to you'.

"The price of disgrace is, apparently, £1,000. Pay, and I am again returned to respectability, my name as pure as daylight. Fail to pay, and the prison door

gapes open, and society shuns me for ever.

"What choice do I have? Of course I must pay, even though I have to remortgage Melcourt to raise the loan. Obtain the letter, for God's sake, and keep this and all others from me, under lock and key. Here is the cheque. Pay off the man immediately.

"I have been outspoken, angry, cruel and perhaps arrogant. You are not vicious, I know you are not, only too childlike and trusting. You will know better now, Toto. You will not mix with such people again. Let us, my dearest, return again to those blessed times of 'once'. Let us seek again the paths that lead to the secret garden where once we dwelt, not with childish credulity, but with the wisdom of more mature years. I wait for you by the garden gate with arms outstretched. Oh, come to me, my beloved. Yours ever, Max."

For a long time, I sat silent; the letter had not surprised or shocked me, for what, I reflected, was surprising about an older man's infatuation for a younger and its inevitable outcome?

Sebastian sat naked on the piano stool, his hair hung loose on his shoulders, his body tensing and rippling in harmony with the music. He had long finished the Stravinsky and was amusing himself by improvisation, drifting from one tune to another, sometimes a popular tune like 'Yesterday', or some dimly recalled snatch of song from decades back. Then, he would drift back to his first love, the eighteenth century, and I could distinguish Bach or Vivaldi, but mostly, it seemed to me, the music was neither familiar nor unknown, but hovered in a twilight world of memories and half-memories. Music evokes and creates images in our minds even more seductively than words.

I was caught up in a kind of trance. At last, I picked up the last letter: *"Melcourt Hall. I do not know how to begin this letter for I am accustomed to write 'Dear', or, in your case, 'Dearest', or 'My Dearest'. I cannot write that now. What, then, shall I call you? Roberts? Who is he? I do not know such a distant person? Shall I, then, call you Anthony, as I did when I knew you first? No, for when I called you Anthony I knew you so little that I believed something good might come from our acquaintance. Toto, then, the name I devised for you one night when we lay together in love? It expressed the* childishness (as I then believed) of your nature, you were a little boy with the sweetest of lisps: 'What is your name, my child?', 'Please, sir, my name is Anthon... Anton... Tonton... Toto'. And it was secret, it was witty, for it expressed the completeness of my love for you. How often I have smiled to think I loved 'in Toto', my love was complete – within you. How often I have spoken this sweet diminutive; I have murmured it in your ear as we sat in a concert or in the theatre. It met with a simple response; your head would turn and your eyes fix on mine. 'Max', you would murmur in reply. Or, you might be in pettish mood, and pout at some imagined default on my part: 'Toto', I would whisper, 'Forgive me, Toto', and you would perhaps remain obdurate, waiting for further pleadings, or unlock your lovely lips and whisper all was well between us, and your name was lost in an ecstasy of sensation.

"So how should I commence writing to you whom I can never again call 'Dear', for whom I have no name?

"I think I never believed you good, even from your very first letter in which you expressed so much, and said so little; I fancied you light, without substance, without virtue. And then, of course, we met and all happened as you intended it should; I beheld your extreme beauty, and I became desirous of it.

"How cunning you were with me, Toto. What a measure you trod in your dance of deceit. How you advanced with arms stretched out and, when I claimed you, retreated in a backward step of 'modesty'. What a blush fell upon your cheek as my lips sought yours, what a withdrawal of hand as mine clasped yours. And what a masterly stroke it was to come to me so tremblingly, so childishly, for against your provocation and your arrogance I had resistance enough, but against your vulnerability, I was defenseless. I took you trembling in my arms, and trembled to possess you. Was this a sin? How could so great a joy be a sin? Nay, it was love, the purest, greatest gift the gods may give to us.

"I was like the hero of some great play by Sophocles, an Oedipus who had the whole of fortune in his fingers and yet let it run away like sand through one fatal flaw. You were my flaw, Toto.

"Already men whisper about me in their clubs, soon many will forget me *as the author of such verse as moved their hearts, and will snigger in their cups and use foul names. My poems will be returned from the publishers. I shall no longer be asked into respectable houses, no longer looked upon as a respectable companion for the young of either sex. All this, perhaps, I would endure for a single taste of your exquisite body – but I cannot. I told you long ago I was not a rich man – and, indeed, you looked a little chastened, for you had reckoned on not less than a cool hundred thousand to line your pocket. But the mind of a predator soon adapts itself. If I had not a million, nor a hundred thousand nor even ten – why, five or three or one would do. Any was better than none.*

"You no longer pretended you were subject to the blackmail of others, there was no need, and besides your importunity was too great. Almost a new honesty crept into your dealings with me: 'Max, I want £500 or I sell your letters'; 'Max, you would be unwise to withhold £300'; 'Who shall not hear the name of Melcourt and not shudder?'; 'Max, "Sodomite" is an ugly word'; 'Mortgage Melcour, Max'; 'Max, a little money, and my body is yours'.

"Well, my anonymous friend, the money is almost gone, I can get no more on Melcourt, my reputation stands as yet. If I tarry longer, my name, even my verse will fall into disrepute and be subject to men's despite. But I would tarry, yes, Toto, I would tarry. For what, you ask, your sapphire eyes gazing prettily at mine, for what will you tarry, Max? I will tell you. I would tarry for your love, even in Hell, I would tarry for your love, but I have never possessed it, nor shall I ever, for there is none to possess.

"I like to think, Toto, you did not know what you did when you set up your scales and placed my life in one pan and your greed in another, and allowed my life to sink down. Perhaps that façade of boyishness concealed – not innocence, no, that could never be – a lack of understanding, a sort of youthful immaturity. I will pretend that had we met when you were older, you would have learned discrimination and would have shrunk from ruining a man who had yet much to give the world.

"Farewell, Toto, I have loved you as no man has been loved by another; I have ventured all for you, and I have lost. I do not reproach you, for a man's life is a small thing – why, there are hundreds of galaxies containing a

thousand worlds apiece; what, then, is the life of one man, even a poet? I hope I may find God, and that He will not punish me for what I do – I do not think he will, for they say He is love and will understand my sins have been in his name. Farewell, my dearest dear, Max."

"Sebastian," I said. "Oh, Sebastian." I could feel the tears running down my cheeks.

He swivelled round on the piano stool and regarded me briefly. "Very sad," he said, "but good for your book and my thesis." Then he turned round again to the piano and continued playing.

If the remark was callous, it also had the effect of making me examine my own feelings. As so often, Sebastian saw to the heart of the matter: I *did* feel the triumph of the researcher. For years, I had speculated on the circumstances of Melcourt's death, and now I knew beyond all reasonable doubt that Max had killed himself for love and, more prosaically, the fear of disgrace. I felt the biographer's delight at what I might achieve, what we might achieve, Sebastian and I; we might complete a tremendous book together. Certainly, we would enjoy the closeness of those who share a secret unknown to the rest of the world. What a source of joy that would be!

'Very sad,' he had said laconically, as if that was enough.

A man's life had been wasted, a great man had been brought low. And he was a man with whom I had been intimately connected, a man whose life I felt I knew, a man whom I loved almost as myself, indeed had often felt we were almost the same man. Of course I was moved, moved to tears, but then, as I have said before, tears come easily to me. I suspected I wept as much for myself as for Melcourt. And the atmosphere was strange, the room in semi-darkness. Sebastian playing – I think it was Dvořák now – a mixture of harmony and discord. 'Very sad, but good for your book and my thesis'. He was right, but not entirely so. There was something else to be learnt and understood from the letters of Melcourt, and I did not know then what it was. I know now.

"Well," he said, cheerfully, from the piano, "not even you suffer as much as Melcourt." His hands ran over the keys in a number of rippling arpeggios. "Not even I am as bad as Toto."

I considered his words, straining my eyes to make him out through the gloom. He was right, I decided: my state was far superior to Melcourt's; after all, Sebastian had not reduced me to penury, disgrace and death. In fact, he had made love to me very sweetly within the hour. My plight and Melcourt's were quite different.

'Not even I am as bad as Toto'. Again I considered his words and, again, I agreed, Sebastian was not machiavellian like Toto; he was merely egotistical, selfish, amoral, venal and mercenary. Besides, he was a Catholic; he attended Mass regularly; presumably, for some short periods of his life, he was in a state of grace. And, furthermore, when he lay asleep beside me with his golden hair all tousled about his face, he was to me utterly perfect, and the concepts of good and evil, and all the uninteresting virtues that men list as mile-stones en route to morality or immorality, did not seem of great importance.

If I had continued with this train of thought, I might have got somewhere with the Melcourt problem and made these last terrible months less incomprehensible. I did not because Sebastian played the National Anthem, stood up, and declaimed:

"There she weaves by night and day
A magic web with colour gay.
She has heard a whisper say,
A curse is on her if she stay."

"What do you mean, darling – I shouldn't have thought Tennyson..."

He looked at me with what I can only describe as a mixture of concern and defiance. "I don't want to end up floating down to Camelot on a bier."

Uncertain as to what he meant, I took refuge in pedantry. "Actually, it was a boat, not a bier."

"I'm sick of shadows, of only looking at the world through a mirror."

"What do you mean?"

"Melcourt and Toto and Reg and Joyce, all letters and biographies, full of half-truths. I feel the presence of ghosts, Jules, intangibles, shadows. They flit about your flat like bats. They get in my hair." And, to demonstrate his point, he tied his hair back with a rubber band which had held together the sheets of Dvořák.

"Skiamachy. Fighting with shadows. But, Sebbie, about the letters..."

"Nothing but words. Vague, nebulous, without substance."

"Words have substance, they have sound and meaning." For a moment he sat in silence, his hands idle on the keys.

"Words," he said slowly, "are only thoughts with clothes on."

"May we not undress each others' words as we do each other?"

"No," he said decisively, "thoughts are prudish things, they do not like to have their nakedness viewed. And quite right, too. They don't bear scrutiny; they are the fat women of the mind."

"I regarded his back sadly. Probably he was right. My secret thoughts of him would seem at best risible, at worst pathetic, disgusting even. And his thoughts of me? Did I really want to know? No, I should not dare look.

"Jules!" Sweet and acquiescent as he sometimes was, he also possessed an inner core of impatience, a reluctance to compromise. "I've told you: I am tired of shadows, I want my tangibles." He shut the piano decisively.

"What do you want, darling?" I asked dully. "A drink, or something to eat?"

"No." He untied his hair. "Actually, I want a fuck. The most unshadowy thing I can think of at the moment is your cock. Which would we both prefer, words running about naked in the air, or your cock in my arse? Which, Jules?"

It was a crude remark and Sebastian – although realistic, outspoken, even outrageous – was seldom crude. Yet he was expressing what I had only felt. In the letters, I had sensed Eros; Sebastian saw the way to realise an intangible idea. Well, I do not suppose I analysed his remark at the time.

How can I remember now? But I do remember pulling him down on the floor and doing exactly as he had suggested.

There was a certain amount of savagery in our love-making which he enjoyed – actually, we both enjoyed (I remember his eyes all topaz and smoky afterwards, with pleasure) – but on a more prosaic note, it left me quite exhausted, and, when I woke up some hours later, I discovered he was gone.

He had not left empty-handed; he had helped himself to the Melcourt letters – they were all missing, the earlier ones from my desk, the later ones from the window seat where I had left them. I was absolutely furious. I went round the flat, banging cupboards and drawers open and shut, not so much in the hope of finding the letters, which I knew were gone, but to relieve my feelings. If I could not thump Sebastian (or indeed bang *him*) I should take it out on something else. How *dare* he take my letters while I was asleep (exhausted by pleasuring him). It was theft, pure and simple. How dare he sneak away? What was he going to do with them? Well, he needn't think he was going to get away with it. Then I caught my little finger in the drawer of my desk and, as I stood rubbing my finger, my anger turned to self-pity.

When I gave him so much love, why could he not return a little of it? I picked up the stapler in my good hand and began fixedly putting staples into a single sheet of paper. He liked it well enough when I fucked him, he liked the size of me inside him, and the skill with which I read his body, knowing every little tremor of him. 'Absolute heaven', he would say, stretching out afterwards, and once, 'You're the best, Jules'. I would have given him anything, he knew he had only to ask. And yet he did not love me. When I had used up all the staples, I picked up the phone. If I could not demand the return of love, at least I could demand the return of the letters. It was engaged. I had a couple of gins and tonics and phoned him again. Half an hour later, he was still engaged and, when I did finally reach him, I got the answering-machine.

"Hi, Seb here – actually, not here – in Melcourt mood. Talk to me after the poem." The first three verses of Melcourt's last poem ensued:

"My love came to me in peacock guise
With plumage bright of hue.
And on his feathers twinkled eyes
Of green and silver blue.
He strutted low amongst the grass,
I followed close beside,
His body gleamed like glinting glass,
The pick of all his pride.
All at once he shrieked aloud
And I stood fast in fear,
He closed his tail, a slithering shroud;
His cries were death to hear."

I did not want to listen to Melcourt at this juncture – particularly Melcourt on treachery. I shouted at Sebastian, or rather, I shouted into the phone, accusing him of thieving, dishonesty, promiscuity and a thousand other crimes. Then, I burst into tears, slammed the phone down, and then went off to bed.

I expect I dreamed about him. I do not remember now. I daresay I dreamed of him; in one way or another, he has always been with me, ever since I saw him first in his lavender suit with beads in his hair when he was a kid of 16.

When I awoke, I felt rejuvinated, calm and rather sensible. I had thought of a plan.

I picked up the phone, listened patiently, and left a message after the poetry: "I'm sorry I was silly about the letters. I know you'll give them back, Sebastian. You're not cross with me, are you? Will you come to Melcourt again tomorrow? No, not tomorrow, I ought to get the car serviced, but Friday. I thought we might have one final bash at *le fils de Toto*. I mean, we could just see. We could just call in, and then spend the day together. They say it will be hot. And we could talk about writing the book. Will you phone me, darling? I don't want to bother you at the flat... Please phone... And what about Italy? Please phone," I babbled.

Eighteen
A Green Smoking Jacket

The following day, my plan seemed less attractive. I failed to get the car serviced and I heard nothing from him. When I awoke on the Friday, I decided not to go; after all, I had not alerted the Roberts, so the visit would come unannounced, and I did not now expect to hear from Sebastian. As always, he surprised me.

"Hi, Jules!" He never needed to announce himself on the phone to me – nobody else called me Jules. There was another thing; whenever the phone rang, I knew before I picked it up whenever it was him.

"Sebastian."

"Jules. Pick me up at 11 a.m. from Poole station. I've got my swag-bag."

"Swag-bag?"

"The letters I stole."

"Poole station? Whatever..."

"*Si, alle undici. Ciao.*"

Why on earth should he be at Poole? *Was* he at Poole? What was he doing there? Best not to ask; but it did seem an unlikely place. I glanced at my watch. I could make it, if I hurried. I spent the entire drive agonising over whether or not he would be there; and I drove much too fast, something I was reluctant to do when not with Sebastian, for although the car was built for speed, I am not by nature a daring driver.

Poole is not a particularly nice place, and Poole station is an exceptionally *nasty* place – even when you can find it. I drove past and round the hideous conglomeration of post-modernist buildings that surround it, vainly searching for the entrance to the car park. I was somewhat agitated when I finally managed to get in and park the car. He was standing waiting for me, amiable and elegant, but my first sensation was of shock. He had cut his hair! The golden shoulder length locks had been castrated. The hair was not exactly short; it was bobbed, making him look even younger and deceptively vulnerable, and altogether more *obviously* desirable.

He waved a large brown envelope at me. It had 'SWAG' written on it in enormous letters. He beamed radiantly (the hair made the eyes look bigger than ever) and came strolling over to the car. I leaned over and unlocked the door.

"I didn't think you'd be here."

"But you came anyway." He brushed his lips against my cheek as he climbed into the car. "You *are* sweet to me, Jules."

"I wanted my letters back," I replied ungraciously.

"Of course; I'll put them here in the door. The glove compartment is full of your pissing pot."

I watched suspiciously as he stuffed the envelope in. "Be careful of them."

"Yes, Jules."

"Are they all in there?"

He turned to me with his hair curled deliciously into his lovely face.

"Would you like to count them?"

"Don't be silly." I touched my lips against his cheek. "What have you done to your hair?"

"That must be a rhetorical question. Do you like it?" I looked straight ahead and concentrated on trying to get out of the infernal car park.

"Of course I like it."

"Really? I thought you might grieve at the shearing of the Golden Fleece."

"No. Which way do we go here? It's one-way; ah, I see..."

"Tell me what you thought."

"I thought – Christ!" I braked sharply. "They should not allow children on bikes!" I relaxed as I joined the flow of traffic into some ghastly main street. "Actually, I thought you looked like the Fra Angelico angel in the *Annunciation,* the sexy one with the multi-coloured wings."

He gave a shriek. "Oh, stop, Jules!" But it was not my foolish words that occasioned his interruption. "That Oxfam shop; there's a most wonderful green smoking jacket. Jules, you must stop."

"There's nowhere to park."

"Yes there is, just behind that little white car."

"Very well. Be quick."

"And I must get some fags and a Mars Bar."

"You won't smoke in my car, and there's all sorts of stuff in the glove compartment from last time. Hurry up."

"Oh, so stern and unbending, like the daughter of time."

"Hurry up! It's a single yellow line."

"I'll buy you something too." I sat and waited. I wondered whether Sebastian or a traffic warden would reach me first.

I stared into the window of a video shop; I wanted to know what he had been doing in Poole, and why he had cut his hair, and yet also *didn't* want to know – like the incident in the motorway services, it was better not to ask. Anyway, he had come back and stroked my hand affectionately and it really had been nothing. Even if he had or did, that was the way he was, that was partly what made him so sexually attractive. So I shouldn't ask. I would think about Melcourt and Toto, instead. Sometimes, I reflected sadly, their behaviour seemed less inexplicable than Sebastian's.

He returned at last, wearing the jacket. He looked, of course quite wonderful, all blue-eyed and gold and green. He was also carrying a paper bag. "Your prezzie."

I peered excitedly into the bag. My enthusiasm was short-lived. "It's a child's plastic gun."

"Yes, and such a bargain, only 50p, and it makes a marvellous noise. Listen!" He demonstrated its cracking sound. "Do you like it?"

"Not much." I was hurt at the trivial nature of the present. "I thought you might buy me something nice."

"But it *is* nice. You know every boy likes guns. And besides, I haven't got any money."

"Enough money to buy yourself the jacket." I felt immensely cross and now disinclined to start the car.

"It was a charity shop. It was my good deed for the day."

"Oh really!" It seemed childish to hang around bickering, and it was a lovely day; too nice to be arguing. "Why the gun?" I asked.

"I thought we could play Melcourt and Toto."

"I think that's a horrible idea!"

"Oh dear, I don't seem to do anything right." Perhaps he was genuinely sorry; I could never tell.

"You do everything right," I said, and we began to see the last of Poole. "Always."

"Do I?"

"No." The sea lay all stretched out, full of boats, on our left, glittering in the sunshine. "But right doesn't come into it, nor wrong. All that matters is that you are here beside me."

"Yes. We'll have a lovely day." He touched my thigh briefly, and then reached into the glove compartment.

"Monster Munch! Jules, you are an angel."

"I shan't stop for lunch," I replied crossly.

"Let's talk about Melcourt, then. Why *are* we going down there, all unannounced?"

"Put your seat belt on, Sebastian."

"I hate wearing seat belts."

"Do as you're told. We are going to Melcourt to see if there are any more letters."

"There won't be. He's given them to us in strictly chronological order, and we have just had the last. Shall I put on some Mozart?" He rummaged about for CDs with one hand, and devoured the crisps with the other.

"What have you been doing with the letters, Sebastian?"

"Don't be so suspicious. I've actually been working on them. I have drawn up an alignment of letters and poems, so we can see why and when he was writing which poems. You know, all that fuss over the sonnet cycle?"

"You have actually put pen to paper?"

"Indeed I have. A hypothesis is in my ungreen jacket and the stolen letters are, as you yourself have witnessed, in the door compartment along with an empty packet of Monster Munch. I will show you what I've done over lunch."

"We are *not* having lunch."

"Of course we are, Jules."

We stopped at a miserable agricultural pub. They had stopped serving – so said the girl behind the bar.

"Is there nothing to eat?" asked Sebastian piteously. The girl, who could not take her eyes off him, said there might be some pies.

"And chips?" he asked. "I must have chips."

"Chips are finished."

"But you could make me some." She conceded that she could. Indeed, it seemed she would be delighted to do so. She turned to stare somewhat less graciously at me.

"Do you want pie and chips, too?" she asked disagreeably. I replied that I did not want anything to eat. I would have a mineral water.

"Ah, drink!" said Sebastian. "To drink life to the lees. It must be ginger beer."

We sat down to wait for Sebastian's pie and chips, I drank my mineral water, and Sebastian had two pints of ginger beer.

"Show me what you have done," I commanded. "I should like to see your notes."

"Oh, look, pickled eggs. I haven't had pickled eggs for years."

As he ate his pie, chips and pickled eggs, I looked at what he had drawn up. He had written the first lines of each letter and listed some dozens of so poems beside each. He had omitted very few. To each letter, he appended a date and one or two general events or facts known about Melcourt. He also suggested the prevailing mood of the letter and its accompanying poems. 'Do the poems explain the letters, or the letters the poems?' he had written. The whole covered some 12 sides of A4, written in ink in his beautiful gothic hand.

"It must've taken you ages," I said grudgingly, looking through the closely written sheets.

"No," he said, his mouth full of pickled egg, "it was very easy." I sipped my mineral water and cast my eye over his work.

It all fell into place beautifully. I agreed exactly with his distribution of letters and poems; even the troubled sonnet sequence, which scholars argue about (some putting early, others late), he had divided up and placed in original and convincing order.

"What do you think?"

"I should have to spend much more time looking at it. One cannot do this in minutes."

"Oh, I could," he said. "Can I have some more ginger beer?" He was infuriating.

"No, you can't, you'll be wanting to go to the lavatory all the time."

"Peeing is a very great pleasure to me," he replied, "you can come with me if you like." I gave him a look of stern reproof – which did not fool him for an instant. He laughed happily. "Ah, well, Jules, in that case, the main thrust of the day will have to be the Melcourt papers."

Nineteen
Flapjacks and Orgasms

"Actually, why *are* we going all the way down to Melcourt again? There won't be any more letters."

I turned to look at him. "So I can spend a day with you."

He smiled. "Silly old Jules."

"Are you happy, sweetheart?"

"Mm." And then he said a lovely thing: "I'm almost always happy when I'm with you."

"Oh, darling, are you?"

"Mm. You're very nice to me – and awfully good at fucking." Set down here baldly, it doesn't sound much; perhaps it sounds a little crude, unromantic even, but Sebastian was not a romantic. He was a dealer in the actual. I have often wondered since if this was not a declaration of love. Anyway, as I say, his words gave me great happiness, and for a long time, I said nothing, unwilling to break the sweetness of the mood.

The whole drive was idyllic: we had the top of the Porsche down, we played Mozart, and Sebastian recited Melcourt's *Polydeuces*. As we passed between the lime trees, perhaps scions of those whose encomium had triggered off my adolescent adoration of Melcourt, I thought how much more fortunate I was than he, since his days with his lover had ended in misery, while mine were spent (I took my eyes off the wheel and looked at Sebastian's contented demeanor and cropped locks) in chequered, but undeniable, bliss.

"It all looks very shut up," he said, as I parked the car outside No. 5.

"Nonsense; it's a hot day, and the elderly can't take a great deal of sun."

"It looks odd."

"I don't think so."

"It's the piss-pot all over again; when we get to the Roberts' bungalow, we start to argue."

"It wasn't a piss-pot, anyway; it was a baked-custard pot."

"The same thing where you're concerned, Jules." He got out of the car in his ridiculous green smoking jacket and beamed at me. The sunlight caught his hair, filling it with little ripples of tawny light.

I spoke severely. "I do not intend going over that tedious argument again."

"Naturally not."

"I'm going to knock on the door, and we shall see if your suspicions are justified, or, as I suspect, entirely unfounded."

I opened the little gate, and we walked down the path; the geraniums which grew in a bucket beside the door looked a little weary.

"There're a lot of blinds down and curtains drawn," said Sebastian, "which rather makes me think..."

"Yes," I knocked peremptorily at the door, "what does it make you think?"

"*Qualcuno è morto*. I'm going to look round the side."

Although I knocked for a second and a third time, I was forced to the conclusion that, yet again, Sebastian was right: one of them was ill or dead, and, unkindly, I hoped it was Joyce; while he lived, there was always the possibility of finding – what could we find? I suspected Sebastian was correct; there were no more letters. What then? Photos, perhaps, or something belonging to Melcourt? Perhaps even the missing Rothstein portrait of Toto, not thrown away after all, but miraculously rediscovered. Perhaps Reg might suddenly start talking, and tell us about his father. Perhaps. My reverie was interrupted.

"We thought we had better come out and tell you." It was the sisters, the two who had invited themselves into the bungalow on our last visit.

"We saw you out of our window, you see."

"As we did last time when you were arguing with your young friend."

"You have come to see Mr Roberts."

They positioned themselves one each side of me. The tall, fat one was armed with a stick. The small, thin one held a plastic pot, rather like the one that had contained my egg custard. I felt we were not unlike the characters in a Greek play, I, the protagonist, and they, the Chorus; any moment now, Sebastian would wheel the bodies out of the bungalow on an ekkyklema.

"Yes, I –"

"Well, you won't be able to," said Fat.

"No," said Thin. And, together, they said: "Mr Roberts has passed away." Fat positively beamed the news. "I expect it comes as a shock to you."

"Yes, indeed. Was it, I mean...?"

Thin bent over towards me, full of ghoulish glee. "A heart attack."

Reg dead, the last link with Melcourt gone. Oddly, I felt not sadness but release. It was good that it should be so, for now that the old tenuous links with the past were broken, it was time to forge something new; now, if ever, it was time to write the book, our book.

"I believe Mrs Roberts had a very bad time." Thin said. She leant towards me, and whispered, "He took a long time to die."

"The ambulance was here two hours."

"We were very distressed."

"Yes, yes indeed. It must have been –" I felt, as always, inadequate. It has always been a puzzle to me that I, who spend my life among words, am so confoundedly inarticulate in social situations.

"Not that he was a close friend."

"Certainly not."

I felt I must make a more determined effort. "And Mrs Roberts, where is she?"

"The warden has taken her into the Hall."

Fat added, "To keep an eye on her, poor dear."

"She couldn't stay here by herself."

"Too many memories."

I tried again. "I wonder whether –" But Sebastian appeared from round the side of the bungalow at that moment, looking thoughtful.

"Your young friend," said Thin. "What a very unusual jacket he is wearing!"

"It will come as a shock to him, too," said Fat, and I could see she was looking forward to going through the whole thing again. No doubt we should have everything from the seizure to the death rattle. She found a ready audience in Sebastian, not, I think, simply because he enjoyed a drama, but because he was naturally sympathetic. He was *actually* sorry – for Reg, for Joyce, even for the sisters, but he also knew how to express this sympathy in terms they would undertand. His blue eyes exuded concern, he held out an arm to steady Fat, and nodded gravely at Thin. He was afraid the whole thing must have upset them terribly, even though the Roberts were not close friends. He, of course, elicited essential information: when it had happened, when the funeral would take place, whether there were any relatives, where exactly Mrs Roberts was now. He might have known them for years. The old women hung on his every word; like teenage girls. Yes, of course they would take us over to the Hall to see the warden, but they really didn't think Mrs Roberts would be in a fit state to see us.

We formed a small procession headed by Sebastian who held Thin's arm. I swear I saw her shoot a look of triumph at her sister; she had got the prize, Fat had to make do with me. I felt rather sorry for her, too. I would rather have had Sebastian than me. And what on earth could I find to say? I needn't have worried, however; death provides its own small-talk. As we walked down the gravel driveway in the blazing sun, it seemed strange to hear the age-honoured words of death: 'postmortems', 'coroner', 'undertaker', 'funeral', banded about like so many motes of dust in the sunlight.

Progress was slow, and we halted halfway up the drive for Fat to catch her breath. We stood in full view of the Hall. In spite of the horrible 1950s additions at the side, and a ghastly porch added to the front, it still possessed a remnant of its former glory, rather like an aged grande dame reduced to penury and forced to buy second-hand clothes. Sebastian, too, must have felt something similar, for he quoted softly:

"Fair mullioned hall, my mother's home and mine..."

"Oh, no," said Thin, "my mother didn't live here. Or have I misunderstood? Did you say *your* mother lives here?"

"No," said Sebastian, "I don't think it's a very motherly sort of place: I think it's more of a man's house."

"It belonged to Lord Melcourt, of course," said Thin, "and he never married."

"I expect he would have done." Thin turned to me instructively. "He died quite young, you know."

"Yes," I said, "I know." How extraordinary it was, I reflected, that an event like Melcourt's death, one that had such importance for me, should have only the slightest interest to another, particularly someone who actually lived here. It was the same, I supposed, with Sebastian; what had Atkins called him all those years ago, 'that young scamp'? – to others, he was no more than a reckless, desirable boy, whereas to me he was the sun and the moon and the stars, the whole bloody firmament. We continued on our way.

"I am afraid," said Fat confidentially to me, "I never really liked Mr Roberts. Of course, I know you shouldn't speak ill of the dead, but he can't hear us, and I always felt there was something rather sly about him." She raised her voice. "Wouldn't you say, Edith?"

"Yes," said her sister decisively, "he came to tea once when Mrs Roberts was unwell, and all my Apostle spoons disappeared."

"What a very useful pot you're holding," said Sebastian to Thin as we stood waiting at the door. "My friend, Dr Collins, has one like it. He puts it to all sorts of uses."

Both the sisters turned and regarded me keenly as if they expected me to produce a pot out of my pocket and do something prestidigitorial with it. Sebastian smiled sweetly, as if to apologise for my disappointing lack of virtuosity; and I thought of how I would like to fuck the hell out of him. Then he smiled even more sweetly, because he knew exactly what I was thinking.

The warden was not pleased to see us. I suspected she had plenty of experience of the sisters. No, it was not convenient to see Mrs Roberts. The horrible, small yapping dog appeared. It remembered my trousers.

"No, Smiler, leave the gentleman's trousers alone; I'll take you out in a minute." She looked at us disagreeably. "Who are you?"

"My name is Collins."

"Carter?"

"No, no. Collins."

"Who?"

"We would so like to see Mrs Roberts," put in Sebastian winningly, but the warden was Sebastian-proof.

"No. She's not having visitors." She looked as if she was about to close the door on us, when the temptation of voicing a grievance got the better of her.

"And now there's the gardens open, and the W.I. teas. They always come when the W.I.'s about."

"Who, the visitors?"

"No. Deaths."

"Tea?" asked Sebastian. "With chocolate cake and scones and things?" Death paled into insignificance beside chocolate cake.

"I should like to look round the gardens," I said.

"And I should like tea," said Sebastian firmly.

"There's always something going on here," said Fat.

"Too much, in my opinion," said the warden, closing the door. It was our cue for departure. Thin was reluctant to part with Sebastian, although I cannot flatter myself that Fat seemed equally upset at the prospect of leaving me. She transferred the Tupperware pot to her left hand in order to shake my right.

"Good-bye, Mr... um... I don't suppose we shall be seeing you again."

"We shall," said the sibling. "We shall all be at the funeral. Mr Salonière has already told me he's coming."

"Oh, good," said her sister, "I *shall* look forward to that. I always enjoy a funeral."

We watched them retreat down the drive, arm in arm. I thought they looked like survivors; it would be some time before one or the other followed Reg Roberts, but whenever she did, I thought the other would derive keen enjoyment from it.

The door opened again abruptly. Apparently, the warden had not finished with us.

"Hey, you still there?" Sebastian looked round and said that he believed we were.

"There's a lot of the grounds cordoned off; the land is sold for more retirement bungalows, although I don't know how I'm expected to see to that, as well. Come here, Smiler. I should be grateful if you'd tell people to keep out. Just tell them it's private. People nowadays will go anywhere."

"Really?" said Sebastian.

"No respect." Sebastian shook his head and his face took on the saddened air of one to whom no depth of human depravity came as a surprise.

She glowered at both of us, lunged at the dog as it tried to get out, and closed the door in our faces.

"Teatime," said Sebastian. We followed some felt-tipped hieroglyphs that passed for arrows, round the side of the mansion, and entered the tea room by a back door. Any fond hopes I had held for seeing the room through Melcourt's eyes were dispelled. Only the high ceiling remained. The room had become purely functional: beige walls and angular tables. There was, however, a sumptuous spread. We queued up, Sebastian loaded his tray ('Clotted cream, Jules!') and I paid. We sat down near an elderly couple enjoying an afternoon out. I drank my tea, and Sebastian tucked in.

"I don't know how you can keep on eating," I said irritably. His eyes had the fixed intensity of huge enjoyment.

"Carrot cake with real bits of carrot."

"Well, hurry up. The garden will be closed by the time you have got through that lot."

"You can't hurry food; it's like sex, meant to last." He surveyed the plate of assorted cakes in front of him. "What shall I have next?"

I was hurt and upset by his crude comparison. "I don't know," I said bitterly. "I don't care whether you have a flapjack or a fairy cake."

"Jules!" He looked quite shocked.

"Food isn't at all like sex."

"Yes, it is. Actually, I think it's better."

"And why is that?" Wretchedly, I thought of all the times I had made love to him, and how his orgasm was, for me, a moment of sacred joy as intense and beautiful as my own. But for him? It meant as little to him as a piece of carrot cake; less, in fact. "Hardly worth making such a mess of my sheets, then."

"No, no, you miss the point. You see, with food, the pleasure lasts much longer. Now, take this flapjack I'm biting into; if it was an orgasm, it would be gone by now; as it's not, I've got at least two more minutes' enjoyment of it." He tucked in happily. "Mm, delicious."

The couple at the next table, an elderly bald man and a thin, angular, sour-faced woman, had stopped talking, and were looking in our direction. I felt thoroughly miserable. Sebastian looked up from the flapjack.

"You mustn't take it all so seriously, Jules," he said, reaching across the table and patting my hand, "sex, cake, ginger beer, drugs, Melcourt, Palestrina; it's all there to be enjoyed."

"And love, what about love, the love that I have for you?"

The couple at the next table were getting up. There was a lot of clattering of cups and banging of trays. Her face was furrowed with loathing for us. I suppose she didn't know anything about love.

"Jules, that's not love. Because I'm pretty, I set up an aching in your cock. I satisfy that aching, and you call that love. Only God knows of love."

"I should like you to know," the man hissed, brandishing his empty tea tray, "that you have spoiled our tea with your disgusting talk."

"Yes," said his companion, "I couldn't eat a thing."

But I noticed their plates were empty.

Sebastian smiled. "You should never let anything interfere with tea," he said.

Like me, they had no answer to Sebastian. He poured out the last of the tea (he loved tea) and assaulted a great chunk of fruitcake.

"I wish you could believe, Jules," he continued between mouthfuls. "You see, God knows how terrible I am, but he forgives me, and one day he will take me to himself to be part of his love."

"What about your sins? Won't you have to expurgate them all in purgatory?"

"No, the church no longer recognises the concept of sin. Besides, I already told you, I shall have the last rites, I shall be as pure as a new-born child, but you, Jules, who do not believe –" his blue eyes were filled with concern and his golden hair was as a halo about his face "– what will become of you?"

"You will have to be like Lazarus," I said grimly, "and lean out of heaven and drop water down at me as I burn in the fiery furnace."

"Yes, so I shall. Mind you take the Tupperware pot down with you." He finished up the last scone.

We set out into the gardens.

Twenty
Un Giardino Segreto

The garden was as uninspiring as the tea room. There was no spirit of Melcourt there. It was all very square: a green, well-kept lawn surrounded by rose-beds, equally well-kept, and apple espaliers ('Not even peaches', said Sebastian), so we strolled rather aimlessly. After we had made two circuits of the garden, Sebastian yawned and said, "It's all very boring, Jules. What shall we do now?" He glanced in the direction of the tea room. "We could..."

"No."

"Well, what then? Have you got any ideas?"

"Yes," I said. An idea had been forming in my mind for some minutes, but I was rather shy about suggesting it. For once, Sebastian misinterpreted my thoughts.

"We can hardly do it here, Jules."

"No, I wasn't thinking that."

"Gosh!"

"I was thinking... You know when you gave me the gun, you said we could play Melcourt and Toto?"

"I wasn't awfully serious. I only bought it because it made a good noise."

"And it was all you could buy me for 50p. Anyway, I *should* like to play Melcourt and Toto, act out what happened." I frowned, conscious of sounding extremely silly.

"Whatever could we achieve?" He turned his head, and the sun glinted in his hair.

"I don't know. I just think –" How could I explain? Here we were at Melcourt, he and I, as they had been.

"Jules, they're dead. They're shadows, ghosts. They're not us."

"You won't even do that for me." I was angry. "The extent of your kindness is to buy me a plastic gun for 50p – because *you* like it, and which you still have in your pocket." He stood with the breeze blowing the cropped hair about his face. Suddenly, he reached in his pocket, took out the gun and pointed it at me.

"What is it you say in your sonnet, Max?"

"To drink from Lethe's timeless streams
The blessed draughts that bring an end to dreams…"

"Come on! We'll go and find the bit of the garden that's cordoned off. That'll be ideal. It might even be a proper old Melcourt bit, not a horrid municipal park bit, like this."

I was somewhat taken aback. "Sebastian…"

His eyes sparkled and he brandished the gun. "Come on, Jules. You said you wanted to." He led the way under the pergola. As usual, I had no reply. Besides, the velvet jacket made a marvellous contrast to his jeans, which, as I have mentioned before, were extremely tight. They delineated the contours of his arse as he stepped over the cordon between the public and private areas, from which hung a sign: PRIVATE KEEP OUT. I was less spry, but followed, my joints protesting mildly. A barbed-wire fence presented the next hurdle; this, too, Sebastian negotiated neatly. I was less eager.

"Horrid to think what damage those little barbs might do." He echoed my unspoken thoughts. "But I am intact, Jules."

"In a sense," I grunted as I squeezed myself between the upper wire and the lower.

A mass of foliage that had once been a hedge confronted us.

"I really don't think..." I began, but Sebastian struggled through where privet reached out to hazelnut.

"It's very easy, Jules." It wasn't: bits of smelly, scratchy leaf did their worst, twigs poked out with intent to blind me, brambles tore and scratched at exposed flesh, but all this was absolutely nothing, for when we finally emerged, the reward was infinite. We stood in silent amazement.

"Oh, Julian," he whispered, "*un giardino segreto.*"

There were, I suppose, in all about 50 yards of wild garden bounded on the one side by the hedge through which we had climbed, and on the other three by high, crumbling red-brick walls. The sight was stunning.

It was as if God had got halfway through creating Eden, and become bored with order and tipped his store of heavenly seed upon it, letting it grow at will. As if the Devil had crept in among the roses, and planted his own nightshades and belladonnas amongst the honeysuckles and agapanthus. Foxgloves and hollyhocks struggled with scarlet poppies, scabious fought for supremacy against staring, moon-faced daises, roses, yellow as malaria and white as leprosy, wept their petals into unmown grass; a small, naked cupid hid his genitalia behind engulfing mallow, while yarrow and feverfree caressed his thighs. We stood fixed in amazement, and I felt the unseen presence of Melcourt and Toto standing beside us. It seemed to me that all my life had been leading towards this moment, all my work on Melcourt, all my love for Sebastian; they would be united in this point of time, in this Garden of Eden.

Here was the very garden where Melcourt had once walked with Toto; perhaps it was 'the wilderness' which he had mentioned in his second letter. Of this he had thought when he wrote to him of the enchanted gardens of 'once'. The garden was then both an actual place trodden by Melcourt, and an abstract concept of his happiness (Sebastian brushed against a great blue bush of lavender, and the scent rose up and the sun glinted on him). And if I was to embrace my lover here, where once Melcourt had embraced his, having feelings so exactly Melcourt's own, should I not, in effect, become Melcourt, and in doing so, should I not unite past and present, lover and lover, abstract concept and tangible reality?

"Sebastian!" I reached for him.

"Later," he said. Slipping from my grasp, he allowed the lavender and mallow to engulf him. A host of red admirals, sunning themselves on the purple phalli of the buddleia tree, was disturbed and fluttered in a brief panic about him, before returning once more to their sybaritic pollen-sucking.

He spoke softly:

"I glimpsed your garden's gorgeous breadth
And felt the scent of scabious flowers
But in them lay a sapphire death
Unholy incense in blue bowers
And, oh, I know the noxious breath
Of belladonna's purple showers."

I stood watching him. Suddenly, he swung round, steadying the pistol with his hand.

"You are going to die, Melcourt," he cried. His scabious eyes glinted, and his hair shone like marigolds; he moved forward with the gun. All my abstract thoughts were dispelled in a minute. Fearlessly, I advanced upon him.

"I know I am to die, Toto," I said, and my calm was amazing, "but you will not shoot me."

I folded my arms and faced him with confidence.

"How do you know I shall not shoot you?"

"You have no need, Toto," I said, "you have already killed me. With your cruelty you have taken the sweetness from my life."

"How foolish you are, Max. I do not know at all what you mean." His eyes looked puzzled; for all his cunning, Toto was not really clever.

"Give me the gun, Toto, and I will explain. No, my dear, do not shake your head at me. You do not imagine I would hurt you, surely? All my troubles have come about from my desire to protect you, always. And even now I would not have one of your golden hairs hurt. Come, give me the gun. I will perhaps have need of it soon."

"That sounds a bit corny," he said. I ignored him.

"Sit down, Toto, and listen to me." He took off his silly jacket and stretched out on the grass. His T-shirt bore the legend 'Libens, Volens, Potens'. Silently, he handed me the gun.

"How can you say I have killed you, Max? You look very much alive to me – particularly about your trousers; your trousers have very much the look of a live man's trousers." He cushioned his head on the green jacket, and prepared to listen to me. The sun was hot overhead. It flickered over the flowers and leaves, and played around his lopped blonde locks; a scent of lavender filled the air. "Tell me, Ju... Max, why I have killed you."

I sat down on the grass next to him. The sun was warm on both our faces.

"I think you always meant to kill me, from the first moment when you sent me your charming letter, so sweetly and calculatedly effusive, and then when you played your courting dance with me, advancing and retreating, spreading your peacock's feathers."

"Good," said Sebastian, "you've picked up on the peacock imagery." He was idly engaged in making a daisy chain.

"And then, when you found you were unable to make the progress you envisaged, you played your trump card. Knowing I could refuse you in your arrogance and even in your beauty, you saw I could not resist you in your weakness, and when you came to me that night shivering, in your nightshirt – 'Oh, Max, I am so cold' – then you knew you had caught me indeed, for against your weakness, I had no defense, no more than a mother her child."

"I think," he said, dimpling, "there was very little of the maternal in your embraces that night. I think, Max, I would choose more robust adjectives to describe your love-making that night, or any night or day, for there is no part of the day or night, Max, when I have been free of your insatiable hunger."

"You are unjust, Toto; if I have demanded, I have also given, more, much more than I have demanded." Having sat down to be beside him, I now stood. I would explain to Toto how I felt.

"What you describe as my insatiable hunger is a thing of which you have no understanding; it is not, as you imagine, lechery, for so far only can you envisage love."

"Love cannot exist between man and man, for love is by its nature a perfection and man is imperfect; he can only offer his own imperfections to God, who is Perfect Love, in the hope that the light of His perfection will subsume imperfection." He threaded another daisy on his chain. His complacency infuriated me.

"I do not want to speak of God. I want to speak of myself." I made him look at me: "Sebastian, there has been no lechery in my acts of love. My every thrust has been a thrust of love, my every..."

"A convenient philosophy, one hard to reconcile with the groans and cries of pleasure that your urgent desires cause you to make."

"Oh, don't give me that." He enraged me as he reclined there, fitting the chain of daisies on his golden hair, letting it cling there like a halo, and all the time, the sun beat down and the smell of lavender wafted over us. "You know perfectly well how I've denied myself for you. 'Jules', always 'Jules', as if my name was somehow ridiculous. 'Orgasms are so disappointing: Oh, Jules, it's better to travel hopefully than to arrive; keep me journeying, Jules, don't let me arrive'. I've done it for you, even when I've wanted you so much."

"This is meant to be Melcourt and Toto." His head rested on the ridiculous green jacket, and the daisies caressed his forehead.

"And what is your repayment?"

"Payment for love?"

"I will tell you what your repayment is: 'Oh, Jules, I'm awfully short of money'. Money, meals, clothes, even that ridiculous car; all bought for you."

"You never let me drive it."

"Once was enough. You are a terrible driver; you are a terrible person."

"Have I ever denied it?" A butterfly rested briefly on his crown of daisies.

"Money... money you wanted, just like Toto."

"At least I have never tried to blackmail you. I could have done. Imagine the headlines in the *Sun*: 'Oxford Tutor Debauches Boy Student'. I wasn't even twenty when you first had me."

Other butterflies joined the first; he was surrounded by flowers and butterflies.

"You took advantage of my weakness, knowing that I, like Melcourt, could resist blandishments, but could not resist your vulnerability."

He removed his 'Libens, Volens, Potens' T-shirt and placed it on top of the green jacket. He stood up, and set about picking flowers – *picking flowers* – when I was pouring out the thoughts of my heart ('Oh, look, Jules, a white delphinium').

"Listen to me!" I cried, my fury rising. "Listen to me, Sebastian!"

"I am listening," he replied, gravely plucking lavender, "but you don't speak truthfully. You'd taken advantage of me before that night."

"Once! Once only, when you tempted me unendurably, reclining, naked and taunting, on my bed."

"But why had you asked me to your flat if you hadn't intended seducing me? Look, how pretty!" He watched a red admiral settle on the buddleia.

"*I* seduce *you*! You had all the wiles of one of Toto's rent-boys!"

"You weren't exactly a virgin -- I was surprised at what you expected from me."

"One night! You know it was only one night. And in the morning, when you were gone, I was glad that you were gone. I deeply regretted..."

"Balls!" He picked a long-stemmed daisy, and sat down to remove its petals. "I was greatly intrigued to observe your crotch at our subsequent tutorial. I do not know how you continued to talk so dully about Tennyson."

"But I resisted you. I did nothing until you came to me that night." It was so vivid in my mind, I, too, began randomly plucking at whatever came to hand in agitation; lavender poppies, even roses. My hand, I remember, was lacerated by thorns. "No doubt you planned it. 'Oh, Julian' – you did not dare to call me Jules then. 'I am so wet, and I have nowhere to go'. You stood at my door, with your golden hair all darkened by the rain: 'Julian, Julian, I have nowhere to go'. They had tired of you, your friends, they had tired of your endless appetites."

"Actually, the lease was up on the house. The others had gone home."

"And why didn't you go home, too, to your father? Why did you stay behind in Oxford, walking through storms to come to my flat?"

"He loves me, he loves me not," he replied, plucking the last of the petals from a daisy. "Because you wanted me, Jules, because your mind sent out telepathic messages of entreaty, and your cock bulged in your trousers at tutorials."

"No, it was because you wanted money. Look at what I have bought you – designer clothes, jewellery, the car."

"You've said all this already, Jules. Ouch, a thorn! There is something you may have not thought of."

"There is *nothing* I have not thought of in connection with you."

"Perhaps it's something you haven't wished to think of, something that Melcourt, too, didn't wish to think of in connection with Toto."

"Well?" I stood against the crumbling pergola, staring at him, my heart full of pain, my eyes full of his flowery beauty.

"Love's a shadowy thing, Jules; it lives in the back chamber of the heart – if it lives at all – and I have told you that I think it doesn't." He removed his crown of daisies, and threw it on the ground. I stared at him miserably. "Love, Jules, can't be proven, but –" he held a rose towards me "– it can be made manifest. A cheque, a car, a meal, are sacraments of love. The Church knows this; that's why we have the

Eucharist, but only in the Eucharist does love actually turn into Christ's body, his love."

"I told you, I don't want to hear you pontificating about fucking religion. I want..."

"Listen. We're mortal. We can do so little, have so little. We live among shadows, but in the giving of gifts, we make concrete the abstract. No one can prove he gives love, but he can prove he has given a pair of his Yves St Laurent boxer shorts. In the giving, he proclaims his love and when his lover accepts the gift, he imagines that his love is acknowledged and perhaps reciprocated."

"Thank you for your illuminating truth," I said. "I see you've been reading the *Ladybird Book of Philosophy* again." I watched him bend down to a rose and sniff at it appreciatively. I was miserable.

"And there's another thing, Jules..."

"Oh, yes?"

"The lover has a darker side. He seeks to buy, own, possess. In fact, he seeks to make the beloved into an object, a tangible expression of love. And in negotiating for this love object, he takes the merchant's pleasure in his trading."

"Stop," I said. "I don't want to hear any more of your ridiculous, simplistic philosophy."

He came over, tucked the rose into the button-hole of my jacket and continued: "The money, Jules, the prezzies, they gave you as much pleasure to give as I had in receiving them. It's as sweet as a kiss to you to hear me ask for something – a meal, or that pink-silk shirt – or to get your cheque book out and write me a cheque. In the handing of it over and in my taking it, there is for you, Jules, a satisfaction as great as an orgasm, 'cos it proves your power over me as surely as your prick thrusting into my arse does. So it was with Melcourt. That's why he had to kill himself; it wasn't fear of dishonour or bankruptcy, but the utter horror of losing the joy of giving to Toto."

I knew there was a kind of truth in what he said, and I hated myself for my weakness, just as Melcourt had, no doubt, felt self-loathing. I wanted to stop the tirade of words and the calumny they brought with them. I looked away from him and my eye fell on the plastic gun lying at my feet. I picked it up and fired at him, on and on, the popping of the shots filling the air. Slowly he fell, folding himself about my feet, and his naked chest was covered in the petals of the red roses, like blood; his body was covered in their torn hearts. And so still he lay, his eyes as blue as the scabious, the delphinium, the lavender, unmoving in their intensity.

I was on my knees at his side. "Oh, Toto," I cried, "my beloved."

And nimbly, so nimbly he rolled over and plucked the gun from my hand, and sat holding it, pointing at my heart. "You could not kill me, Max," he said, "but I can kill you."

I grabbed for the gun and we rolled over and over fighting for its possession, but when I had prized it from his hands, I threw it away, held him beneath me, and began to kiss him without restraint. He returned my kisses.

We undressed because we knew that Melcourt and Toto had done so, perhaps on the very spot on which we were. And then I made love to him, as Melcourt had done to his beloved. The consummation was very sweet, sweeter than it had ever been because I was both Julian and Max, and he both Sebastian and Toto.

"Ah," he said, "the joys of necrophilia. No one has ever thought that the corpse enjoys it as much as the living."

I wasn't angry that his comment should be so trivial, for he was Sebastian and I his lover who had gained, for whatever reason, the greatest of human joys from him.

"Could it have happened like that?" I asked.

"Necrophilia?"

"Don't be silly. Did Max try to shoot Toto in a moment of anger, and miss, and then did Toto shoot him in self-defence? I was so sure before that it was suicide, but now... did Toto shoot Melcourt?"

"No, of course not," he replied, lazily plucking rose petals. "I've told you how it was. Melcourt killed himself because he couldn't live without giving to Toto. And besides, he couldn't have brought himself to destroy Toto's beauty. He couldn't have coped. Death isn't kind to the human body." For a moment, he looked quite solemn, and then he laughed. "Only I, Jules, am beautiful in death."

"And what had Toto to gain from Melcourt's death? His money was all gone. Perhaps poor Max shot himself here in this very garden, but death did not come easily to him, and he dragged himself indoors. Perhaps even in death he thought to prevent suspicion from falling on Toto by dying in his own gun-room."

A silence fell between us. At last I said: "And I, Sebastian, what shall I do when I can no longer buy you clothes and meals and write you cheques?"

He reached up and took a strand of my hair between his fingers. "Silly old Jules," he said. "You've still got lots of money – and you're much more sensible than poor old Max." He pressed his cock against mine. "Shall we do it again?"

We stayed until the heat went from the afternoon.

Twenty-one
Junk Food

"Jules, will you drop me back at Poole station?" I accelerated in my bitter disappointment. How could he ask that after this afternoon, when we had almost become Melcourt and Toto? No, after we remained ourselves and yet knew them, we had consummated the union of the four of us. How could he? I did not expect to dissuade him, for it was always I who bowed to his wishes. But this time, for some reason, he weakened.

"Oh, very well."

I accelerated again in case he changed his mind, and when we were safely away, I asked.

"Why Poole, anyway? What were you doing in Poole, of all God-forsaken places?"

"My father lives there."

"No, he doesn't, he lives in Kent."

"*Eh bien.*" We lapsed into silence, and he put on Elgar's Violin Concerto as we drove through a village where every other house seemed to be thatched or half-timbered. I imagined leaving Oxford and settling into rural domesticity with him. We might, I thought, keep geese, and a pig or two in the orchard; I pictured myself in a Harris tweed jacket, and Sebastian in green wellies and, to be honest, very little else.

"Rather hungry, Jules."

"We'll eat at home," I said.

"But it takes you so long to cook."

"I have curry in the freezer. I'll only have to put it in the microwave, darling."

"Can I have something to keep me going?" He opened the glove compartment and peered inside. It was empty, except, inevitably for the Tupperware pot.

"Nothing," he said sadly, "except your commode."

"I'll buy you junk food when I stop for petrol."

"Mars Bars and Coke?"

"Yes, darling." And anything else in the world, I might have added, as long as you stay sitting at my side. We stopped off at a post-office stores and I bought him food.

"Do you think the car has a bit of a list to the left? I asked as I started it up.

"No," he said, opening the biscuits, "cars can't write."

"Silly." I took my left hand off the wheel and stroked his thigh affectionately. He smiled amiably and opened the Coca-Cola.

When he had consumed my bounty (a can of Lilt and the family-sized bottle of Coca -Cola, a Mars Bar and a packet of Boasts), he said, "I have to tell you something." I braked and incurred flashed lights from the car behind. Fear gripped my heart.

"What is it?" I asked roughly. I ran the whole gamut of my fears: he had Aids, he was going to leave me, to blackmail me. Intermittently, I would wake in the small hours of the morning and worry about such things. Usually, I chose to ignore them. I turned and looked at him.

"Keep your eyes on the road, Jules. You really will kill us both. Don't worry, it's not about me – not really."

"What, then?" I was a little reassured. "Tell me."

"After the curry." And I could not coax him. He put his head on my shoulder and fell asleep.

For a while, I worried about whatever it was he wanted to tell me; but only for a while. With his bobbed gold locks on my shoulder and

Mozart in my ear (Concerto No. 21 in C major), I felt life was too good to spoil with pointless speculation. I thought again about the book we should write together, and I believed I should have no difficulty in persuading him now, since the afternoon in the garden had brought us (all four) so inextricably together.

As he slept and I drove into the setting sun, my heart swelled within me.

Twenty-two
Chicken Curry in Bed

"You're going to be shocked, Jules."

"Am I?"

"Mm."

To be honest, I had completely forgotten Sebastian's earlier words of warning – partly, I suppose, I didn't want to think of them, and partly because other pleasant activities had intervened. I thought they might intervene again.

"Tell me then, sweetheart." I felt rather relaxed and unbothered.

We were sitting in bed, eating chicken curry out of the casserole dish with fork and spoon and fingers; only the bones were left, and Sebastian took the last piece of naan bread, wiped the inside of the dish with it, and ate it slowly.

"I want to wash first; I'm all covered in curry. I smell horrid."

"You smell lovely." I sniffed at him appreciatively. "Like some exotic creature of the East." I started reciting:

"Thy body is a white and glistening chalice
Wherein the incense of the levant's found
Oh, let me live..."

"Bloody Melcourt," he interrupted as he got off the bed. "I'm going to have a shower."

He came back, his hair water-darkened and the gold suffused into bronze. He removed my purple and green striped towel from his desirable hips, and came over to the bed.

"Well?" I asked.

He got on to the bed and sat astride me, his cock nestling against mine. "They are forgeries," he said. "They are all forgeries, the Melcourt letters."

I felt a sensation of violent nausea, and I pushed at him roughly, "Don't be so stupid. Of *course* they're not forgeries!" I spoke very loudly so I should not have to hear my thoughts. I began to turn on to my side to show him how far I disassociated myself from him and his words. He refused to be dislodged, either physically or verbally.

"They are forgeries."

"They're not!" I turned to face him as he sat securely on my thigh. "Do you imagine, after years of studying Melcourt, I cannot recognise his writing? He wrote them. You *know* he did." I spoke automatically, calmly even, but in my innermost soul I sensed the sound of truth and I knew fear.

"No, Jules," he said, climbing off me and lying down sadly at my side, "we've been duped. Reg has fooled us."

"Balls!" I said, but I spoke for the sake of speaking, to put off facing the facts. "Why should you think they are forgeries? My God, I have studied Melcourt for twenty years, I know his style, I know his handwriting... And anyway," I concluded lamely, "if by some extraordinary chance they are not genuine, why on *earth* should you attribute the forgery to Reg?" But even as I said it, I remembered many things: the old man with his chin sunk down to hide the craftiness of his Toto-eyes, the sisters and the story of the Apostle spoons, Joyce and her question – 'He hasn't given you anything, has he, dear?' (Did she *know* he was a forger?) But of course he wasn't! He *had* got the letters from his father.

"Can I have a cigarette, please, Jules?"

"No."

"Please?"

"Oh, have one!"

He went and foraged round in the pockets of the green jacket, picking it up off the floor. "Well, now." He lit up. "I think we can be a little forgiven for being such pricks – neither of us likes to be thought stupid, do we? I mean, the writing was perfect."

"I know, I went to the Bodleian and checked it against the letters there."

"But you didn't have them professionally authenticated, did you?"

"I was happy to rely on my own judgement," I replied. "I am not exactly a novice in these matters."

"Yes, I know, and Reg did a brilliant job; he must have taken hundreds of hours – and copied and recopied hundreds of the pages, but, of course, if he went wrong, he just crossed it out heavily: there are a number of crossings-out in the letters, more than in the Bodleian ones. No, it wasn't the writing that alerted me."

"I suppose," I said slowly, "it was the content: you saw what I did not, that Melcourt did not write those letters. There was something wrong with the style?"

He lit his cigarette with an expensive-looking lighter I had not seen before. "No, I didn't doubt the content – I didn't have a problem with the letters per se. Like you, I heard Melcourt in every sentence." He peered into the casserole dish; it was lying on the floor by the bed. I am normally punctilious about such matters, but tonight was not the right time for bothering with trivialities.

"What, then? Why should the letters be forgeries? Why should Reg..."

"Stop wittering, Jules, and listen. I'll come back to Reg in a minute." He climbed into bed, adjusted the pillows and made himself comfortable. I frowned disapprovingly as he flicked his ash into the casserole dish.

"It was when I compiled that list of poems that went with the letters. I wanted to see how the poems reflected the moods of his letters, to see how you could trace his approaching end through the poems indicated by them. I had that first edition, the one you gave me, and I started casually; I thought it would be difficult; but you see –" he stubbed out his cigarette and folded his hands behind his head "– it wasn't difficult at all. It was easy. In no time at all, the poems corresponded with the letters. Do you remember, in that pub, you said is must have taken ages, and I said no, and you thought it was just me showing off again. But it wasn't; it really *was* easy, because someone had already done the work, matched up the letters with the poems. Do you remember, I wrote a note: do the poems reflect the letters or the letters the poems? I mean, it was all too neat. The amused and light-hearted early poems going with his first letters; the poems of foreboding going with the later ones, and so on." I lay next to his warm, damp body, thinking furiously.

"You mean that someone, maybe Reg, made arbitrary groupings of Melcourt's verses, and then wrote appropriate letters?"

"*Si*. Some we know the dates of, and others we have to guess at, since publication dates don't necessarily reflect the chronological dates. Anyway, you know all that; God knows, you've written enough papers on it. It seems you and Reg came to the same conclusion: happy, cynical and mildly suspicious, 1893; carefree and ecstatic, 1894; worried and finally despairing, 1895. Once you've got that worked out, you concoct the letters to back up your theories."

"So? I still don't see why they shouldn't be written by Melcourt. And –" I sat up, triumphant "– what about the paper water-marked 1892, the same as other extant letters are written on?"

"I'll come to that later. Ah, wandering hands, Jules... mmm. I've told you why my suspicions were aroused: they tied in too exactly. No relationship goes gradually one way or the other; there are ups and downs. Look at us. When you threw me out for a mild case of infidelity..."

"I found you sucking off your bit of rough in my bed."

"Exactly. So your poems, if you were to write them, would reflect that, and they would strike a discordant note in your later poems of glee, reflecting your delight in my return to your bed. But there are no discordant notes in these letters. Each letter is a neat stage in the downfall of Melcourt.

"Well, perhaps."

"I am always suspicious, Jules, when things are too clearly set out. Life, people, they're awfully vague and shadowy. But as you so rightly say, that isn't proof – where's the rest of that wine gone? I'm *thirsty*." I handed over the bottle and he took a swig.

"You said nothing to me." The hurt had begun to sink in. "All that time, when we were in the car together, and in the pub, when you showed me how you had matched up the poem and the letters, you said nothing. You never so much as hinted. All the time in the garden. Why didn't you tell me?" I turned and looked beseechingly at him.

"Jules," he said, kissing me gently on the cheek, "it's better not to alarm you when you're driving, sweetie, and you liked the garden so much, it seemed a pity to spoil it."

"Why didn't you tell me before?"

"I wanted to be sure before I told you. I wanted to check."

"Days, you've known, and you said nothing." I was reproachful – but was mollified by the kiss. "That was why you took the letters – without consulting me. What did you do with them?"

"I took the letters to a friend of mine in Poole."

"A friend skilled in forgery?"

"Oh, I wouldn't exactly say that."

"But how did you check against the original letters?

"I borrowed an original from the Bodleian."

"You mean you *filched* one?"

"There's a guy who works in the stacks..."

"Oh, God!"

"One has to make little sacrifices."

"A *sacrifice*?"

"Of course. And I say to my friend in Poole –"

"– With whom you, doubtless, spent the night."

"– To my friend in Poole. 'Tell me, Benedict, are they, or are they not forgeries?' And he looks very carefully and doesn't respond immediately. It takes him some time, but eventually he says, yes, he thinks they are. And he points out two little things; the cross-stroke of the 't' is a little too exaggerated – you know how Melcourt wrote elegantly, but not extravagantly – and the tips of the 'f's, the bottom bits are ever so much more rounded. Shall I get them and show you?"

"Do you mean to say you have been walking round with the stolen letter from the Bodleian in your jacket pocket?"

"No, of course I haven't. You know quite well I've been walking round like Robin Hood in my new Sherwood green jacket; the letter is in my other jacket." He smiled happily.

His composure infuriated me: "Do you realise you have committed a criminal offence?"

"Several, I should imagine."

"Don't be so bloody smug and pleased with yourself. It isn't just you, you know; you involve me, as well. I'm probably an accessory after the fact."

"True. I wonder how many years they'll send us down for? Perhaps we'll be able to share a cell."

"You may scoff."

"It's quite safe, Jules."

"Why?"

"Well, nobody except you and me wants to read Melcourt. Come on, Jules. Don't be silly." He twisted a lock of my hair round his index finger.

"Well, just suppose that I accept they are forgeries. And, don't forget, the paper was watermarked 1892 – if I accept this, and I don't say that I do, why should they be Reg's forgeries? Why should...?"

"Do stop going on, Jules." He pulled down the duvet and looked meditatively at our respective cocks.

"What are you doing?" I asked crossly.

"Looking at the shape of things to come."

"No," I said, pulling the duvet up. "Go on with your hypotheses."

"Well, now," he said, conceding and lying back," I have thought a lot about this; and I've tried to see Reg as a young man."

"You think he did them when he was young?"

"Don't be silly. You could *hardly* see him doing them with his chin all sunk down as we saw him. No, I see him as a young man, interested in the relationship between Melcourt and Toto. Perhaps he is gay himself. I think he is."

"Yes, I suppose Toto's son might be."

Sebastian looked at me meditatively, then said slowly, "Perhaps he's not Toto's son at all."

"What!"

"What do we know?" he went on. "Merely that his name is Roberts – a common enough name. That he lives at Melcourt; well, Joyce comes from Melcourt. They might've gone back there to live for her, not him."

"There's Venice and Lady Ellen." I felt miserable. My hand sought his cock for consolation.

"It's all hypotheses, shadows. We know that Reg is brought up abroad, but we don't know it's in Venice. His mother is called Nell, but that doesn't mean she was called Ellen. She may have had a title, she may not. Joyce's 'real lady' could mean anything; certainly none of this proves that Toto married Lady Ellen and had Reg. I told you at The Randolph that I wasn't convinced. In fact, I shouldn't think Toto married at all."

"Well, Bosie married after Oscar Wilde's death."

"Reg just throws in that mention of Lady Blythe for authenticity. He'd read the Horatio Brown letter like you. And don't forget, Reg himself never claimed to be Toto's son. Joyce never said he was, either. If he is, why not say so?"

"Steiner."

"Oh, Jules, you know what you always say about Americans. Sloppy scholarship. Besides, you told me Joyce said Reg couldn't say anything to Steiner because Reg had just had his stroke."

"Hmm."

"Actually, you can't claim to have a grasp on any facts at all. You've been merely massaging them. Talking of grasping and massaging..."

"No! I want to hear the rest of your theories, and you'll need to concentrate."

"How mean you are, Jules."

"Carry on."

"Well, as I say, I don't think Reg is Toto's son at all – not that it matters; what interests me is why this guy Roberts goes to all these lengths to forge letters, and the answer must lie in the question of cash. Do you remember when we went down and found the place all locked up, and I did my Miss Marple bit and went round the back?"

"Did you see something?"

"No. That's it."

"What?"

"I looked in through the windows and thought, 'poor old things, fancy getting to the end of your life and having so little to show for it'. Then I came round the front again, and saw you talking to the two old biddies and thought no more about it. It was only later that it occurred to me he must have forged the letters to sell. Perhaps he wanted some money to marry Joyce, but didn't have any. He had some miserable job as a schoolmaster somewhere, paid almost nothing. Perhaps he'd been teaching Melcourt's poetry, thought of his own name, Roberts, and thought he'd try to make a bob or two. I don't know – I suppose he wrote the biography first, to make money that way and, when it was poorly received, became disappointed and decided to forge the letters. Perhaps he tried to sell them, and either nobody wanted them, or else he got caught. Anyway, poor old Reg didn't get anything out of them, so he was stuck with them. And when you came along..."

"He didn't ask for any money."

"He wasn't up to very much, Jules, was he? I mean he didn't do a lot of talking. He was a very old man; all that was left to him was craftiness.

He was probably working towards getting some money from you, only death came first."

"But..." I eased myself down the bed. "They were wonderful letters; how did this man Roberts write such letters? We are talking about the same man who wrote *Max Melcourt: A Life*."

"I don't know. Perhaps he didn't write them. Perhaps someone wrote them for him. Perhaps Joyce did!"

"I don't think that's very likely."

"It's all very well for you to lie there sneering, Jules. Think of a better reason."

He lay smoking another forbidden cigarette – the circumstances were exceptional.

"You still haven't explained why the letters shouldn't have been written by Toto. It seems to me..."

"No. Think, Jules. Poor old Melcourt commits suicide, or possibly Toto kills him. Either way, everybody who is anybody knows Toto's mixed up in it somewhere. He's finished. What he wants to do is to keep a low profile; the last thing he wants is to be touting about letters from Melcourt."

"Let me get it clear," I said. "You are saying that all the Melcourt letters are forged, on the basis that they are too tidy?"

"Obvious."

"And having taken that premise on board, you have them checked by some dubious friend –"

"Mmmm."

"– who declares them fakes. Then you have to decide whose forgeries they are."

"Mmmm."

"They can't be Toto's because he wasn't in a position to sell Melcourt's letters, so the most likely explanation is that the forgeries are done by Reginald Roberts, who may or may not he his son. The motive being simply to make money?"

"Yes; he stole the sisters' Apostle spoons. He was always short of money. For a while I thought it might be chagrin – you know he'd tried to present the homosexual angle on Melcourt and couldn't find a publisher – but I knew it wasn't when I looked in through the back window of the bungalow and saw how pathetic it all looked."

I returned to my old grievance. "So you were thinking all this yesterday while we were driving back and you didn't bother to tell me any of it." I had, over the previous weeks, fallen into the way of imagining I possessed the whole of Sebastian's confidence. I did not want to be reminded that this was not necessarily the case.

"I wanted it clear in my head. I was worried, you see Jules, about the water-marked paper. I couldn't quite figure it out. I had to let everything sort of brew together in my mind. And suddenly it all became clear.

"When?" I inquired suspiciously.

"You know we were talking about food?"

"You are always talking about food."

"More specifically about flapjacks. I said flapjacks were better than orgasms, but actually I was wrong: flapjacks don't clear your mind in the same way. You know how it is, Jules, when you've just come, all sorts of pictures flash into your mind with extraordinary clarity."

"Do they?" I felt great sadness to think of Sebastian's mind filling up post-coitally with a series of comic-strips while my own was conscious only of the joy of him.

"Yes; and you remember how good it was in the garden; just as the deliciousness of it all was going off, I saw Joyce's face."

"Joyce's face?" I asked faintly.

"Yes, wart and all and I knew how Reg had got the water-marked paper; it had come through Joyce. You remember Joyce's grandmother and mother were housekeepers at the Hall. Her grandmother probably filched it when she left and, with no thought, gave it to Joyce. Probably seeing a box of virgin paper with the water-mark on gave Reg the idea of forging the letters. Joyce must have known what he did with it, all the forging, and so on; that was why she was so anxious that he shouldn't give you the forgeries. Probably, there had been trouble before, and she didn't want it to start all over again. You can imagine how pleased I was to see Joyce's wart and the wart-er-marked paper... What's the matter?"

I flung myself on to my front and began to weep convulsively. All the time we had been talking I had remained calm, even managed to laugh a little. My acceptance of the fact of forgery had come almost instantly; perhaps, I thought, I had known anyway and pushed the knowledge aside. After all, why had I not had the letters authenticated, it was the obvious thing to do? Was it because I had wanted them to be genuine so much, I had not dared to put them to the test? But the letters themselves, marvellous as they had been, were only part of all my hopes and aspirations.

"Jules, what's the matter? Jules?"

But I couldn't explain. How I had longed to write the Melcourt book with my beloved, using the material known only to the two of us. The letters were a discovery we shared, it was *our* secret, something that he could not share with others, as he shared himself. I had spoken (fancifully as I see now) at The Randolph of the great importance I attached to our book; I had compared it to a child, our child. But it was not so. My love was, after all, fruitless. Our child had been still-born, no, it had not even been conceived. But this was not all: that consummation in the garden had been, to me, a moment of unbearable poignancy and beauty, bringing together (as I then believed) the four of us, Melcourt, Toto, Sebastian and I. But to *him*, it had meant nothing more than an opportunity to solve an intellectual puzzle. The false nature of the letters symbolised Sebastian's absolute indifference to me.

"Don't cry." He stroked my shoulder gently. "It's not the end of the world, you know. Melcourt and Toto still existed, do exist in the poetry."

"It's not Melcourt!" I said furiously, raising my head from the pillow. "It's you. Oh, God, I don't want to talk about Toto or Melcourt, only about me and you. All I have ever wanted is your love."

"Dear Jules!"

I lifted my head and stared at him. His hair was dry now and returned to its glistening gold. Even as I raged against him, I was conscious of his extraordinary desirability.

"Speak to me, " I sobbed, "be nice to me."

"Julian, of course I am fond of you. I admire your work, I admire your good taste. I am grateful for all the things you have given me. The fucking is great; but I have always told you, sweetie, that fucking is only fucking, and that love is for God."

I buried my head in the pillow. In his way, he had always been honest with me; he was not vicious as Toto had been. He could not help it that he did not love me. I lay in misery, shutting the world out, thrusting my head blindly into the pillow. At last, I sensed him get out of bed. I could hear him moving about.

"I'm going to clear up the curry debris, Jules, and then I'm going to find a bottle of something in the kitchen because this is all finished, and we'll sit up and drink it together and be a bit jollier. Honestly –" he bent down and kissed my neck "– you mustn't get so uptight about things. I'll stay the night, if you like."

I reached out for his hand. "Sweetheart."

"You see, Jules, you're much luckier than Max."

He disappeared into the kitchen (I found later he had eaten all the Camembert), and returned with brandy and glasses.

"Sit up," he said, adjusting the pillows behind my head. He let his fingers travel idly about my body. "Do you want to talk Melcourt?"

"No," I said sadly, "I don't think so."

"A little, perhaps, before we bury him along with Reg on Friday."

I was surprised. "Do you still want to go to the funeral?"

"Of course. I want to see them all ritually buried, don't you?"

"What do you mean?"

"The whole lot, Jules." He took my hand and let it rest on his cock. "Reg, Melcourt, Toto, the letters, the whole bogus mystique of the biography thing."

"Meaning?" He was exquisitely formed.

"You've got to forget them, disassociate yourself from them."

"What about the book, *our* book?"

"I daresay –" his hands moved expertly about me "– we'll find something else to do."

"Shall we, darling?"

"Mm." He raised his head for a moment. "I mean, Melcourt things don't seem very successful, do they?" First Reg's book, then Steiner's, and then the bogus letters."

"What about *my* Melcourt book, the thing I have devoted years of my life to. I must finish that."

"No, Dr Collins, you can't."

"Not even a book on the poetry?"

"No, for what is the poet but the man?"

"All right," I said, dismissing my life's work in two words. "I won't write the book if you promise to come to Italy with me."

"Not Venice. Toto will come gliding past in a gondola." He folded his arms behind his head and his eyes closed.

"Where would you like to go?" No reply. I augmented my words with a more tactile reveille. The blue eyes opened briefly.

"Not now. Sleepy. Busy dreaming."

"What are you dreaming about, sweetheart?"

"Flapjacks." The eyes closed firmly, and my hands were set aside.

I lay for a long time, exposed like a piece of barren land subject to the vagaries of climate. I basked in the warmth of the sunlight of Sebastian's body, but I also shivered with the icy winds of disappointment and suspicion. Sebastian had suspected the letters were forged, yet he had not shared his suspicion with me. And he *had* stolen the letters from me, even though he had now returned them. Why had he returned them? Only because he knew they were fakes. Would he have returned them to me if they had not been? Why had he taken them to Poole? Probably, he had intended selling them. Probably, he loved me as little as Toto had loved Max. He deceived me and sponged off me quite shamelessly. Did he, like Toto, intend to utterly ruin his lover? Dark clouds loomed and dispersed as I listened to his even breathing, and gazed at the golden hair upon the pillow. Biography, he said, was dangerous: I was not Max and he was not Toto; I did not need to imbue him with Toto's vices. I sighed. I loved him. I turned and looked at him. How lovely he was, his cheeks flushed, and his supple body so glorious next to mine. Let him sleep.

I slipped carefully from him and went to the study to get the letters. I thought I would search through them for some final proof or disproof that they were fakes. I took them out of the envelope he had marked 'SWAG' and looked them over. I got the one from the Bodleian out of Sebastian's jacket and compared it with the others. Sometimes it seemed that they were identical, but at others that the 't's and 'f's were, as Sebastian had alleged, a little exaggerated. There were a good number of crossings-out, but the forgery, if such it was, was skilfully done. Even in his last letter, Melcourt's handwriting had been subtly altered, had become less orderly, as if to reflect the failing of his life. And yet, probably, the handwriting had been only that of the forger – of Reg – who could no longer bother to keep up the pretence. I could have them checked if I wished. There were experts a plenty in Oxford who could tell me within minutes whether or not they were genuine. I need not to go to Poole. I could take the letters the following day, but I knew I would not; although I believed them fake, as long as the question remained open, I could maintain an illusion that once a red-haired man like me had written upon water-marked paper to a man with whom he was besotted. I returned the letters to the envelope, laying aside the genuine article to be returned to the Bodleian the following day, although it, too, now assumed a spurious air, as if by contamination with the rest. Besides, Sebastian had enjoined me to forget the ghostly figures of Melcourt and Toto. I must learn to commit Melcourt, Toto and the letters to the past.

I suppose I must have nodded off, and was awakened by sounds from the kitchen. He was foraging. "Sebbie!" I called.

"Jules!" He appeared at the door, dressed in only a T-shirt. He held a bread roll in either hand; each dripped with something red, I suppose he had found the strawberry jam. At the sight of him, my heart thumped in my chest and my cock stirred. However, practicality muscled in:

"Don't drop jam on the carpet!"

He licked the red from the outside of one of the rolls. "What are you doing, Jules? Here you are, with the best four-poster in the world, it's in the middle of the night and neither of us is in it!"

"You wanted to sleep. You were dreaming about flapjacks."

"Really? Was I? I wonder if I enjoyed them."

"Well, you preferred them to me."

"How horrid of me! I shall have to make it up to you." He came over to the cushions and placed sticky lips on mine. His eyes fell on the pile of papers.

"You haven't been going over the letters again! I thought you agreed we were going to forget Melcourt?"

"I was trying to stop thinking about you."

"Is that so difficult?"

"Yes."

He lowered himself into the cushions, a roll in each hand, and regarded me gravely.

"Jules, there is something I forgot to tell you about Reg and the letters."

"Forgot?" I queried. "Or purposefully misled me about?" My heart leaped. "They are genuine after all! Reg told you. He..."

"No."

"Oh."

"You know I told you he didn't say anything, when you were at the pub with Joyce, and I was alone with him?"

"Yes." He had finished one roll and was licking round the second. "Well?"

"He did say something." The words were muffled.

My heart leapt. "Stop eating and tell me properly!"

"Well, when he handed me the letters, you know, those last three?"

"Yes?"

"He said..."

"Yes?"

"Well, he sort of muttered and I couldn't catch it to start with; but he kept saying it. "

"*What did he say?*"

"He said, 'They are best gone, got rid of', or something."

"He told you to destroy the letters?"

"Well, more or less." I sat up, indignant and amazed.

"Why didn't you tell me this *before*?"

"I don't know. I expect I forgot." He threw the rest of the roll into the fireplace.

"Really!" I heard my voice, high with exasperation. "You painstakingly tell me about your theories of Reg and his forgeries – all of which, it seems, you formulate simultaneously with having an orgasm –"

"Afterwards, actually."

"– then you don't even bother to tell me that he actually wanted the letters destroyed. I mean it puts a whole new complexion on matters. Did he tell you to destroy the ones he'd given to me, too?"

He yawned. "I don't know. It was very difficult to tell what he *was* saying."

"You are so devious!"

He licked his fingers. "Anyway, what does it all matter? They're only fakes."

"Well, why did he give them to you – to me – if he wanted them destroyed? Why?"

"Jules!" Sebastian was very seldom annoyed, but he was now. "You're always asking 'why this, why that', as if everything has an answer, or everything is like a bread roll with a certain size and shape. Only *things* are like that; people and their motives are all crumbly and half-eaten, like that." He pointed at the fire. "I don't know why Reg gave you or me the letters. He was very old; he must have been at least ninety-three. He was very confused. Perhaps he actually forgot he had faked the letters and only remembered something needed writing on Melcourt; when he saw you, he really did want you to write the biography. Perhaps Joyce found they were gone, got worried, and told him to destroy them. Or perhaps..." He paused and touched my cock thoughtfully. "Perhaps he *did* tell you to destroy them."

"He most certainly did not!"

"Well, perhaps he just liked playing games with us – particularly if he was Toto's son. I'll tell you what, Jules –" his eyes danced as they did at the prospect of pleasure "– let's destroy them!"

"What?" I was confused.

"The letters, like Reg wanted. Let's get rid of them. Let's burn them!"

For a moment I was appalled, but only for a moment; I saw, as always, Sebastian was right. The letters were the tangible evidence of Melcourt and Toto, those shadows who stood between Sebastian and me. Perhaps, I thought, he, as much as I, wanted to be free to love. Why else should he be so anxious to persuade me to forget them?

"Yes," I said slowly. "Yes. I think you're right." I saw them now, not as letters at all, but simply as obstacles to our love. I reached for them; I couldn't get at them quickly enough. I gathered them into a bundle.

"I have a better idea." He smiled at me gently. "We'll cast them into Reg's grave on Friday. There will be a pleasing finality about it."

"But darling, you..."

"I'll do it, Jules. I'll see to it." He placed the letters in a neat pile on the table. He smiled. "Do let's take off that ridiculous dressing gown." He knelt down beside me, untying the belt and letting it fall open. The feel of his mouth was a tangible pledge of our future.

He was as good as his word, and stayed the night, though I could not persuade him to spend the next day with me. After he had gone, it occurred to me that the placing of the letters in Reg's grave was not really a feasible idea at all, but then, with Sebastian, one never knew what might be done. Furthermore, he had taken the letters, so presumably he intended trying. Anyway, I reflected, none of it mattered; with Reg went Melcourt, Toto, the letters, and everything that had cast shadows between Sebastian and me. For long years, Melcourt had been with me, almost, as it were, as my alter ego. Now, like some actor who has taken his fill of encores, he was making his final exit. There would be no more curtain calls for him or for Toto; they would leave the theatre by the stage door and go wherever actors go who will return no more. All was over, finished. And the theatre was empty.

But not for long. It was time for a new venue, a change of scenery, and a new production. There was a month of vacation left; I would persuade Sebastian to come to Italy with me, and we would make love all the time, without the voyeuristic presence of Max and Toto.

Twenty-three
Farewell to Reg

As I sit here (in the piazza at Massa Marittima), gathering my thoughts together to write at length about the day that preceded that most terrible, unspeakable night, I am amazed that I remember anything of it at all. Why have my thoughts not shrivelled into nothingness, subsumed in the horror? But I *do* remember. I remember with extraordinary clarity: in going over and over the events of the night, the tiny threads of thought which link one thing with another bring with them memories of the advent of the event, in addition to the event itself. Well. It is possible I deceive myself. Perhaps, after all, it was not as I remember. Perhaps it was not.

I had arranged to pick Sebastian up from his flat in the Iffley Road. I was looking forward to this; I felt that to be received into his flat as readily as he was received into mine (in whatever state it was in) heralded a new open stage in our relationship. The fact that I might pick him up from there was tantamount to an assurance I would find him on his own. I had been there only once before, and had the door opened by a naked, ithyphallic youth of Egyptian appearance. Both he and Sebastian had been high on some narcotic. But now I might go with impunity. I was looking forward to it immensely, to all the business of 'calling for' a loved one, the knocking on the door, the being told not 'mind the muddle but come right in'. I wondered what his flat was like (he never spoke of it). I imagine he spent little time there. My mental extravaganza even went as far as picturing a photo of myself (I had once shyly given him one) propped up on the bedside table; but I don't think, even then, *that* picture held much conviction. Anyway, I was looking forward to the day ahead. As ever, the gods gave with one hand and took away with the other.

Coming back from Melcourt on the afternoon of our garden discovery, I had mentioned to Sebastian I thought the car had a list; there was something odd about the steering. The next day, I had taken it into the garage, and the man agreed it should be looked at: of course, he couldn't do it that day. I could bring it in the next day. I told him I was going to a funeral, and needed the car. He was, as is the wont of such people, impervious to persuasion; he was a humourist, too. He said he could fit the motor in 'before you pop your clogs, mate'. I was not amused. I drove home, cursing cars in general and Porsches in particular. I did not even bother garaging it. I left it outside in the road as a kind of reproach. I toyed with the idea of driving it, but decided against it, I have always been extremely safety-conscious. I rang Sebastian. Unsurprisingly, I got the answering-machine.

"*Hi, Sebbie here. Did you know Melcourt is dead? Would you like to hear his last words before you leave your message? It's about a peacock.*"

I had never liked the poem, coming as close as it does on Melcourt's death; it had always made me feel uneasy. I did not enjoy hearing it five times:

> "*He closed his tail and spread his wings*
> *And fluttered low above*
> *And every moment closer brings*
> *The time to die from love.*
> *Oh, every feather has an eye*
> *Of blue or silver leaf*
> *And every eye shall watch me die*
> *Of love and pain and grief.*"

After six further calls, I got him. He was not in the least put out by the news. "We'll go by train. I want to go to London tomorrow, anyway. I'll go straight from Waterloo the next day, and then get a taxi."

"Can't we go together?" I didn't like to think of him spending the night alone in London.

"Obviously not. Never mind, we'll come back together on the train. Trains are such fun."

"Oh, Sebbie!"

"We'll have a picnic on the way back. Funerals make you awfully hungry."

"Will you spend the night with me afterwards?"

"Of course; lots of fucking amidst the remains of the funeral feast. Nice alliteration."

"And talk about Italy?"

"And talk about Italy."

"Really?"

"Really."

"I love you, darling."

"I know you do. See you at Melcourt. Take care!"

So, we went separately. My train was forty minutes late. I had to wait a further 20 minutes for a taxi. The man was new; he had difficulty finding the way. When I arrived at the church, they were well into 'My Song Is Love Unknown'. I tried to slip in at the back, but some busybody of a female church warden – now I think of it, I believe it was the woman who had been doing the flowers in the church on my first visit – conducted me to the front; everyone (including Sebastian, gleefully) watched my progress up the aisle. I provided a welcome distraction from the gravity and tedium of proceedings, but at least my progress enabled me to see everyone. There were a number of familiar faces: the two sisters were there; Fat sported an extraordinary hat, more suited to a wedding than a funeral. It burgeoned with bright-blue roses and had, I noted, the effect of totally blocking the view of those behind it. Thin was all in black and looked like an archetypical witch. Next to them sat the pudding lady, even more enormous than I remembered her. She was again clad in turquoise, with touches of black – I believe it was the same tracksuit top dressed up. I remembered that the Tupperware pot was still in the glove compartment of my car. I doubted she would see it again. Perhaps she thought she wouldn't, either, for she glowered at me quite horribly. I wondered whether Joyce had told her I had made off with it, or perhaps she attributed its non-return to the light-fingered deceased, whose spoon-theft, I suspected, would be common knowledge. The sheropody was there, only just discernable beside the bulk of the pudding lady; I wondered if she would take the opportunity of drumming up trade. The warden sat in the second row, looking harassed; I was pleased to see the medieval custom of taking dogs into churches no longer held good.

Sebastian sat to the left of the aisle; he looked wonderful. His hair shone and his eyes were studiously grave. He was wearing another suit I had not seen before. I know little of fashion, but the name Versace seemed appropriate. That, however, might well have been prompted by the fact that the subject of Italy was in my mind. I had determined to make him finally agree to coming on holiday with me.

Sebastian was not alone. Next to him stood (we were on to the Responses) a man of extraordinarily unpleasant appearance; he was big-built, and his suit looked as expensive as Sebastian's, but unlike Sebastian's, his was both too tight and too loose: it strained across his stomach and flowed over his shoes. (I looked back covertly.) His hair was close-cropped, and he wore gold-rimmed glasses, which might well have been of genuine gold, for his watch certainly was; and there was an earring. His skin was tanned, and I instinctively felt this was due to ultra-violet rather than to natural reasons. He had a number of chins; he looked greasy, self-indulgent, smug and rich. Already I loathed him, and I loathed, too, his proximity to my lover.

Sebastian smiled at me in an unfunereal way as I passed. I was put into the front row next to a woman whom I identified as 'the cousin'. She looked even more disagreeable than she had in the photographs.

She was undoubtedly enjoying herself and spoke the Responses in a particularly unctuous way, as if she had a special relationship with God from which the rest of us were excluded. I turned my attention to the Vicar, who was intoning some interminable prayer in an irritable voice. I also caught him thumbing surreptitiously through the Prayer Book – probably looking to see if there was anything he could miss out. He glowered horribly; presumably, he had not counted on his congregation including an open-eyed heathen like me.

Surreptitiously, I looked at Joyce. She was wearing her usual bland and slightly bewildered air, but did not look unhappy. In fact, she looked – not pleased, exactly, but relieved. Of course (I knelt), there might be many mundane reasons for this. She was an old lady and Reg's death (if at least the sisters were to be believed) had been singularly distressing. He had gone; it was over. Such things bring relief. But I did not think that altogether accounted for her blithe air (the wart seemed to positively *gambol*). I thought of the limited number of facts I knew about Joyce and Reg and their life together, and concocted a theory: Joyce married late in life. She might have been the maid of Melcourt, but she had somehow missed her chances, and had settled for Reg, around her fortieth year. Too late, anyway, for children. It had been a bad bargain, for Reg had no money.

"Aaaaamen," from the cousin, slightly after the rest of us. The Vicar bade us rise. He seemed maliciously pleased, as he watched us struggle to our feet. The cousin looked decidedly aggrieved and sighed loudly; glancing back, I saw the witch-like sister glower horribly as if she would like to confer some ghastly transformation on her. I pictured the cousin metamorphosed into some amphibious state. On the whole, I thought, it would be an improvement. The organist played the introduction to the hymn slowly and inaccurately.

I returned to my musings: they had so little money that Reg had forged the letters. She had found out. What was her reaction: shock, disapproval? No, probably a sort of unhappy non-comprehension. Anyway, it hadn't done any good. Perhaps it had even been disastrous.

Had the police been involved? Then he had written the book, and that hadn't been any good, either. Furthermore, what was it like living with Reg? Pretty miserable, probably (surely we hadn't got to get down on our knees *again*?). Perhaps he was gay. If he *was* Toto's son, he might well have been. If he wasn't his son, intense interest in Melcourt suggested an interest in gays. Sebastian had said he might be. Did Joyce have *that* to take on board as well? No wonder she looked bewildered. Then he was sly, underhand, a thief perhaps. Poor Joyce. Perhaps today was the happiest she had known for 40 years.

The Vicar began to do his spiel. What would he have to say about Reg? I glanced back at Sebastian; he was all grave attention. His companion could hardly have sat closer. Who was he? He must be some relation or friend of the family. Not even Sebastian would bring a pick-up to a funeral. And what a pick-up! I shuddered. The Vicar, I was pleased to note, was ill at ease. It seemed he knew as little about Reg as the rest of us, and probably disliked him in equal measure.

"*This* modest *man*," he was saying, "*who spent so many years imparting knowledge to those young souls whom God had given into his charge...*" Heavens! I hadn't thought of *that*. What had he got up to with all those young souls? Was that another cross that Joyce had had to bear? "*And we here who have known this... fine member of the parish, have entered his house, have entertained him in ours, we who have been –*" he was going to say 'privileged', but obviously couldn't bring himself to utter such a blatant falsehood, and contented himself with "*– situated to see his last mellow years spent in the company of his dear wife, Joyce* (he was on safer ground now) *may now rejoice that he is now safely with the Lord, in the hands of the loving Father.*" He was romping home. He had got rid of Reg, doubtless he was looking forward to his £15.

Joyce didn't cry, not even when the coffin passed through. I watched it go: the wreath looked dog-eared, as though someone had picked up one that had already seen service in the churchyard. Perhaps it had. There goes the last link with Toto, I thought. But perhaps it was no link at all. Probably I would never know now if he was Toto's son.

Of course, I could find out; I had only to ask Joyce, but I knew I never would now. After all, what was the point?

The coffin was not bound for the churchyard, but the incinerator at the crematorium. Sebastian and I would have no opportunity of throwing the letters into the grave. Perhaps Sebastian had never intended we should, perhaps he did not even have the letters with him. What did it matter? I had thought I had known so much – of Melcourt, and Toto, perhaps even a little of Reg – whereas I knew nothing of any of them. That did not matter, either. All that mattered was to bury the ghosts and to move into an untramelled future, I and the beautiful young man whose body I possessed and who stood behind me, feverently saying the Lord's Prayer. I gazed round at the mock-Norman architecture, the indifferent stained-glass and the rows of solid oak pews. I might be sitting where Max had once sat. Perhaps Toto had sat next to him in as close a proximity (I glanced back apprehensively at Sebastian and his neighbour – but it was all right ; he was singing *Dear Lord and Father of Mankind* in a lusty and open manner) as they. Yes, I might be sitting where Max had once sat, but, there again, I might not, and did it matter if he *had* sat there? Sebastian had decreed that we forget the whole thing; the whole Melcourt mystery and mystique should become as much dust and ashes as the corpse of Reg presently being shunted off to the crematorium.

We came outside in our various ways, Joyce conducted importantly by the cousin, the warden harassed and haggard, darting looks, from side to side as if in searching for the horrible little dog; Fat, with the hat now precariously balanced at an angle, (obviously weighted down to one side by the blue roses), Sebastian swinging his hips, closely attended by the loathsome stranger. I was advancing to stake my claim, when I was attacked by the officious church warden who had ferried me to the front of the church.

"Come along, Mr Carter. The hearse is waiting."

"I beg your pardon?"

"Your place with the family, Mr Carter."

"But I... "

"Come *along,* Mr Carter. The hearse can't wait."

As I stood there feebly protesting that I wasn't Mr Carter, and that I had no wish to ride in the family funeral car (only to be beside my lover), the Vicar came up and virtually manhandled me into the car, giving me a vicious shove in next to the cousin, and shutting the door against my escape. He gave me a triumphant wave; I swear he was taking his revenge for my having had Joyce's baked custard, and not having listened to his account of the flower festival. As we drove off, I caught Sebastian's eye; he smiled gleefully. Such situations delighted him.

I shall not dwell on the time spent at the crematorium – which was, fortunately, less than a mile away – as it does not bear upon the events I chronicle. Suffice it to say that I was, as always, woefully inadequate, and I stood about, fruitlessly wondering whether Sebastian would appear, and speculating uneasily about his unpleasant companion. In the event, the funeral party comprised only the cousin, the Vicar, myself and, of course, Joyce. Her wart moved gently in the breeze, but, again, she shed no tears. No-one thankfully, seemed inclined to linger, and we were back in the car in a matter of 15 minutes. Reg's end had been as insignificant as his life.

On the way back to the Hall, the cousin maintained an important silence to suggest that her grief was of a higher order than Joyce's or mine. Indeed, I thought, it probably was. I was slowly acclimatising myself to Sebastian's injunctions to bury Melcourt and Toto along with Reg. If anyone had told me, two or three days before, that I should abandon my life-long study of Melcourt – and, indeed, do so quite happily, I should have laughed him to scorn. But now this had happened, I did not grieve for Max, Toto or myself. The Melcourt era was over, I felt, and a new happier epoch was about to open. I should no longer live in the shadows with Max but in the light with Sebastian. It would not always be plain sailing; even today, there was the stranger, intending, I was sure, to seduce him away from me. But what of it? My darling belonged to me now.

Joyce, too, seemed to be looking towards a happier future.

"What lovely roses there, in Mrs Gordon's front garden!" She exclaimed as the car wound its slow way up the hill to the Hall. "Of course, she always has horse manure for them." I made a noise that could be construed as interest. "It comes from a farm in those black plastic bags," she added. The cousin sighed loudly and pursed her lips at this show of levity. All three of us were, however, dry-eyed when the car disgorged us outside the Hall.

We were guided through to the tea room, where Sebastian and I had so recently discussed the relative merits of orgasms and flapjacks. The cousin went before, her eyes fixed upon the sandwiches with a look of pious avidity. She almost forced poor Joyce into a chair.

"Sit down, Auntie, while I fetch the sandwiches."

"Oh, yes," said Joyce happily, "I do like a nice sandwich. Reg never liked..." A look almost like contentment came upon her face; she would no longer have to consider Reg's likes. I remembered Reg's chair in front of the electric fire. Now Joyce could have the comfort.

It would be hard to say which was more unpleasant, the cardboard bread and putrid meat of the sandwiches, or the paraffin viscosity of the sherry. The Vicar, however, (who had disrobed in record time) had no qualms at all, and I could see he intended to make a clean sweep of both. I smiled maliciously; he would meet his match in Sebastian. Sebastian – where was he?

In dribs and drabs, they all arrived. I amused myself (as I kept one eye on the door for Sebastian) by watching the various techniques for attaining food: the cousin loaded up a plate with sandwiches and bore it aloft, like some heavenly sacrament, before making her way over to Joyce. She made a great play of offering them to Auntie, but I noticed it was she who ate them, crusts and all.

The Vicar made no bones about the sandwiches; he had taken the precaution of having a plateful already reserved for him behind the hatch. He ate these with gusto – no doubt in relief at having got over the business of Reg's encomium so neatly. The two sisters shared a plateful; I heard Fat remark to Thin that this was the first and last occasion that anyone had got something for nothing out of Reginald Roberts. I waited impatiently for Sebastian, and gazed about the room. Nobody spoke to me except the warden.

"You aren't Mr Carter at all," she remarked accusingly, and her odiferous little dog jumped up at my trouser leg, clung to it with it with its front paws, and began to take pleasure from my calves. I calculated the angle, then flicked my foot. It gave a yelp; I hoped I had rendered it impotent.

"No," I said looking round for Sebastian, "my name is Collins." She looked at me disbelievingly and indicated the cousin. "You aren't Mrs Carter's husband, then?"

"No. My name is Collins."

"Well, I can't think *why* you got to go in the car, then. Here, Smiler, don't do that. Dirty boy." She looked with dislike at both of us, and moved on.

"Ah, yes, Mr Collins?" It was the pudding lady. "Have you got a Tupperware pot of mine?" The turquoise bosom heaved in indignation.

"Good heavens, Julian," said a familiar voice, "haven't you given it back yet?" He grinned as we turned to him, all golden sweetness. "He's a devil for Tupperware."

"I've never known such a place as Melcourt for things disappearing," said Fat. "I lost all my Apostle spoons, you know." She looked darkly in the direction of Joyce, who waved merrily back. She was clearly enjoying herself.

"What a very beautiful hat," said Sebastian. "You couldn't spare a rose for my button-hole, could you?" And, of course, she did.

"Who's your friend?" I hissed at him when she had finished the business of putting the rose into his button-hole ('There, you do look nice', from Thin).

Sebastian smiled. "You'll never guess."

"Tell me."

"No. You can find out for yourself. I have to go and eat sandwiches."
I watched him pat the warden's dog as he passed. It was working away
frenetically at the leg of the sheropody.

"Dr Collins!" An unctuous, transatlantic voice assailed me.

"I'm sorry, I don't think I know..."

"No, of course not. I learned your name from your gorgeous young
friend."

"Indeed!"

"My name's Steiner."

I gazed at the swarthy features and the gold-rimmed glasses with
repugnance.

"You may have read my book *Max Melcourt: the Gay Lord*. It's sold a
few thousand in the States."

"Oh, really?"

"Not bad. It's just amazing how well old Victorian gays go down
there." He beamed at me. He wore a gold bracelet. "I believe you do a
bit of writing yourself, Dr Collins. I hear you know a thing or two about
old Max."

A thing or two about old Max! I, who knew everything that was
worth knowing about Melcourt, had virtually *been* Melcourt. I, who
would have written the definitive book of all time about him, but who
had been gazumped by this loathsome American.

"I believe I am the... English authority on Lord Melcourt."

"Yeah. I may've read your stuff. I don't remember."

"My work is academic rather than popular."

"That's where you guys slip up." He stuffed a sandwich into his
mouth whole and continued speaking with his mouth full. "You
academics want to keep all your information to yourselves. I believe it
should be accessible to everyone, every kid in the street. Look at that
film they made of *Romeo and Juliet*."

"Have you come to England just for the funeral?" I gritted my teeth,
I would find out what he was doing here.

"Ah, no. I was in England on a little business."

"How did you learn of the funeral?"

"I saw the advert," he replied, smoothly.

"An advertisement for a funeral?"

"In the obits. I thought I'd come down and say goodbye to old Reg."

"Did you know him?"

"Nope, I only met him the once; I came down when I was doing the book. Thought he'd maybe have something to tell, him and Joyce. Figured out he might be Toto's son."

"And did he tell you he was?"

"Yeah; he said something. Anyway, I couldn't hang my ass about in England for ever. You get anything, Professor?"

"No." We both gazed at Sebastian who was holding an entire dinner plate of sandwiches. He was working his way methodically, intensely, through them. I glanced at Steiner, almost with pity: he might have written his silly book, and sat next to Sebastian in church, but he was only an outsider. All he saw was a boy eating sandwiches with enjoyment, he did not know, as I did, Sebastian's imperative needs, for those were known only to me, and only I satisfied them. This very afternoon I should fill him with delicacies, and this very night, I should do to him what Steiner would doubtless give all his gold watches and bogus American qualifications to do. I felt quite sorry for him.

"When are you going back?" I asked.

"I'm flying to New York tomorrow." He consulted his gold Rolex. "I'd better be going. Good to meet you, Professor."

I watched him make his way across the room to Joyce and offer some banalities. He waved to Sebastian and was gone. I felt a sense of relief, linked with malicious delight. In spite of his glib assertion, he had obviously got no more from Reg than I. And I was relieved for another reason: he wouldn't come sniffing round Sebastian once on other side of the Atlantic. Steiner, Melcourt, Toto and Reg were all behind us. I gazed round the tea room, and saw nothing but formica-topped tables and plastic chairs. There was not a trace of Max to be seen. Melcourt Hall was no longer the country estate of a minor

Victorian poet; it was simply a rather second-rate home for old people.

Steiner's departure had acted as the catalyst for general departure – and the sandwiches were gone. There was nothing to detain the devourers. Even the cousin was looking about her with obvious boredom.

Sebastian made his way over to me; he regarded the empty plate sadly.

"Well," I said, "I suppose I'd better phone for a taxi."

"I've got us a lift, Jules," he said. "The sheropody will take us."

"What, to the station?"

"Well, I've asked her to drop us off at Waitrose."

"Why?"

"The food. A picnic for the train." We made our way over to Joyce. The cousin regarded us with suspicion.

"I have *so* enjoyed our meetings, Mrs Roberts," Sebastian was saying, "not today, of course."

"Oh, I've enjoyed it," said Joyce, "they gave him a beautiful send-off." The cousin cleared her throat. Sebastian put the empty plate down on a near-by table, withdrew the blue rose from his button-hole, and tucked it into the lapel of Joyce's jacket.

"There," he said, "you look much more cheerful now: black is so horrid, isn't it? He leant down and kissed her withered cheek, wart and all, then took her hand and held it to his lips. "Try and let a little happiness into your life, Joyce," he said. "God wants us all to be happy, you know."

We all three looked at him: the cousin's expression softened; if she had been capable of smiling, she would probably have done so. Joyce gazed up at him with a sort of wonder, and, for a moment, I saw the Maid of Melcourt, some 70 years since. I do not know what my face expressed; perhaps little, for I always tried, in Sebastian's company, to conceal my intense love for him. My own conventional farewell was, of course, a dreadful anti-climax. I muttered, 'Condolences', and turned swiftly away.

But Joyce surprised me. "You're writing your book with your young friend," she remarked blithely, "a collaboration."

One or two people turned to stare at Joyce's unexpected erudition, and I could see Sebastian leaning forward attentively.

"You want to take care you don't fall out," she said. She nodded (she had not put on a hat for Reg) and the wart trembled. "People do, you know. Reg's book… " But we were not to hear what interesting factor might have occasioned her confidence, for the cousin returned at that moment from a fruitless search for more sandwiches.

"There, there, dear," she said, "you mustn't upset yourself." Useless to protest that Joyce was not going to upset herself, only divulge some priceless piece of information: useless, for Joyce was swept away by the intervening bulk of the pudding lady.

She looked accusingly at the cousin. "A few nice desserts would have made all the difference," she said. I didn't catch the cousin's reply, for the sheropody materialised from behind the pudding lady.

"Are you ready, then?" she asked aggressively. There was nothing more to be said.

Twenty-four
A Feast from Waitrose

The car journey with the sheropody offered no opportunities for discussion, since Sebastian was bidden to sit next to her in the front. I, relegated as always in Sebastian's company to the back, listened while he made polite conversation. The sheropody was, in spite of her small stature, as uncompromising in her driving as she was with her clippers – we nearly mowed down a bicyclist and a lollipop lady. Nor was she any gentler in her remarks: "Mrs Roberts will be better off without *him*" she stated, "the nasty old man." She had seen it all happen before; either the bereaved died within the month, or else they developed a new lease of life. It was her opinion that Mrs Roberts belonged to the second category. There was a great deal more such talk; she seemed to me as unsavoury as the feet of her clients. I waited impatiently for Waitrose. I wanted to talk to Sebastian, I suppose to reclaim him, assert my rights (whatever I imagined *those* to be). Furthermore, there were a number of subjects I wanted to raise: what had Steiner been doing in Sebastian's company, had Joyce meant anything by her unexpected use of the word 'collaboration'? Well, I wanted to chew over the whole funeral thing in the cosy exclusive way friends do when they return from the exequies of one they do not greatly care about. Besides, I might have agreed to bury Melcourt, but I wanted one last gnaw at the carcass before I let it go.

The sheropody dropped us off, and Sebastian bade her an effusive farewell, my own being rather less ecstatic. We watched as the tiny figure (scarcely visible above the wheel) drove off, scattering a party of Japanese tourists who stared after her with resignation.

"Now," I said. But Sebastian was not to be drawn: he had, he said, more important things on his mind.

"What things?" I asked testily as we entered Waitrose's portals. He seized hold of a trolley.

"Well, it's so late in the day, Jules, what if they've sold out of scotch eggs?"

"Oh, really!" But it was no good trying to hold a sensible conversation with him; the sight of so many delicacies on all sides had much the same effect a herd of impala would have on a predatory cheetah. He was out to make a killing. I pushed the trolley round in silence, and he went to and fro to the different counters, emitting cries of delight.

"Duck pâté with orange, and tiny tomatoes. How scrumptious! Can I really have whatever I like, Jules?"

"Of course," I replied, "why do you ask? You know you can have whatever is in my power to give you." I felt suddenly very weary.

He noticed my mood. "We'll talk about it all, Joyce and Steiner and everything." He stared at me pensively, a box of profiteroles in one hand and a carrot cake in the other, then, quite suddenly, hurled them both into the trolley. Two middle-aged ladies smiled indulgently at him. He smiled back. "I ought to be more careful, oughtn't I? I might have injured someone. Imagine the headlines: 'Carnage Caused by Carrot Cake', 'Death by Doughnut!'

They found Sebastian terribly funny. They came and peered in the trolley. "It looks as if you're having a party."

"Oh no," he replied, "just a picnic. Would you like to come?" I pushed on in silence, brow furrowed.

The girl at the till said he had chosen all the things she liked best.

"Then I *must* have good taste," he said. I got out my credit card. The bill came to £139.73, but there *were* two bottles of champagne.

We carried three plastic bags apiece, and made for the station; I could wait no longer.

"What about Joyce's comments about collaboration, Sebastian?"

"Oh that's easy."

"Is it?"

"Mm. I think we turn right here, the sheropody said."

"So?"

"Well, Reg writes his book with a friend –"

"Is Reg in a relationship with the friend?"

"Oh, yes, I should think so, but they fell out, let's say, perhaps over the letters. Perhaps Reg tries to pass the letters off as genuine, and the friend found out Reg deceived him and –"

"Perhaps the friend is the forger?"

"No, I don't think so. I think Reg was forgery material. Anyway, they fell out, and Reg lost heart in the book. Perhaps the friend threatensed to expose him if he used the letters – look, there's the station!"

"So he wrote the miserable book? And would Joyce be pleased, do you think, that the friend had gone?"

"Oh no! Joyce was madly in love with the friend... Oh look, it's only down here. And now," he said, as we turned the corner, staggering under the weight of the bags, "what do you want to talk about; Steiner or Joyce?"

Suddenly, I felt tired and irritable; it had been a long day, what with the trains, the crematorium, Steiner and the rest of it; now, with the plastic bag handles digging into my hands, I reflected I was too old to be chasing about like this; I felt like airing a grievance. After all, why shouldn't Sebastian share some of my discomfort?

"Neither. I want to know where the letters are. You said we would cast them into the grave."

"There wasn't a grave, Jules. You could see."

"Where are the letters? Why didn't you bring them?"

"I did."

"Where are they, then?"

"In my pocket."

"All of them?"

"Yes, Jules, all the letters are in my pocket, but..."

"Yes?"

"Why are you so bothered? They're forgeries."

"Let me see them, anyway."

How foolish I was! After all this time, what did it matter whether he had brought the letters or not? Melcourt was nothing any more. It was all finished. I suppose I was experiencing the emptiness one feels at the end of something – after all (apart from Sebastian), Melcourt had been my life. It wasn't so easy to stop thinking about him.

He put down the bags and began extricating an envelope from his inside jacket pocket. I was suddenly filled with contrition; my carping seemed so mean and shabby.

"Put them away!"

"Are you sure?" he proffered the envelope.

"Of course I'm sure. I'm sorry, darling."

"It's all right . I should be just as suspicious of me, if I were you."

"Tell me about Steiner."

"In the train, Jules. Look, there's the entrance. I don't care. And nor should you, sweetie. We're finished with them all. If we have to wait for the train we can start the picnic in the Waiting Room."

He was flushed from all the hurrying – not, of course, hot, red and sweaty like me, but pink and glowing as if he had just been making love. The sight of him moved me tremendously: I felt I should like to stand up in the middle of the station car park (we had just come in through the gate) and make a great peroration on the subject of my love, after which I should have had him bend over the waste bin while I fucked him ferociously.

"Sebastian?"

"Jules." He smiled. Undoubtedly he knew what was on my mind. "There's a train coming in, Jules. We must run, I bet it's ours."

I clutched my three plastic bags and went panting off after him. He ran before, and I kept my eye upon his hips. In all the world, there was nothing to my eyes as beautiful as the body of my young lover – or that is how I see it now. That is what I *think* I felt. But I cannot be sure: after all, who can be certain of the past?

We nearly missed the train; the station man had just closed the last door and stood poised with his arm up, but then he caught sight of Sebastian, and everyone had to wait while we got on to the train.

We made our way up an interminable length of corridor, Sebastian embarking on what I can only describe as a sort of Royal Progress: teenage girls lowered their eyes and tossed back their hair, toddlers held up sticky fingers, elderly couples nodded approvingly. I banged against people's legs with the plastic bags. Sebastian apologised for me profusely.

"Gosh, sorry. Is your leg all right ? Would you like a scotch egg? Whoops, do be careful, Jules... What a pretty dress your daughter's wearing; does she like scotch eggs?" And so on. It was a long way up the train to First Class.

As we reached the buffet car that divided Second from First Class, he said, "Jules, can we have some BLTs?"

"No, we can't!" I shouted, exhausted, embarrassed and exasperated. "I've just spent over £139 on bloody food. Come on!" Someone emerged from a lavatory, and stared at me in amazement.

"And there're flapjacks. You know how I feel about flapjacks."

I banged down the bags. "One flapjack, please," I said to the man behind the counter.

"Two."

I turned and glowered at him. "You're so fucking spoilt and greedy," but I had to mutter sotto voce so the man wouldn't hear.

"But one is for you."

When we finally got to First Class, I found us seats at a table on our own, well away from the inquisitive eyes of others, and sat down thankfully amidst the bags.

"I haven't got a ticket, Jules."

"I bought one for you in Oxford."

"You *are* kind to me."

I was tempted to pursue this, salve my wounded pride and purse, make some capital out of it. Maybe follow it up with some reference to my love for him, and hint at my desire for some reciprocal assertion. "Sebastian..."

But he had already begun to unpack the bags; I could not compete with the food.

He spread out the spoils on the table, and surveyed them gleefully. "Smoked salmon, moussey bits, lovely scotch eggs, tiny tomatoes and gorgeous poached trout. Oh, and champers and strawbs. You *are* kind."

"Yes, aren't I?" I said.

"Do you like it all, too?" He popped a couple of stuffed vine leaves into his mouth, and the delphinium eyes filled with concern.

"Not as much as you."

"Oh, Jules, you make me seem such a pig." He eyed a pork pie gleefully, slipped a hand under the groaning table and stroked me deftly. "Are you a little bit happy?"

"I am happy to see you happy."

He smiled and removed his hand to undo a packet of watercress. "Iron," he said, "it's full of iron, awfully good for you."

"Can we talk about Italy?"

"Oh no, not now. I want to eat and gossip and drink the fizzy. And for you to play with me under the table. Funerals give me the most enormous erections. I've been in agonies ever since the ham sandwiches. I wonder if anyone noticed."

A picture of Steiner's face, leering at Sebastian as he ate his sandwiches, presented itself. I felt a momentary stab of jealous anger. "I'm sure Steiner did. He couldn't take his eyes off you."

"People often can't. But, unfortunately, they *can* take their hands off. Please, Jules."

Huh! I felt the satisfaction of the successful male animal. Steiner might well have glimpsed the delightful bulge in Sebastian's well-cut trousers, he might have looked, but only I could have. Have and have again. Poor Steiner. I saw him in my mind's eye, sitting, disappointed and miserable, on his lonely flight back to the States. I felt it was I who had dispatched him from Melcourt, even from the shores of Britain.

"No. I'm going to open the champagne, and besides, the ticket man's coming."

He was a surly individual who scowled at us both and spent a long time scrutinising the tickets in the hopes of finding something amiss.

"Gosh," said Sebastian, "You must be awfully tired after all that reading; would you like a giant prawn?"

"No, thank you, sir."

"A pork pie?"

"No, thank you."

"Can't I tempt you with anything?"

"No, *thank you*." He walked on down the train. Even Sebastian was not always successful.

"What a dreadful man Steiner was," I said. I sat back to enjoy indulging myself further with discussion of my vanquished rival.

"You would have disliked him anyway, whatever he'd been like; even if he'd looked like me."

"Not if he'd looked like you, but he didn't, he looked exactly as I imagined he would."

"He can't help how he looks. Do hurry up and open the champagne. Put your handkerchief round the bottle. We don't want any unseemly spurting, do we?"

"Stop flirting with me. I am not going to do it for you here, much as I'd like to."

"Neither flirting nor spurting?"

"No."

"Why not?"

"Because there's a man with a lap-top two seats behind you."

"Perhaps he'll do it for me, instead." The champagne cork went off like a bomb. The lap-top man nearly overturned his computer. "I love champagne out of plastic cups," said Sebastian.

"How did you come to have Steiner sitting next to you in the church? Did you flirt with him, too?"

"Of course not. I never flirt. Heavenly champagne. Should we offer some to Mr Lap-Top?"

"No. When did you meet Steiner?"

"Oh, I got to the church early, *hours* before you, and he was strolling about, poking about at the gravestones, you know, and I asked him if he was looking for Max and he said he was. These profiteroles are simply gorgeous with a dab of salmon mousse."

"And what else did you talk about? Don't drink all the champagne."

"Oh, he said who he was, that he'd written a book, and had I read it?"

"And what did you say?"

"I said, yes, of course, because I had; and Jules, I said how both I and my supervisor had found it extremely useful. I said we had made thorough use of almost *every page*. And then he talked about how he'd tracked Reg down to Melcourt – he was awfully proud of his detective work, and, well, basically that he had tried to get information out of Reg, but couldn't because of Reg's stroke, and Joyce wasn't very forthcoming. He put it down to his being American."

"I should have put it down to his being Steiner. So he didn't pursue it?"

No, he couldn't see much mileage in the business."

"Why did he say that Reg was Toto's son?"

"Apparently, it was the one thing Reg did manage to tell him. Or rather, he mumbled something, and Steiner thought that was what he said. Anyway, he thought – quite rightly, as it turned out – that it didn't much matter, as Reg didn't have long to go anyway."

"Typically sloppy American reasoning."

"Actually, I think he meant it kindly; he said he thought it would please Joyce."

"And then what did you do?"

"Goodness. You should have been in the Gestapo, Jules – perhaps you were."

"Ha ha. Carry on."

"We talked a bit, and I showed him Melcourt's grave, and then the Vicar tipped up, and then lots of people started arriving, and Steiner said could he sit next to me in church? I said yes. Is the inquisition over?"

I fed him with an éclair, and he put his elbows on the table and smiled engagingly. "I think Joyce was pretty pleased to see the end of Reg, don't you."

"Well, the sheropody thought so."

"Perhaps she loved him."

"Who, the sheropody?"

"No, silly, Joyce." He thought for a moment. "I don't think anybody could love Reg, do you?"

"Who knows? He may once have had a 'friend'." I paused. "Who can judge others' reasons for loving?"

"Oh, don't let's be serious."

"All right . Have some more champagne."

"You *are* nice to me."

"I know."

"Do you love me very much?"

"More than anything else in the world." For a moment, his eyes looked troubled, and I took his hands in mine.

"It's all right, darling," I said, "it's my problem, not yours."

"Really?"

"Yes, I don't expect too much of you."

"Jules." He took my hand.

"Yes."

"Would you forgive me whatever I did?"

"I hope I shan't be put to the test."

"But would you?"

"Oh, I expect so." I laughed merrily – as foolish people do.

"Really?" he asked again.

"Really." I reached up and stroked one silken strand of his hair. I caught sight of the man with the lap-top. He was hastily packing it up. An ageing gay was more than he could take after a hard day at the office – or perhaps he was simply getting ready to get out at Reading. After all, it was the next stop.

"What will you do without Melcourt?" Again his eyes looked troubled and I was absurdly touched.

"I don't know; I don't much care. I'll find someone else – Housman, Noel Gordon, Horatio Brown..."

"They don't have to be gay."

"No, but they probably will be. What else should I do, Enid Blyton?" I was suddenly struck by a thought. "What about your thesis? It rather falls apart without Melcourt, doesn't it?"

"Well!" He shrugged in his elegant way. "Whatever I do, it won't be anything to do with biography".

"There's nothing wrong with biography. I have published three."

"Yes, Jules, I know. And they were very good."

"Thank you."

"Because –" he began dipping tomatoes into the pot of cream "– you weren't *involved* with them, Cory and Swinburne. Oh yes, I know you were very interested, but you stood apart from them. You didn't identify with them as you do with Melcourt. You've almost believed you were Melcourt, and I, Toto. And don't forget the mirror."

I took a cheese straw and bit into it, thinking of the time he and I had made love in the garden, thinking of my fantasies with the mirror, and all the times when I had enacted Melcourt and substituted the figure of Sebastian for Toto.

"It's playing about with shadows," he said, "We know nothing about Melcourt, Toto or Reg. We can only reinvent figures from our imaginings; put the flesh on the bones; actually, I'm not sure we don't manufacture the bones as well. You see, there isn't any Melcourt or Toto or Reg. There was once, but that's different. Now there's only nebulousness."

"Nebulosity."

"Actually, I think you can use either, Jules."

"Possibly."

"You saw Melcourt through the veil of your own personality and Toto through the veil of mine, or rather through two veils, the veil of your *perceptions* of me, and then through your own perception of him. About Reg, we only conjectured. It's like your Tupperware pot."

"Really!" I smiled at him; I was happier to indulge his nonsense than to brood on my own past follies.

"You say it contained baked custard."

"It did. You could check with Joyce."

"My bet is that Joyce doesn't remember. She didn't ask you for it."

"She's hardly likely to at her husband's funeral."

"Joyce has forgotten, Jules."

"Well, there's the pudding lady. She even asked me about it, you heard her."

"She doesn't *know* whether Joyce gave you the baked custard. That was why she was asking."

"Well..."

"And I claim it contained another substance – which sometimes you agree to and sometimes you don't. I maintain then, that we can never prove that the pot contained custard – or pee – or nothing at all."

"That's as may be. The pot exists; it's in the glove compartment of the car."

"You don't know. Someone may have broken into your car and stolen it."

"Doubtful. Anyway we could go and look in the car on the way back."

"But it might not be the same pot. You might have substituted another one."

"You are very silly," I said affectionately and I refilled his plastic cup of champagne. "Anyway, I should recognise that pot anywhere."

"So you say, Jules; so you believe." He dipped a chicken leg in the pot of cream.

"When I sit with my legs touching yours, and look at you all blue-eyed and glossy-haired, I do not much care about metaphysics." He laughed, and his fingers flickered about my groin beneath the table.

"If we can't prove the pot, we can't prove people, who are so much more complicated than Tupperware pots. All we can have is the 'through the glass darkly' sort of perception. Perhaps we'll see it all clearly in Heaven."

"Well, I doubt you'll see Toto there."

"Oh, God's mercy is infinite."

"It must be, if you anticipate God allowing *you* in, darling."

"I've told you, I'll make sure of the last rites."

"And what is your heaven?"

"An infinity of flapjacks. You'd like it, Jules. You must convert."

"I'll make sure of my flapjacks in the here and now," I said.

"Here and now?"

"Don't be pedantic. I mean tonight."

He pouted and started on the strawberries. We finished the champagne as the train came into Oxford.

Twenty-five
Betrayal

There are ten thousand ways of making love; I am not speaking of positions and techniques, for those are irrelevant. I mean moods, I suppose. One can be tender, violent, languorous, passionate – there are a thousand adjectives one could use to describe the act of love. Sometimes a mood is initiated by the one, sometimes by the other, and often a mood descends, initiated by both or neither, but for the lover, besotted by his beloved, the greatest joy is his when the object of his affections chooses on his behalf, and his choice is one of sweet tenderness. And so, that night, it was for me.

We had showered together and gone to bed: the first act was brief and business-like. We ate our flapjacks, so to speak, quickly and greedily. The train journey had given us an appetite. Afterwards, Sebastian went off to the kitchen and brought in the remains of the Waitrose feast and the other bottle of champagne. We lay eating and drinking (Sebastian having the lion's share of each) in a relaxed and contented way. I began to talk of Italy. "We'll drive around Tuscany," I said, "since you don't want Venice, just going where the mood takes us. We'll do Siena and Lucca, but most of the time, we'll just do this."

"This?" He asked, rolling over on to me, Sebastian was always good at kissing, but I had never known him as lovely as now; at one moment his tongue was flickering, quick and sharp like a spat of flame, at another it rolled languorously around mine, enclosing it as firmly as a cock within a fist. And then it was an adventurous, roving, buccaneering tongue, changing tack and moving down to explore my armpits, nibbling, biting and rasping, burying and foraging among the gnarled red hair. Then it descended again, skimming across my belly like the tips of an angel's wings before swooping down and exploring, with grave and tender attention, all those secret places of my arse, before opening his lips wide and firm and soft and wet, to enclose my straining cock. But it wasn't his mouth I wanted, it was him. Now I raised his legs above my shoulders and entered him, reaching up and up to fill his hungry, aching, biting arse with the essence of my love. And all the while he, who was always silent, moaned for me to give him my very being.

Ah, how I should like to set it all down here, for I remember every tiny detail of it, second by second, from the moment I entered him until the moment when he shuddered about my cock. I shall not do so, for words cannot capture memories nor encapsulate actuality. Let me just say it was – as I believed then – the perfect consummation of love.

Modestly, sweetly, he slipped from me and I took him in my arms and held him, gazing at his beauty. And he? He lay tranquil, returning my gaze with a look of such sweetness, it would be impossible to describe. Slowly, he reached up for a strand of my hair, and solemnly twirled it about his finger. Then he lay back, content, and his eyes closed in sleep with his finger still wound about with my hair. If I have ever known happiness, I knew it then.

A shrill sound broke through our sleep, and we both awoke, I sleepily, he immediately, clear-headed.

"Oh shit," he said, getting out of bed, "it's the mobile."

"I didn't know you had one."

"I haven't," he said, going into the bathroom from where the sound was coming. "It belongs to someone else. It's in my jacket pocket."

"Who?" But he was gone. I listened for the ringing to cease, and heard him speaking, although I could not catch the words. I was not particularly bothered, partly because I was still sleepy (it always takes me a while to become fully alert) and partly because I was not interested in the phone call per se, only annoyed that it had taken him out of my bed. I wanted it to be over, and him to come back. I wanted (I ran my hands over my cock) to fuck him, fiercely, to punish him for leaving my side. He was gone a long time. Whoever it was was not concerned about expense.

Time passed; I lost interest in my cock and became more alert. What was he doing? I thought I would get up and see who it was he was talking to, tell him to get off the phone. But I didn't. Perhaps even then I sensed it was better not to know.

At last he returned, the phone still in his hands, and I felt him beside the bed, gazing down at me. I switched on the bedside lamp and the sudden flood of light caught him in all his glistening beauty. Lines, not from Melcourt but from Milton, came to me:

> *"… in his face Youth smiled celestial,*
> *And to every limb suitable grace diffused,*
> *So well he feigned."*

The description was, of course, of Lucifer, God's fallen angel. For a moment, Sebastian stood, an apotheosis caught in an instant of time. Then his expression changed. Like Lucifer, he could not pretend for ever.

Guilt was not an emotion I connected with him. In the course of the many horrible things he had done to me, I had never known him look guilty, but he did now.

"What is it?" I strove to hide my fears and became aggressive. "Well, why don't you bloody well get into bed? There's no point standing there looking stupid." (As if he could!) "I want to go to sleep… Too tired to fuck. Hurry up… "

"Julian," he said, sitting down carefully on the bed at my side, "I…"

I said nothing. Fear stopped my mouth.

"I'm not coming to Italy."

Oh, well! I felt a blessed sense of relief. That wasn't the end of the world, was it?

"Very well, darling. We'll go somewhere else. Perhaps –"

"I'm not going anywhere with you. *I'm* going somewhere else."

I tried to calm myself, resorting to rationality.

"Might I inquire where?" I clenched my fists and squeezed the words out. I would not allow thought to intervene.

"I'm going to the States."

"America?" I was still sleepy and did not make the obvious connection. I had been to the States on a number of occasions, but always to give papers at conferences, so the country had become synonymous in my mind with academia. Perhaps Sebastian had been offered a post at some university?

"I am going to California."

"The university?"

"No."

I could make no sense of it, and I took refuge in sarcasm. "I see. You intend to make a film. Hollywood, perhaps?"

"Yup."

"Oh, for God's sake, Sebastian!" Anger rose to protect me. He took my hand and I shook him off. Thoughts struggled about in my head and came twisting out like worms, like snakes. I must be calm, rational, superior. I must not show I was worried.

"May I ask for details of your sudden meteoric rise to fame?"

"Oh, Julian, I'm sorry." He went to the bedside table to look for cigarettes. "Do you really want to know?"

"No. Yes."

"You won't like it."

"I don't imagine I shall." I laughed bitterly, fully awake now.

"It's Steiner."

"Steiner?" I gave another laugh to show how little I was concerned with this mention of my rival's name; but the sound which came out was like no laugh I had ever heard; it was hardly human at all.

"Shall I go on?"

I said nothing; I was incapable of sound. He sat down on the end of the bed. I could dimly make out his face in the mirror and he, perhaps realising this, stood up and moved away.

"He's making a film about Melcourt, or, at least, a friend of his is. He's writing the script. That was why he was at Melcourt, looking for atmosphere and stuff. Listen, Jules." He had obviously made up his mind, but sounded awkward, fumbling for words. Guilt makes mutes of us all.

He put down the mobile phone and picked up his cigarettes, but changed his mind and did not light one. "I had met Steiner before," he went on hurriedly. "You see, when you rang, you know, after you'd gone to Melcourt the first time, and left that message and told me about the letters, I thought they might be worth quite a lot of money. I thought I'd contact Steiner and see if he'd like to buy them."

"I see." My words emerged as a whisper.

"Jules... it's not as bad as it sounds."

I had no strength for speaking. He sat down on the bed at my side and tried again to take my hand. I pushed it away.

"I got him through the internet. I didn't have any definite plan. I just thought I'd sound him out. I didn't really expect to hear from him and, anyway, I was using the college set-up, and you know how hopeless it is; it's always crashing."

"Yes, yes," I said, "it does, yes... " For a brief, flickering moment, my brain clutched at the subject of computers: didn't we both dislike them? Why shouldn't we talk for ever about computers, and other safe and neutral subjects and avoid, even forget, other things? "Only last week, I ..." My voice died away.

He disregarded my interruption and continued. "Anyway, I sent his publisher an e-mail. I was lucky; he was in Europe – in Amsterdam. I rang his hotel; it was so easy. Would I care to meet him, all expenses paid, and so on!"

"You went from my bed to his."

"No, I didn't think of fucking him."

"Of course you did." *Of course you bloody did. It's all you're capable of: fucking and food... stuffing the orifices of your body...*

"Jules, I was thinking of selling the letters..."

I heard my voice, querulous like an old woman's; "Behind my back, cheating and...You must have been planning it while you were in bed fucking me."

"But I *didn't* sell them!"

"You didn't have them to sell. I only had the two then!"

"I could have taken them, but I didn't!" He stood up and began walking about the bed, tugging at the curtains as if to shut out the presence of his reflection in the mirror, but for some reason he could not get them to close; his guilty double stalked him about the room. "I met him in Amsterdam and –"

"I don't want to know. I only remember that you sent me a card from Amsterdam – I *believed* you wanted to show me you thought of me, and all the time you were fucking my enemy, trying to sell him *my* letters..." My voice trailed away.

"But I came back, Jules; I didn't stay with him for long."

"You were in Amsterdam for ten fucking days at least!"

"I didn't know he was coming to England, I didn't know he was writing the Melcourt script, and –"

"Of course you did! You lie and cheat so much you can't distinguish truth from lies, you little shit!"

"No; I didn't know. Really, Jules. I met him in Amsterdam; we fucked, he gave me money."

"Yes, yes!" My voice rose in triumph that he had inadvertently shown me further proof of his viciousness. "Money, that's the other thing you care about. He gave you the shorts, didn't he?"

"Yes. And the suits."

"And you said... you said you would steal him the letters from an *ageing bloody queen*..." I was now nearly beside myself.

"No, of course I didn't. I said I'd see if there were any more letters and let him know."

I sat up. I was shaking so much, I had to clutch the bedcovers to steady my hands. I took some deep breaths; this was not the way forward. I had to regain some sense of control over my treacherous emotions. "So you waited until the right moment, and took them from me... You stole them..."

"Three of them were mine, actually, Jules, the last three, the important ones. Anyway, they were *fakes*, for Christ's sake!" He stared at me defiantly. Anger had almost taken the place of shame.

"But you didn't know that at first."

"I had my suspicions. I did ask you if you had had them authenticated." He picked up my dressing gown from where it had fallen at the side of the bed, and began to put it on.

"Don't touch my fucking clothes!"

"Very well. I'll shiver."

"Shiver as much as you damn well like!"

"I shall shiver far more than I'll like," he pouted, his old flippancy returning. "But you're wrong about the letters, about it not mattering that they were forgeries. Once I was sure they were fakes, it put me in a quandary. I didn't know what to do about them. In a way, I felt better about selling them to him, as they were fakes – I wasn't hurting you, I even thought of telling you."

"Yes, you could have explained it all while I was inside you, and you were –"

"Jules, don't! How could my selling forged letters to Steiner hurt you? You should have been pleased – a fine blow against the enemy."

"I lack your deviousness."

"Yes; you're *much* too honest. Anyway, I was the smallest bit worried about selling fakes, Americans and lawyers and things, so I thought I would just think it over. And I *didn't* contact him."

"What restraint you showed!" Like him, I began to feel cold.

"He contacted me. He rang me that afternoon after we had been reading the last letters. I had just got home. He was very... persuasive."

I remembered how he had taken the letters and how the phone had been engaged for an hour, and afterwards he had not returned my call – his mind had been too full of his plans with Steiner – yet the night before, he had lain in love with me.

"It wasn't really the money."

"No?" I sneered.

"No. It was... it's difficult to explain. Yes, I did want to make money out of the letters, but it wasn't just that; after all, I knew I could always get money out of you."

"Yes. You could always do that."

"It was more of an adventure; that's how it started. I wanted to see what Steiner was like, see what I could do with him. Fuck him, because he was Steiner. I wanted to get Melcourt out of my system – and you, Jules. I *wanted* to betray Melcourt and you. I *wanted* to cut loose. But I *didn't*."

"Why?" I uttered a single, choked interrogative for 100 questions – but I wanted the answer to just the last: *Why had he not cut loose from me?* But he did not answer.

He continued. "He asked me to meet him."

"In Poole?"

"Yes. It seemed an odd place, but, of course, it's only about 30 miles from Melcourt, and, as I say, he was researching the Melcourt area for atmosphere. He wasn't as gullible as I thought about the letters. He had an expert with him, a man called Benedict something. He had a look at the letters and... anyway, I told you what he said. So the whole thing was a non-starter. But Steiner wasn't just interested in the letters. He wanted –"

"Spare me!"

"No, not just that, something else. Anyway he asked me if I would be interested in helping him write the Melcourt script. I'm awfully cold, Jules."

I thought of Sebastian's head bent over a table next to Steiner's, and

I thought of how I had imagined Sebastian's head next to mine as we wrote our Melcourt book together. The cold spread through me.

"No wonder you told me not to write the biography."

"Oh, Jules. It wasn't cut and dried; life hardly ever is. I told you not to write the book because the letters were forgeries and you were too involved with Melcourt, Toto and me, Jules. I'm only 21, I can't marry you." He stubbed out his cigarette and began pulling again at the bed curtains, but still could not get them to close.

"I don't want you to – now. Leave the bed curtains alone. You'll pull them down."

Impatiently, he pushed them apart, and his reflection came, once more, clearly into view. I experienced a frisson of perverse satisfaction that he could not escape the guilty figure who was both himself and yet also, in some bizarre way, a witness to his guilt. There was another witness too: Melcourt, who looked down at us both from the wall.

"Steiner asked me if I would co-write some of the script for him –"

"Which you've already mentioned. So, you leapt at the chance of prostituting your talents and writing a tabloid version of Melcourt and Toto – a sort of *EastEnders*."

"No, actually, Jules, I didn't. I didn't trust him, I thought he wasn't really interested in my intellectual abilities."

"Indeed!"

"To be honest, I didn't take it seriously. So I said bye-bye and went to meet you at Poole station. And we went down to Melcourt, and I was *honest* with you!"

"You, *honest*?"

"I *told* you the letters were forgeries, and I *told* you your involvement with Melcourt was dangerous. We fucked and it was good, and I said I'd come to the funeral with you. I decided to forget Steiner. I even suggested burning the letters. And that was to be the end of it. Then you rang and said you didn't want to drive, so I thought maybe I'd go up to London and see Steiner after all, before he went back to the States."

"WHY?" I screamed the word at him.

"I DON'T KNOW! I'm always *telling* you, one doesn't know motives afterwards, not even one's own.

"Why?" I repeated. "Why? WHY?"

He shrugged, "To sell the letters, fuck, talk about the script, get money, get a lift to the funeral, go clubbing: I *like* London!"

"London? I thought he was staying in Poole?"

"Yes, he had been; but he was spending a few days in London before going back to the States... He didn't know about the funeral."

"You told him?"

"Yes."

So nearly had Steiner gone, left the country, disappeared for ever to wherever he had come from. Only the Porsche had stood between me and happiness.

"So –" I fought to maintain calm "– you stayed the night before the funeral with him in London?"

"Yes."

"Did you enjoy yourself?"

"I don't know." For a moment he paused. He must have felt something akin to shame; perhaps he saw the pain in my eyes. He bit his little finger. "I don't remember. I expect so; I always enjoy fucking."

Despite his blatant self-interest and lack of real remorse, he looked so vulnerable. I was reminded of the night when he had come to me with his hair all wet from the rain. I thought again of my phone call. If I had not rung him, telling him the car was unsafe to drive, he would not have seen Steiner again. All might have been sweet between us. He began to fiddle again with the bedroom curtains, and because his actions were awkward, I suddenly knew there was more to come.

"Jules..." He stood at the end of my bed, naked and exposed. I watched his body reflected in the mirror and I remembered how only a few days before, I had made love to him in front of that very mirror;

that was another time, another life, even, when we had been happy, when we had Melcourt and Toto with us. I waited. The seconds dropped like lumps of hot lead on my shivering body.

"It wasn't just the script writing."

"No?" My mouth was dry.

"When I met him in Poole, he gave me money – a lot of money – to have my hair cut. He didn't say why. He just asked me to do it."

"And?"

"He wanted to study me, to see if I was right..."

"Right? Right for what?"

"He didn't say then. He only told me yesterday."

"*What*, for God's sake?"

He threw back his shoulders and stood very straight and still in front of the mirror, as if he had deliberately chosen to confront me there, to force me to consider the whole of him, his beauty and perfidy, for both were there, inextricably mixed. 'Look at me!', his body seemed to proclaim, 'how tangible, how beautiful, and yet you know no more of my heart than you do of the figure reflected in the mirror'. I stared at him, bemused, not knowing what to say; then he shook back his hair as if tired of waiting for my reaction, and said, "He offered me the part of Toto in the film."

"Just like that?" I spoke automatically; I had not yet fully understood what he was saying.

"Well no, there was nothing in writing; it all depended on a friend of his back in the States... but Steiner thought... well, you see, he was putting up a lot of the money."

And there is was. The enormity of Sebastian's betrayal began – finally – to sink in. I became conscious of the cold leaving my body; I felt a searing heat sweep through it. I knew then of Medea's gift to Jason's bride, Glaucé – a garment that burnt and bit into the flesh, and the more she strove to remove it, the more deeply it ate into the flesh, even to the bone. With every word, Sebastian's confession embedded itself more cruelly into me. He sat down abruptly on the end of the bed.

His head fell forward, and all his golden hair caressed his cheeks.

"And who... and who –" I could hardly say it "– is to play Melcourt?"

"Steiner hoped to play it himself."

I thought how I had thrust so gravely and serenely within him in the absolute perfection of love, only half an hour ago, and with what sweet skill he had responded to me. Afterwards, he had held a strand of my hair in his finger as he slept. All was false: it had meant nothing to him at all! He was merely amusing himself until he should go off with Steiner and ruin my life for ever. Questions poured out. My grief could not be contained. "*Why* did you come back here? Why didn't you... *go off with him after the funeral? Why did you... pretend? Why?*"

"I hadn't decided, Jules, I –"

"You thought to test the quality of the *fuck* before deciding. You thought to compare the duration of the fucking orgasm... to see if..." I was sobbing now. "Obviously I wasn't *good* enough!"

"No, Jules!" He stood clutching his arms about him trying, I suppose, to keep warm. "It was because it *was* good. Yes, you are *very good at making love*. I am *not* inhuman, I *am* fond of you. I like you fucking me, I like it very much."

Coughing and sobbing still, I felt the heat of my fury lessen a little, and lay watching him as he stood gazing at me with his huge forget-me-not eyes. He stopped clasping his body and his arms fluttered with an odd awkward motion (he who was never awkward) as if he would reach out for me, to take me in his arms. I felt a stabbing in my heart, a desire to forgive him, to beg him to stay. And for seconds, perhaps as much as a minute, we gazed at one another. I desperately wanted to fling myself out of bed and enfold him in my arms, but could do nothing; I no longer had the strength or skill for speech or movement. At last he dropped his gaze, and spoke brusquely.

"You see, Jules, I don't want to fall in love with you."

For a moment, hope flared up in me. "Oh, Sebbie." In that sentence, I almost had from him everything I had ever wanted, an assertion that he might... that we...

Suddenly the sweetness went.

"That's why I *am* going to the States with Steiner." Hope was extinguished. As he spoke, he pulled again at the curtains, and, this time, they slid smoothly across and his reflection disappeared. "Best for everyone, really – particularly me."

I spoke with difficulty. "Why did he phone you here?"

"To tell me about contracts, and things."

"You didn't know for certain before?"

"No."

"It was nothing to do with being frightened of falling in love. You were amusing yourself until Steiner called."

"Oh, *Jules*, don't you *understand*, even now?" He sighed and ran a hand through his hair; then he began to speak emphatically. "Things AREN'T fucking cut and dried! I could have gone back with Steiner after the funeral, but I didn't because I'd promised to come back here and fuck you. Anyway, I *wanted* to. I *like* fucking you – I *told* you. It was wonderful tonight, but I *don't* want to spend the rest of my life with you."

He was now what he had always truly been – the willful adolescent impatient of restraint. Through the veil of love I had not seen it.

"I want to get away from the shadows. I want to go. I want to be a star. I want to have fun! I want the tangibles – food, sex, cars and my picture in *Hello!*"

Like the tide, all the loveliness of him ebbed away; all these years, the waters of his love had come lapping towards me, touched my toes, and I had prepared to fling myself into his depths, but even as I stretched out my body towards them, they ebbed away and away, receding into the distance, further and faster, to lap on another shore. One always forgets the sea does that. He would never be mine, had never even truly considered it. His beauty, wit and charm he would remove from me as casually as he ate my food or took my money. He would give it all to Steiner, to a thousand other men; he would make a film, not caring whether or not it distorted Melcourt's life, his worth. 'Not even I am as bad as Toto', he had once said. He had lied. I was consumed with hatred and anger.

"*Toto had nothing on you*! He was kindness its fucking self compared to you. You... you disprove your own theories. 'We cannot know these people', you say, 'they are shadows'. But what *you* actually do is take them over. You have taken Toto and improved upon him, he is surpassed by your own *fucking* loathsomeness!"

"Jules, you mustn't... " His slim shivering nakedness drove me mad with rage; but my body was numbed; I would like to have struck him, or fucked him, do anything to get rid of the hurt; but my body wouldn't move. I sought relief from my terrible pain.

"Get out!" I yelled, "Get out of my life, get out of my bedroom, get out of my house! Take your disgusting, stinking arse somewhere else! Let the whole fucking US of A have it, if they haven't already." I went on shouting, my words becoming more and more incoherent. For a while he sat on the end of the bed, watching me in silence. I was exhausted at last. "Get out," I whispered. They were the only words which would come.

"Very well." He stood up and walked out into the bathroom. I heard him moving about, getting dressed. I stayed in bed, listening to him, hating him, waiting for him to go.

At last, he came into the bedroom and stood in the doorway. "I hadn't decided to go off with Steiner when we made love, you know. It was for real, Jules."

"Get out!"

"Julian."

"Get out!"

My brain reacted and tried to find other words, but it lacked the skill. I was filled with numbness, could not reason. I only knew two words, could no longer remember any others. Nor did I want to call a halt to them. Like a tap that one cannot turn off, the words continued: "Get out! Get out!" It became an incantation, soothing, like the repeated lines of a nursery rhyme, "Get out! Get out!"

For a moment, he stood in the doorway. His beauty, even then, was extraordinary. I can see him, the slim lines of his body shown to perfection by the perfectly cut suit, his hair falling about his dazzling face, the enormous eyes gravely fixed upon my own.

Yes, all this I can see; but there is another thing, and I do know if I saw it then. Sometimes when I think of it – that picture of him – I think I *did* see, and at other times I think I did not. I pray, or perhaps I persuade myself, that I had not seen that he held the keys of my Porsche in his beautiful hands.

Twenty-six
The Loss of the Tupperware Pot

He didn't get very far – perhaps a mile or so. I heard the sirens, both police and ambulance, and knew it was he. Driving was perhaps the only thing that Sebastian did badly. He never wore seat belts. He had also drunk most of the two bottles of champagne – and the steering on the car was faulty. For that reason, I hadn't driven it.

I knew it was him and I didn't go. The police, when they came, couldn't make me, either. They took me, instead, to the Radcliffe Infirmary, where I stayed for perhaps two or three weeks. I can't say now whether or not I was mad, or just pretended to be. I didn't have to identify his body (there were no other casualties), attend an inquest, or go to the funeral. I think all these duties were carried out by his father.

It was obvious to the doctors that it would be some time before I could return to work. The college was very good: I could remain on sick-leave almost indefinitely; my illness attracted sympathy since unconventional behaviour was unknown for me. Everyone was very kind and understanding. Even Sebastian's father called, and when he was told I wouldn't see anyone, he left me a very decent note exonerating me from any blame in connection with the car. I didn't reply.

The college put me on Sabbatical; I had earned it, and it was suggested that I write a book on the late Victorians, in particular, Max Melcourt, about who apparently, I knew a lot. I said no. I was unhappy with biography. I felt it impossible to obtain an understanding of a dead person. "I think," I said to Williams, who came and took me out to lunch, "with Herbert the poet, that, you know, we see now through a glass darkly." I paused, then said, "then we shall see face to face."

Williams cleared his throat and briefly picked his nose.

"What do you mean by 'then', Collins?" He spoke to me carefully, as if he was afraid I would break.

"In Heaven, of course."

"And how do you define 'Heaven'?"

"Easy."

"Really?" He explored his other nostril. "Aquinas and co. can take a leaf from your book, eh, Collins?" He tried to laugh, but stopped when I didn't.

"Yes," I replied, "Heaven is simply a question of flapjacks."

He changed the subject quickly and asked me about the car.

"It was a write-off," I said cheerfully, "Sebastian wrapped it round a lamp-post. It's a vivid metaphor, isn't it, 'wrapped round'?"

He cleared his throat and tried again. "Hope you didn't lose anything in the wreckage, papers and so on? Weren't you working on something?"

"Yes," I said casually, "Sebbie had some nineteenth-century letters of mine. They're gone now."

"Good God!" He almost leaped out his chair, "I hope you had them properly insured!"

"No. They were fakes."

"Oh, yes, ah, I see." He didn't, and he was embarrassed.

"Actually," I said, "I was more worried about something else."

"Ah, yes. I'm sorry, Collins. Poor young Sebastian, we all thought very highly of him." He paused, then thought better of something. "*Intellectually*, I mean, Salonière had a fine brain – if you recall, I was instrumental in getting him his college place. I..."

"No, I didn't mean Sebastian!"

"Oh!"

"No, nor Toto..."

"Toto... oh, is that...?"

"Not real, any of them. All from our imagination. Nothing tangible there. *Nebulousness.*"

"Don't you mean 'nebulosity'?"

"No, I *don't!*" I thumped the table and all the glasses on it danced. "Either is right. I have it on the highest authority."

"But... going, er, back to your comments... I'm not sure I follow your line of reason..."

"Never mind, Willy boy," I said, and I remember being angry at his slowness. "You must've heard," I went on, "I lost a large, blue, Tupperware pot, and the fucking insurance people won't give me a penny for it!"

"Oh..."

"They *say* it wasn't worth anything; but I know they're just being devious. Actually..." I leant forward confidentially, "I know they don't believe it was there in the first place." I laughed, and he knocked back his port so fast, he almost fell over himself getting to the door. He sent me a note the next day, with the address of a 'charming little place in Switzerland'. It had, he said, done wonders for his sister when she had her little trouble.

I wrote, turning down the Sabbatical, and gave in my resignation instead. "I don't think," I wrote "that the study of Max Melcourt has any further relevance for me." They said it was the poetry, not the man, which was my area of study. "As I've read his personal letters," I replied, "I can't separate them." Only when I sealed the envelope did I remember the letters were fakes. It didn't seem to matter much.

I should take time to reconsider my decision, I was, of course, to do nothing hastily, they said. I felt sorry for the President, the Bursar, the Fellows, the whole lot of them; the age of political correctness had come; they had a madman among them, and yet couldn't be shot of him. I wrote, stressing my decision; I even added a word of warning, "I don't want," I said, "to be with young men who may remind me of my former young friend." Then they said my resignation would be accepted. I wrote, thanking them for their acceptance. I told them I was going to exchange literature for art. I was, I think, a little pompous in my assertion: "The painter catches reality more readily on his canvas than the writer upon his page." Who said that? Anyway, it *was* all rubbish; what am I doing now if not writing a biography?

Twenty-seven
Italy

Seven months (to the day) after Sebastian's death I left for Italy. Like other men of letters, Byron or Browning, say, (but *not Melcourt* who, as far as I know, never left England) my reasons were complex, only partly understood by me, even. I'll explain.

Human beings are extraordinary creatures, particularly in their ability to defend themselves from trauma. So, when the police came to report Sebastian's death, my mind flipped, because it knew, I suppose, that it couldn't deal with the horror. I went, quite literally, berserk and had to be carted off in the modern equivalent of a straight jacket. I've always been strong, and my size and my madness nearly defeated them. One part of me watched them, detached, as they called for reinforcements. I think I gained some satisfaction from that. This phase passed. I was taken in and shunted between a number of psychiatrists. One was himself mourning the loss of a (gay) partner and preferred talking about his own problems to mine. He assured me that he'd experienced rage, too, and I mustn't be scared of expressing my feelings. I told him quite truthfully that I was numb, because my mind had moved into a different protective state: it completely blanked out the events of that night. It told me that Sebastian had merely moved *temporarily* out of my life, as he had so often. I was released, and went back home and prepared my lectures for the next term. However, my mind protected me from my subconscious: I think I've mentioned that

265

I have a weakness for 'imaginative reconstruction'; up to this point, I could always keep control over it: I knew, or I thought I knew, the difference between reality and imagination. Now I lost it. I began to dream. My dreams weren't confined just to nighttime. I began to dream during the day, as well, so it seemed more rational to stay in bed. After a week, I stopped washing, and only got up to indulging in huge eating binges. I bought and ate the kinds of food Sebastian had loved.

I began seeing him in many forms: sometimes he appeared as Toto, gleaming and beautiful. 'Why did you kill me, Max?' he asked sweetly. Sometimes, he appeared with Steiner. I watched them fondle each other, and I hated him. Sometimes, he appeared so horribly disfigured, and I could only recognise him by the fixed intensity of his delphinium eyes. 'God won't let me into Heaven, Jules,' he said, 'because you stopped me from having the last rites'. Another time, he was in a brothel in Amsterdam. He was wearing pink-suede shorts and eating flapjacks. Once, I found him lying underneath me, and my bed was sodden with sperm.

They took me back to the hospital. I sat patiently while they carried out tests on me. Fortunately (or unfortunately) I have a good brain, I played them at their own game, and told them what they wanted to hear. I must have convinced them, because they let me go. I didn't, however, go back to bed; instead, I took to sleeping on the rug in front of the fireplace in the study. For weeks, I never went to bed at all.

Even then, I didn't avoid the dreams; Sebastian was as unpredictable dead as he was alive, but I had to discover how to live with his ghost, and the ghosts of Max and Toto. When Sebastian had spoken about burying the past along with Reg, I hadn't known about ghosts. And when ghosts come to haunt you, you have to find out what happened to change them into their shadowy state, because only then can you lay them to rest.

I didn't know whether I loved or hated him, whether I should pray for his forgiveness or whether he should intercede with God to give me his – if he *was* with God because he'd died without the Last Rites. I didn't know whether or not I was responsible for his death – or if, indeed, he had brought about mine: my life as I'd known it was over. Until I could understand it all, my brain couldn't heal; it didn't know whether to mourn a lover, or be happy at the death of an enemy. Beneath my thoughts were my feelings, as battered, bloodied and mangled as the body of the one I had once loved.

A colleague of mine (Atkins, I think) had given me the address of a seminary in Tuscany. I thought it would do as well as anywhere else, but I did consider the logistics carefully: Italian winters can be very cold, and I didn't want to have physical as well as mental torment. Before I committed myself to going, I found out that the priests catered for visitors whose tastes were not ascetic. My room would be heated, have hot water and a comfortable bed. Also, they told me, Tuscan springs come early; by April, there would be warmth and sunshine. So it was decided. I settled my affairs, put my furniture, fittings and so on (including the Melcourt portrait) into store, and left the flat with an agent.

Everything went almost exactly to plan; the seminary was – I should say 'is', as I'm still here, six months later – fine for an eremitic man like myself. I had my room and creature comforts, was treated with consideration and left alone. It was all I needed.

As the weather got warmer, I took to sitting out in the seminary garden, and made a lot of notes on the sequence of events (yes, he *had* contacted Steiner as soon as he heard me reading the letters into his answering-machine; had contacted him *again* after our first trip to Melcourt, when he'd made me drop him off at the corner of Holywell Street), and I considered his motives: what game had he been playing with Steiner and the letters? Had he really sold him the letters (I'd never seen them after he'd taken them away that night, saying we would throw them into Reg's grave). If he hadn't, where were they now? At the police station, along with the Tupperware pot? Where?

During March and April, I kept busy trying out different permutations, telling myself I must get everything clear. Fool! Coward! I knew perfectly well that none of this mattered in the least; there was really only one issue: had I *seen* the key in his hand? Had I *known* that he would take my car and kill himself? Was I responsible for his death? Had I killed him, my darling, my beloved...?

I found a new delaying tactic. I had told the college that I'd swap literature for art. Very well, then, I *must* make a start on this. I would become an artist!

Twenty-eight
I Sketch the Duomo

I took care over purchasing the materials – the pencils had to run from HH to BB, the charcoals must be of different thicknesses, there should be lots of water-colours, *especially* the blues... must cover every shade from... delphinium... to forget-me-not. Paper had to be the best. I carried with me a thick sheaf of paper wherever I went.

I also bought a folding canvas stool – after all, it was almost May, and the weather was balmy. I've become something of a familiar figure about town; I think I'm pointed out to tourists as a kind of curiosity, though not for the colour of my hair; over these last months, all different areas of it have turned quite grey. I've also lost weight; I'm quite svelte now. Sebastian *would* be impressed, though... perhaps not: 'I like size, Jules,' he would say, although he may have been talking about my cock. Anyway, in respect of my thinning, grey hair, I had bought a hat, a kind of panama, which shaded my eyes when sketching, so, as I say, there was no real danger of anyone laughing at my hair – any more than there is of someone taking hold of a lock of it, and keeping it wound round his finger while he sleeps.

As I say, I set about my sketching, always choosing the most solid objects, buildings, not people. I was amazed to find how bad my sketches were (I covered them over when people passed). However, I kept on throughout June and July, using drawing as an excuse to put off investigating Melcourt's motives – and my own. The day came – I can't remember the exact date; anyway, it's irrelevant (although I know it was before 15th July) – when I finally thought about it.

I was seated at a table in the piazza. I had a jug of chianti in front of me and the remains of some excellent crostini (I reflected sadly that there would have been no crumbs had Sebastian been there). I was sketching the Duomo. The lower part of façade is quite stolid despite its graceful arches, but at the top it becomes... ethereal, with spires losing themselves in the sky. I did a lot of careful cross-hatching with a BB pencil and concentrated.

When Sebastian had stood beside my bed, pulling the curtains and telling me of his intended betrayal, I hated him. Often, he had made me utterly miserable, but I'd never hated him; and I'd always forgiven him; but this time, the sum of his crimes seemed overwhelming. I hated him then – with a violence born from bitter disillusionment. I had thought that, at last, he loved me and, at one fell swoop, my illusions had all been swept away.

The Duomo sits perched uneasily on the top of 17 rather worn out, shallow steps; it was difficult and time-consuming to draw each one, and to get the perspective right; every time I moved in my chair the whole view seemed to shift and I would have to start again. As when I used to play games while waiting for Sebastian, now I said, 'When I've done the steps (all 17), then I'll look at the questions: *Did I see the keys in his hands? Could I have stopped him, or, did I see? Did I instigate his death?* I shuffled my chair – a passing tourist blocked my view – now I'd have to start the steps again! I would think of the questions later.

I couldn't put it off indefinitely, go on cheating myself for ever. I put down the pencil. 'Well?' I asked. But the brain was crafty. 'How can I answer your questions?' it replied, 'didn't Sebastian tell you that motives aren't cut and dried? How *can* you know?'

But there was a more honest side to me; 'You must look at the question, Julian, you must look in the dark places of your heart.' 'How can I?' I cried in anguish – I think I cried out loud, because the family of Americans at the next table got up and took a table further away from me. 'Well,' said the rational part of me, the true Julian Collins, 'You know what you should do. You've known for months. Look at Melcourt's motives if you can't look at your own; your lives have run parallel. Did *he* want Toto dead? If so, then you must be as guilty.'

So, I had to go back to Max Melcourt to find out the truth of what had happened that day in the garden. And when I say 'that day in the garden', I mean *both* days in the garden, the day Melcourt died there, and the day that Sebastian and I played with the plastic gun. Had Melcourt wanted to kill Toto? I, Sebastian? Had we both wanted our lovers' dead?

I took a well-sharpened pencil and started on the six rounded arches on the Duomo's façade: they were slim but firm; shouldn't be too difficult. I put down the pencil and took a great gulp of chianti. I must be careful: in Melcourt's guilt I'd find my own. *Had Melcourt bought a gun to kill his lover?* Toto had, perhaps, suggested some betrayal, as Sebastian had me. To Melcourt, drained of money, reputation failing, this was the final straw. He had decided to kill Toto. Perhaps he planned to shoot, and then put the gun in Toto's hand, and hoped the thing would be put down to suicide. Thankfully, I saw this was *so* unlikely – Melcourt could never have killed Toto in cold blood, least of all in his own garden. He'd no more bought a gun to kill Toto than I'd bought the Porsche to kill Sebastian. Neither of us could have premeditated our lover's death. Of that, at least, I was innocent. Well, then; had murder been attempted in the heat of the moment? I finished the chianti and the rounded tops of the arches, took a fresh pencil and started outlining the great bronze doors.

Perhaps the gun was Toto's. 'Boys like guns', Sebastian had said. It was true; he'd really bought it for himself; perhaps Toto, too, had fancied a pretty gun – or maybe it'd been a lover's gift: 'Look, Max, what Bothwell has given me. He says its action is like his own, hard and merciless. What can he mean, Max?' And Max, unable to take any more, had snatched it from him, shot and missed and turned it on himself.

A good enough hypothesis, but there was no evidence for any of it. None. And, most importantly, no evidence to suggest Toto's presence at the scene of Melcourt's death, or evidence to suggest Melcourt intended anything other than killing himself. Whoever'd forged the letters had thought Melcourt's death quite straightforward; he'd killed himself because his life was finished. His own death was all that mattered then. I sat back, almost satisfied. Melcourt hadn't wanted Toto's death, nor I Sebastian's.

But (I regarded my representation of the dome critically) if Toto hadn't been present at Melcourt's death, why had he disappeared so quickly afterwards? The gun used wasn't Melcourt's, so it *could* have been Toto's. Might not Melcourt – might not I – goaded beyond hope, have wanted his lover dead? For who can measure the speed with which love can turn to hate?

I sighed and put down my pencil again. I knew as little about my own motives now as I did about those of Melcourt – probably I should never know. I glanced at my sketch of the Duomo; it was barely recognisable.

I crumpled it up and left it beside the empty bottle and the remnants of the crostini. I picked up my pad and pencils, and left a generous tip (although the priests had told me to leave nothing: 'The boys are idle and sinful; they spend it all on cigarettes and the lottery'). I began making my way up the steep incline towards the seminary; I was quite well-known now, at the tabacci, at the Hotel Chris, the Pharmacia (for sleeping pills) 'Buona sera, Signore', 'Gracie a lei'. I liked the shapeless old women in their black, the slim, green-eyed youngsters of both sexes. Nothing would ever be much good again, but they were something – a little less than friends but a little more than shadows.

I began the steep ascent past the Arch of San Francisco, and watched two vespas come abreast of each other and disappear off to the left, to the happy sounds of hooting and laughter. It was like that, I thought, with our lives, mine and Melcourt's: for a while, they ran parallel, before veering off and disappearing into the dusk. But there the parallel ceased. Melcourt used up his life and died for his love. But I did not die for my love of Sebastian, it was he who had died and I who now gathered my breath for the last pull up the hill to the Seminary.

Melcourt had been marked for death as soon as he'd replied to Toto's first letter. Though I'd felt unreasonable (at the time) intimations of trouble when Atkins told me Sebastian had gained a college place, I had, mostly, survived. I stopped and rested my arm on the ancient hand-rail, and stared at the shuttered window of the Optician, who was never open. Why had I been spared, when he hadn't? From inside the Optician's came the sound of English pop music.

Sebastian had always told me it was dangerous to play with parallels. I might have looked like Melcourt, but I was no more he than Sebastian had been Toto. Toto was vicious, but Sebastian wasn't; there was no malice in him. All he'd ever wanted were his tangibles. I stopped halfway up the steep hill to the Seminary to look over the town. With the sharp rays of the setting sun, a tremendous revelation came to me: Sebastian wasn't bad at all; he was, in fact, supremely good!

When we made love that last time, I hadn't been wrong in believing his love was a pledge. Hadn't he looked at me and said, 'It was for real, Jules'? I had a sudden thought: of course, he hadn't intended going to the States with Steiner at all, nor had he allowed Steiner to touch him. He had invented the whole thing to save me from ruin and death, had simply sought to leave me in such a way that I would stop loving him, and not be ruined, like Melcourt. As he was more brilliant, more beautiful, and more promiscuous than other men, it followed that he was more intuitive and fearless. He'd traded his death for mine.

I felt so euphoric at the thought of his sacrifice, I almost ran the remaining hundred or so yards up the hill. However, when I reached the top, I saw the theory for what it was, a delusion. Unlike the eponymous saint, Sebastian had *never* shown signs of a desire for martyrdom. He hadn't taken the Porsche to kill himself, but to get away as quickly as possible from an unpleasant situation. There had been so many glaringly obvious examples of his immorality. I might just as well claim that Toto was all good and Melcourt all bad. Melcourt's obsession with Toto had caused the tragedy, just as mine with Sebastian had caused his death. I thought wryly of Sebastian's egg custard philosophy. Nothing was certain, neither events nor character.

I crossed the road, narrowly avoiding another vespa, and went into the Seminary garden. An aged priest who had, over the previous two weeks, been erecting a low fence round some desiccated fig trees, looked up and gave his usual greeting: *"Buona sera, Dottore."*

"Buona sera, Padre," I returned.

We had never got any further than alternating *"giorno"* for *"sera"*, but today, for some reason, he indicated the object of his labours and volunteered, *"Sabatto, lo finerò."* He must have wondered why I didn't reply, but turned away and went quickly into the Seminary. I didn't mean to be ungracious, but I didn't want him to see my tears. That coming Saturday was the 15th of July, the anniversary of Sebastian's death.

I had little sleep that week, and afterwards, couldn't get back into my former pattern. If only I could, I told myself, establish some facts: *was* he good or bad, was *I* innocent or guilty? I remembered a ghost story, told by the author Pliny, of a husband's haunting by his dead wife; only when he found her gold sandal and burnt it, did she stop bothering him. I was, I suppose, looking for Sebastian's 'gold sandal' – not that I wanted to stop dreaming of him; I didn't, though dreams of him brought nothing but discomfort; I woke from my dreams with painful erections which were only soothed by fierce bouts of rough masturbation, which left me sore, exhausted and sleepless.

One day followed another, summer passed into autumn, and I could see no end to my miserable existence.

Twenty-nine
A Letter and a Parcel

Post takes a long time to get to Italy, and to an obscure Seminary in Tuscany, even longer. Besides, I received little post after the first couple of months. Initially, people treated my stay in Italy as an eccentric holiday. They thought I'd be back. I received journals, college documents, summons to committees, reports and articles. I sent very few replies. But, one day in November, I received a small parcel with the postmark, Dorset. It contained a wrapped oval-shaped object and a letter. I opened the letter first:

Melcourt Hall

Melcourt

2nd October 1995

Dear Mr... ('Carter' was crossed out and 'Collins' put in) *I'm afraid I always get your name wrong.*

There's been a thing that's been worrying me for a long time now, and I've made up my mind to write, although it's difficult with the arthritis in my hands. It was seeing that Mr Steiner again at the funeral that got me worried, because what he put in his book wasn't right, and I heard him say he had sold a thousand copies. Oh, dear. Of course, I can't do anything about that now but I don't want you getting it wrong when you write your book.

Well, you see. Reg wasn't Mr Anthony Roberts' son at all – but when Mr Steiner was here before, Reg had just had his stroke and his speech wasn't very clear – and of course I'm a bit deaf.

So it was all a muddle about him being Mr Anthony Roberts' son – Reg wasn't a relation at all, it's me that's the relation.

You see, Mr... the name's gone again... I'm Mr Roberts' grand-daughter, although I don't talk about it outside the family, the truth being very disgraceful and I shouldn't be telling you this now, if I didn't want you putting it in your book all wrong, like Mr Steiner did. You see, Mr Roberts had got round my grandmother (I think I told you she was housekeeper at the Hall) and he was with her, so my grandmother told my mother, when poor Lord M shot himself.

And after that, Mr Roberts couldn't get away quick enough. He went off to live abroad, or so my mother told me, and he went off in such a hurry that he left all his things behind with a lot of letters, and it was my mother's belief that Mr Roberts had been blackmailing Lord M with them. Anyway, and I don't like writing about this, Doctor, but after Mr Roberts had gone off, my Grannie found she was expecting my mother, and she kept the letters in case they came in useful, if you know what I mean, but she never done anything with them, and nor did my mother, not wanting to have anything to do with it all. To tell you the truth, she only told me about Grannie and Mr Roberts when she was dying. Of course, after she'd gone, I had a look at the letters, but I couldn't make anything of them, with all that poetic talk. And then when Reg came down, doing his research and we got friendly, I told him about the letters. He was over the moon, and the long and short of it was, we got married and I gave him the letters. No good came of it, because they weren't nice letters, it seems, and when Reg read them he hit the roof and called my father all sorts of names. He said he had always loved Lord Melcourt's poetry, and now it was all spoiled for him, and of course I was very shocked. Anyway, he told me to destroy the letters, which I did; but I don't know how it was, Reg must have kept some back. I suppose he couldn't bear to part with them. All the heart had gone out of him over the book. 'I'll just say the minimum, Joyce', he told me.

It was after Mr Steiner came asking whether Reg was Toto's son... and there was such a muddle, with Mr Steiner writing about Reg being Toto's son, I was so worried. And then it was in the book! Oh, dear. I mean, you can get into dreadful trouble for having false information published, can't you? And then Reg seemed to keep thinking about Lord Melcourt, and I fancied he'd still got something although he was very close about it. 'If you've got anything, Reg', I said, 'you must destroy it; and I shouldn't like anything being printed about my grandfather'. It's one thing to read something in print, but it's another when it's about your own relatives.

But I think Mr Steiner's visit must have started something off in his brain, for he didn't say anything, but he was very excited when he got your letter. I didn't really want you to come, but he got the warden to ring and ask you. And I wondered if he had given you something, although you said he hadn't, and I know doctors have to say on oath that they will speak the truth, but I did wonder. Then it was all right , because he told me your young friend had got rid of all the letters for him. So I'm not worried about that. Reg was very fond of Lord Melcourt's poetry. Poor Reg. And he was so disappointed. I daresay he wouldn't have married me but for those letters, but we got along all right , he was a good husband, and I miss him. My cousin thought I should be crying at the funeral, but I had promised him I wouldn't, when he knew he was going. 'I'll be brave, Reg,' I said. And I was, wasn't I?

Anyway, Mr Carter, I shouldn't like you to write anything about my grandfather, even though it's so long ago, and he was not a nice man. I hope you won't do.

I'm sending you the enclosed, which I found when I was sorting out after Reg passed on, because I remember how interested you were – and perhaps if you have this you'll spare a thought for me and not write about you-know-what in your book.

Yours,
Joyce Roberts (Mrs).

PS I believe you've got a Tupperware pot belonging to the pudding lady. If you're ever passing I should be grateful for it back. They're very useful, you know.

I read the letter, sitting on the end of the bed in my cell-like room. After I had read it and taken in its contents, I put it down and thought about all the implications. I forgot altogether about the parcel. I sat still and silent until darkness filled the room, but didn't switch on the light. The shadowy blackness seemed more appropriate.

Well, now that I knew what I had spent so many years trying to discover, how happy I should once have been! The letters were genuine. Melcourt's death hadn't been accidental; he had shot himself. Toto hadn't shot him, since, at the time, he'd been consoling himself with the housekeeper. Max hadn't tried to kill him, so I must also be innocent. So many later mysteries were also solved: why Reg's biography had been so meagre, why he had parted with the letters so surreptitiously, why Steiner had believed Reg to be Joyce's son. On the other hand, perhaps Sebastian had managed to sell him the letters, and Steiner now had the originals... But it didn't matter; none of it mattered.

I'd spent my life pursuing inessentials, concocting ridiculous theories about them, but of the *essential truth*, I knew nothing; I never had.

Surely it was Reg with his meagre biography who had seen Max with greater clarity than Steiner or I, for Reg had written only of what was incontrovertible, he had not attempted to fight with shadows. And as for Joyce, whom I had utterly dismissed, she had been the one true link with Melcourt.

I had invented a character for Reg, seeing in him some of the craftiness of Toto and a vague physical resemblance. I had even thought him a thief. This I had imagined merely because of the idle remarks of two old women; I had thought him gay, whereas in fact he had not even known of Melcourt's homosexuality and had been shocked by it. I had thought him selfish, because his chair had been nearer the fire than Joyce's! I had assumed his book had been written with or by another – simply because Joyce had, in quite another context, mentioned the word 'collaborate'. Out of all these hints I had concocted an imaginary character. On every count I had been wrong.

He was simply an old unexceptional schoolmaster, a loving husband who had once written a poor biography of a Victorian poet.

How arrogant and smug I'd been with my poetic alignments and theories. In fact, almost everything that I'd 'proved' had been wrong. I had no evidence to suggest that Melcourt was like me in any respect, other than having an obese figure and red hair. Toto was not gay, but a bisexual – hence the tryst with the housekeeper. Even Joyce's motives I had misinterpreted. She had not been uncaring at the funeral, simply very brave.

I had played with intangibles. I thought of the antique mirror that hung opposite the bed on the wall of my bedroom at Oxford. It seemed a paradigm for my delusions. Incredible to recall that I once believed I had seen Toto and Melcourt through it. The only time the mirror contained reality was when Sebastian had come over it, and covered its surface with sperm.

And Melcourt's poetry; no, it wasn't for his verse that we admired him, but because we had avidly read his verse for its homosexual content and connotations. Neither Melcourt nor his poetry had been worth any more than the treatment it had been given by Steiner!

And Sebastian; how foolishly I had tried to understand and analyse his motives. Only his tangibles had meaning, and now the beauty of his own tangibility was gone for ever.

For an hour, perhaps two or three, I sat in the darkness and thought. 'Words are only thoughts with clothes on,' he had said. But when thoughts themselves have no body, what is left?

At last I remembered the parcel. I wrestled with the sellotape. There was a brief note included: it was from the cousin. She had found the parcel packed up, she wrote, ready for sending: 'Auntie Joyce has suffered a heart attack and gone to join dear Uncle Reg'. She would be grateful for the cost of postage. Parcels abroad were expensive. She had had a lot to do, cleaning up after Auntie. On the back of the parcel was written in angry capitals, 'Sender: CARTER'. I felt that she thought I was to blame in some way.

The parcel contained a picture; the glass was broken, but the portrait itself was unharmed. It was an exquisite miniature of a very beautiful young man. For a long time, I sat gazing at it in wonder.

The young man gazed back at me, proudly conscious of his beauty. Was this Toto, the missing Rothstein portrait that Melcourt had once commissioned? Was it Reg in his youth? Perhaps a friend or brother? Perhaps this boy was merely the artist's own creation. No wonder he'd reminded Joyce of Sebastian: the golden hair, the eyes the same larkspur blue, and the expression was Sebastian's, sweet and open, dark and sensual. But it wasn't him. It didn't matter that it wasn't.

As the young man looked at me, mockingly proclaiming his anonymity, his laughter explained what I had not understood: it is not a question of identity, historical data, facts, 'proofs'. All are unimportant, ephemeral: they slip away: but they leave behind the only thing that matters. The essence; the essence is immortal, indestructible. The essence of the picture was Beauty, and the power (both terrible and inconquerable) of Love.

Love (Eros) had transfigured Melcourt's life and my own. From its suffering and glory, Max had made his poetry and it had given my life a kind of glory. That it had also brought destruction and death didn't matter; it had been inevitable. All that mattered was the eventual knowledge that it had, and did, exist. 'Now we see through a glass darkly, then we shall see face to face'.

To search for the truth about Melcourt, or, indeed, anyone, was as pointless as trying to catch the butterflies that had flitted about Sebastian's head in Melcourt's garden, or to identify the figures reflected in my bedroom mirror. How right he'd been, my lover, with his joyful possession of a green smoking jacket, his pink-suede shorts, his pheas'n'salmon mix, his Palestrina, his flapjacks and his fucks; for he knew that such things gave a solidity to the insubstantial.

All that mattered was the discovery of the essence, love, Erotic Love, his and mine. Erotic Love is both terrible and beautiful, but the beauty outlives the terror. It's immortal, and he who has possessed it once possesses it for ever. I had been such a man. The portrait told me so. I raised my lips to his.

Now I was free once again to love him. I tossed the letters aside, and held the portrait close. I lay back upon my bed, happy. I'd always loved him. I loved him from that first moment when he had come into my room for his interview in his lavender suit with beads in his hair. I loved him in those years before I knew him, while I watched him so svelte and successful about the college. I loved him while I taught him. I loved him that night when he came to me drenched with his hair in curls about his beautiful face. I loved him when I fucked him and when we slept together. I would always love him. The portrait told me so.

Now there was just one thing I needed to know. I spoke with a number of priests (there are plenty at the Seminary), until I found the one who would confirm my views. Some, of course, were limited and stupid men: when I spoke of Sebastian's carelessness of conventional morality, his indifference to the deadly sins, the fact that he'd died in mortal sin, they shook their heads and denied him Heaven.

Dom Gentile was different; he understood. He was an educated man and he spoke perfect English. We sat beneath a crucifix in the Seminary's small chapel, and he explained to me what I should do.

"Sometimes," he said, "our Lord creates a thing of outstanding beauty: a perfect lily, a shining panther, a man of strange imaginations, like the artist Bosch. Through such things, such people, God gives us an indication of the variety and the majesty of His power. He doesn't ask us to understand them, to pass judgement on them; He alone can judge. Perhaps your friend was such another."

"But his mortal sin, Father?"

"He loved God."

"Yes, with all his heart."

"God doesn't turn away those who love him. And your love, too, was divinely given."

"Shall I see him in Heaven? Do we see again those whom we've loved?"

"For God, all things are possible."

"And for Man, for one who's loved deeply; for me?"

"God's love is infinite. If you belonged to God's true church, then you would understand."

It was what *he* had said: 'Convert, Jules', he had said as he lay beside me, gazing at me with eyes full of concern.

Dom Gentile was an astute man. He quoted the passage from the Bible about the camel passing through the eye of a needle, etc. I sighed and he paused. He asked me if I was a rich man. I replied that my father had left me a good deal of money. He nodded. He said that a rich Catholic could make endowments, pay for novenas and masses. He expressed it all very delicately (being both Italian and ecclesiastical), but I understood money had clout, in Heaven as on earth. It would buy me peace of mind, and it would save Sebastian from Hell.

It cost me a fair amount, but I welcomed the expense; spending money on lovers had always been a pleasure to both Melcourt and me. After all, if Sebastian had come on holiday with me to Italy, as I'd so often begged, I would have definitely spent as much. It was my last and, I hope, my best present to him.

Thirty
Red Feathers and Blue Feathers

They had told me at the hospital it would be good for me – 'therapeutic' (how I hate Greek-based jargon) – to set out my memories of everything that had disturbed me: not just his death, but everything which led up to it. They were kind; one of them even went to the trouble of buying one of my earlier biographies (the Swinburne, I think).

"Of whom, then, shall I write?" I had asked. And those who had listened (and even, I was astonished to learn, actually taped my ravings) told me to write about Sebastian, Max, Toto, Reg, Joyce, even myself.

"But I don't know any of them," I replied. They smiled at me in their efficient way.

"Perhaps you will come to know them," they said smoothly. And I smiled and said I'd prefer to sketch.

Nevertheless, as you can see, I took their advice; during my stay here in Massa, I've spent most of my time writing.

Some may call me inconsistent. I've dismissed biography as meaningless twaddle, but have spent some hundreds of pages (and quite as many hours) writing my own!

But this isn't biographical nor autobiographical. How could it be, since I can't corroborate any of the events, characters or conversations included in it? If I've written anything, I've written a hypothetical autobiography which shows the nature of the man presented and the man who presents. Are they the same? Perhaps not. In the course of writing this... account, I've come to understand the flexibility given to the author by the insubstantiality of the nature of biography. Take biography a stage further; create a new genre. I'll call it epibiography. Allow me to explain.

Imagine me, for the sake of argument, seated at my usual table in the piazza. I have my chianti and crostini, but no drawing materials, since I now realise I have absolutely no artistic ability. From this position, I watch a middle-aged man struggling (as I've done so often) up the steep hill to the Seminary.

Now, with regard to this individual (identity unknown), I can't say for certain that he *will* attain his goal, and enter the Seminary gates, nor can I say he won't reach it, for I've no evidence to support either hypothesis; so, in the writing of *epibiography,* I can describe his joy on attaining his goal, his relief on seating himself on the stone bench outside the main doorway... or I can amuse myself describing his being accosted by robbers, his loss of consciousness on being beaten up, and his subsequent death on the road. In writing my own *epibiography*, I may conclude by describing my growing boredom with the seminary, my projected return to England and my fêted return to Oxford, or I may describe my slow disintegration on Italian soil. Both are equally uncertain.

There is, however, one point of absolute certainty: my own death. Naturally I can't (at present) tell you about it, but I can with absolute certainty state: 'J Collins. Obibit'.

My dying is of little interest: it won't be of interest to myself once it's happened, though it may be of some interest as I come closer to the event, who knows? Certainly, it'll be of no concern to the reader, whose only reaction may be to sigh: 'Thank God, he's finished'. But suppose he's not finished? I've discovered yet another new genre: *epithanatography.* I can depict my life after death since there can never be anything to disprove it. The use of tense will be tricky; I'll do my best:

"Goodness, Jules, what a long time you've been! Whatever have you been doing?"

As always I shall conceal my delight on coming face to face with him; I cloak it in severity.

"I have spent some considerable time in Purgatory – mainly on your account."

"Oh, Jules!"

"And what have you been up to here, Sebastian, amidst all these gold and crystal fountains? I see nobody encumbers themselves with clothes here. I trust you have behaved yourself."

He will laugh delightfully, his face all flushed with rosiness.

"Do you like my wings, Jules?"

They will cover his shoulders in a cloud of soft whiteness, shading towards the tips to delphinium blue. They will move gently in the celestial breezes.

"Of course I do," I shall say crossly, "they are exactly the colour of your eyes."

He lets a loose delphinium-blue feather drift towards me.

"Mm, it's awfully clever, isn't it? The cherubim took absolutely ages, well, not ages because time doesn't really happen here, but, anyway, they took an awful lot of care to match up the right colour."

He looks, perhaps a little insubstantial, but sweeter than ever.

"I am not sure I like the idea of your dealings with cherubims, Sebastian."

"Oh, Jules! They took much longer matching up the reds for your wings. They said the last time they used that particular gingery ochre was..."

Tentatively I begin feeling my shoulders and back; I twist my head round in horror.

"Sebastian! I have pinions! Most enormous red pinions!"

"Yes, Jules. Max will be awfully pleased; he's always hated all the seraphims staring at him. Now you're here with the same colour wings."

"Is Max here?"

"Of course. And Toto."

"Toto? How on earth...?"

"Not on earth, Jules."

"In heaven, then."

"Oh, the rumour is, he dimpled at St Peter; he's the tiniest bit susceptible, and Toto is awfully pretty."

"Sebastian, you haven't...?"

"I've been waiting eons for you, Jules, all the time you were in Purgatory – just because it took you so long to convert. And I did try to fill the time in innocently and I spent centuries doing nothing but eating ambrosia and playing the harp; the Palestrina is awfully difficult."

"I'm here now, darling."

"I'm so glad, Jules."

"Sebbie, I love you."

"I love you too, Jules." *(This time he will not be lying.)*

"The wings, Sebbie... I'm not sure, they do get in the way a bit."

"No they don't; I'll show you – but don't you want to meet Max and Toto first?"

"No," I shall say decisively, "after all, we have all Eternity for them. I should like to..."

"Oh, Jules, so should I. "

And the air shall be full of feathers, red mingling with blue, and angels shall sing to the music of the spheres, and Sebastian and I shall taste the everlasting sweetness of the heavenly flapjack.

Dear Atkins

I fail to see any problem vis à vis the Collins manuscript. I should quietly destroy it, if I were you. After all, it's not as if there are any friends, family or loved ones to be affected, is it? Alternatively, you could send it back to the priests: Italians never understand English.

Of course, his great hero, Melcourt, died young. What a pity Collins can't enjoy the parallel. Not, of course, that I imagine there was anything suspicious about JC's death: any number of things could have caused it. I shouldn't wonder if it wasn't something brought about by his sexual mores and, of course, he always drank too much. If it was cancer, well, I should call it a Benign Malignancy, shouldn't you? Better dead than mad.

A couple of small points: a) was Collins' reference to you and 'the closet' libellous? (b) I certainly do not regard any idiosyncrasy of mine as risible.

Yours truly,
John Williams

PS. A thought occurs to me: you could send the manuscript to Steiner. He might make a film of the whole thing – particularly if he were to set it in Cambridge, rather than here.

PPS. Did you work out the last line of the Nutella limerick? JW.

Bend Sinister:
The Gay Times Book of Disturbing Stories

Edited by Peter Burton

A deeply disturbing collection

This new collection, nominated for a Lambda literary award, is packed with chills and thrills from thirty gay writers. It ventures into the world of the sinister and the disturbing, with flashes of sheer horror.

Authors include: Sebastian Beaumont, David Patrick Beavers, Perry Brass, Christopher Brown, Richard Cawley, Jack Dickson, Neal Drinnan, Francis King, Simon Lovat, Stuart Thorogood, Michael Wilcox and Richard Zimler.

Across a range of nationalities and approaches, one thing is guaranteed: something out of kilter, something dangerously askew.

"A collection of startling originality… a welcome addition to the canon of gay literature" City Life

"[An] excellent anthology of horror, fantasy and crime… a chillingly good read" ★★★ Big Issue

"A lively, eclectic collection… Highly recommended" The List

"Breathtakingly different… incredible 'tales of the unexpected'" Our World

"A superb collection of disturbing tales" ★★★★ OUT in Greater Manchester

Out now UK £9.99 US $14.95
(when ordering direct, quote BEN427)

How to order

GMP books are available from bookshops including Borders, Gay's The Word, Prowler Stores and branches of Waterstone's.

Or order direct from:
MaleXpress, 75B Great Eastern Street, London EC2A 3HN
Freephone 0800 45 45 66 (Int tel +44 20 7739 4646)
Freefax 0800 917 2551 (Int fax +44 20 7739 4848)
www.gaymenspress.co.uk